as swallows fly

a novel

L. P. McMAHON

VENTURA

This book is published by Ventura Press
PO Box 780, Edgecliff NSW 2027 Australia
www.venturapress.com.au

ISBN: 978-1-920727-51-2 (paperback)
ISBN: 978-1-920727-57-4 (ebook)

NATIONAL LIBRARY OF AUSTRALIA
A catalogue record for this book is available from the National Library of Australia

Cover and internal design by Alissa Dinallo
Printed and bound in Australia by Griffin Press of Ovato Book Printing

FSC www.fsc.org MIX Paper from responsible sources FSC® C009448
The paper in this book is FSC® certified. FSC® promotes environmentally responsible, socially beneficial and economically viable management of the world's forests

To my family – Penny, Claire, Will,
Alastar, and George

'The worst loneliness is to not be comfortable with yourself.'
– Mark Twain

'Because one believes in oneself, one doesn't try to convince others.

Because one is content with oneself, one doesn't need others' approval.
Because one accepts oneself, the whole world accepts him or her.'
– Lao Tzu

prologue

Melbourne

Twenty-three years earlier

Kate shut the car door and limped across the lawn. Her mother had already reached the front door. She pushed it open and marched down the hallway, her heels echoing on the floorboards. Kate waited until she disappeared and went to her room. She eased herself onto her bed and rolled on to her side, shivering as she bent up her knees. Next to the window, the hibiscus was in bloom. Its hot pink flowers glowed in the early afternoon sun. Her father had said it would do this when they planted it.

She was still curled on her bed, the sun long gone from the plant, when her mother walked into the room. She placed two tablets and a glass of water on the table beside the bed.

'The doctor said you should have these. You'll need two more in the morning.' She paused. 'Are you all right?'

Kate looked up, her eyes moistening. 'It really hurts, Mum.'

'The tablets will help.'

'I feel dirty.'

'I'm sure you do.' Her mother's skirt rustled against the pillow as she moved close to the bed. Her perfume descended like a cloud. 'Who was the father, Katherine? It's time to say.'

Kate rolled towards the window and stared at the shadows outside. Her hands curled into fists.

'It was him, wasn't it? I'm not blind.'

There was a long silence, longer even than the afternoon had been. Then, her eyes closed, she made the slightest nod, hoping even as she did that her mother would miss it.

Footsteps retreated to the doorway.

'Can we leave this place?'

The footsteps stopped as the words filled the room.

'You've ruined your life and now you want to ruin mine as well? Of course we're not leaving.'

She was almost asleep when the front door opened and quietly closed. A minute later, distantly, the car coughed into life. It was the last thing she heard until morning.

part one

Rural Pakistan

Five years earlier

1

The man in the faded turban at the front of the dray clicked his tongue and drew the mule to the side of the hot bitumen. Malika waited for the policeman and the boy – Tahir, he had mumbled once – to get off before clambering down herself. They waited at the roadside for a car and then a bus to pass, before hurrying across. Their feet stirred up the white dust that lay everywhere around them as they followed the path to the village, coating Malika's leggings and the policeman's black trousers, just as it had whitewashed the roofs of the homes that lay ahead.

Passing wooden gates, they followed a corridor between bleached, mud-brick houses to a clearing where the branches of a giant fig tree spread wide, almost touching the buildings. The policeman motioned for them to wait beneath the tree and crossed to the far end of the clearing, where two old men were sitting cross-legged in the dust. They looked at him as he squatted in front of them.

The air was cool under the branches. Malika marvelled at their size, at the way the roots grew down from them towards the ground, as if searching for a home. The morning had been long and her mouth was as dry as her stomach was empty. She sat and picked up a dusty leaf, rubbing it between her fingers. She smiled as her fingers became speckled white and the leaf's deep green colour emerged. It was the same dust that had lain across the road they travelled on that morning, with the train line constantly beside them. The policeman had told Tahir that the line connected the towns of the north with Lahore and the other great cities of the south. Malika liked the thought of towns being connected, if only by dust and noisy trains.

When the policeman returned, Malika and Tahir followed him to another part of the village. They stopped in front of a hut and the policeman called out a name, waiting until a woman emerged from inside. She stood in the shade at the doorway, her arms folded. The policeman took off his hat and wiped his balding head with his handkerchief.

'Peace to you, cousin,' he said.

'And to you,' she said. 'It has been a long time. Why do you come to visit me now?'

'I have a favour to ask.' He turned to the children.

The woman followed his gaze and looked back at him. 'Two children is more than a favour, cousin.' She turned to a young woman who had emerged from the next hut. 'Fetch some water, Nadia. They will be thirsty.' She turned back to the policeman. 'Even one child is costly, Razzaq.'

'They are old enough to work. They will work hard. They are good children.'

She looked at the children again and her eyes narrowed. 'They are not of the same blood.'

'No.'

'What happened?'

'A bus accident in the mountains east of here. God looks after his own. Their parents were not lucky.'

The woman's eye dwelled on the boy's white jubba. 'He is Muslim,' she said.

'He will change.'

'We will see.'

The policeman smiled and wiped his head again. 'There is a small problem with the girl, cousin. She has not spoken since the accident.'

The woman stepped across to Malika, held a finger beneath her chin and looked into her eyes. Malika looked back. The woman's eyes were dark; not hard, but without humour. She missed her mother's face.

'When was this accident?' the woman asked.

'A month ago.'

The woman turned to him. 'She is pretty. She will survive. Has no one called for them?'

'We have contacted the boy's family. But it was a love marriage and the family see the accident as kismet. They say his lot has been ordained.'

'And the girl?'

'Unusual. No family other than the parents.'

'That is kismet also, cousin. What do you want from me? You have not come from the city with them merely to talk.'

'You have longed for children, cousin.'

'My husband is dead. How can I provide for two growing children?'

'They can work. They will provide for themselves.'

'The girl has no dowry.'

'I will do what I can.'

The woman scoffed. 'You have two daughters of your own. How can you provide another dowry on a policeman's salary?'

'I know what it is to have daughters, cousin. I will do what I can.'

'The boy will rebel.'

'The girl is Christian. They need a home. It is not forever.'

'You say that, but no one has come forward.'

'Not yet.'

'No, not yet.'

Nadia brought water and the woman sat them beneath a vine canopy that hung between the two huts. As the policeman and the children drank, she squatted in the shade, sipping her own cup and looking deeply in front of her.

'How many summers have they seen, cousin?' she asked at one point.

'For the boy, we think twelve,' he responded. 'It is harder to know for the girl. Perhaps the same.'

Keeping her gaze on the ground, she sniffed in reply.

Finally, she turned her head. 'A month,' she said, fixing her cousin with a stare. 'I cannot afford longer. I am sorry for their plight, but we have many mouths here as it is.'

The policeman smiled and nodded. 'May good fortune find you, cousin.'

The policeman waved to them from the dray that would take him back to the station two hours down the track. He said he would send money.

'It will be needed,' the woman said.

She talked to the children on the walk back to her hut.

'You are mine, now,' she said. 'I am a good woman. I will not beat you if you do what I say. I will care for you, but you must help for the good of the village. I do not know of your past lives. They are over. Here, we must survive. We have crops in the field that need to be worked and animals that need to be tended.'

'I am Muslim,' said Tahir.

'Your past life is over,' she repeated. 'We must work together to survive. Your family has not come forward to claim you and you must do what you can to survive.'

'I am Muslim,' he said again and turned away.

Malika looked at the woman and the woman stared back. 'I am Ayesha,' she said.

Malika said nothing. It was important to say nothing. If words slipped out, memories might slip in. She wanted to be away, just away. The policeman had not let her see her parents' bodies. Malika had wanted to, but perhaps it was better he did not let her. This way she could believe that one day her parents would return. They could come now, to the village, to take her back to her own village in the hills, where clear streams fed trees that erupted in the summer with leaves and fruit. It was a game she played some days until the sun was low in the sky. But always the game ended as night came.

'Come,' said Ayesha, holding out her hand when they reached her hut. 'It is time to eat lunch. Then you must work. In a month you will be gone from here.'

A month passed and no word came from the policeman. Three months. Ayesha knew no one would come. Malika had begun to talk, at least a word here and there, mainly in response to the woman's kindness: a thank you for extra rice or a goodnight as they lay together on the bed. One night after working the fields, she collapsed on the earthen floor inside the hut and began to cry. Ayesha stayed with her during the night, stroking her skin and bathing her forehead. She told Malika no one could change the past, no matter how unjust. Everyone must do what they could. When the first birds chirped and the sky lightened, Ayesha lay down next to Malika and began to snore. Malika looked across the room to Tahir. He too had stayed awake during the night, at one point turning his face to the wall and covering his ears.

The men called to collect the children for work soon after the first sun crept across the lane. Ayesha said they needed rest, but the boy rose from his bed to join the men in the fields. Malika woke late and helped prepare dinner at the fire. In the afternoon, Ayesha brought out her dowry chest, a large tin box. Tin to keep out rats, she explained, adding that it had cost her father a month of labour. Her parents had hoped for a large family from her; they had given her clothes and vestments for baptisms and first communions.

'But,' she said, 'the Lord took my husband young, barely a year into our marriage.' She smiled at Malika. 'Now my parents are gone, I am too old for children, and my dowry box is without purpose.'

Malika looked at her. 'My mother had a dowry box also,' she said. 'It is gone now.'

The woman nodded. 'It is good to hear you speak,' she said.

Later, Malika made tea and they sipped the warm, sweet liquid as the fire glowed and the light outside faded. As they drank, Ayesha reached into her glory box for a parcel wrapped in muslin cloth. She opened it to show fabric and needles, with reels of cotton and scissors of different sizes.

'Do you know how to sew?' she asked.

Malika nodded. She took a piece of fine cotton and a patch of material from the basket and showed the woman the cross-stitching her mother had taught her. Her fingers played deftly with the needle, first on one and then the other side of the fabric. She completed a pattern and showed Ayesha, who could see it was beyond the skill of the village. It would sell for a good price.

That night, Ayesha took her ideas to the elders in the village. She showed them Malika's stitching and spoke to them of profits. It was resolved that the girl would no longer work in the fields. She would mix with the village girls, learn to work in the animal pens, wash clothes and organise food lists. Twice a week, she would teach the girls her craft.

The next Monday, well after the men had picked up Tahir, as morning light spread across the land, Ayesha took Malika to meet some of the village girls and young women beneath the fig tree in the square. They became interested when Ayesha showed them Malika's stitching. Rolling out a ream of cotton cloth to protect against the dust, they sat around her in a circle and the session began. It was a slow process; their hands were not as agile as Malika's. She would hold their fingers and patiently guide them across the fabric, talking as she did, explaining what they were trying to achieve.

She had mixed little with the village girls until then: the older girls had tolerated rather than welcomed her and the younger girls were busy with their own games. Now though, some of the girls began to linger outside her hut in the mornings and accompany her to the centre square. They waited for her when the clothes needed to be washed, walking beside her to the creek beyond the rail line, smiling and shyly touching her skin. Sometimes she would smile back and at night, as she lay next to Ayesha, the grey blanket that covered her life carried a little less weight.

Malika slowly settled into village life: the morning smells of barley porridge in the smoky hut as the weather cooled, the shared pleasures of an evening breeze in the square, eating goat's cheese and listening to the choir sing after Mass on the last Sunday of the month, when the priest would visit. She knew which small avenues afforded the best shade and which dogs to avoid. But it was not her home. It was a place to rest as she waited for life to bring another change. She knew the truth of what the visiting priest called Limbo, the home for lost souls. And as memories of her past life became more distant, so too did they become more accessible. Sometimes, she would even welcome them.

One day Fatima, one of the sewing class girls, brought a bag of sweets. Her mother had bought the sweets at the bazaar for her birthday, and told her to share them among the other girls to ensure good fortune stayed with her for the year to come. Fatima stood the girls in a line and handed out the sweets, one at a time. When she reached the end, she turned and began to work her way back. The bag was large, and Malika saw the process would be slow. She tapped Fatima on the shoulder and, taking the bag from her, told her to count the girls while she began to count the sweets.

'How many?' she asked Fatima, when she herself had finished counting.

'Twenty-two.'

'And a hundred and seventy-eight sweets,' Malika answered after a minute. She thought a moment. 'How many did you not already give two sweets to?'

The girl turned and counted back from the end of the line. 'Seven. And then there's you,' she added.

'And how many did you want?'

Fatima blushed. 'It is my twelfth birthday.' She hesitated. 'It is customary here –'

Malika nodded. 'To have one for each year.' It had been the same at her home.

Fatima nodded. 'But everyone else?'

The answer appeared in Malika's mind like a warm glow. 'Make sure each girl has nine sweets.'

'And you?'

She shrugged. 'I will have what is left.'

Fatima held the bag high and the other girls gathered, first for their sweets but then around Malika. They looked at her as if she were a wise man or an elder, pleading with her to show them how such tricks could be done. They took her across to the base of the tree, and needlework was forgotten as they sat on the cotton ream and Malika spoke to them of arithmetic and the games that numbers could be made to play.

When their mothers and the day's chores called, Fatima came to Malika, a smile curling her lips, her hands behind her back. 'How many sweets did you think would be left?' she teased.

'I thought five.'

Fatima shrugged as she handed across two. 'I wanted to save you more, but Rashida took the others for her brother.' She held out the bag. 'It is no matter. You can have some of mine.'

Malika shook her head. 'Perhaps the boy is sick.'

'I know she took them for herself,' said Fatima, pulling the bag inside her clothes. She glanced at Malika and hid a smile behind her hand. 'How will she find a husband? She is already as big as a water buffalo.'

'Perhaps she will marry a nice fat boy buffalo,' said Malika, and Fatima giggled.

As she walked back to Ayesha's home, Malika wondered if her parents – in whatever place they were – would be pleased with her. She wanted to tell them that she was making friends and helping the village, that she honoured what they had taught her. She needed to tell them about her day, from when she first opened her eyes in the morning to what she saw in her dreams at night. She forced herself to think of the morning and of the girls' faces as she explained how numbers fitted together. Numbers had always come easily to her. Even as a small girl, still too young for school, she had helped the older children understand the secrets they held. Later, she didn't need the formulas the teacher taught in the classroom. She could look at the numbers and the answer would appear in her mind. As she tried to explain to her mother once, it was like seeing them as different colours.

The following morning, some of the girls brought paper and pencils to the square, arriving with them clutched in their hands.

'It is better we do our stitching first,' said Malika.

The next night, she lay awake in bed wondering what to tell them, where to start. She wished she had a book to help her. She could feel Tahir listening in the darkness from the other corner as she turned and fidgeted beside Ayesha's warm body. She hid her fears beneath her clothes as she dressed in the morning, and then set the fire for chapattis. In the end, she made a decision to start with arithmetic, although she remembered only a few of the laws and formulas her teacher had begun to show her. She half hoped they would forget about the number games, but after a token effort with their stitching the girls wrapped their handiwork in cloth and placed their packages at the base of the tree before gathering around her. Malika took a deep breath and began.

After some weeks, Malika resorted to writing down number problems at night, so there was something for the class to start with during the day. Sometimes, Tahir stared at her in the faint glow of the kerosene lamp, his dark eyes flashing. He asked her once, in a whisper so Ayesha would not wake, what she was doing.

'It is a game for the other girls,' Malika whispered back.

'Games are for children,' he said, and rolled over to the wall. Minutes later, she heard him snoring. For a few moments, they were in time with Ayesha's loud snorts, and Malika lowered her head and smiled.

In the class, she began to recite numbers, forcing the girls to remember them in sequence, and giving them simple problems to work out in their heads. It didn't seem to matter what she did or which tasks she set, the girls were always on time, bubbling with excitement and eager for the next lesson. Soon, they would not leave until their mothers came looking for them, and some walked around the village reciting their tables or explaining division and multiplication to their brothers.

One day, the elders called Malika to an evening meeting. Ayesha stood behind her as she explained her lessons to the circle of stone-faced elders. Ayesha stayed when Malika was asked to walk home. The next morning, Ayesha told her that the elders had banned the classes.

Malika ate her breakfast slowly and later that morning spoke to Fatima at the latrine.

'We must continue our work,' Fatima said. She directed the hose at the concrete gutter and waited as Malika followed with the broom.

'They could make things worse,' said Malika. 'They might stop our stitching, too.' She paused her sweeping to take a breath then, holding it, she shoved the excrement into the bucket at the end of the gutter. She exhaled. 'We should be careful.'

'That is true,' Fatima nodded.

Malika leaned on the broom. 'I have an idea. We have paper and pencils. We can pass problems between us. So we do not gather together, except for stitching. I could make up a code.' Her face became doubtful. 'Perhaps it is too dangerous.'

Fatima's face beamed. 'No! That is a good idea, my friend. It can be our own secret code.'

'We will need to be careful of displeasing the elders.'

'What of Ayesha? She is almost an elder.'

'She will not mind,' said Malika.

One Sunday, the priest arrived early for Mass. He manoeuvred his small, red car along the largest of the lanes and parked it at the edge of the square, beneath a branch of the fig tree. He stood for a moment, his hands on his hips, and then wandered over to where the children worked on their sewing. One of the mothers now supervised the children to make sure they worked. The priest gazed at the gathering before smiling at the woman.

'May I speak with them?' he said to the woman, who ordered the girls to lay down their work.

The priest was easily the tallest man that Malika had seen, taller even than the policeman. His hair was red like autumn leaves. His accent spoke of foreign lands as he told them of the child Jesus visiting the temple, and how his holiness was visible even then, even by those who didn't believe. Malika had heard the story before. She glanced at Fatima, who had been working on a puzzle that Malika had given her that morning as they threw grain to the chickens. Fatima nudged the girl next to her and slipped a folded sheet of paper in her hand. The girl waited until the priest had turned away before leaning across to Malika. But she was not careful enough and the woman saw the folded paper in the girl's hand.

'What nonsense are you making, Lubna?' she hissed. She stepped between the girls and snatched the note from the open-mouthed girl, before burying it in her clothes.

'What is that?' the priest asked.

'It is foolishness,' said the woman. 'A foolishness the elders have forbidden.'

'May I see it?'

The woman hesitated but then did as he asked, looking at Malika with malice as she handed it across. He scanned the note for a minute, then looked up. 'Who wrote this?' he asked.

Malika stood and he beckoned her forward as he read the note again, this time frowning.

'What is it?' he asked finally, looking in her eyes.

'It is a puzzle,' she answered.

'They are lines without meaning.'

She took the paper. 'No, it is a code,' she said. 'Each line is a different number. We are deciding what size the square would need to be if all the harvest from the field had to be stored here, if it reached the same height as the wall.'

'The elders have forbidden it, Father,' said the woman again, staring at the seated children. She clutched at her robes. 'We must work, not play idly.'

The priest held up his hand and turned back to Malika. His eyes narrowed. 'And what is the answer?'

'The others are working on it,' said Malika, looking around. 'I do not want to spoil it.'

The priest laughed. 'Perhaps that is because you do not know it.'

'Three and a quarter chains on each side,' she said immediately, looking at him.

'How do you know?'

'I saw the answer when Tahir told me they hope to fill three silos this year.'

'But the silos are round.'

'Cylinders. Yes.'

He leaned forward, his hands on his knees. 'My name is Father Louis Andreas Salvador Prader.' He smiled when she hesitated. 'My friends call me Father Louis.'

'Then I will do that,' said Malika. The girls were behind her, she knew, but none of them had moved. She felt the woman's anger at her back too. Father Louis seemed about to talk again before changing his mind. He handed back the note. 'You say you saw the answer. Do you mean you calculated it?'

She shook her head.

'Then tell me how you explain it to the other girls.'

'I do not know how. I see it, then I work it out as I explain it.'

'Sit with me,' he said. 'Let us spend some time together.' He spoke to the woman. 'Rasheed, please, could you make me some tea? I will watch the children.'

That afternoon, after Mass, Father Louis spent time talking with the elders in the large building that served as the church on the Sundays he was there. It was a long discussion. As she always did on such days, Malika relaxed with the women and girls in the square, but on this day she had to try hard to ignore what was happening inside the church. She ate the late lunch, drank tea and made jokes, laughing at the young children as they ran around chasing each other. Older boys had begun a game of cricket on the other side of the tree. While she sat, her eyes kept drifting to the path she knew Tahir would take to the square. He was not forced to come to Mass, and instead usually worked in the fields in the morning.

He arrived grasping a scythe, his slender limbs now strong with muscle from the field work. His skin glowed in the afternoon sun. He had long grown out of his *jubba*, and wore the same grey top and pants as the others. But the village barely saw him outside the Sunday meal, and even then he would take food from the table and either sit alone or occasionally find shade with a few of the older boys from the field and watch the activities in silence. Tahir did not mix; the whole village knew that. Sometimes though, she knew he looked at her, especially when she was looking anywhere but at him.

Long shadows had formed across the square by the time the priest came out of the hut. He walked across to Malika. 'I think we have an understanding,' he said.

She looked up. Sweat moistened his face, as if he had been working under the sun. His shirt was wet too, with an acrid odour that caught the breeze.

'Treat Father with respect, girl,' scolded Ayesha, pushing her to her feet.

'You must stop the teaching,' Father Louis said, gazing into her face.

She nodded. In the corner of her eye Fatima was pretending not to listen.

'You will not teach,' he continued, 'but I will bring you books on the Sundays I take Mass, so I can teach you.'

'I can learn alone.'

'Mathematics, perhaps. But you might find English more

difficult.'

'What is English?'

'Another language.' He smiled, showing many large teeth. 'You will see.'

'And Fatima?'

'I'm sorry.' He shook his head. 'The elders will not relent.'

2

The summer rains passed and her second autumn in the village approached. Malika saw her girlhood departing. By the time the winds from the north had turned cool and the harvest had given its last, she found she was already taller than Ayesha. Her breasts had swelled, and in the cracked and scratched mirror next to the door, her lips were fuller, her hair long and strong. Her heart jumped to see she was like her mother. She began to wear her hair the way her mother had worn it, using a band to keep it off her face. One day, she found an old magazine in Ayesha's tin box. It had a faded picture of a pale-skinned princess on the front. She must have been a princess; no one else could have been so beautiful. When Ayesha was out, Malika would practise pulling up her hair and turning her face the way the princess did in the magazine. It annoyed her that unlike the princess, dark hairs had begun to grow from beneath her armpits.

When frost began to cover the fields in the mornings, Ayesha said it was time for Tahir to sleep with the men in the large shed at the end of the village. He looked at her a minute, his face immobile, and then he picked up his small bag of belongings and stepped out of the hut into the cold sun. Ayesha looked at Malika as he left.

'It is better he goes now,' she said. 'He is already looking at you and the village is starting to talk. He needs to be with the other men.'

As she went about cleaning the breakfast dishes, Malika did not tell the woman what had happened a week earlier. In the glow of the fire embers, as she prepared her hair for sleep, she saw him watching her from his straw mat. It was a look that chilled her heart and made her turn away, clutching her hand to her breasts. That night, with the faint smell of smoke in the air, she lay in the dark beside Ayesha, listening to three people breathing. She asked herself why she feared his stare. The next morning as they ate their barley porridge, Tahir had spoken his customary few words to her and the woman before leaving for the fields. Malika decided some things were best forgotten.

She rarely saw him after he left the hut. She did not miss him but they shared a past and, apart from Father Louis who now came every second Sunday, he was her only contact from the world beyond the village. Each morning and evening as the men passed on their way to and from the field, she would look out for him, hoping he might also look for her.

The winter set in hard, with freezing nights and colder mornings. Rain had not fallen since the autumn, and slowly its absence crept into the village talk. Everyone knew the number of days since the last rain, and when the creek beyond the rail line slowed to a trickle anxiety began to mix with fear. It sat among them as they gathered at night and it was in the eyes of the women as they scanned the horizon uneasily during the day. A single cloud was enough to fill the conversation for the morning. The men left early to make the most use of the light and were at their ploughs even as the women cooked breakfast. Malika hoped she would be asked to walk with the group to bring the men food. They joked and teased in ways the women did not. But usually it was the older women who went, and she and the other girls were given empty bowls to clean.

Some mornings, on her way to the deepening well for the day's water, Malika's feet would first take her to the outskirts of the village. She would stand between the tracks on the train line, watching as the men in the fields shouted at the lumbering water buffalos that were yoked to ploughs, while a string of women and older children walked behind, clearing the waste. Then, she would look along the tracks and gaze far into the distance until they became a single point. She wondered what a great city looked like. Once, as she turned and picked up her buckets, she saw Tahir. He was working a plough on his own while the men were busy with another that had stopped midfield. She smiled at his resolute figure standing pencil straight behind the giant animal. It saddened her that he kept himself apart from the rest of the village. He did not join the nightly prayers for rain and a good crop; instead, after drinking deeply from the buckets left in the cool of the tree, he would disappear to his quarters. The men talked of seeing him there on his knees, praying.

Beneath the fig tree as they prepared their wares for the bazaar, the women asked Ayesha, 'We have given him life. Why does he not show us gratitude?'

She shrugged. 'He chooses not to be one of us. How do I know what he thinks?'

As the drought deepened and whispers and resentment grew within the village, Father Louis intervened.

'Christians and Muslims believe in the same God,' he said to the congregation one Sunday at Mass. 'In God's eyes we are one. To believe means we must accept His ways as we must accept all His people.' He scanned the room, challenging each of them with his stare. 'All His people,' he repeated. 'Christ died for the sins of all men, not just the faithful. Belief is nothing if it is not seen in our actions.' He proceeded to speak to them of Job and of the need to persevere, not to lose sight of hope. They had not heard the sermon before and the villagers' hearts were more open as they ate lunch that day. A woman took a plate of food and some water across to Tahir. Wide-eyed, he took it from her, eating it quickly but then disappearing soon after. As those who saw him leave looked at each other and shook their heads, Malika followed him down the path. She found him among the ploughs, in the field behind the shed.

He didn't look up as she sat on a plough handle behind him. She waited as a minute passed.

'Hajira was kind to bring you lunch.'

He shrugged.

'They want to help you. We all want to help you.'

'I do not want help,' he said. He looked to the distance. 'I want justice.'

'Can I do nothing?'

'Only Allah brings justice.'

She stood and folded her arms. 'Why must you be this way?'

He paused, then turned to her. 'My family saw it. The policeman said it when he brought us here.'

She remembered the day they arrived on the dray.

'It is my test,' he said. 'My fate. Allah is truly great.'

He turned away and she stayed for a moment, before walking back to the village. Close to the square, she dropped her head so her hair fell forward and her face was hidden from those returning to their huts. She deviated around the square and waited inside her hut until her lessons with the priest began.

Once the crops had been sown and Christmas had passed, Malika filled her spare hours with her lessons. Her night-time studies forced Ayesha to buy more kerosene for the lamp. Father Louis brought Malika four books: mathematics, chemistry, physics and English. They spent their time on English before Christmas. She needed the new language to make sense of the other books. She laughed the first time she opened the English book; it started where the end should have been. Dressed in his white shirt, with a gold cross on each collar, Father Louis took her through simple and then more complicated English passages. After a few months, he insisted that they speak only English when they talked together. He gave her lists of words to learn from one week to the next. By the end of winter, she could read simple books and began asking for more. The mathematics book she completed in a month; the same period for chemistry and physics combined. He tested her when they met. She saw the answers before the priest had finished reading the question, laughing when he turned to the end of the book to check.

As they pounded the clothes clean at the creek, Fatima would sometimes ask about her studies. The pain in her eyes prompted Malika to begin teaching her secretly, on afternoons when the women were cooking together in the square. She tried first with mathematics.

'Let us solve two equations at once,' she said, opening the book and laying it flat on the bed.

Fatima read through the chapter with her as they sat on the bed. At the end she turned to Malika. 'I do not understand this *x* and *y*. How can they be numbers when they are also letters? And then, how can the same letters be different numbers in the next question?'

Malika nodded. 'Let us look at physics.' She opened the book and flicked through the pages to the first chapter. Atomic structure. Despite her translation, it was like showing a blind person the sun. The concepts were beyond her. After a few tries Fatima rolled back on the bed with her legs in the air.

'Too hard!' she laughed, and poked out her tongue. She picked up the English book. 'Let me try this.'

To Malika's surprise, she took to the words with ease. After only a few lessons, she could say the words clearly; her tongue found a way around syllables that Malika still found difficult to pronounce. Once, Fatima corrected her pronunciation and Malika fumed, smiling reluctantly when her friend placed a worried hand on her wrist.

As the days warmed, Father Louis and Malika came out from the large hut to sit beneath the great tree after Mass. He brought more books, as well as pens and paper, and spoke to her of things outside the village. She began writing in the new language, sometimes tasks the priest set and sometimes purely for herself. Father Louis would take it all away with him on Sundays and return her work covered in comments, and sometimes corrections, when he next arrived. Sitting at a makeshift table made from an upturned wooden box, they discussed and argued, sometimes hard, and it was not beyond Father Louis to slap the table or the tree beside them to make a point. Malika found herself doing the same. She surprised herself by the way her feelings were set free at these times. When she knew she was right, no force in the world could turn her. Entranced, jealous or bored, the young men of the village sat on stools around them or sprawled along the nearby wall. Occasionally, she would glance up as Fatima crossed the square and once, Tahir stopped on his way. He stood for a moment listening, before squatting near them. She felt his eyes on her as she tried to convince the priest of her solution to a maths problem. When she had finished, the priest handed her the solution the professor at the university in Lahore had given him. She read it through and saw she had made an error right at the start. She blushed and looked up. Father Louis smiled and winked at her.

'But I know calculus,' she pleaded. 'I do.'

'The professor said everyone does this the first time. Even him.'

She nodded and bit her tongue. When she looked up, she saw Tahir disappearing around a distant hut.

After spring came the heat and then the harvest, although the older men shook their heads as the grain only half-filled the silos. Fortunately, and to the relief of the whole village, rains followed. The men smiled easily enough through the mud on their way to the fields, knowing that God had blessed their lives for another year.

When not studying, Malika's chores were her life. She worked with the other young women to fetch water from the well or wood from the large shed, and to ensure the vegetables and herbs were well tended. One time early in the morning, as she stood at the edge of the village, a flight of swallows flew past a nearby tree and swooped across the nearby fields. She watched the rhythm of their flight, the way the birds moved as one and yet didn't. She frowned as she studied them, seeing how the birds on the edge deviated beyond the reach of the others, sometimes returning, sometimes not, and how the whole flock would then close on them to stay intact. The pulse of their movement was like a beat within her chest. It was only when Fatima, washing basket on her hip, called to her that she returned to her chores.

One morning, Ayesha could not get out of bed. Malika felt her cheeks and forehead. They were burning.

'You have the fever,' she said.

The woman nodded. 'Before you leave, you must fetch me some water.'

'I will stay,' said Malika.

Her heart beat strongly and her hands trembled as she filled the pail with cool water at the well. Ayesha's body radiated heat as she sponged her down. The older woman smiled and held her hand as she finished.

'It is good you are here.'

Malika told Fatima and the others when they arrived for

her that she needed to care for the woman that day. The day turned into a week. Ayesha became confused, calling out for her husband in the early hours of the morning. Malika could hardly get her to take the water she offered. The other women came; the husband of one of them had worked as a hospital orderly in the Great City.

'She needs hospital medicine,' this woman said.

'Perhaps Father Louis will have medicine when he comes,' said Malika.

'We should pray,' said another woman. She got to her knees.

In a circle, they recited the rosary three times as Ayesha moaned in the corner. Malika had prayed fruitlessly many times to her parents, waiting for a sign they heard her. It never came. But her chest heaved to think of life with Ayesha gone. She bowed her head and swore to the Divine Mother she would offer her life to God if she would intercede.

Three days later, against the expectations of the elders, and after Malika had completed countless decades of the rosary, Ayesha called to Malika in the early morning, asking her for some of the broth she could smell. Malika burned her fingers as she heated the soup and poured it into a bowl.

'Not too fast,' she said, as she pushed the spoon against the woman's lips.

Ayesha swallowed, gasped and smiled, and squeezed Malika's fingers. As she lowered Ayesha's head to the mattress, Malika bowed her head and wondered what the Divine Mother would ask of her.

As the season passed, Malika and Fatima began to spend more time with the other young women. They would gather in a group in the square after dinner as the days lengthened, and talk. Malika noticed that now, instead of telling how they would search the world as they had once dreamed, they now spoke of making their lives inside the village. Some were already eyeing certain young men, knowing their parents were in discussion. Now and then, the talk would turn to Tahir, who was as tall as a man and had hairs on his chin.

Fatima shuddered as she spoke of him. 'He lives with hate,' she said in a low voice, and the other girls nodded. 'I pray I am not in his thoughts.'

Malika admitted as much to herself. She never saw him smile and his chosen isolation had become a festering sore on the village's conscience. Though a part of the village, he was also separate. She wondered how someone could live as he did. She wondered how long he would stay.

One morning, when the worst of the summer rains had past, Malika set off to clean the goat pen. Their enclosure was at the far end of the village near the water buffalos, each as far as possible from the train tracks. Ayesha had explained to her that before Malika had arrived, the water buffalo pen was closest to the rail line. One night a buffalo broke loose and was killed by an overnight train. It was a loss the village could not afford.

She was astonished to see Tahir at the goat pen. The week had been busy and Malika had not seen him. He shrugged when she arrived, then turned away and began sweeping. He pushed the goats away from the dirty straw beneath them before scooping it away with the broom. Seeing what needed to be done, Malika filled her arms with clean straw and threw it onto the ground as Tahir made space. One goat had just delivered a litter and together they picked up the small, pink forms and placed them into the first pen, which was now clean. For a moment as they each held a tiny kid, their eyes met and Tahir's features softened. It was as close to a smile as he had shown her since he left the hut. Malika wished he would show her more.

They mucked out and swept the rest of the pens in silence. The goats brayed and urinated immediately on the clean straw when it was placed beneath them. It made Malika roll her eyes. As usual, Malika knew Tahir looked at her when he thought her back was turned or that hair across her face prevented her from seeing him. She had grown to like it, their secret.

They had almost finished: the old concrete trough was filled and they only needed to lay down fresh straw in the hutches. They leaned on their straw brooms for a moment before beginning. On her right, Malika noticed the lactating goat lying on its side. Its fresh litter had backed it into a corner, but there were more kids than teats. The runt, its tail wagging furiously, blind and bleating, had missed out again nudged aside by a sibling. Tahir watched for a minute, his face expressionless. Then without warning, he dropped his broom and stepped forward to the litter, pulling the bully off the teat. He held the offending kid high in one hand as he encouraged the smaller one forward. He watched for a moment until it latched on.

Without glancing at Malika, he took the hapless animal to the trough and, with both hands around its neck, plunged it deep into the water. He didn't lift it out until it lay still in his hands. It was over before Malika could think to act but her heart stopped as she watched. Tahir dropped the dead animal beside the trough. He stared at it a moment and then turned and walked out. He passed Malika on the way.

'Kismet,' he said, without shifting his gaze from the horizon.

She could not move until he had gone, as she could not think that afternoon or sleep that night. The black fire in his eyes as he passed had scorched her soul, and she knew she would never understand him.

By autumn, the afternoons were beginning to close in. One such Sunday, lessons finished, the sun suspended above the rooftops, Father Louis told her she was ready.

'For what?' she asked.

'It is time you sat the test,' he said.

She shielded her eyes from the sun to look at him. 'What good is a test when there are chores to be done?'

He sighed and looked up at the giant trunk of the tree, his eyes following the branches to the sky.

'Do you know where this tree came from, Malika?' he asked.

She shook her head. 'It has always been here.'

'Before you and me, certainly. But the village built itself around this tree.' He stood, picked up the box and began the walk to the car. Malika followed him.

'Do the elders not know the answer?' she asked.

'Such trees do not belong here. But here it is.'

'It does the village much good,' she said.

'It is already dying. Have you not seen the way its leaves

drop before each summer?'

She nodded. She had seen that, this year in particular. 'What will become of it? Of us?' she added.

'I do not know.' He opened the car boot and placed his box inside. 'But there are many other trees that would grow well here.' He got into the car and smiled at her. 'I will return in three weeks. Study hard.'

She watched until the car disappeared into the haze and dust.

Another priest came with Father Louis the next time. He was called Monsignor. They said Mass together in the large hut, which had been set up as usual. The unexpected arrival of the older, quiet man with the weary face and pink-lined black garments brought out the entire village. They barely fitted inside the building. Communion took twenty minutes. The older men said afterwards that a Monsignor was more important than a cardinal.

After Mass, the Monsignor sat in a chair beneath the fig tree and asked to see Malika. She stood in front of him, answering his questions patiently. She saw Ayesha and Fatima at the side and wished they were near her. She glanced at Father Louis, but he shook his head.

'Child, are you ready to sit this test?' The Monsignor said eventually. His voice sounded as tired as his face looked.

She nodded.

'It is an important test.'

It was important to Father Louis, too. 'Why?' she asked.

He smiled as he turned to Father Louis. 'The papers are in

the car, Louis,' he said.

Tucking them under his arm, the Monsignor took Malika back into the church. As they stepped across the threshold, she caught a glimpse of Fatima before he shut the door and locked the world outside.

The shadows were long across the square when Malika walked outside. Her eyes lit up when she saw Fatima rise from beneath the fig tree and cross the square towards her, then her legs wobbled without reason as her friend held out her hand.

'Did you finish?' Father Louis' voice was anxious as he emerged from a hut.

She nodded.

'Was it too hard?'

'No, except,' and she smiled, 'except the part where I had to write in Arabic.'

The priest nodded. 'That should be of little consequence.' He looked up as the Monsignor emerged from the chapel.

'We must go, Louis,' he said. He looked at Malika. 'We will know the test results soon.'

Father Louis leaned over and placed his hands on Malika's shoulders. He looked straight into her eyes. 'Whatever happens, you did well today.'

She nodded.

'Eat dinner now and then rest.'

The two men began walking to the car.

'She has a singular gift,' she heard the Monsignor say.

'I hope she did well enough,' the priest responded.

'God reveals His own.'

Fatima turned and gently pushed Malika towards her hut. 'Your face is pale,' she said. She danced lightly around her. 'But Ayesha has promised a special meal tonight. For both our families.'

'She is kind,' said Malika. Her hand reached for her friend's.

'You are family for us both,' said Fatima.

Father Louis brought the news three Sundays later. As he knocked at the hut, his smile told Malika she had done well. 'Too well,' he said, laughing. He showed her the papers and then picked her up in his arms. She shrieked and Ayesha laughed. Malika could not remember another time when she had laughed.

The priest put her down and straightened his shirt. He turned to Ayesha.

'We must talk.'

Ayesha's face changed. 'Will we need tea?'

'Perhaps tea is a good idea.'

'Malika, go and find the elders,' said Ayesha. 'Tell them Mass will be late today.'

Ayesha and Malika ate dinner in silence that night. Afterwards, the older woman left to speak with the elders. Malika was in bed when she returned. She turned off the lamp as Ayesha's head found the pillow, then lay on her back listening to the rats scurry across the roof.

'It is settled,' said Ayesha in the dark. 'You will leave in three Sundays.'

She sighed. 'I must leave?'

'Father says this village is no place for you.' She paused. 'Thinking of you will bring gladness to my heart.'

'And you?'

'I survived before you came.'

Malika placed her hand on Ayesha's arm. 'I will miss you.'

'You always have a bed here.'

'I will come often.'

The Friday before she was due to leave, Tahir stood at Ayesha's door in the late afternoon sunshine and called for Malika. But it was Ayesha who appeared from the darkness. She leaned against the doorway and looked at the strong young man before her. Not even sixteen summers old and already the black hairs on his face were enough to form a beard. A stranger then, a stranger now. She folded her arms.

'Greetings, Tahir,' she said.

He bowed his head. 'Greetings, Ayesha.'

'What do you wish of Malika?'

'I wish to watch the sunset with her on her last night.'

'There is a party planned for tomorrow. Is that not enough?'

'We arrived together. It is right we should say farewell together also. There are things I wish to say.'

Ayesha hesitated.

'Wait here,' she said.

She spoke to Malika inside the hut.

'Perhaps he wishes to make amends,' she said. 'And I know my leaving will be difficult for him.'

'Perhaps Fatima should go with you.'

Malika smiled. 'He is Tahir,' she said.

'A man cannot be trusted with a young woman alone.'

'We arrived here together as children. Now God has smiled on me and I am leaving. I know his pain.'

Ayesha's eyes stared at her, the light from the lamp flickering in their depths. Finally, she stepped outside.

'She must be home by dark,' she said to Tahir.

'I wish to talk to her.'

'Why can you not talk here?'

'She will be home by dark.'

They walked in silence to the edge of the village, crossing the railway line as a golden sun hung low over the wheat. They stood on the edge of the field.

'Your last night in the village will be filled with stars,' said Tahir, looking at the sky.

Malika nodded. It had been a mistake to come. She could barely look at him. The image of the baby goat beside the water trough welled in her memory. It made her heart beat fast.

They followed the edge of the field some way along before Tahir stopped at a small tree. He sat beneath it and beckoned Malika. She knew they were further from the village than usual, and sat a little distance from him. Tahir ignored her as he looked up.

'From my first night here, I knew I was in a prison,' said Tahir. He continued gazing upwards. 'For me, nothing has changed.'

'I will return one day,' said Malika.

'Why would you?' he asked. He turned to her, but she looked away.

She didn't hear him, didn't feel him move until it was too late, until he was almost upon her. His weight and his speed easily pushed her back. She gasped as her head hit a tree root and, dazed, tried to push him back. But he grabbed her wrists and pushed them into the dirt and cold dust.

'Tahir, what are you doing?' She tried to move, even to wriggle, but his heavy thighs straddled her legs. The weight of his body made her pant.

'Tahir, stop. You must stop this. It is madness.'

Why did she whisper? Why did she not shout out loud? Would anyone have heard if she did? Or did part of her ask for him? She did not know. Then his hand was between her legs ripping her dress wide and exposing her thighs. Her eyes widened as his knee forced her flesh apart.

She screamed with what air was left within her lungs. He was still for a moment – did he pause? – then he raised an arm and his broad fist struck down against her face, cracking bones with its force. She yelped from the pain and he punched her again. Harder. Across her cheek. And her world went black.

She woke to a world of silence, where he was inside her, and lived an eternity as he pumped her until there was nothing left. She stayed true to that world when he rose and ran, leaving her to the gathering dusk. She made not a sound as blood trickled down her throat, and trembling fingertips across her face spoke the awful truth. She was mute when Ayesha found her beneath the star-filled heavens and took her home, one step at a time, where she bathed her and washed the blood from her clothes.

'We will find justice for you against this criminal,' she said, as she placed her gently on the bed. 'My cousin will bring him to us and the elders will decide his fate. Revenge will soothe your pain.'

Her hands began to stroke Malika's forehead, but with the last of her strength Malika pushed her away.

'Revenge will not return my honour, and it will not bring back my face,' she whispered. They were the only words she would utter for the next month.

The next day, her groin bleeding, her face throbbing as if to burst, she lay in bed and stared at the wall. When Ayesha stepped out, she climbed from the bed and limped across to the mirror. She gasped. Her face belonged to another. Her nose was flattened and swollen blue, impossibly twisted. One eye was closed from the swelling on her cheekbone. She gasped again in pain as a fingertip gently prodded. She gazed at herself for as long as she could bear, until pain or her shame dragged her back to the bed, where she stayed until Ayesha returned in the evening.

part two

Melbourne

Present day

1

Her mother's car was still in the driveway. Kate parked hers outside, halfway up the hill, and turned off the ignition. She leaned across the seat and looked through the window at the red-brick house with its high-pitched roof and sagging front garden. It stared back at her. They were like two long-term acquaintances who had never quite hit it off, never really at ease in each other's company. She had hoped for more. She had wanted it to be a home.

She stepped along the winding path to the small porch in bright sunshine, trying to ignore the weeds growing thickly between the bricks. She had meant to clear them, as she had meant to water the parched garden before the funeral. On one side of the porch the front wheel of a rusted barrow was buried in garden foliage, the same place she had left it in the winter. Around its legs, fine strands of yellow grass reached almost to its belly.

Faint clattering echoed from the kitchen as she let herself in. The caterers had arrived. She exhaled in relief as she stepped into what had once been her bedroom. She looked around. It was like the wheelbarrow, untouched since her last stay. The drapes were still spread wide and the oak dresser, with its large oval mirror, was pushed hard against the wall. Two lilac-coloured pillows were neatly placed behind a pink cushion at the head of the bed, and her quilted spread was stretched drum-tight across the mattress. She perched on the edge and rubbed her palm back and forth across the spread, her bare arm pale against its creamy hue. It was her mother's wake and she might have been about to perform an operation: her feelings on hold, a task before her to complete. It had been the same at the funeral. She wanted to tell herself it was the shock.

Through the muslin curtains, a young woman in a white shirt and black pencil skirt turned off the street, carrying a tray of glasses. They rattled faintly as she walked down the driveway and disappeared around the back of the house. It was about to start. Kate glanced at herself in the mirror, then slipped her feet into her only pair of heels. She brushed out her hair, retied her ponytail, and checked the mirror again. Her mother's friends could be merciless and, numb or not, she didn't need their scrutiny today. This was about survival.

Barbara, the caterer from Maidstone who had saved her late on Friday afternoon after five knockbacks, smiled warmly as Kate appeared at the kitchen door.

'Nearly there,' she said. Fitting a hand inside an oven mitt, she pointed at the trays of pastries and small pies spread across the kitchen bench. 'Just need to put these in now.' She paused. 'Are you all right, dear?'

Kate nodded and smiled. 'I'm fine.' She eyed the lines of chicken and avocado triangles on the long white plates in front of her and her stomach clenched.

'I could only get two girls given the short notice,' Barbara continued. 'I can help, though, once I get things under control here.' She waved away a loose strand of hair. 'I'll just need five minutes to freshen up.' She creaked the oven door open, squinting from the heat, and pointed to the trays. 'Pass me the pies, will you, dear? Julia and Kaylee are setting up the bar in your lounge room. I know it's carpeted, but we thought for your mother's wake ...'

Kate nodded as she passed the tray across. 'Good idea.'

She crossed into the lounge, smiled at the suddenly silent girls, and poured a large glass of wine. Then she stood at the window, sipping, and looked out at the empty street.

An hour later, she nudged and twisted between people across a room transformed. She hadn't been to a wake before – or couldn't remember her father's as a young child. It came as a surprise to find it had its own kind of rhythm, its personal sense of order. Neighbours arrived first, as supportive as they were dry-eyed. They moved smoothly from the front door to the food trays and the bar before wandering the house, glasses charged and necks turning. She hid a smile; she could see herself doing the same. Her mother's colleagues and high-heeled clients were next, in sombre dress and suitably modest bling. Most had clearly overdone the work across the years: filler, Botox and tell-tale, discrete skin nicks seemed a condition of entry. The occasional name was familiar to her from long ago. Some though were truly shaken, their faces tear-stained or their lower lips quivering as they introduced themselves. It was touching, comforting in a detached sort of way, and she was left with a vague sense of regret for what might have been. Regret she could handle; she was used to it.

A few men turned up last as if on cue, each walking through the front door and then gathering one by one around the empty fireplace. She didn't know them, but she could guess. Her mother didn't like to be alone. They were awkward in one another's company. One placed an elbow on the mantelpiece as he gripped his drink, the others conferring with lowered heads. One of them, Thomas – Tom, he corrected himself – kept blowing his nose. Grey-haired and pale, he pursed his lips and shook his head at her offered tray. She placed a hand on his shoulder as she turned, and he reached for his handkerchief again.

She spotted Father Mike in the corner of the lounge room on her second, or possibly third, time through. He must have slipped in. He had changed out of his vestments since the funeral, and now all that distinguished him were two gold crosses, one on each collar, which gleamed above his brown leather jacket. He looked up from the woman he was talking to, his lined face opening, eyes widening, when he saw her. She smiled back.

She was too far away to make herself heard. She pointed to her tray and raised an eyebrow. He waved his hand. 'Later,' he mouthed, winking as he adjusted his glasses and focussed again on the woman. Kate nodded and moved on. Father Mike. She had struggled as a child to know whether to call him that, or Uncle Michael, or simply Michael – which was his preference, he told her once. But her mother had branded such a liberty as precocious: words that at the age of ten had carried a forbidding ring, the tone lifelong control. In the end, her mother had settled on Father Mike. But just when she'd become used to it he left, and they lost touch. She looked back at him as she left the room. He had turned sideways and was still listening to the stout, middle-aged woman whose earnest look was at odds with her colourful dress and necklace of turquoise nuggets. His wine glass was empty. He would find a way to detach himself soon, she was sure.

She rescued a fresh plate of pies from one of the waitresses, who was busy taking a selfie with some glam woman she vaguely recognised. Balancing the plate in one hand, she grabbed a bottle of bubbles from the bar with the other, crossed back into the kitchen and headed down the outside steps into the back yard, where a profusion of thirst awaited. Forcing a fixed smile as she poured, she made it to the shade of next door's jacaranda before Barbara appeared at the top of the stairs with two more bottles. They nodded to each other and Kate's face softened for a moment.

Gaynor Sweeney, owner of the high-end beauty salon where her mother had worked, tapped her on the shoulder. Kate twisted and tipped the last of the bottle into her glass without thinking. She was the only woman Kate could recall who could get away with a bright lime dress and green eye shadow.

'Thank you, dear.' She brushed back her coppery hair and placed a chubby hand on Kate's arm. 'I'm so sorry about your mother. What a shock. So sudden. We're all still reeling.'

'Thank you, Gaynor.' She nodded. 'Yes, well I guess heart attacks are like that.'

'Are you coping?'

'I'm okay.' Her eyes roamed the yard before returning to Gaynor. They would need more bottles soon. 'Really, I am. But thank you.'

'The service was as good as it could have been. Such a long way out to the cemetery at Fawkner afterwards, but that can't be helped.'

'Not easily.'

Gaynor narrowed her eyes and tilted her head. 'Will you miss her?'

Kate hesitated. 'Doesn't everyone miss their mother?'

The older woman smiled faintly. 'Of course. And we'll certainly miss her. She was our anchor: a magnet for our clients. In all her years with us, she never lost her looks. Between you and me, it took an awful lot of work, but the end product – none of us could believe it.' She smiled and narrowed her eyes slightly. 'I think you must have her – genes. Your job must help, of course.'

'What do you mean, Gaynor?' Her cheeks warmed.

'The way she was able to keep her youth. There's barely a line on your face, either.'

She forced a smile. 'Being on the right side of forty probably helps a little. And,' she added, 'for the record, I'm a plastic surgeon. You might be confusing what I do with cosmetic surgery.'

'Well, she was a wonder, however she pulled it off.' Gaynor checked her watch and gulped the last of her wine. 'I'd best go. We open again at four.' She placed her glass on the empty pie plate. 'Good luck, dear. Remember, call me if I can help.' She toddled off around the side of the house as Kate headed back up the stairs.

An hour later the lounge room was mostly deserted; people leaving as quickly as they had arrived. Kate was helping one of the waitresses feed a tray of glasses into the dishwasher when Father Mike's tall figure appeared beside the bench.

She straightened and smiled. 'Time finally for a chat?' she asked.

He tapped his watch and shrugged. 'I have to get back,' he said. 'I'm sorry. Mass at six.'

She handed the tray to one of the waitresses. 'I'll walk you to your car,' she said.

They ambled up the hill, the priest with his head down, hands deep in his pockets. Kate's head ached behind her eyes and her feet were sore in her heels. The golden glow of the late afternoon seemed wasted on them both.

'I must pay you for today,' she said.

He glanced across at her and smiled. 'We're family, Kate. Long separated I know, but still family.'

'A donation to the church, then.'

'Families do things for one another,' he said, faintly. She had to concentrate to hear him.

He turned to her when they reached his car, shielding his eyes from the sun. 'It would be good to reconnect.'

'I'd like that.'

'Let's make it happen.'

'Will you miss her?' she asked.

He paused as he thought about it. 'It was a shock when you rang. I should have kept in touch more.'

He seemed about to speak again, but a passing car slowed

and then stopped further up the hill. They watched distractedly as it reversed awkwardly into a parking spot. Father Mike rattled his keys loose from his pocket and smiled as he opened the car door. 'Let's find a time to talk.'

'That would be good.' She smiled.

She waved as the car started downhill, then shifted her gaze to the slim, blonde-haired woman she recalled vaguely from the funeral, now walking towards her. A memory stirred and she frowned, before awareness lifted the veil. It was her gait that did it – the lightness of step, square shoulders swinging rhythmically, her body effortlessly connected. Only one person walked like that. She drew a breath.

The woman held her hair to one side and her grey eyes creased in smile as she approached. 'Hello, Katie. Long time.'

'Lucy.' She smiled back. 'I hardly recognised you.'

'Too blonde?'

'Just too long, I think. You've lost weight.'

'I'm really sorry I'm late. I had a midday meeting I couldn't get out of. I only found out yesterday.'

'How did you find out?'

'Mum rang. She and Dad are in France. She asked me to go for her.'

'I'm glad.'

Their eyes met.

'I'm really sorry about your mum, Kate.'

'Thanks, Luce.' She paused. 'She really liked you.'

A breeze rustled the trees as they turned downhill. Ahead of them two women Kate didn't know were leaving the house. Heels glinting in the afternoon light, they waved as they headed for their cars.

Kate waved back and then clicked open the small gate at the top end of the block. She pushed away a low-hanging bush as they followed the curved path to the front door. 'Are you hungry? There's an abundance of food left.'

Lucy patted her stomach. 'I had a sandwich after the funeral. I needed something before the meeting.'

'I have to hang with the stayers for a while, but then I'll need a drink.'

Lucy placed a hand on her chest. 'Now that's more like it.'

'Is North Carlton too far?'

'I'm sure I could manage. Somewhere special?'

'Just not here.'

'You know,' said Lucy, as they stepped onto the porch, 'I expected you to be in shock.'

'Me too,' Kate replied. She pushed on the front door.

Lucy hesitated as the door opened and the steady rhythm of a familiar song became audible. 'Fleetwood Mac, Kate? At your mother's funeral?'

'Wow! One of the waitresses must have put it on.'

'Sure.'

'Well, whatever. Anyway, it's better than silence.'

Kate parked in the space beneath her apartment in North Carlton and headed back to the main street. Lucy was still in her car, fixing her make-up.

'Done?' Kate asked, when she finally emerged.

'Natural only gets you so far these days,' she said. She slipped Kate a look. 'For most of us.' She stepped around the car and glided her arm inside Kate's.

'Meaning?'

Lucy laughed. 'Oh, come on, Katie. It's been twenty years and you'd still make a fashion statement with my picnic rug. I was hoping you'd gained five kilos and a few wrinkles: given the rest of us a chance.' Kate blinked hard and Lucy squeezed her arm. 'Hey, I'm just jealous. Let's get a drink.'

They sat at a rickety table on the pavement outside the corner pub. Around them, numerous couples and a few small groups were also enjoying the evening cool. Behind, the pub walls were alabaster in the fading light. Across the street, a floodlit park was still green from the spring rains. Behind a row of bordering trees, blurred shapes sprinted up and down chasing a ball. Voices – shouts, and the odd whistle – punctured the traffic hum from the main road nearby.

Kate and Lucy sipped their drinks and spoke of old times, as the sky darkened and cicadas kicked into life in the surrounding trees. A waiter with rolled-up sleeves refilled their wine glasses and placed a bowl of nuts on the table. Kate crunched on a few, washing them down with her wine. She found herself staring blankly at passing cars, their headlights bright. For the first time since the two solemn-faced policewomen had stood on her front porch that night with the news, her insides churned. Maybe it was the wine, or perhaps it was because everything had been done. Reality began when the ceremonies finished. She glanced at Lucy, who had been watching her.

'It's been a long day,' Kate offered.

'Tired?'

'Yep.'

'Missing your mum, even a bit?'

Kate shrugged.

A frown crossed Lucy's face. 'I'll be inconsolable when my mother goes. When either of them go, for that matter.' Her voice was quiet. 'I know it has to happen, but as long as it's years away – decades, even – I'm okay.'

Kate drained her glass. 'It was better once I'd moved out. I'd ring her sometimes, help out in the garden. We'd talk a bit. Maybe I should have done more.' She looked for the waiter. 'So,' she said, 'what did you end up doing?'

Lucy leaned back, folding her arms. 'Nothing as impressive as you. I finished school in Sydney, got into and dropped out of journalism, then travelled for a bit. Got back to Melbourne ten years ago and did a naturopathy course. I thought I should have something to show for all the faith and money my dad invested in me over the years.'

'Do you like it?'

'Sure. Part-time it's okay. My problem is I like doing too many things.' She tilted her head. 'I'm easily bored.'

They smiled and fell silent. Kate held out her glass for another when the barman finally approached.

'You didn't get in touch after you got back to Melbourne,' she said, when he left.

'I wasn't sure I was welcome.' Lucy paused and looked down. 'I wrote to you from Sydney, Katie. I wrote even when I was overseas.'

Kate nodded and her cheeks warmed. 'VCE and then the medical course drowned me, I think.'

'I guess they must have.'

Kate looked across to the park, still frenetic with lights and footballers. She remembered a path ran around the edge.

'Too late for a walk?'

'Not for me.'

They finished their drinks and set off along the narrow bitumen track, the grass beside them as bright as noon beneath the lights. Almost halfway round a ball charged at them from nowhere, pulling up ten metres ahead. Seconds later, two men in training gear and neon boots arrived, panting heavily. They stopped a few metres away and stood grinning at the women.

'Hi, ladies,' said one. His receding hair was streaked with sweat and his top clung to his chest.

'Hi, yourself,' said Lucy. 'Shouldn't you get your ball?'

'We thought you might like to join us for a drink. We're just finishing.'

'Perhaps in another life,' said Lucy. 'My husband's waiting in the car.'

'What about your friend?' said the other, his hand on his hip.

Kate looked at him a moment before stepping onto the grass and walking towards the ball. Passing it by a few metres she turned, ran, and then kicked it as hard as she could towards the other players in the distance. Rousing cheers echoed across the pitch.

'Game over,' she said to the men. She waited until they shrugged at each other, then continued along the path.

'That was so cool,' said Lucy, as she caught up.

'I can't believe I just did that,' said Kate. 'My heart's about to jump out of my chest. Keep walking.' She glanced back, but the team was already heading towards the exit.

'No! It was the same thing you did to those guys in the bar in Year 10. Remember? You took their beers outside and locked the doors when they went out to get them.' She giggled. 'Then we slipped out the back. I miss those days. You had such balls.'

Kate lowered her head and waited until they had walked a little farther. 'Are you going to tell me about your husband?'

'It was two years ago. And yes, I was going to tell you – before *Real Madrid* turned up.'

'Good decision?'

'Definitely.' Her golden head nodded as they passed beneath a lamp. 'The best.' She breathed deeply. 'I thought you would be mad I hadn't asked you to the wedding.'

'I didn't deserve to be asked, Luce. Where did you both meet?'

'You won't believe this. He walked into my therapy room one day saying he had heard good things about me.' Her hands moved in front of her as she talked. 'I got halfway through his details and then told him I couldn't see him anymore.'

'Really?'

She laughed. 'And then I asked him out.'

Kate smiled, despite herself.

'Anyway,' she continued, 'His name's Hamish. He's a lawyer. Allens. It's some firm in the city. He's away more than he's home at the moment.'

'Never thought you'd marry a lawyer,' she said.

'Never thought I'd get married.'

As they rounded the far bend, Kate leaned against a lamp and flicked a stone out of her shoe. They headed back.

'Will you take some time off?' Lucy asked.

'Can't. I have to make up a whole day as it is. I've organised rooms first thing in the morning.'

'No one to help?'

'Everyone's just so busy.' The statement was as true as the question.

Lucy's phone buzzed. 'It's Hamish,' she said, tapping the screen. 'He's landed safely.' She began tapping a reply. 'He's in Perth for a week.'

They reached the entrance to the park then crossed the side road as they headed for the cars, ignoring the cheers from the soccer team outside the pub.

'Plans for tonight?' Lucy asked.

'I'll pick up some stuff from my place and head back to Kew. I thought I'd stay there for a few days. You know, clean it out.' Her insides were queasy at the prospect. 'It'll need to be evenings. Evenings and weekends.'

'Any thoughts about the house?'

'None.' As far as she knew, her mother hadn't made a will. Even if she had, there was nothing to say Kate would get any of it. Her church-going mother might have left the three-bedroom house to the institution that sanctified her life. Not that she needed anything her mother owned.

'Mum and Dad took six months to get everything sorted when Grandma died,' said Lucy, as they reached her car. She dug into her bag for her keys.

'I might cut back on the public work for a while, at least until I can clean the place out. I've got months of leave due, now that I think about it.'

'I can help while Hamish is away. I'm good at cleanouts,' Lucy added, her head down. She finally held up her keys and smiled. 'A hug, for old times' sake?'

Kate clung to her for longer than she intended. It was a small thing, insignificant really, and almost certainly unnoticed by Lucy, who slipped into her car as Kate crossed the road. She hovered on the far kerb, as the indicator light on Lucy's red Fiat blinked, and then merged with the traffic. She didn't know how long she stayed there. Right there, at that spot. Ten minutes, maybe more. What relevance did time have in her life just then? Eventually, she turned and strode back to her car, forcing herself to make a list of what to take to her mother's. It helped to avoid thinking of Lucy's wedding.

Kate studied her duffel bag from the end of her old bed. It was bursting. She hadn't expected to bring nearly as much. She drew the curtains, undressed, and paced the room. Unfinished business. She had put it off for days now. She glimpsed her face in the mirror as she headed down the corridor to her mother's bedroom.

Disapproval seeped from the plaster walls as her feet sank into the carpet. She passed the bed and turned into the ensuite, stopping at the dressing room. It was in darkness. She flicked the switch and the large mirror on top of the dresser burst into life, the show-lights around its edge waiting for their glamorous celebrity. Light bulbs. Forty-three, precisely. She had counted them as a child, sitting before the mirror as her mother fussed over her, and then later as her mother did the same to herself. The scent of fragrance was stifling – cloying. When had she last been in this room? She pulled open a drawer. It was chock-full of cosmetics, some costing as much as she would spend on herself in a year.

She sat at the mirror and looked around. Behind her, the wardrobe seemed to go on forever. But lose the clothes, the shoes, the expensive accessories, and it was as tired as the rest of the house. She glanced at her reflection and, on an impulse, drew her rich auburn hair behind her head, letting it tumble down her back. She tilted the mirror towards her, forcing herself to look. For once. To stay and look. Her skin, forever pale, was ivory smooth in the unforgiving light. As a child, days outside had been few – her mother aware before her time of the effects of the Australian sun. Her pool-blue eyes stared back at her, uncertain within their almond-shaped confines whether to be amused or irritated. Or afraid. Their corners creased as her full lips chanced a hesitant smile and her hands, with their strong surgeon fingers, rose to the tiny lines that appeared. Then, like a falling veil, her fingertips traced the contours of her cheekbones and the smooth curve of her jawline, before finally resting at the base of her neck.

She stayed there a minute, steadying herself, before she stood and leaned forward, her palms flat on the glass top, her breasts full and mirror-close, her long thighs squeezed against the dresser's smooth edge.

'Would it have helped if you'd talked?' she whispered to the stranger before her, watching as the mirror merely fogged and slowly cleared.

2

Kate woke early, the sun through the window a vague promise above the rooftops on the far side of the street. She blinked a few times, orienting herself, and swung her feet onto the carpet. She went about her morning routine much as she had done as a teenager: quick shower, token dabs of moisturiser on her face and neck, her hair dried, brushed and quickly tied back. On the days she was operating, it was always in a bun. And sometimes, like today, because it was practical. It was all about minimums, though she had relaxed the routine a little over the years: these days she carried a brush in her bag, and allowed herself a smear of lipstick if giving a talk or demonstration – undertakings she had learned were as much about winning your audience as they were about content.

The drive to her rooms took longer than she had expected, and she was late as she drove into the underground car park. She hurried into the reception area where Sam, the practice secretary, was at her computer behind the desk. She swivelled in her chair as Kate walked in, her round face looking up as she brushed her hair aside.

'Sorry to hear about your mum,' she said.

Kate picked up the files and patient list for the morning. 'Thanks, Sam.' She forced a smile.

'I would just die if my own mother passed,' Sam continued, her eyes back to the screen. She punched a button. 'She's got two young kids of her own, and then I'd be stuck with them.'

Kate blinked and her mouth opened. 'Well, let's hope,' she said, finally. She tucked the files under her arm and strode across the carpet to her room.

She was behind her desk scanning the patient list when Sam's head appeared at the door. 'Your first patient's arrived.'

Kate looked up. 'Thanks.' She smiled and held up a finger. 'Before you leave, I see Mrs Costello's booked in again. I saw her a month or so ago. Everything was fine.'

She shrugged. 'She confirmed yesterday.'

'I see.'

Sam shut the door and Kate spent a few minutes reading the referral from the GP for her first patient. She read it twice. And then a third time, her mind refusing to engage. She slapped a fist against her thigh as she walked to the door, paused, smiled, and opened it.

Faces and problems began to file in and out of the room, most needing surgery either sooner or later – and those that didn't requiring a referral elsewhere. A double-booking, both patients needing to be seen, put her well behind. At least Liz, her practice nurse, could sort most of the post-op wounds in the anteroom between offices. She paid her above-rate but she was worth every extra cent: a work ethic that belonged to the past and clinical smarts that couldn't be taught. Typically, she had left a condolence card on Kate's desk that morning. She was halfway through her list when Liz called her in.

'Bit of a problem with this one,' she said from behind her mask, as she propped the door open. 'It's Len,' she whispered, as Kate joined her in the small space. She remembered him well, a farmer from Gisborne who had fallen onto a box of broken beer bottles outside the pub one Friday night. He sat in the chair beside the examination couch, his arm extended. Beneath the overhead spotlight a grubby wrap, which a week earlier had been the bandage she had used in theatre, lay open on either side of his forearm. His stubbled face smiled when Kate appeared, and he wiped his free hand on his overalls, as if about to shake hands.

'Hiya, doc.'

'Hello, Len.'

He glanced at his forearm, and then at her. 'Might have a spot of trouble here, doc.' He had made her smile the last time she saw him, too.

'Let's have a look.'

His hand was as big as a steak, his fingers like sausage rolls – each fingernail bed and palmar crease invaded by soil and deep grime. An open wound extended from his wrist to halfway up his forearm, stitches yawning as yellow-green pus oozed from swollen flesh. An angry, red tinge encircled the cut. The skin flap she had painstakingly harvested and laid in surgery never had a chance. 'What happened, Len?'

The man shrugged his massive shoulders. He had been gazing in fascination at his forearm.

'You know you could have called me. Should have.'

'I thought it was okay.'

'Did you take time off work as we agreed? You said you had someone to help.'

He shrugged. 'He had to go to Sydney.'

'Okay.' She sighed. 'This might need antibiotics through a drip. In hospital.'

'Can't do it.' He shook his head. 'Crop's right to go.'

'I hear you.' She frowned, and looked across at Liz. 'Let's remove half the sutures, swab it, clean it out and I'll start him on cipro and Flagyl. God knows what's got into it from the soil.'

'Will it be all right, Doc?' his thick eyebrows pushed up high.

'I hope so. Can you see your GP the day after tomorrow? And please call me if you're not well.' She held up a hand as his mouth opened. 'I mean it. I'll see you Friday.'

Peter, a boy of seventeen, was next. His GP had called her last Friday morning. His mother had been in tears in his office after finding a black mole buried within his long curls. One look when he arrived at her rooms and Kate forced him into a theatre spot the same afternoon. She got him back when the pathologist had confirmed her fears.

Peter and his mother were forced cheer and fresh smiles when they came into the room. They sat down and she braced herself.

'It's a melanoma,' she said, watching them carefully as she spoke. 'It needs a wider removal.'

'And my hair?' Peter asked.

'I'll have to shave off your hair on that side, yes.' She paused. 'And you might need a skin graft.' A large one.

He swallowed and nodded, his eyes bright.

Kate braced herself. If she had read his mother right, her

silence until now was hardly a sign of what was to come.

She glanced at the clock as she shut the door. The appointment had put her back the better part of an hour.

Around midday, Sam put through a call from HR at the public hospital. Kate had left a message for him on the way to work. The man sounded sympathetic.

'It's called 'personal leave' these days,' he said cheerfully. 'And you have six months that you can take.'

'I was thinking of a few days.'

'Whatever. Just tell us when you're ready to come back. You'll need a medical certificate, but I'm sure you can manage that.'

It was past one by the time she got to the last name on her list. The planned mug of tea had proven as elusive as her toilet break and, as Sam brought in the last file, her trembling fingers reminded her that twenty hours without proper food was too long.

'Stephen said I can take my half day early if you're happy,' said Sam. 'Angus and I are choosing our lounge suite.'

'I guess.' She frowned. 'What time does Deb start? Is there someone to answer the phones?'

'I've put on the answering machine.'

'Can she come early, perhaps? You know how busy the phones get and we advertise that the rooms are open until five.'

Sam shrugged. 'I'll text her.'

'Perhaps do that because, Sam,' she lifted her voice as the door began to close, 'we actually do need someone here before you go.'

The door slam was predictable but not loud enough to take

it further. Kate stood behind it a moment before calling the patient in. She smoothed her top and skirt and made sure her professional face was firmly fixed before stepping into the waiting room. The woman outside leapt to her feet as she did and Kate ushered her in.

'Mrs Costello,' she said, slipping behind the desk as the woman sat. 'I thought we were done. Tell me what's wrong.'

The woman facing her was about her age. She had straightened brown hair that fell thickly around her face, an enviable taste in clothes and jewellery, and hands that were used to having other people work for her. She took a breath and looked directly at Kate.

'They're not big enough.'

'What do you mean?'

'Well, it's obvious, isn't it?'

'I disagree. And we did discuss this.'

'I know.'

'At length.'

The woman nodded.

Kate looked at the cleavage she had spent two hours operating on more than two months earlier. Leading up to that had been a series of glossy pamphlets, samples of different sizes and weights, and internet promos. They had met half a dozen times until she had seemed certain.

'They're just not what I thought they'd be.'

'I see.' She paused. 'Is your husband unhappy as well?'

'He – well, he thought they would be bigger too.'

'You don't think he'll get used to them?'

'It's not that simple,' she said.

Kate stood up and looked out her narrow window onto the street below. The traffic was thick. These days it was always thick. Even five years earlier – or was it six – when she had started here, there was a kind of rhythm to it, a pattern of ebb and flow that somehow gave it character. Not anymore. The cars extended from the traffic lights below the rooms all the way down the hill, irritation and heat simmering off the waiting bonnets. She closed her eyes.

'Let me have a look,' she said, without turning around.

'Same as before?'

'Please. Tell me when you're ready.'

'Does that mean you can redo them?'

'It means I'll examine you.'

She was sitting at the table in the tearoom, her hands clasped around a large mug, a mouthful of double-dipped Tim Tam dissolving on her tongue, when Stephen Campbell's long legs and expensive belt walked past.

'Why do I do breasts?' she asked.

'I didn't think you did.'

The kettle clicked behind her and began to hiss.

'Occasionally I break my own rules. Every time I do, I regret it.'

'Send them to me.'

'She seemed like she was sorted. Nice lady, we got on. Now, they're not right.'

'Husband found someone else?'

'Maybe.' She gulped her tea. 'I gave her a C cup; anything more with her frame and her back would give out.'

'Tell her that.'

'Made no difference.' She tipped the blue packet looking for another biscuit. It was empty. 'Damn it!' She slapped her hand on the table.

There was a pause. 'Should you be here, Kate?'

She shrugged and he dropped onto the chair beside her, his craggy face serious for a change. He took off his glasses, one eye's gaze not quite matching the other as he looked at her. It made it impossible to know which eye to focus on. It had been the same when she was training with him, but she hadn't felt comfortable asking him which one she should choose. She finally did when he and his then wife had taken her to dinner after her final exams. A couple of wines down and she said if they were going to work together, she had to know which eye to look at. He had stared at her and for a heart-stopping moment her career evaporated in front of her. Then Elena leaned across and placed a hand on hers. 'It's been the same with me for twenty years,' she said. Only then did he laugh and wink at her, first with one eye and then the other, and they toasted a new beginning. He and Elena separated the next week. It had nothing to do with her – she knew that – but a brooding sense of involvement stayed with her nonetheless, as if she'd been witness to something she didn't understand. Needless to say, she still didn't know which eye.

'Go home, Kate,' he said. 'God's sake. Why couldn't you ask one of us to fill in today?'

'I'm fine. Anyway, I've still got my inpatients to see. Martine was only able to cover yesterday. And then I've got a late clinic.'

'Where?'

'Malvern.'

'I'll do it.'

'It's Wednesday, Steve.'

'Yeah, but the golf's tweaking my back at the moment. Glad of an excuse, to be honest.' He studied her again. 'Go on. Get out of here.'

'I can do it.'

'The good news is you don't have to. Anyway, you've covered my arse before.'

She raised a hand in defeat. 'Okay. Thank you. I'll sort the inpatients. I've only got three, and Martine thought two of them were almost good to go yesterday. By the way, did Sam speak to you?'

He looked vague. 'Maybe. Something about a couch, I think.' He picked a mug from the rack and spooned in coffee. The water followed.

'She wants to leave early, again.'

'Oh!' he sipped loudly, 'Well, as long as the patients are sorted, I guess.'

'I'm not sure you can bank on that.'

'Deb starts at two. She'll fix it.'

'At the moment, Sam's got attitude with a capital "A".'

'I'll talk to her.' He nodded and paused. 'Unless you want to.'

The butterflies began in the pit of her stomach as if they had been listening. She swallowed. 'I'm supposed to be the junior partner.'

He grinned. Well, it was worth a try.' He checked his watch. 'Better get back to it. It's Cabrini this afternoon, right?'

She nodded. 'Four o'clock.' She rubbed her face with her hands, energy draining from her like love withdrawn.

'Are you sure?'

'Go on. Get out of here.'

The melanoma in the boy's scalp two days later went deep, deeper than the original biopsy had indicated. Deeper even than she had feared. The scalpel in her gloved hands was almost through the shaved scalp before she found the margin. She swapped glances with Dave, her anaesthetist.

'Not good,' he said, his mask pearly green in the reflected lights.

'Not even slightly. I'll contact Myron Davis when I get out. This boy's going to need everything the oncologists can throw at him.'

'His family came with him into pre-op.'

'They're close. That's my job this evening.'

He squeezed on the ventilator bag and checked the heart monitor. 'Times like this I know why I chose anaesthetics.'

The windows along the hospital corridor were dark by the time she got to Peter, his face pale to the point of angelic beneath a headful of bandages. He was deeply asleep. Dave had made sure he'd been given enough narcotics. The family stood around his bed: strained, tearful, hopeful. The father looked at Kate when she walked in and moved to the armchair at the end of the room, putting his head in his hands and staring at the floor, as if deep in thought. It was he who, twenty minutes later, wouldn't let her leave.

She stayed with them for another ten, explaining again what she'd seen in theatre, and that it was now a matter for the oncology doctors, stressing as she did so that recent advances in treatment were highly effective. She hoped to God the new drugs that Myron Davis, the head of oncology, was crowing about were as good as he claimed. They nodded, somehow finding a smile as they thanked her. When she turned to leave the father moved across and stood in front of her. His face was pale and his hair mussed as he looked her in the eye.

'He's not going to get through this, is he, doc?'

She took a deep breath and squared her shoulders as she gave him the answer he already knew, the one he would have given anything not to know.

She closed the door and slunk from the ward, hugging the railings along the wall and keeping her head down as she passed the nurses' station. Her thighs trembled on the stairs down to the car park. She checked her phone on the way down. Three texts from Sam, same patient: Mrs Costello urgently requesting another appointment. She threw the phone on the front seat as she got in the car.

In bed back at her mother's the moon was a beacon through the muslin curtains. She tracked it across a barren sky, finally dozing off as first light touched the morning sky.

Lucy had texted on Friday night saying she had kept Saturday free. Kate's finger hovered over the screen as she was about to reply. A catch-up had been comforting; reconnecting was another matter completely. Old friendships, like parents, were embedded in the debris of the past; debris she had spent her life escaping. As a teenager, she had locked Lucy out of her life. It wasn't just Lucy. She couldn't face anyone after what had happened: mortification and guilt haunted her every moment;

her mother had made sure of it. Would she do it again? She was on the verge of forming an excuse – she was an expert – when something Stephen had said to her as she left on Tuesday came to mind. 'Why don't you spend some time with friends,' he said, as she collected her things. 'At times like this, they can help.' On the way across to her mother's she had tried to think of someone. But apart from Stephen and maybe Mel, his current wife, in short bursts, there was no one. It had been the same the last time she'd thought about it. Her Christmas list was all but non-existent. Almost of its own accord, her finger began tapping. Anyway, seeing Lucy one more time didn't mean it would go anywhere.

Pausing at the entrance to her mother's lounge room, she removed her scarf and eased a strand of hair behind her ear. The room had been turned into a tip, now filled with half-packed boxes, piles of clothes, and accumulated stuff from over the years. Some of it she remembered from when she still lived there.

Lucy lay stretched out on the cushion beneath the bay window, a magazine and the remnants of lunch in her lap. She had arrived that morning as promised, bringing a baguette and the last three days' mail from the letterbox. She raised her head as Kate entered.

'Nearly done?'

'Getting there.'

'It's hard work sorting.'

Kate looked at her and put her hands on her hips. 'It must be.'

'Hey!' said Lucy, 'I brought lunch. Anyway, you have to decide about most of it. One thing I'll say,' she put her feet on the carpet, 'your mother could hoard. Did she throw anything out?'

'Not much. She hid things, as if it was too good for "now" – whatever that meant.' She picked up a bag. 'I found six sets of sheets in the garage. Ten or more new towels. And a dinner set she'd never used.' She put up her hands. 'Take what you want.'

'I'm a bit fussy about those things. I'll have a look.' Lucy wandered over to a collection of photos hanging on the wall.

'Who else but my mother would hang pictures of herself around the house?' asked Kate.

Lucy peered more closely. 'You look more like her now than you used to.'

'Don't say it.'

Picking up a Stanley knife and a roll of tape from the mantelpiece, she ripped off several lengths, each about sixty centimetres long. She had become an expert. Lucy helped, squeezing the sides of the box as she taped it shut.

'You know what I find funny?' said Lucy.

'What?'

'After all your bitching about this place, you've moved in.'

'I'm just cleaning it out. I'm going to sell it.'

'But you could have done that and stayed at your apartment. Or got packers to do it for you.'

'That's funny?' Kate frowned. Had it just been a long morning?

'How long will you stay, then?'

Kate shrugged. 'Once I finish I'm out of here. But it is closer to work. Well as close. Sort of.'

'You see? You said you hated this place.'

'I – does it matter right now?' She pasted on the last length of tape and straightened, staring at Lucy, who raised her hands.

'Not to me.'

'Me, either.' Her arms ached as she looked down at the box. 'Let's get this down to the others.'

They dragged it to the small recess outside her mother's bedroom where the other boxes from the morning were stacked. While Kate counted and labelled them, Lucy fussed with her hair in front of the hallway mirror.

'You know,' she said, 'I was just saying that what you're doing here at this place isn't the same as what you've been saying. Even the night after the funeral you seemed a bit vague. I thought then it was just me.' She leaned into the mirror and pressed at a blemish. 'There's nothing wrong with that, I mean it's your mother's place. It's just surprising after what you've said.'

'Thanks. I heard you,' she snapped.

Lucy looked at her, her mouth agape as the years fell away. Best friends once, the bonds of the past had not proven enough. For a moment, Kate thought Lucy would walk, but instead she smiled faintly.

'Well, you know best,' she said. That seemed as far as she could go to a resolution. She drew back from the mirror and picked up her bag. 'Anyway, I'd better go. Hamish is home in a couple of days, and I haven't shopped all week.'

'I'll keep going here, I think.'

'Okay.' Lucy smiled again.

'I'll see you out.'

After she left, Kate pulled a bottle of wine out of the fridge and opened it in the shade on the back steps. The hurt in Lucy's eyes had been plain as she climbed into her car. Kate would make amends, she would. She leaned her head against the window and poured another glass. Why couldn't friendship be more like surgery? Simple. Clean. Together you and your scalpel got rid of problems and everything was well. But then a patient like Peter came along and even a scalpel didn't help. She stayed on the steps until the afternoon drifted towards evening and the mosquitoes hovered around her bare ankles.

The mail Lucy had brought in earlier was on the bench. When she finally went inside, she began to leaf through it. Nothing special until she got to the last one. She turned it over. A plain white envelope, except for the address of her mother's solicitor on the back. She swallowed, and fumbled in the drawer for a knife.

Her eyes quickly ran down the page. No will, so the house should be hers, although the formalities might take twelve months. It preyed on her mind as she headed to the bedroom and then as she stood under the shower. A week earlier, she had been ready to put the house on the market. Now that she could sell, would she? Hadn't Lucy's question been the same, more or less?

She found the photo in her mother's desk the following Saturday. She had approached the locked bureau reluctantly, fearing secrets might be held in the nooks and pockets of its wood panels. Mostly it proved to be receipts and insurance certificates, and the predictable letters from her mother's various men over the years. Finding the house title deed was a relief.

The photo was the last of a pile, buried in a small box down low at the back and covered by a few faded letters. It was dated 1975. She checked the back, where her father's neat writing identified the three people standing on the beach. Beside her father – looking even younger than she remembered him – and mother, was a youthful Michael Cunningham. Tall and square-shouldered, he was oddly disconsolate, standing slightly separate as the other two beamed at the camera. Her mother had her head against her father's chest and her arm around his waist. Her other hand was on Father Mike's shoulder. She hadn't known the three of them went so far back. She had known Father Mike as a child, especially after her father died, then saw him again in her twenties, almost by accident, when he had returned from years in India and Pakistan. She nestled the photo in her purse and put the box in a mostly empty plastic tub, together with a few other family mementos she had found. One day she might look at them again.

3

There was a message on her mobile when she got up Tuesday morning. Father Mike. She took advantage of an empty tea room and a break between operating cases to ring him back. Mug in hand, she sank into one of the worn-out lounge chairs that formed a ring around the walls. Tucking one foot under her scrubs she dialled with her free thumb.

His voice was reserved, quiet, lacking the easy reassurance of the week before. He asked to meet that evening and they agreed on seven o'clock, or as early as Kate could make it. She frowned as she hung up.

Stephen appeared in the doorway. 'Good to go? They're waiting.'

She followed him down the corridor to the theatre washroom, pulling on a mask as she entered.

She joined him at the sink. He glanced at her as he began scrubbing. 'You are coming to our Christmas drinks again this year?'

She forced a few stray hairs beneath the elastic rim of her theatre cap. 'Christmas Eve?'

'Of course.' His eyes creased behind his mask. 'Can't change an institution.'

'I think I might have pencilled it in after the last one.' She flicked on the taps, the water immediately warm on her wrists and hands.

He chuckled. 'It did go on a bit, didn't it? Felt a bit sorry for the young ones who went home to early starts. Didn't stop them drinking my booze, though. Anyway, Mel's desperate to show you the extension. Been this year's obsession.'

'Sounds great.' She pumped the soap container and pulled out a nailbrush from the container on the wall. 'How did Wednesday go?'

He looked at her blankly.

'My rooms at Kew.'

'Oh, yeah.' He nodded. 'Fine.' He winced as he straightened. 'Think I really need to give the golf away for a while. Just as my handicap's finally improving.' He reached for a nailbrush. 'I didn't know you bulk-billed them.'

'Not everyone.'

'I don't do that.'

'Oh.' She tried to think who might have been on her list.

He flicked off the taps with his elbows and picked up a sterile towel from the tray behind them. 'They dress like they've got nothing, and the next visit they're showing you photos of their trip to Europe.'

'Some, maybe.'

Hands high, he headed to the swing doors, pausing with his back against them. 'They work it out.' He winked at her. 'I'm good, but I'm not cheap.' His eyes rolled. 'So don't ask me why I'm still working public. See you in there.'

She finished scrubbing, switched off the taps with her elbows, and followed him in.

The second case was trouble from the start. The man had been in a fight. His heavy, tattooed arms and two long scars on his neck said it wasn't his first. They managed to expose the fractured nasal bones easily enough, but when Kate tried to fix the septum into place, it wouldn't budge. She looked across at Stephen, who smiled knowingly behind his mask. He could be such a pain.

'We focus on one area and forget the others,' he said, circling the exposed field with his finger. 'This chap's had his face bashed, not just his nose. You have to remember that. If we operate just on his nose, we may miss the central issue. The art of anatomy is much underrated.'

'Shall we get the faciomax guys?'

'No need. The bones simply want to be in their correct positions.' He pointed to the computer screen at the end of the theatre. 'If you check the films, there's a small but important angulation of the zygoma. Normally, we mightn't touch it. In this case, there's just enough pressure to cause havoc. Watch now.'

He chose a large probe from the tray beside him and angled it into the area beneath the cheekbone. There was a soft crunch, a grinding sound, and suddenly the pressure on the nasal bones resolved.

'Now try the nose again,' said Stephen, fixing his gaze on her beneath the spotlight. 'Then I'll plate the zygoma.'

She blinked. 'That was really good, Stephen.'

He grinned. 'Just when you think you've seen it all.'

She smiled as she slowed along Studley Park Road, just before it ran its long course downhill to the river. She knew this place, this red-brick wall of mystery with its profusion of green-leafed trees on the other side, but she hadn't known it was a Jesuit house. In her early days at university, the bus would stop at this corner with a throng of schoolboys cramming the exits, all bags, blazers and skinny legs. Somehow they fell, pushed, fought and jumped their way through the doors onto the kerb and then, their bags over their shoulders, raced the bus along the pavement until the road diverged, the bus pulled ahead, and they would look on, beaten. In those days, she would ask herself if her own child might have run to get ahead of the bus too – perhaps even beat it – and if she would ever get another chance to find out.

She turned the car through the open gate at the end of the wall, her tyres crunching on the pebbled drive as she cruised beneath long-established trees. Green lawns and deep garden beds were spread wide on either side. Near the bottom of the slope, a building large enough to be a schoolhouse rose monolith-like from the white pebbles. She drove round to the side and parked in a scooped-out area, beside the century-old walls. Fixing her hair behind her head, she stepped out of the car and climbed the stone steps to the entrance. The front door handle turned in her hand and she let herself into the over-large foyer as Father Mike had suggested. It was impenetrably quiet. All around, heavy-framed portraits and faded photos interrupted aged, dark-oak panelling that seemed to soak up what little evening light could enter. Stale smoke and the faint, acrid smell of old men lingered.

A door creaked to one side, and an orange jumper came towards her. She smiled as Father Mike extended his arms.

'Sorry about the lack of light. Few visitors at this time of day,' he explained, as they embraced briefly. He looked back at the door he had come through. 'Would you like a drink?'

'I'm fine.' Kate glanced around the room again. She shivered. 'Shall we go outside?'

They tracked back down the steps, crossing the pebbled car space, and continued down the slight incline until the land flattened and meandering paths crisscrossed through well-tended garden plots, thick with vegetables. Kate chose a track at random and they strolled between head-high vines, the traffic noise in the distance barely audible.

She held out a hand and let it drift, feather-light, through staked beanstalks. 'I used to wonder what lay behind that red-brick wall on the street,' she said.

'I sometimes still wonder that,' he replied. He pointed to a row of peas and neatly spaced lettuces in front of them. 'I planted these at the start of spring. Each year they grow faster.'

Nearby, at another plot, an old man in a faded t-shirt and black Wellingtons had his back to them as he watered a herb garden. His hose dripped as he fanned a sprinkler across the plants with the same deliberate lack of haste she had noticed in Father Mike. The man turned when the priest called him, rotating his head just enough to see them with both eyes. He nodded.

'Brother Amos has been here for forty years,' said Father Mike, as they ambled towards the end of the garden.

'That's a long time to live behind a brick wall.'

'It's a long time to live anywhere.'

He plucked two ripe tomatoes from a nearby vine and handed her one. He bit into his and sucked deeply, his white hair and the redness of the fruit luminescent in the evening light.

She took a bite and looked at him.

He nodded. 'You were right. It is time we talked.' He threw the last of his tomato into the garden and they began walking. 'We received bad news from the high commission a couple of days ago. Two of our Pakistan missionaries, one of them Australian, have gone missing. It appears it happened over the weekend.' He glanced at her, his eyes troubled. 'Time is of the essence.'

She studied his face, his set jaw. 'You're going there, aren't you?'

'I worked there for many years. I may be able to help. And,' he added, 'they are ultimately my responsibility.'

'When do you leave?'

'The earliest flight is tomorrow night.'

She nodded slowly, her head moving in time with each step. He could have told her this on the phone this morning. 'Is there anything else?'

He put his hands in his pockets and glanced at her. 'Kate, I also have a favour to ask of you – if you are willing. There is a girl there that needs to come to Australia. Assuming I am successful, she would benefit from having a friend here.'

'A girl from Pakistan?'

He nodded.

She thought for a moment. 'This hasn't just happened, has it?'

'There have been efforts to get her out for six months, but it has been complicated. Now there is a sense of urgency.'

'Is she connected to the missing priests?'

'She has known my friend, Louis, there for some years. He believed she was in danger. It seems that he was right.'

Her hands clenched behind her back and a stubborn lump rose in her throat, pinching her voice as she spoke. 'What do you want me to do?'

'We have negotiated a place for her to board at your old school. I need someone to help her. Perhaps let her stay with you for a few weekends until Easter. I know you are very busy.'

She cast him a sideways glance. 'The school told you about me, didn't they?'

'They did mention your name.'

There was a time during her surgical training when she had billeted foreign students on occasion. Before work took over her life. She knew what it was like to feel alone at school.

They left the path and began climbing the rise, the grass crisp beneath their feet. Around them, birds swooped between the trees.

'Will she go to school here? Would it be for the whole year?'

'We hope so. She will also be at the university. Louis believes she has a great gift,' he added.

They reached the top of the garden and he leaned against a large oak, the traffic now loud on the other side of the wall. The yellow top of a bus rumbled past.

'Why me?' she asked.

'I do not have a lot of time. And if the news is bad, she will need a friend. '

'I don't know if I can commit to that, Father.' She sighed. 'My life is overfull as it is.'

'Sometimes a full life is glad of diversion.'

'And sometimes it's just full.'

He nodded and smiled, pushing himself off the tree as she swatted a mosquito on her leg. They began back.

'What will it mean if I can't?'

'Something will work out.'

'I can't promise anything.' Her words came of their own accord.

'Whatever you can do will be much appreciated.'

They had almost reached the stairs at the bottom of the drive when a thought occurred to her. She had almost forgotten. She put her hand in her pocket and pulled out the small photo she had found in the bureau at her mother's. 'I meant to ask you about this.'

A smile came to his face as he studied it. 'I had forgotten about this,' he said.

'What was my mother like as a young woman?'

'She was very beautiful.' He paused. 'Though at times she lacked heart.'

She wasn't sure if he was talking to her, or to himself. 'She could be like that later on, too.'

He lifted his gaze from the photo and looked at her with a softness that told her he knew more about her past than he had ever said.

'Perhaps having a heart only causes trouble,' Kate added.

'Any heart can make mistakes. There is a difference.'

An Asian man in a white shirt appeared at the top of the

stairs. He nodded his head deferentially. 'Will you be joining us at dinner, Father?'

Father Mike put a foot on the lowest step. 'I'll be right there, Phillip.' He turned to Kate. 'It is time,' he said.

'People have depended on me before,' she said. 'I let them down.'

'With trust, there is always that chance.'

She looked, but in the gathering dusk, couldn't see his eyes. 'Don't be away too long,' she said.

She didn't hug him. She knew he wanted her to and part of her wanted that also. But she wasn't used to hugging her father's brother and besides, she decided as she drove back to her mother's, she was cross with him. Cross he got her name from the school, cross about this girl that he wanted to drop in her lap, but mainly – *mainly* – she was cross that he knew about her past.

By the end of the week, it was everywhere. She listened to the report on *PM* as she drove to Carlton for more clothes and to feed the few plants she kept around her bare-walled apartment. They had to be hardy to survive; she had chosen them for that reason. She sat at the round table, chewing on sushi as she listened to the SBS reporter from Pakistan. He was doing his best, but either he didn't know anything or he had been gagged. The information was in the public arena, and at the same time it wasn't. No sign or mention of Father Mike. The TV images had been fuzzed by glaring lights and hieroglyphic captions. Bearded men in khaki robes flashed across the screen, one shoving an outstretched hand at the camera.

She watered the cactus and the two hydrangeas on the back patio, ironed a week's worth of clothes, slung them over her arm and locked the front door. As she headed to her car it crossed her mind that Lucy might have been right. It was strange that she was spending all her time at her mother's. This had been her abode for five years – by all definitions her home. Except it wasn't.

The newspaper headlines the next morning created their own truth. She read the articles as she waited for coffee. 'Find Our Priest!' the *Herald Sun* thundered, but the pictures were the same indecipherable camera shots as were shown the previous night on TV. *The Age* was much the same, apart from an editorial deploring the rise of terrorism and its tentacles that reached across the globe. Nothing new. No requests for money, no internet releases. Just gone. Inevitably, it was the top story on her car radio that afternoon as she drove to her rooms. But again it was a rehash, and she sensed that already interest was beginning to wane – no story without new information. The non-committal voice of the foreign minister that night was the death knell: a tragic but random attack; everything that could be done was being done. Kate translated that to mean the two men had been abducted.

Her suspicions were confirmed a few days later with a half-hearted segment on *The 7.30 Report*. The journalist could only allude to unnamed emissaries who had been sent across as Archbishop someone asked for prayers and understanding. His unwavering gaze at the camera was a welcome change from the blinking, hesitant apologist of several months earlier, 'deeply regretting' the epidemic of child abuse in the Church. She had received a short email from Father Mike when he arrived mid-week, but since then, nothing. By Friday, all air-play had gone the same way. The parochial waters of political infighting and a pending Test series had closed over the 'heroic missionaries who sadly might have just risked too much' – as one mournful reporter put it. Further publicity, and the pressure that could be applied from it, would only occur now with hard news – or possibly if the First Test was a washout.

The next few weeks passed in a haze of work. At the public hospital, it was a stream of casualties, from deep lacerations to severed nerves, usually after a potent mix of drugs and boozy nights or, from the fringes of the state, complex patients needing intricate solutions – a euphemism for coordinating two or three surgeons at once. The private side was just as busy if less intense, with its pre-festive run of skin cancers requiring attention before another summer of sun, and rescuing botched cosmetic procedures that had overstretched plausibility. She was rarely home before midnight. She grew used to waking in her old bed that creaked when she rolled over, familiar too with turning left for a shower in the morning, and left again at the end of the street for work.

She coaxed and pleaded with Lucy for a drink of atonement one Friday night, weaselling time from work to get there early. It ended with them both soaking drunk and shivering in the blast of an icy wind as they waited on Exhibition Street for an Uber. Lucy told her halfway through the evening she had the social skills of a Carmelite nun.

'No offence,' she added, pouring herself another glass and staring over the rim.

'None taken,' Kate replied. She raised an eyebrow. 'I guess that makes us one-all.'

Lucy raised her glass. 'Let's drink to the future!'

Inexorably, Christmas approached. It was a season that always baffled her. The rules she had learned as a child belonged to another life, where her father, home from work on Christmas Eve, would speak of Santa starting his trip from the North Pole for all good children. And her stomach would churn and her eyes become round as she remembered the times she hadn't been good at all. Then her father would laugh and she would too, and she was sure – she was *sure* – sometimes, so would her mother. Once, years later, she told her mother she missed the Christmases they'd shared as a family. Her mother had simply stared at her, her pristine face taut, as if what her daughter said belonged to a script she didn't have.

Perhaps to hide the emptiness, or possibly to avoid reliving the past, most years she volunteered to be on call at the hospital. It had become a habit that the other surgeons now relied on – to see their kids and drink more booze, basically. And she had come to enjoy her Christmas Days in theatre – carols playing through the speakers and Santa hats a rite of passage for any anaesthetist unlucky enough to be on call. But it was the lacerations and facial wounds, and the occasional failed suicide attempt, that kept her there.

Her one obligation for the festive season was drinks on Christmas Eve at Stephen's. From experience, she arrived by Uber – Mel drank like the desert sand, and they would knock off a bottle or two together as Mel tried to set her up with some new 'suitable hunk' she had met. Kate let her do it because it gave them something to laugh about together.

Stephen answered the massive double door when she rang the bell. A blue jacket over an open shirt and freshly-ironed pants had to be Mel's doing. 'Kate!' he beamed, standing back and holding out his hands.

'Getting an early start I see, Stephen,' she said, as he held her wrist and kissed her cheek.

'You betcha!' He stood back and looked at her. 'Wow! Great dress. You should wear them more often. Let me show you around.'

He led her into a room big enough to have accommodated her whole apartment. It had completely changed since her visit twelve months earlier. Smelling of fresh paint and new rugs, ornate parquetry glowed beneath rows of downlights set into the high ceiling. Along the inner wall, statues and artworks nestled in alcoves, and marble steps at the end divided a bookcase set into the wall. A waitress appeared at the top of the steps, balancing a large tray.

'This way,' said Stephen, nudging her elbow.

Bypassing the forty or more guests – at this stage still standing awkwardly in groups – he ignored the doorbell and took her across the room to a wall of glass at the front of the extension. The city sprawled before them, invading the room like a giant TV screen. She could make out the logos of the nearest buildings, count the individual floors left alight. Directly below them a dark ribbon of water wound its way silently between the freeway and the flood-lit gums from neighbouring properties.

'You've been busy,' she said, turning to him.

He grinned. 'Do you like it?'

'It's – amazing. Is Mel happy?'

'Are you serious? It's her baby. Months in the planning and a whole year rebuilding. But look at it. What gets me is the engineering.' He waved an arm lengthwise along the floor. 'Under our feet is a single stretch of iron that took two cranes to load into place. Two.' He leaned towards her ear. 'She needs a new project for next year.'

'What's he saying about me this time?' Mel approached with two filled flutes, somehow managing to coax her hair behind her shoulders as she did. Her dress hugged her curves and then fell naturally to graze the floor – except there was nothing natural about it. She passed a glass to Kate. 'Here almost five minutes and still no drink. Unacceptable.' She raised her glass and looked at Stephen. 'Here's to projects.'

'Here's to finishing them,' he said. They smiled.

She turned to Kate, her earrings sparkling as they caught the light. 'Speaking of houses, Stephen tells me you're squatting at your mother's. That must have its moments.'

'It's okay. Fine, actually.'

'What will you do with it?'

She shrugged. 'Sell it when I can, I think. It needs a lot of work.'

'Well, my advice is to wait until March. No one with the money to buy a house in Kew hangs around Melbourne in January. And with all that back-to-school stuff the world goes crazy in February.'

Kate sipped her champagne. 'It might take a little longer

than that.'

Mel turned to Stephen. 'You're suddenly quiet.' She winked at Kate. 'I normally don't get a word in about real estate.'

Kate took a longer look at Stephen, who winced before draining his flute and placing it on a nearby table. 'Is your back okay?' she asked.

'Just a twinge.' He beamed. 'Not a problem.'

'Good enough to go cycling with his mates for three hours this morning,' said Mel. 'He thinks these parties just happen by themselves.'

'As my bride points out,' said Stephen, 'I can still cycle.'

'So, dear, take some Panadol and let the rest of us enjoy the party. Kate didn't come here to hear anyone whining.'

'I did ask,' said Kate, instinctively protective. Though their banter hadn't changed in the five years she had known them.

'Thank the Lord for loyal colleagues,' he said, selecting another flute from the tray as the waitress passed.

Mel surveyed the gathering crowd. Something about her movements – or maybe it was her profile – made Leah Costello pop into Kate's head. A boob job had been Mel's project the year beforehand, cheekbones and nose the year before that.

'Oh, God,' said Mel, 'the CEO did come.' She leaned into Kate's ear. 'I'll be back. I've got just the man for you this year. No joking. And,' she stared into Kate's eyes, 'he said he might drop in tonight.'

'Can't wait,' said Kate.

'I'll bring back a bottle just for us.' She winked.

Mel found her again when the numbers in the room – it was really more of a hall – were enough to make it crowded. She guessed a couple of hundred. Champagne had morphed into cocktails and still wine, the barmen in one corner were working their shirts and braces off, and laughs and occasional screeches drowned out the string quartet that had begun playing shortly after she'd arrived. Taking Kate's arm, Mel dragged her to a padded bench beside one of the bookcases at the base of the stairs. She filled Kate's glass with the promised bubbles, refilled hers, and they rested back on the stacked cushions.

'You're looking very pleased,' said Kate.

She smirked. 'Knowledge is power.'

Kate waited. Or tried – but it was her third glass or maybe her fourth. 'Okay, I'm interested,' she said.

Mel shook her head. 'Next glass,' she said.

Kate skulled and held out her glass.

Mel refilled and touched the side of her index finger to her fine nose. 'All I can say is the hospital's new professor of surgery has arrived from London. More importantly,' she added, 'he's here by himself.'

That was it? She was disappointed. The rumour had been circulating for a couple of weeks, though no one had seen him yet. 'They advertised everywhere about six months ago,' she said, 'when Graeme left. Big shoes to fill.'

'Well, it's sort of hush-hush I gather, while he finds his feet. And he's an ENT surgeon,' she added, looking mystified, 'which Stephen says never happens. He must be brilliant.' She swooped on the bottle resting beside her heels and restocked their glasses. 'We had him here for dinner last week. Stephen will see him a lot, I think. You know he still does all those public sessions, don't you? I don't know why. The money's hardly worth it.' She leaned across and placed a hand on Kate's forearm. 'One thing I can tell you for sure. He is *cute*.' She looked at Kate with the intensity of the converted. 'And I mean cute.'

'Maybe he's gay.'

'Not a gay vibe in sight,' she said, confidently. 'My guess is he's divorced, and he's come here to get away from it. I can understand that.'

Kate finished her glass. Mel actually seemed serious. Serious and sloshed was not a good combination for Mel. Nor for her, she decided as she tried to stand. Had they really finished the bottle? She looked around. Stephen wasn't anywhere and he was tall enough to be visible across the room. Mel said he was most likely in the kitchen putting his culinary skills to use. Or getting another box of wine. Kate checked her watch. Almost eleven. Maybe boy wonder wasn't going to show after all. Regardless, it didn't matter.

She waited until Mel wandered elsewhere, then booked an Uber and slipped out the front door. She would gush a thank you note in the morning. As a couple, they were anything but tight; the celebrations seemed to grow with each year. She trod uncertainly down the steps towards the front gate, glad of the tiered lights. Halfway down, she passed a man in a tweed jacket. He looked at her as he climbed past, and she returned his vague smile. She turned when she heard him trip behind her.

She retraced a couple of steps and reached out to help the figure still picking himself up. 'Are you all right?' Her voice sounded loud in the stillness. With the mansion behind them and the illuminated steps at their feet they could have been in a theatre.

'No problem at all,' he said. 'Thank you. Absolutely fine.' He straightened, brushed off his pants and adjusted his glasses. He looked into her face a long moment before extending a hand. 'Andrew Jamieson. Very pleased to meet you.'

English as a red bus. Younger than she expected. For a professor. Slim too, unlike Graeme. His hand was warm and firm. 'I'm expecting an Uber,' she said. 'Kate, by the way.'

'Of course. Delighted. Kate.' He pushed on his glasses again, making her smile.

She turned back down the steps, holding up a hand and waving as she continued. 'Enjoy the party, Andrew.'

'Thank you!' floated back the response.

She exhaled at the bottom step and let her head settle. Awkward. Very. She didn't need awkward in her life.

A few minutes later, inside the Uber as the driver did a three-pointer, she looked up at the mansion above. With its stone walls and sweeping lights, it rose from the earth as if meant for eternity.

4

The slight figure in the black niqab stood in the queue to get off the bus. Father Louis was waiting for her in the fading twilight. She waved to him across the small crowd that was waiting to board, working her way between them as they surged around her.

'I know my way back, Father Louis,' she said, touching his arm. 'In the dark as well as the light.'

'Then you can show me,' he said. 'I have come with news.'

The bus rumbled past as they began walking, a grey cloud of exhaust fumes rising behind it.

'Is it someone in the village?'

'Not that I have heard. Your visa has come through.'

She remained silent. 'I do not wish to leave here,' she said eventually.

He directed her down an alley where they walked beneath washing strung between high buildings. The smells of dinner were strong. Some families were cooking outside in the cool evening; they greeted the black-clad girl and the priest as they passed. At one point, where the alley narrowed, they were forced against a side wall with the other pedestrians, as a taxi drove through. The driver waved, nodding his head as the cab inched its way forward. Nearby families watched from each side as they held back their goats and skinny dogs.

Father Louis spoke again. 'The school and the university professor you have been writing to in Melbourne both wrote letters to support you. Is that not a good thing? You will learn a great deal.'

'Yes,' she said. 'That is a good thing.' She paused. 'But the university in Lahore is good, too. And,' she continued, before he could interrupt, 'the one in Islamabad is very good, if Lahore is too close. Can I not learn as much there?'

'Perhaps,' he said.

They turned onto the main road, where traffic crawled and angry horns sounded. Bright lights from shop windows and open stalls made the priest look pale. She imagined she looked the same. They stepped around a beggar and then another, Father Louis stopping as usual to drop a coin in their bowls. Malika waited for him. During the past two months he had met her at the bus stop whenever he was in town. Each time they would take different routes back to the religious house, and many times he had told her she must do the same. 'Mix up your walk on the way home,' he would say, encouraging and scolding her at the same time. 'Do not be predictable.' And she had tried to do as he asked.

It had become important since Father Louis spoke to her of a man he had seen in the shadows as he walked from the bus stop one evening. 'It was Tahir. He was taller than I remembered,' Father Louis said, 'his face was full with beard. There was another man beside him.'

The mention of Tahir had stilled Malika's heart for a minute.

Then she wanted to forget it, to believe her priest had made an error. In Lahore, there were so many men who looked the same. But Father Louis' face was grave as he looked at her and it stayed with her. As the days became shorter and the evening shadows longer, she began to see threats as she walked to the house from the bus. Mornings were different. Sunny laneways spoke of family life as women in their hijabs farewelled their sons – and sometimes daughters – in their smart suits and briefcases. And she would laugh at herself, yet knowing that the same laneway in the evening would again breathe its own danger and fears. For despite her protestations, they both knew she was glad to see him, for fear clung to her like a cold that wouldn't leave, forcing shapes into the shadows. Was something truly there, crouched within the gloom, waiting, hiding more misery? She did not wish to think of it, simply could not.

'I think,' said Father Louis, 'it would be better for you to stay with friends until you are ready to leave. The Bhatti family is a good family. They will care for you as their own.'

'They are Muslim?'

'Yes, and they are good people. I trust them. I think you will like them.'

'Must I leave?' Her heart ached to think of it.

He put his hands in his pockets and his voice dropped. 'You remember the bird I found on the doorstep in summer?'

She nodded, and her shoulders tightened. It was after they had returned from the village, where Ayesha had made them a special banquet. It was a dead swallow. He told her it had flown into the door. She had not believed a swallow would do that.

'The creature lay on top of a letter. It was not really a letter, just a few words.'

Her spine tingled. 'You did not tell me this.'

'It was two weeks after I saw Tahir.'

'What did the letter say?'

'I cannot remember.'

She looked at him, but his head was still down. Did she really want to know? 'When should I leave?' she asked.

'There is much still to do. We have time.'

'What am I running from, Father?'

He smiled at her and put an arm on her shoulder. 'If I was sure, I could go to the police.'

'They have not helped in the past.'

'Most police are still good people.'

They reached their house and he knocked loudly on the front door.

'Who is that?' a woman's voice asked through an open window upstairs. 'You will wake the dead with such noise.' Her head appeared at the window and she gasped. 'Oh Father, forgive me. I will come now.' She disappeared.

Father Louis grinned at Malika. 'It is good for me to be back, too.'

'Is Daniel with you?'

'He says hello. He will return tomorrow. He is helping build a well in the north. He boasted to me last week that he converses in Urdu now. He is very proud.'

'He makes me laugh.' She especially liked his blond hair.

'It is good you get on well. But he must return to Perth soon to complete his studies.' He smiled. 'I am sure you will be able to keep in touch.'

The door opened, the woman's face behind it, and they walked inside.

In her room that night, neither her work nor the street noise beneath her window were enough to calm her thoughts. Her body needed to be held, her mind assured that everything would be well. The prospect of studying in a new land had sounded magical when Father Louis first mentioned it. An escape, somewhere new, a different culture. But the wait on her passport became interminable as they bore endless trips to the bank, the passport office, and then the special government agencies needing to confirm her orphan status. While they waited, news reached her that Ayesha had suffered another episode of fever. Her other mother – as she now called her – had recovered, but Malika's guilt gnawed. She was no longer a part of the village. When she travelled to see them now her friends would make a special meal, as if she were an important guest. And they had their own lives, some their own husbands. Fatima had become distant, focussed on her dowry box and preparing for marriage to one of the elder's sons. When the passport finally arrived, she had wanted to throw it out the window onto the busy street, let the trucks and speeding motorbikes destroy it, crumple the pages and tear her hideous photo to pieces. Instead, she hid it in the drawer beside her bed, deep inside her least favourite physics textbook.

The visa had been worse. And it was strange that as her departure became possible, her dread and the risk of danger more real, her desire to leave dwindled like a flame fed with green wood.

Daniel and Father Louis joined her for the meal the Bhatti family threw for her farewell. The women in the house danced for their guests, laughing as they fell over their children who were trying to do the same.

After the meal, Father Louis and Daniel took Malika up onto the roof, where the sky was velvet and the air cool enough for Malika to need her wrap. She was to leave for Australia in the morning. Father Louis sat in the rocker to one side; Daniel's head was golden beneath the light on the other.

After much laughter and stories, Father Louis produced a small package. 'It is for your birthday,' he said, holding open a small box so a watch face caught the light, making it gleam.

She covered her face with her hands for a moment. 'But my birthday is four months away,' she said crossly, as she wiped away tears.

The two men smiled.

'It is better that than a farewell present,' said Daniel.

Then they were gone.

5

There was a brief email from Father Mike just after New Year's. It arrived as she was waiting for Lucy, who had asked her to her family's place at Lorne for the weekend. She scanned the message on her phone. It was sent in short, almost staccato sentences. He was in an internet café in Lahore. He was all right. Yes. That was the main thing. He was all right. No mention of the girl or the missing priests, and nothing about when he might be back. But he was all right. She wondered why he hadn't called, or emailed more often, then admonished herself. There could be twenty reasons. He had been in touch and he was all right. She tapped out an equally brief email as Lucy walked up to the front door, bags in hand.

'So, how long does this trip normally take?' Kate asked, switching on the headlights and nudging the accelerator as they came off the West Gate Freeway.

Lucy was staring out her side window as an orange car sped past, its engine roaring. It ducked in front of them then braked hard, forcing Kate to do the same. 'Two hours, if we actually get there,' she said.

Kate fumbled for her phone in the centre console. 'Find us some music?'

They stopped for dinner at Airey's as dusk was settling on the warm, salt-laden air. A few seagulls screeched above them as they climbed from the car. Kate placed her hands on her hips and eased back gently. She really needed to get back to her yoga. After a quick meal they set off again, passing through a silent Fairhaven and then hugging dark cliffs along the Great Ocean Road. Waves breaking far below echoed at random. They kept chatting, Kate trying to ignore the eerie sense of isolation as the car's headlights strayed off the winding road and lit up the impenetrable bushland. Occasionally, a flash of light appeared in the darkness out at sea. Fishing boats, Lucy explained, as Kate chanced a peek across to her left. On the far side of Big Hill, she let an insistent pair of headlights pass. Its red tail-lights snaked in front of them before disappearing around a bend.

They entered a stretch where trees bordered the road on both sides, their branches close enough to touch. As she navigated a tight bend, a kangaroo hopped in front of them. Kate swore and jumped on the brakes. They screeched to a stop and the roo looked into the headlights, chewing, before scratching its hide and lazily hopping back into the bush.

Lucy laughed and clapped her hands together. 'I love the Surf Coast. Things like this happen all the time. Dad actually hit a roo once when I was a kid, which wasn't funny at all, but you just never know what's going to happen.'

Kate's heart was still thumping as they started moving again. 'Am I going too fast?'

Lucy yawned. 'It's fine. We're nearly there.'

The house was tucked in behind the town, halfway up a steep hill. A full moon hung above the waterline as they pulled into the drive. Kate sat spellbound, but Lucy was already halfway out of her seat.

'Drop the bags at the door,' she said. 'I'll get the keys. And make sure I turn on the hot water if you want a shower in the morning.'

Half an hour later, after unloading tables and chairs onto the deck, they sipped tea and gazed at the water through silver gums, the moon already clear of their reach.

'How about we kayak in the morning?' said Lucy. 'The water's calm enough.'

'Sounds good,' said Kate. She wrapped her hands more tightly around her mug. 'I'm not so great in the sea, though.'

'We've got life jackets. We can paddle out to the pier. It's so much fun.'

'Sure. Okay.' She gulped her tea, almost burning her mouth.

Her paddle bit into the glistening water as she tried to keep up with Lucy's steady rhythm in front. Her arms rotated the same way in her orange vest, but they lacked Lucy's fluidity. A jetski scooted up and down in the distance, its droning enough to upset the quiet.

'You don't often see it like this.' Lucy half-turned, rocking the yellow hull slightly and forcing Kate to grab the sides. Her feet pushed hard into their stalls.

'Smooth as,' she replied.

'You're doing fine,' said Lucy, grinning. 'Don't worry; you

can't drown in these vests. It's impossible.'

Kate scanned the horizon, her hands still on the side. 'Why are we the only ones out?' She didn't count the jetski.

Lucy began paddling again. 'Just early, I guess. Though not that many people kayak this far out.'

They were about halfway there. Maybe not quite. Kate could barely make out the people on the beach now – the only visible objects on the thin strip of sand were umbrellas, beginning to sprout like multi-coloured toadstools as people set up for the day. Along the shoreline waves echoed faintly, while behind, the shopping strip and a rash of individual dwellings signified civilisation, defiant against a forest of gums that descended from the surrounding hills like a besieging army.

A small swell slipped beneath them and Kate swallowed. She looked into the water, where spears of sunlight plunged into green-blue depths. It was just a matter of time before a large fin appeared beneath them. They were sitting ducks.

'Come on,' said Lucy. 'Let's make for the pier.'

Kate squinted. 'Are you serious? It's miles away.'

'It's easy.'

Kate exhaled, bit her lip, and dipped her paddle into the water once again.

The noise from the jetski increased. They stopped paddling as a young guy with sunglasses and iridescent board shorts grinned while he circled, and circled again. He waved, before racing off.

Before long, the umbrellas on the beach had become pinpoints. Kate's chest heaved, the sweat on her face and palms not just from the exertion – or the sun. She couldn't see the bottom, couldn't go on. She was about to insist that they turn back when Lucy tucked her hair behind her ears and laid down her paddle inside the hull.

'I'll be right back,' she said. She unclipped her vest and stood up in her seat. Steadying herself, she launched over the side like a twelve-year-old, making the kayak rock like a cradle. Kate clutched the sides. Lucy surfaced a few metres away with a wide smile. 'Coming?'

Kate kept her hands on the side of the kayak and shook her head.

'The water's not even cold.'

'I'll swim when we're closer in.'

The jetski was returning, whining as it sped across the surface, spewing spray in two high arches behind it. Kate watched as the guy approached. He wasn't slowing. Just as she thought he was going to ram the kayak, he made a sudden turn sideways, pulling up abruptly, but the momentum of his wake hit a second later and, before she could react, the half-metre wave flipped the kayak over. She screamed as she fell into the water.

'The paddle!' she spluttered as she surfaced.

'It floats,' said Lucy, swimming to it. 'I've got it. Arsehole!' she yelled at the back of the receding jetski. It was already twenty metres away.

Kate thrashed her legs and arms as she bobbed in the water. 'What the fuck is he trying to do?' she yelled. Fear made her numb, though she was sure Lucy had lied and the water was actually freezing.

Lucy swam to the front of the kayak and pushed up on the

near side while pulling on the other. A brief resistance and it rotated right side up. Then, dumping the paddle on board, she pulled herself up onto the hull. With the vest high under her chin, Kate splashed-swam over and tried to do the same. But at the last moment, her vest caught the rim and she slipped back into the water. 'I can't even see the damned bottom,' she shouted.

Lucy reached out a hand. 'Work your way over here. I'll pull you up.'

'It's okay,' said Kate, her fingers fiddling with the clip on her life vest. 'Let me get this damned thing off.'

Back in her seat, she pulled her hair forwards. She squeezed it and, twisting it into a whirl, flicked it onto her back. She shivered in the whisper of breeze, as she reached forward and took the paddle Lucy held out.

'So,' said Lucy, 'we go back?'

Kate looked again at the water. There was no bottom. There never would be. She set her jaw as she looked at Lucy. 'If you can make it to the pier, so can I.'

They leaned back on the wide mustard-coloured couches after dinner, their feet stretched forward. Two empty pasta bowls and half a bottle of red were splayed on a low table in front of them. The breeze had strengthened, making the towels on the deck railing flutter. Through the landscape windows in front of them, the panorama of a pink and indigo sky was intoxicating. White cockatoos circled in flocks between the trees, their screeches easily penetrating the room.

Kate picked up the bottle of red and poured another glass.

Lucy's was still half full of water.

'A glass after dinner at least?'

Lucy shook her head. 'Water's fine tonight.'

Kate shrugged and eased herself back again. 'You are so lucky to have this view,' she said. 'To have this house.'

'My parents keep talking about selling, but they've been doing that for the last ten years.'

'Why would they want to?'

'Mum thought they would move down when Dad retired, but they're both obsessed with golf. I think it's what's kept them together.'

Kate sipped on her wine and stared at the empty deck. 'I'm sorry I made all that fuss today in the water.'

'Don't be. That guy was a real prick.'

'I just need to see the bottom when I'm in the sea.'

'It's not that deep. I used to dive down to the bottom when I was a kid.'

'It's just me.'

Lucy picked up her water. 'We still made it to the pier and back.'

Kate placed a hand gingerly on a smarting shoulder. 'I got burnt.'

'Unavoidable here in the summer.' Lucy squinted at her before draining her glass. 'Your face is fine.'

'How long are you on the wagon?'

She shrugged, yawning. 'Maybe just tonight.'

'So, I guess a trip to the pub's off.'

'We can go if you'd like. Or there's the cinema.'

'Not sure I feel much like anything, to be honest.' Kate stood at the window. The sky was still bright, while the world was all but dark. 'Do you mind if I sit on the deck?'

'You okay?'

'Just need to think.'

'Sure. I'll make some tea. Here.' Lucy tossed her a couple of blankets from the couch. 'Take one for me.'

Lucy handed Kate a steaming mug and sat beside her. This side of the house, up close against the window, they were protected from the breeze. She leaned her nose into her mug and inhaled. 'Mum buys this from somewhere around here. She won't say where.'

Kate nestled into the folds of her blanket, holding her mug close. 'It smells good.'

They drank in silence as darkness crept around them and the lights from inside shone on their faces.

'Anything on your mind?' Lucy asked eventually. Her goose-bump arms pulled on her blanket.

The moon had begun to edge above the surface of the water. Kate's eyes were glued on it as she answered. 'You remember Father Mike? He was the priest at Mum's funeral?'

'Sure.'

'He wants me to look after this girl who might be arriving from Pakistan.'

'That would be so cool. How old is she?'

'Fifteen or sixteen, I think. It might also be a nightmare. Worms, scabies, dental caries.'

'I've got some great therapies for those things.'

Kate turned, her eyebrow raised. 'Caries?'

'Maybe not caries.'

'And then, I'm never home.' She sighed. 'I told you he was my uncle, didn't I?'

Lucy shook her head. 'I don't think so.'

'Dad's brother. Anyway, at the moment he's over there risking his remaining heartbeats, while I'm here enjoying myself.'

'You can't be everywhere.' She sipped her tea loudly. 'So, effectively this girl's a kind of temporary refugee.'

'I'm not really sure.' She put down her mug and turned. 'You're pregnant, Luce, aren't you?'

She blinked and looked down. 'Maybe. I've been late before.'

'Well, if it's more, then that's wonderful.' She got up and hugged her tight. 'I never thought the day would come.'

'Don't!' She pushed her away, smiling. 'You're putting the moz on me.' She pulled her heel up onto the chair beneath the blanket. 'I won't tell Hamish until I'm sure.'

Kate told Lucy her secret later that evening, sitting on the double bed in her room while Lucy sat back against the pillows, lengthy shadows from the bed light flung along the wall. It just came out. She hadn't told anyone before. Lucy listened with wide eyes, her hand on Kate's thigh, frowning now and then but no more, and Kate found, to her surprise, that long-held secrets can be let go. Or at least shared.

'Well, that explains a lot,' Lucy said when Kate paused.

'Like why I cut the friendship?'

She nodded. 'And also later. Did the nuns ever find out about the abortion?'

Kate shook her head.

'Still,' said Lucy, a half-smile on her face, 'it would have made an interesting dilemma. Their brightest student, pregnant.'

'Didn't live up to that exactly either, did I?'

Lucy rolled her eyes. 'Oh, you bombed bad, girl. Fell apart. Only made it through plastic surgery. Give yourself a break. I would have dropped out, that's assuming I could ever have got in.' She rubbed her shoulders and then stood, wrapping her dressing gown around herself before sitting back on the bed. 'I used to wonder if you were with him,' she continued. 'Every morning at swimming training. It was like there was no one else at the pool.'

'He said he wanted us to run away together.'

'Did you believe him?'

'I did, at the time.'

'Kate, you were what, fifteen?'

'Almost.'

'We were in Year 10. Kids.'

'I knew what I wanted.' She sighed and looked at Lucy. 'And I knew that Mum liked him. Really liked him.' She looked at the ceiling. 'Angus Parker, the swimming coach. We used to talk about him, each of us pretending we couldn't care less.'

'So it was a competition.'

'Yep.'

Lucy leaned forward and hugged her. For once, Kate let her. As they broke away, Lucy looked thoughtful. 'What happened to him? Did he find another school? I imagine a swimming coach could –'

Kate held up a hand. 'There's more.' Her fingers trembled as she pulled at a strand of hair. She took a deep breath. 'Mum got it out of me – that it was him – and he ran. I felt dreadful. I had betrayed the man I loved. We had a pact not to ever tell, and I did. He knew what would happen if they caught him.' She smiled against the pain that was rising in her chest. 'He parked his car on the West Gate Bridge, Luce. That's how they knew.'

Lucy pulled some tissues from the box beside her. She wiped Kate's cheeks.

'I'll never forget the look of triumph on Mum's face when the cops rang. We were eating dinner.'

'She turned him in, Kate. Not you.'

'I still betrayed him.'

'He didn't have to jump.' Lucy's gaze was steadfast. 'Nor give you concrete shoes for the rest of your life.'

'Guilt can be hard to shake.'

'He had alternatives. You were a child.'

They sat together silently on the bed for a while.

'I need a drink,' Kate said, finally.

'I'll join you,' said Lucy. 'How am I supposed to sleep on all this?'

'No alcohol for you,' said Kate, firmly. 'You're having tea. And I'll join you.'

The rain woke her in the dead hours of Sunday morning. It started as a patter, then rose to a drumbeat on the tin roof, waking memories she thought long buried. But they were still as fresh as they were raw. Her insides cringed and her legs were wet with perspiration when she thought of what she had told – and as she remembered more. Her eyes were wide as morning crept into the room.

The rain continued at breakfast, bouncing off the deck and saturating the already wet towels. The cockatoos were white dots scattered among the gums. By late morning, with rain still falling in sheets across the valley and clouds stacked grey behind them, Kate decided to head back. Lucy was expecting Hamish anyway. They hugged tight and Lucy waved from the small verandah as she headed downhill.

Stephen called Monday morning, while she was stuck in traffic. He wouldn't be in. It wasn't a complete surprise; he had grumbled his way around the rooms on the Friday.

'It's the back again,' he said, his voice tinny through the car speaker. 'I might have to sit this out a day or two.'

'What can I do?'

'Hang on, I'll just get comfortable.' The phone clunked. He was panting slightly when he spoke again. 'Sorry, bit of spasm.'

She checked the rear vision mirror before changing lanes. They both knew he wasn't going to be in that week.

She found ten minutes alone with Sam in the consulting rooms when she arrived. Stephen had rung her, too.

'I'll reschedule most of his patients to next week,' said Sam, scanning the screen in Stephen's office. 'There's only three or four, mostly post-ops that needed to be seen today.'

Kate nodded. 'Tack them on to the end of my session, or mix them in. I'll work it somehow.'

'Doesn't your hospital clinic start at one?'

'Yep. I'll have to ring them.' She took the files that Sam had placed on the desk.

'And Stephen's got his inpatients still.'

'He said you had a list of them.'

Sam blinked. 'I used to.'

'But?'

'It was a waste of time. He always managed it.'

Kate chewed on her lip. 'Is there any way of finding them without troubling him?'

'I could call his Glenferrie Rooms,' she said. 'They might have a list.'

'They might well.' She tried to avoid the edge in her voice, but it didn't quite work. 'Let me know if you have a problem.' She could ring him from the car later if she had to.

Someone called out from the empty reception area. Patients were starting to arrive.

'We'd better get out there,' said Kate, getting up from the chair. Stepping through the waiting area she smiled at an oversized, middle-aged man at the reception desk as she headed for her office. 'Sam will be right with you.'

But Sam followed her into the room and shut the door. She stood there; her stilettos pointed straight ahead, her arms folded. 'Is he going to be all right?'

Kate glanced at the clock as she sat down. 'He's just getting some scans done. Sounds like he's had a bad weekend.'

'But he always works. Even when he had his gall bladder out two years ago. It was on Friday afternoon. He turned up for work on Monday still.'

'We're all human.' She waited, but Sam didn't move. 'Yes, Sam?'

'There is one more thing. This being the start of the year and all.' She pulled her hair back and smoothed it behind her head. 'Can I sit down?' She dragged a chair to the desk. 'I asked Stephen about a raise the other day before the break.'

'A raise?' He hadn't mentioned it to her. She remembered exactly the last time they'd spoken about Sam. 'Sam, I know Stephen thinks we pay you very well.' She smiled. 'And in fairness, this really isn't the best time.' She needed her out there. Patients walked if no one was at reception.

'It never is.'

'Okay. I guess you're right on that.' She sighed. 'Anyway, Stephen's the one who employs you.'

'You're still a partner, aren't you?'

Kate raised an eyebrow. 'Can we talk about it later in the week?'

'So that means it could be delayed a week. Or even more.'

'We can backdate it if needs be.' She breathed slowly, counting five in and then the same out.

Sam's eyes narrowed for a moment before she nodded and headed for the door. She turned as she reached it. 'You know, this place would go under if it wasn't for me.'

'I'm sure you're right.' She did her best to smile until the door shut. 'Maybe because that's your job,' she added in a whisper. She picked up the first file. The referral said 'carpal tunnel'. She flipped the page to see if the nerve conduction report was there. She remembered the large man at reception now. He had pushed hard for the op on the underside of his wrist to be done under a local. But it all went pear-shaped when he got to theatre, with sweat erupting on his face and his heart rate dropping to fifty. Dave, her anaesthetist, had quickly wheeled him out. Eventually, they fitted him in at the end of the list, but it was under a general. He wasn't happy. 'Missed my lunch with the guys,' he complained. 'We should have gone with the local.'

'Maybe next time,' she'd said. She smiled. Well, here was his chance.

She phoned the public clinic on her way there. Margaret, the clerk the switchboard put her through to, told her to relax. Eight patients hadn't shown, so they had to reschedule anyway. 'I do hope Mr Campbell gets better soon,' she said as she hung up.

It was the sort of comment that made her glad she had stuck with the public system. She and Stephen had talked of it occasionally, once as they'd waited outside the boardroom for a meeting or presentation. Mel was there too, so it was at best semi-official. 'One thing's for sure, it's not for the money,' Stephen had laughed. Mel scoffed. 'At least pretend to be honest, Stephen. You like being the head of the unit.'

'I think we both like that, dear,' he had grinned, putting a hand on her shoulder.

'Myron wants me to get some rest,' Stephen said when she rang again. His voice sounded stronger. 'The codeine's helping. But more tests Wednesday.'

'Perhaps we should just plan on you not coming back this week.'

'Good idea,' he said, after a long silence.

It was straightforward. She would pick up his private inpatients, and do what she could with his rooms. He thought Martine and maybe Andrew Tan were back that week as well. 'They'll both pick up whatever you throw at them – though most of the patients can wait a week.'

'I'll speak to Sam,' said Kate. 'Did she mention a raise to you, by the way?'

He paused. 'Weeks ago. Vaguely. I was non-committal. I didn't know it was urgent.'

'She's counting the minutes.'

'I think her boyfriend's getting at her. They want to buy a house. You know she's already getting as much as the hospital interns.'

'What do you want to do?'

'Let me think about it. Maybe it's not the best time to play it tough, though.'

'Things aren't great, are they?'

'They've been better. Have you got any ideas?'

I'd sack her and find someone new, she wanted to say. 'Let's talk when you've had a think,' was what came out.

Later that week, she picked up some new cushions and other homemaking pieces in the sales. She would move them to Carlton some time. In the meantime, she could use them at her mother's. With a couple of artistic-looking lamps and a matching vase for the table between the couches, the lounge room became a place where she could rest at night but also get her paperwork done. She stared at the vase for a minute. It was empty, hollow to its core. She went to pick some flowers from the garden.

6

Kate counted the ruler-straight sandstone steps as she climbed to Stephen's front door. Pre-dinner Sunday, as he had asked. Rain clouds loomed – threatening but, unlike the drenching at Lorne two weeks earlier, going no further. It would be a harsh summer. She paused at the step where Andrew Jamieson had stumbled and smiled. Prof Jamieson. They had seen each other a few times since then. Each time they seemed to stop and find something to talk about. He made her smile. She reached the top step, drew breath and knocked on the door.

Stephen greeted her with a winning grin. He was moving more easily, able to duck around her and take her coat as she slipped out of it. He placed a hand on her shoulder as he led her into the lounge; it was even vaster without the Christmas guest list. He crossed to the vacant doorway, calling to Mel before joining Kate on one of the white leather couches.

Mel joined them, gliding on her heels as she carried flutes and a bottle of champagne. Full of chatter as bright as her bangles, she sat beside Kate and aligned the flutes along the coffee table. Only after popping the cork did she glance at Stephen.

He nodded. 'I'll stick with black tea.'

Mel put down the bottle and headed for the kitchen. 'Be right back,' she said. 'Kate, do you want to pour?'

Kate's eyes followed her. Something wasn't right. Had they been fighting? When she returned they drank silently for a few minutes. Kate was unsure whether to start a conversation or to wait. Her instincts told her to wait. Eventually, Stephen cleared his throat and turned to her with a smile. 'What's Sam up to?'

Normality. She fished in her bag and handed him the list their receptionist had passed to her on Friday, as Kate rushed from the rooms. 'Seems more than she's worth to me.'

He scanned the page before peering over his glasses. 'But as I said before, awkward timing to see her walk right now.'

'So we give her what she wants?'

He pressed his hands together and placed them beneath his chin. 'It's interesting, isn't it? You and I both not on par for a couple of months and she moves in with a list of demands.'

They both watched as Mel swayed back into the room with Stephen's tea. She was impossible to ignore. She sat down next to Stephen.

'It's also the start of the year,' Kate continued. 'If you're going to do it, it is the right time.'

He rubbed his stubble with one hand. 'Her boyfriend works in HR at the hospital. Did you know that?'

She shook her head.

'Did you put in for leave after your mother died?'

'Three days, I think.'

'So together, they would have had access to both our leave forms.'

'You think they're colluding?' She frowned.

'Who knows? But she may as well be the executive assistant to the PM if we give her this.'

'She wants to be called the "rooms' manager".'

His eyebrows shot up. 'With a staff of one?'

Mel stood up. 'Listen to yourselves. She's a fucking secretary.' She stormed back to the kitchen, returning with a tray of crackers fanned around a slab of cheese. She stabbed the knife into the cheese before cutting a corner. 'What is happening to the world? Did she even finish school?'

'You employed her,' said Kate, turning to Stephen.

'And you're a partner.' He smiled briefly. He looked suddenly weary. 'I'm not going to be able to get there for a while. Can you talk with her?' He raised the papers in his hand. 'See if you can soften these demands a bit.'

'And if she won't?'

'Let's talk again.'

He closed his eyes and eased back into the couch, his body sinking into his clothes. For a minute or two, he didn't move. Anxiety filled Mel's face as she and Kate swapped looks.

'Stephen.' Mel's voice was suddenly softer.

He opened his eyes, blinking a moment. He glanced at Kate and took off his glasses, slowly cleaning them on his shirt.

'Enough of Sam for the moment,' he said. 'I have a favour to ask. You can say no, and please do if it doesn't work for you.'

Kate put her flute down and sat back, crossing her arms. Mel was silent beside her.

'I need someone to carry the public hospital work. The head of unit stuff. For a while,' he added.

'Your job.'

'Yep.' He looked at her. 'It's not as bad as people think.'

'Meaning? Time wise?' Her eyes narrowed.

'With theatre lists and admin,' he pursed his lips. 'About three sessions. Maybe less than that.' He smiled encouragingly.

'This is more than a favour, Stephen.'

'It is.'

She inhaled as she thought about the realities: chairing unit meetings and managing bruised egos. 'You know a couple of the surgeons used to be my teachers.'

'I'll talk to them. Andrew said he would help you find your feet. You'd only be acting up for a while. Minding the shop.'

Mel's gaze on her was like a laser as Kate stood and walked to the glass wall in front of the couches, folding her arms. It was impossible, any way she looked at it. Three sessions meant a day and a half, when she already needed an extra day in her week. 'Stephen,' she began, 'I –'

'Martine's happy to cover my private work. She'll do more besides – you know what she's like.'

'How long?'

'Three to six months.' His face twisted. 'Six.'

'That's not a short time.'

'No.'

They fell silent again.

'Tell her, Stephen, or I will.' Mel drained her glass and poured another. 'He's got cancer, Kate. We found out last week.' She edged across the couch and laid a hand on top of his.

'Cancer?' Her voice rose despite herself. 'What sort?' She asked as much to give herself time as wanting to know. Cancer.

Stephen. The two didn't mix. This was Stephen. He had always been there. A part of her life.

'It's myeloma.' He smiled bleakly. 'Not a great cancer to have.'

She closed her eyes and leaned her head back against the glass. 'The back pain?'

'It seems so.'

The thought made her spine tingle. 'I'm so sorry,' she said. 'For you both.'

He smiled again and Mel's fingers slipped between his. 'They say it's almost curable these days,' she said, her voice defiant – the same tone that would have sliced through any potential issues with the builders. 'But he needs time for the treatment cycles before a transplant.' She looked hard at Kate, her flute resting at her lips. 'We're going to beat this.'

Kate gave her a small smile. Without a medical degree she would have said the same thing. 'How's the back pain going?' she asked Stephen.

'Better, since I've stopped pretending it's not there. The radiotherapy has helped a bit.'

'It was a miracle,' said Mel.

Kate turned back to Stephen. 'I'll do it,' she said. 'Of course I'll do it.' She shut her eyes. 'Just be around when I need you.'

Their eyes met in a moment of understanding and the corners of his mouth turned up as he nodded. 'Good for you, Kate.' He placed a hand on Mel's thigh. 'Second thoughts, honey. I think I will have that champagne.' She opened her mouth but his hand was already up. 'I'll stop when the chemo starts.'

They talked until it became apparent there was no more to say. Kate found herself retreating behind her medical mask; Stephen did the same. It was a form of protection. Their language drifted into jargon, then to witnessed or even apocryphal cures. He had myeloma – one of the better sorts to have if you were going to have myeloma, they agreed – and treatment these days was so much better.

He saw her to the front door, but she lingered on the porch, her anxiety rising now they were alone.

'Do you want help getting to chemo or radiotherapy?' she asked. 'I could easily swing by. Just tell me.'

He shook his head. 'Mel should cover it.' He dropped his voice. 'It might at least cut down on the champagne bills.'

'It's not curable, is it?' She knew the answer, but needed to hear him say it.

He looked at her for a hard moment. 'We both know what's going on, Kate.' He smiled. 'Good luck with Sam.'

The sun made a brief appearance as she headed down the steps. It lit the leaves on the trees, as if a late showing was better than none at all. She sat in her car until the clouds gathered again and the faintest of showers passed over, pockmarking the dust on the windscreen. Her fingers trembled as she used the spray and wiper blades. She blew out hard. Stephen's news had taken her by surprise. No. The tingling down her spine even now as she thought about it and the hollow sensation in her gut as if her body was on auto, her head floating in another space, were more than surprise. She was in shock. It was not unlike her initial response to her mother's death in a way, but for whatever reason, this – Stephen – cut with a different blade altogether.

She typed a text to Lucy, stopping as she was about to send it. Lucy didn't even know Stephen. What more could she do than say 'sorry'? Everyone would be sorry. She tossed the phone on the seat opposite. It was her problem and she had to deal with it.

On Tuesday morning she met Sam in her office for half an hour before the first patient was due. She couldn't see another way to handle it. If it all went pear-shaped, she would bail and discuss it with Stephen. Dressed in a business jacket and skirt, Sam's brown eyes flicked around the office from the other side of the desk, her plump thighs pressed together. As Kate feared, compromise was out.

'You guys earn a fortune here,' said Sam. 'I deserve a home for my future family as much as you do. My hours are just as long. Richard says you're on massive salaries at the public, too.'

'Richard's your boyfriend?'

She nodded.

'What have you been saying about us?' Kate asked quietly.

'Nothing more than general talk.' She shrugged, and flopped her hair free from under her jacket.

They stared at each other.

'He works at the public hospital, doesn't he?' said Kate. 'In HR, I think Stephen said.'

'So?'

'You know it's not a good idea to share information like that about us, don't you? Stephen and I would regard that as an invasion of our privacy.'

Her face went pale. 'I wouldn't do that. We wouldn't.

Richard's completely discreet.'

It was easy enough after that, though the compromise she was able to force – ten per cent increase compared to twenty-five – all but dissolved in the smug satisfaction in Sam's eyes at the end. Kate said she would get her new contract done in a week.

'What about back pay?' said Sam, standing. 'You agreed on that the other day.'

'That was before you and Richard started talking about me,' she said, and smiled.

Sam's eyes flashed but she shrugged.

'But there may be room to move.' She remembered the idea that had let her fall asleep the previous night. She leaned forward. 'What would you be prepared to do a Saturday morning session for? I know it would be additional on what we've just discussed.'

'Four hours?'

'Yes.'

'Every Saturday?'

'Uh-huh.'

She thought a minute. 'I'd do it for five hundred.'

Kate blinked. 'That's a lot, Sam.'

'Double rates, plus inconvenience, travel. It's half my weekend.'

'It's four hours.'

Sam didn't move.

Kate forced a smile. 'Okay. Thanks. I'll think about it.' She would come up with another plan.

The morning was crowded but potentially manageable until

Liz, her nurse, phoned in sick, which meant she had to take down and dress all the post-ops. She was gloved, with her fingers in the middle of an open wound when Sam knocked on the door.

'There's someone called Ellen on the phone,' she said, poking her head in. 'Professor someone's PA?'

Kate looked up.

'She's checking you're on target for the meeting this afternoon.'

Kate's heart dropped. Ellen had rung her on Friday between theatre cases. She'd completely forgotten. She glanced at her watch. 'Can you see if three is okay?'

Sam's head disappeared, returning a minute later. 'He said "just for you". Ellen said to tell you.'

'Thanks.' Kate's cheeks burned behind her mask. She glanced an apology at the elderly patient in front of her.

She didn't get away from the rooms until almost three. She would ring ahead as she drove. She hurried out of the lift in the car park, only to see Leah Costello walking towards her. She quickly stared at the ground but it was too late, and all she could do was smile as the attractive, tanned woman hurried across. Her hair was shorter; it bounced off her shoulders as she approached.

'This is a surprise,' said Leah. 'I'm just here seeing a friend. I was going to call you.'

Kate smiled. 'How are things?'

'I'm fine. Well,' she paused. 'Not exactly. But I wanted to tell you I won't be coming back.'

'That's okay,' said Kate. 'Found someone else?'

'God no!' Her lips smiled but there was pain behind her eyes. 'You were absolutely right. I don't need anything more than these. In fact, not even.' Her hands cupped her breasts as she looked down.

'I'm glad to hear that,' said Kate. She frowned. 'Look, I'm running a bit late –'

'I kicked him out,' said Leah. 'My husband. Part of me felt bad, but I just had to. We both needed space.'

'Oh, I see.' Kate bit her lip. Andrew would have given up on her already, no doubt. 'I'm sorry to hear that.'

'I found them in bed.' She laughed and looked up at the concrete ceiling. 'It was another man.'

'Wow!' said Kate. 'Really? I'm sorry, I mean –'

'No, it's okay.' She pulled a tissue from her bag. 'I'd kind of wondered for a while – you know I'm not that bad looking – and why these,' she looked down, 'were never good enough.'

'Will you be all right?'

'In some ways, though lawyers can only do so much.' Her lip quivered. 'The rest will take a while.'

They smiled at each other, and Kate wondered if she might have got to like the woman beneath the façade. 'You're not really here to see a friend, are you?' she said.

Leah sighed. 'I knew you would cotton on. Blood tests. He said it was all okay, but this wasn't his first time.

'Didn't he use condoms?'

'Mostly, he said.' She dabbed her eyes with a tissue. 'Mostly! Would you take mostly?'

Kate sighed. 'I'm so sorry, Leah. I hope everything's okay.'

She nodded, smiling, her eyes teary. 'Thank you, Kate. Can I call you Kate?'

'I think it's about time.'

Myron, the head of the oncology unit, caught her a couple of days later as she was stepping out of a lift. His team trailed behind him in procession. His pug-like face broke into a broad smile when he saw her.

'Just the person we were discussing.' His stubby fingers pushed their way into his pockets, as he drew close. 'Remember that boy you sent to us? Peter Mason?'

'Of course,' she said. 'Responding well to the magic drug?'

'Hardly.' His bottom lip drooped as he looked at her over his glasses. 'He's not done well at all. I'm staggered – it's hardly ever this resistant. We're checking with the company in case they have some ideas.'

'When do you see him next?'

'Oh, sorry!' His eyes widened. 'He's here now.' He snatched a look at his team. 'He's not going anywhere.'

Her hand rose to her mouth. 'It's only been a couple of months.'

'Yeah. It was right through him though once we started to look.'

One of the registrars behind him coughed, and he checked his watch before turning to them. 'Get going, guys. I'll be right there.' The throng drifted off up the stairs and he turned back to Kate. 'Sorry. Pathology meeting.' He drew closer again. 'You're probably too busy – but his mother would love to see you. Time's short for that kid. He's on Level Four, if you get a chance.'

He paused and glanced around, lowering his voice when he spoke. 'I heard on the grapevine you're acting head of unit now. Congratulations!'

She raised an eyebrow. 'Prof wasn't releasing the news until next week.'

'Stephen told me,' he said, smugly. 'We discussed you as his replacement.' He winked. 'You owe me.'

He hadn't changed since they were medical students. Always inferring he was in the driver's seat. But he did care for his patients. 'Level Four you said?'

'You can't miss him. Next to the nurses' station.'

She knew the room well. She had called on oncology patients there for urgent skin grafts or troublesome growths. It always ponged of over-ripe flowers and air freshener, meagre attempts to cover grief. She got to it at the end of her rounds, but had thought of little else as she scooted up and down the various floors with her new registrar. He had called her Dr Davenport.

Exiting the lifts, she walked halfway down the corridor to the central work station. The nurse in charge smiled at her, and asked if she could help. One advantage in staying in one place for a while was that you were known. Kate explained, and the nurse crossed the corridor to the room opposite.

'He's in here,' she whispered, opening the door slightly. Kate flashed a smile as she left. She took a breath and clenched her fists before slipping in quietly.

Most of the room was in shadow, apart from the bed. A soft lamp shone on a crocheted blue rug. Beneath it, a boy, pale as the sheets, lay in the middle of the bed. His cheekbones and forehead pushed taut the skin on his face as his pyjamas swallowed what was left of his body. She watched as his breathing started and stopped and, after an agonising wait, began again.

Someone stirred in the shadows at the end of the bed. Squinting, she could make out his mother, who had her head on her hands as she leaned forward on the mattress. She lifted her head and squinted at Kate.

'Dr Davenport,' she said, after a minute.

Kate raised a finger to her lips. 'Kate,' she whispered.

'It's all right.' She turned to her son. 'He won't wake. We had half an hour with him this morning.'

'I'm very sorry, Mrs Mason,' she said. 'I didn't know he was so sick. I would have come earlier.'

'You must be so busy with the ones you can help,' she replied. 'I understand. And it's Jane.'

Kate moved to the side of the bed and squatted beside her, placing a hand on her forearm. Neither spoke for a minute. Outside the room, someone dropped a tray. The clatter was followed by muffled commotion.

'He never forgot the time you sat with us,' she said, her voice quiet in the darkened room. 'I didn't thank you either.'

'He was hurting.'

'He used to say that you're the most wonderful doctor.' She stared for a long time at her son's face. 'I would do anything to take this for him. Anything,' she rasped. A tear fell on Kate's hand. 'You know that, don't you?'

Kate nodded, and smiled bleakly. 'But it just doesn't work like that.' She turned back to her son.

Her legs becoming numb, Kate pushed herself to her feet.

A few minutes later, the father and their teenage daughter, Angie, returned. They had all decided to stay the night and Angie dropped a couple of takeaway pizzas on the chair at the end of the room as they walked in. They gathered around the bed. Kate shook the father's hand, who kept dabbing his eyes with his hanky as he asked questions she knew he must also have asked Myron. Eventually, she sensed they wanted to be alone. Before leaving, she held Peter's hand a long minute.

When she finally left the hospital, she let her car guide her to Victoria Street, where she parked and found a near-empty eatery still serving food. She sat at a laminex table, chewing on the deep-fried chicken and rice combo that fed the gnawing ache in her stomach. She drained her water glass and poured another. First her mother, then Stephen, and now this. Her mother used to say that bad news came in threes. 'You watch,' she used to say, 'it'll be three strikes.' Was this the last then? She hoped so, though her mother had rarely been right when she was alive.

Another strike did come. It arrived as a phone call in the middle of the night the following week. She was on call and her hand fumbled across the bedside table for her phone. She stuck it to her ear as she rolled onto her back.

'Yep.' She rubbed her forehead, tensing for what waited at the other end. On call was a drag. It was the only word for it.

'Kate?'

'Father Mike!' She threw off the covers and found herself perched on the edge of the bed, clutching her nightdress around her.

At times she could barely make out his words, coming as they did in random moments of lucidity etched from the background static. Once, he cut out so long she thought she had lost him. He was in a village, north of Lahore. The local priest had fled following death threats and the villagers were frightened. Taliban versus Christian. She was sure he said Taliban. 'A lot of hype,' the voice crackled.

'Are you all right? Safe?' Her words seemed loud in the dark.

'Yes, but Malika,' he answered, among the crackles. Then, '... on the plane. She will need a friend.' The last sentence was as clear as if he were in the next room.

She nodded. Stupidly. 'The other priests?' she called out.

'I think gone, Kate. Nothing's certain.' His voice was hollow through the crackles.

'Will you get out?'

'I hope so. Soon as –' the line sputtered again before, '– worry.'

'Are you okay?' She needed to hear it.

'Kate, I must go.'

The line went dead.

She threw the phone on the bed and rubbed her hand across the rash of goosebumps that had erupted across her shoulders, pushing away the vague nausea that washed over her. Where the hell was he? How much danger was he in? Outside, there wasn't even the start of a moon.

For the first time that week, she left work on Friday while the sun was still in the sky. Heading back to her mother's, she showered and then sat out the back in what comfort the shade provided, the backs of her thighs instantly moist on the warm metal of the chair. She drank several glasses from a jug of cold water she had revived with mint and lemon, and opened a bottle of wine. Overhead, the clouds were tinged red as a low-hanging sun promised more of the same the next day. A couple of wines down, she got up and wandered round the side of the house, stepping between the twin ribbons of the cement drive. Fifty or so years ago someone must have thought it would suit the place. Now it just looked suburban. And tired. At several points, the concrete had split, and soil and the occasional weed pushed up broken slabs as if they were tiny tectonic plates.

She wandered down the path to the front, pulling her still-damp hair behind her back, and turned to the run of saplings along the fence line. The trees stood together in a group, their tops in full sun, leaves limp from a week of summer heat. How had she not noticed them earlier? Was she so self-absorbed? She plucked a leaf from a lower stem and brought it to her nose, inhaling. Then she went across to the garden hose, unrolled it and gave the tap a hard turn. As the nozzle spurted into life, she pointed the stream to the sky, smiling as it sparkled in the sunlight.

Dragging the hose across to the saplings, she softened the jet and pointed it at their roots. A summer like this could kill them. She soaked the bed until puddles formed and water ran in streams down the drive. This was what she was born for, the reason she had chosen medicine: to help, to make others better. Whether that was people or plants, in some ways it didn't matter.

It came to her then, the decision she had delayed since Father Mike's phone call. She would do what she could for this girl. It didn't make sense, and yet perhaps it was the only thing in her life right then that did make sense. She probably wouldn't need to do much at all, perhaps just a phone call to the school now and then, see if she was all right. The odd weekend, maybe. They might already have it sorted and the poor thing would just need an occasional meal and a shoulder. A friend, Father Mike said. She could do that, surely.

part three

1

Malika lay in bed, watching the morning sunlight play off the open window. The images danced on the wall like spirits. Outside, the branch of a eucalyptus tree rustled in the golden light, just as they did in her village. The men there would be grumbling by now as they stirred from their dark beds, the frost hard on the ground. Later, when breakfast was cooked, Ayesha would join the other women in the warming sun as they took food to the fields. Fatima would be with them. Malika's fingertips reached for her watch and traced the contours of the delicate leather band before resting on the smooth glass. She sighed and reluctantly checked the time before throwing off her coverings and stepping across to the bathroom. Pulling open the door, she locked the adjoining access and turned on the light.

She filled the basin and splashed water on her face before pulling her garments down from the shower railing. She patted them, relieved to find they had dried overnight. She slipped on her pants and ducked her chin as she drew the plain tunic smoothly over her head. Then, turning her face away from the mirror, she brushed her hair and tied it behind her head.

She heard a stirring in the room beside her. Chloe was awake. A window squeaked open, followed by a loud yawn. Malika quickly unlocked the connecting door and stepped back into her own room. She pulled the door shut and picked an apple from the bowl on her desk, standing at the window chewing slowly. The leaves on the eucalyptus were lit bright and small birds played in the early sun, hopping from branch to branch and back again. She had found a fig tree in the school grounds the day before. It was in the middle of a square, surrounded on three sides by a building of glass that Mrs O'Bryan, the boarding school teacher, told her was built especially for science. The tree rose high into the sky and spread its boughs wide like the great tree in her village, but its branches had not yet sent out roots in search of the soil, and the leaves that had fallen to the ground were barely larger than those of other trees outside her window. Even so, she had rested for a time on the wooden bench around its base, breathing in its coolness and hoping its discovery was an auspicious sign.

Chloe's door on the other side of the bathroom opened, followed by a sharp click of the lock. The yellow note stuck to her door the day she'd arrived had made it clear. 'Bathroom's mine from 6.30 to 7.30.' As the shower spluttered into life behind her, Malika sat at the workbench beside the open window and opened her laptop. She had much to do.

An hour later, she closed the cover and returned to the now empty bathroom. Standing at the mirror, she washed her hands and cleaned her teeth. Then, resting her hands on either side of the basin, she gazed into the mirror, forcing herself to look at the broken face that was now hers: skin stretched like tight leather across her nose, her nostrils forced sideways – one gaping wide like a worm's mouth, the other beneath it a slit that was barely visible. On either side of her nose her face had developed into two uneven halves. One sunken cheekbone pulled her eye down and flattened her cheek. It made her look like Kara, the old woman in the village who had woken one morning with half her face unable to move. She touched her cheekbone gently. Father Louis had taken her to specialist doctors in Lahore. They had done what they could. She had hoped they would have at least stopped the aching.

She reached beneath the basin for her hijab, running her fingers along the material for a moment before slipping it on. She made sure the veil and nose cover were fastened across her face, and only a slit of her eyes and her forehead showed.

Ping-Mei met her on the stairs. Like Malika, she had her laptop under her arm.

'Didn't see you at breakfast,' said Ping-Mei, starting down the stairs in front of her.

'I ate in my room. It is very pleasant there in the mornings.'

'It was disgusting. It never changes. But I've lost a kilo already since the start of term. So I'm not complaining.'

At the bottom of the stairs she handed Malika her laptop. 'Hold this a minute.' She put her hands behind her head and pulled on either side of her ponytail, tightening the band. 'Did you get away for the weekend?'

Malika shook her head. 'It was cancelled.'

'Bummer.'

'Last minute change, Mrs O'Bryan said.' She shrugged. 'It was fine.'

'My sister was in town. We cruised like I cannot tell you.' She took back her laptop and opened the door, letting Malika pass into the bright sunshine. 'Her bank had taken out a room at the Westin. I mean!' She rolled her eyes. 'It was so awesome!' She leaned into Malika's shoulder. 'I've made up my mind. She said she'd get me into merchant banking with her. Have to work my arse off now but,' she grinned, 'it'll be worth it.'

'That is great!' said Malika. 'What is merchant banking?'

Ping-Mei's jaw dropped. 'You're shitting me.'

The door opened behind them and Chloe appeared. Her hazel eyes narrowed slightly at the sight of Malika and Ping-Mei together, but she smiled as she came up to them.

'Hey guys, where is everyone?'

Malika marvelled at her straight, golden hair – how it gleamed in the sun.

'Already gone,' said Ping-Mei. 'Hels and Marie got a det on Friday for being late.' She shook her head. 'Year 11 and they're still giving us stupid dets.'

Chloe sidled up to Ping-Mei, taking her arm. 'Well, we can say we were helping out the new girl.' She flashed a smile at Malika. 'No way she'll get a det.'

'We'd better move it,' said Ping-Mei, checking her watch, 'we've got a double with Batters. Batters and a pre-test on Monday morning – nothing about that combo in my horoscope this morning.'

The tree-lined path turned into a corridor between two white buildings. 'Drama School and my personal torture chamber, the Music School,' Ping-Mei had pointed out to her on the first day. Once past the buildings, they joined the main school avenue that reminded Malika of the bazaar near her village. Girls of different ages and sizes were pouring through the entrance gates farther down the hill or stepping out of large cars in the parking area, all of them in uniform as they made their way up the slope towards the classrooms.

Girls laughed and chatted as they passed her, just as the women at the university in Lahore had done when they were away from the men, who always complained about women studying with them. When she first began, many of the women did not wear hijabs. 'It is our right,' they told her. 'This is the new world.' But after the bombings in Iqbal Park and around the city, even Christian women began to cover their hair and their faces, seeking safety in devout conformity. She had other reasons to conform: she detested the sight of her own face, and the world would feel the same.

Malika stopped on the avenue as Ping-Mei, Chloe and some other girls headed towards their classrooms. Ping-Mei turned.

'Good luck with Stella,' she said, raising both thumbs.

Malika nodded behind her veil, and continued up the slope before reaching a white staircase. She clutched her laptop to her chest as she climbed three flights, pausing to catch her breath at the top.

The secretary was waiting for her. Her hair was very red and her face pale from make-up. She smiled in a way that was not really a smile, as she led Malika to a nearby door. Knocking, she showed her into a large room. The size of the room took Malika by surprise. She gazed at the high ceiling and then the wide stretch of carpet around her. It was large enough for three families. Perhaps they slept there at night.

A tall woman with pale brown skin was getting up from behind a desk as large as the bed Malika had shared with Ayesha. She crossed the carpet, her arms swinging loosely. Her hair was dark and short, like a man's, and her teeth when she smiled were as white as chicken eggs. Her smile was very wide, with much pink lipstick around her lips. She said her name was Ms Catalano. Up close, she was very tall.

'I am so glad to welcome you to our school, Malika,' she said, extending her hand. Her dark eyes were warm.

Malika shook the principal's hand, as she had been taught. Her dress was very fine with intricate stitching, and she marvelled at the skill of the woman who had sewn it. How much help must she have had?

'Normally I meet our new girls when they arrive, but the start of the school year is such a busy time.' She smiled. 'I know Mrs O'Bryan would have made sure you were comfortable for the weekend.'

Malika was glad the woman did not stare at her eyes, but instead returned to her desk and pointed vaguely to the chairs in front of it. She frowned as she stepped across the carpet. Ms Catalano, who was also Ms Stella Catalano, made knowing what to call her difficult. Ping-Mei had called her 'Stella', but the secretary, Ms Gatt, had not said that. Then there was Mrs O'Bryan, and Mrs Batters' class, which she needed to find again after this meeting. But the students all had double names too – as far as she could tell without titles. She would ask Ping-Mei about this; why some had first names but others, it seemed, only titles and last names. It was much simpler in Pakistan. Normal people had one name: Ayesha, Fatima, Malika. Important people were the same, except they had a title before their name. The principal's fingers tapped silently on the desk as she smiled again, and waited for Malika to sit down. Behind her, between two large windows, a crucifix hung on the wall.

Malika breathed softly behind her veil, as the principal put on glasses pink like her lipstick and leafed through a folder in front of her, nodding from time to time as she turned the pages. 'Ah, yes,' she said once, her mouth twisting a little and her dark eyes looking troubled as she glanced up. Malika shifted her gaze. Two small birds on the window ledge outside were taking turns to perch and fly out, briefly, only to return and do it again. She could sense a rhythm in their actions and let her mind join them. Finally, Ms Catalano put the folder aside and leaned forwards, her hands clasped.

'This has been a long journey for you, hasn't it, Malika?' she said. 'It has been for us all, to be honest. There was a time when I didn't think we would get you here. But I am glad we've been able to help our friends, Father Michael and his team, as well as you of course. They seem quite taken with you.'

Malika's heart lurched. 'You have heard from him? Or from Father Louis?'

The principal's lips tightened and she shook her head. 'Not yet. But we continue to pray for them – and for everyone over there.' She smiled. 'We hope soon there will be good news.' She smoothed her hair with one hand. 'Well, we had better get down to business, so you can get to class. Did you bring your passport?'

Malika reached into her clothes and pulled it out.

Ms Catalano flicked through it before holding the front page sideways and glancing up at Malika. 'I am very sorry, and I know this will not be easy for you, but I do need to ask you to remove your veil, so I can verify your passport photo.' Her eyes were sad this time as she smiled. 'Would you mind?'

Malika hesitated a moment, then nodded and removed the pin beneath her chin, freeing the hijab from its clasp, letting the two sides of the fabric fall straight. Placing the pin on the desk, she eased the fabric over her head and laid it on the desk. She had anticipated the sharp intake of breath from the principal as she looked up. Everyone had been the same. Even Father Louis.

'Thank you.' Ms Catalano's eyes remained sad as Malika picked up her headdress. 'Do you intend to wear that the whole time you are here?'

'Yes.' She reached for the pin.

'The girls might ask you about it. Some might not understand.'

'I know that.'

'Even parents might not understand.'

'I am sorry. I do not want this to be known as my face.'

The principal watched solemnly as Malika reattached her hijab and veil. 'Our pastoral care deacon starts back next week, Malika. I know she would like to see you.'

'I am fine. Thank you.'

She smiled. 'Perhaps we can talk about it again in a few weeks. Now, to your billet. Mrs O'Bryan tells me Dr Davenport will collect you after your session at the university this Friday. We normally expect our billets to pick up their students from the school. However, there seems little point in making you both come all the way back here if you are in the city.' She paused, as if reconsidering the plan, then her lips stretched wide again. 'It is slightly irregular, but I think it will work. I'm sure you'll get on.'

She handed a yellow envelope to Malika, who opened it, leafing through the papers and photos inside.

'She is very beautiful,' said Malika, picking out a photo.

'She was an asset to our school when she was here and has done very well. I know she will have your best interests at heart.' A patch of sun appeared on her shoulder as she eased back in her chair. 'There is one more thing before you leave. While you are at the university you are your own self of course, but you are also a representative of our school. Our uniform signifies who we are and where we are from. And the University of Melbourne is a highly prestigious place.' She paused. 'Do you understand what I mean?'

'You wish me to be in school uniform when I travel to the university.'

'That would be very helpful.'

'And my …' Malika pointed.

'Your hijab and veil. Yes, I have discussed this with some of the other teachers. Under the circumstances, we feel it is all right as long as you are wearing the uniform.'

Malika breathed deeply. Father Louis said that the ways of the elders and the ways of the young were different. 'But fortunately,' he would add, as he smiled, 'the Lord creates options.'

Ms Catalano stood and Malika did the same. 'Please know you can come to me anytime at all, Malika. I have an agreement with our missionary friends and I won't let them down. I want you to consider this your home while you are here.'

Malika's eyes darted to the older woman's face and she stretched out her hand. 'May I have my passport, please, Ms Catalano?'

The principal frowned and put her palms together. 'We do normally hold on to all passports during the term. For safekeeping, you understand.'

Malika's hand didn't move as their eyes met.

Ms Catalano sighed. 'Be careful with it,' she said, as she handed it to Malika and headed to the door. A tanned hand reached for the handle. 'I do hope you enjoy your time with us, Malika.' Her smile was very wide.

'I am very grateful to everyone for their help,' Malika replied, holding tight to her passport and the envelope inside her veil.

The classroom was silent when she arrived. Mrs Batters was not like any of her previous mathematics teachers. A large, older woman in a dress of bright colours, she smiled in welcome when Malika opened the door, at the same time raising a finger to her lips. Malika followed her to a seat at the back of the room, passing Chloe who, head down and chewing on her pen, ignored her. Mrs Batters placed the test on her desk as she sat down.

'There's half an hour left,' she whispered. 'Do what you can.'

Malika scanned the square room as she settled. Ping-Mei was two rows across. She sneaked a smile at Malika and waved. Malika waved back. She liked this room. She had not seen walls as clean or windows as large. The windows in the classrooms at her university in the Great City were caked in grime and had fans that only sometimes worked. Here, fans did not seem to be needed.

Mrs Batters came up to her. 'It is a rather long test, Malika,' she whispered. 'Perhaps you should get started.'

She nodded, and opened the booklet.

Mrs Batters handed the exams back on the Thursday, commenting briefly to each girl as she walked around the class. Malika was in the same seat as before, with Chloe directly in front of her.

Well done, Chloe,' said Mrs Batters, smiling. '71% on a pre-test is excellent.'

As Chloe glowed, Malika glanced at Ping-Mei who was rolling her eyes. She mouthed '55' and smiled, showing her a thumb pointed to the ceiling.

Mrs Batters stopped in front of Malika and raised an eyebrow as she handed Malika's test back. 'Extraordinary,' was all she said.

Chloe spun around. 'What did you get? Tell me, tell me!'

'Malika got 100%,' said Mrs Batters, speaking to the class. 'Now everyone knows, so let's move on. Congratulations, Malika.'

'What!' hissed Chloe. 'In a pre-test?' She reached for Malika's paper.

'Turn around and show a little decorum please, Chloe.' Mrs Batters' voice had dropped a degree. 'Malika can show whatever she likes to whomever she wants when she is ready.'

'Show me?' Chloe mouthed at Malika, when Mrs Batters had turned her back again.

Malika sighed and handed her paper across. Chloe flicked through it feverishly.

'But where're your workings?' she whispered, pointing at the mainly single statement answers or diagrams that filled the pages.

Malika shrugged. 'I did not think they needed workings.'

Shaking her head, Chloe passed the paper back and turned to the front. She didn't turn again for the rest of the class.

'I've never seen anyone nail a pre-test in Spesh maths,' said Ping-Mei that evening. 'I mean it's stuff we're supposed to do in the coming semester, so, like, you're supposed to get it wrong and find out where you need to work.' She thought a minute. 'I guess that means you already know it. That's so cool.' She jumped off the bed and pulled down some books from the high shelf above her desk. Dumping them on the desk, she pulled out a bottle that was three-quarters full of a clear fluid.

'My sister got this for me on the weekend.' She angled it against the light. 'Got through more than I thought. Guess its baptism the other night was more like a confirmation.' She shrugged. 'But an effort like yours deserves a celebration.'

She fetched two glasses from the bathroom and poured bright raspberry cordial in each before spinning open the top on the bottle and filling the glasses a quarter full with the clear liquid. She sat back down on the bed and passed one of the glasses to Malika.

'To Spesh Maths!' she said, taking half the glass in a gulp. She shuddered. 'Prefer the bar at the Westin, but it's not bad. Not too bad at all.' She stretched out her legs and stroked her black ponytail with her free hand. 'You gotta try it at least.' She took another sip and closed her eyes. 'I'll finish what you don't have.'

Malika held the glass beneath her nose. Raspberry, and also something else. She couldn't place it. She pulled her veil across enough to let the glass in and tasted it. Sweet and then burning down her throat. Her mouth tanged. She wiped her lips. 'What is this?' she asked.

'Vodka.' Ping-Mei took a smaller sip. 'The best. You can't buy this sort here.'

'Alcohol?'

'Of course. Oh my God!' She put a hand on Malika's leg. 'You're Muslim, aren't you? I should have checked.'

Malika laughed and took another sip. 'No. I am Christian, like you.'

'My mother says we're Catholic, not Christian.' She shrugged. 'I don't really give a shit.'

They wriggled their feet on the bed together. Another sip and Malika's head began to swim. 'I think that's enough for now,' she said, reaching across to put the glass on the desk.

'Tell me,' Ping-Mei exchanged her empty glass for Malika's, 'if you're not Muslim, why the veil?'

'It is my preference.' Malika glanced at her.

'But it must be so uncomfortable. Like just then, with the glass and all.'

'Sometimes it can be. Yes.'

Ping-Mei frowned a moment and their eyes met. She held up a hand. 'Whatever. That's cool.' She raised her glass. 'Here's to veils and preferences. Next time I'll find a straw.'

Malika slid her feet up so they were flat on the quilt. She hugged her knees. 'Ping-Mei, I need your help. Ms Catalano told me I must wear my school uniform when I leave the school, but this I cannot do.'

Ping-Mei looked puzzled. 'Do you mean your face? Is it such a big deal? I mean, not being Muslim or anything.'

'My hijab and veil are permitted.'

She frowned. 'I'm now totally confused.'

Malika sighed. 'I am not used to showing my legs in public places.'

Ping-Mei looked at her own legs splayed out on the bed. 'My legs are one of my best attributes,' she said.

'You have very beautiful skin,' Malika agreed. She paused. 'But that is not what I mean.'

'Oh.' Ping-Mei nodded and leaned back against the wall a moment, before bouncing off the bed. She knelt down and pulled out a pair of black tights from her set of drawers. She threw them at Malika. 'Tights. They'll be a bit hot, but I guess nothing like what you're wearing now.'

Malika nodded as she held them up. 'It is a good option.'

'Best I can do right now. Try them and let me know.'

'Thank you.' She stood up. 'I have a meeting at the university tomorrow. I must prepare.'

'You have a meeting at a university?' She twisted her face. 'Well, I guess I have to pull my finger out, too. Merchant banking, remember?' She studied herself in the mirror, pulling her hair one way and then the other. 'Out for tonight, I think. Definitely.' She picked up a brush. 'Shall we go to the library?'

Malika considered this a moment. 'Yes, I think that will be fine.'

'Cool. Okay, see you downstairs in ten. Don't forget to brush your teeth.'

'Vodka makes your teeth dirty?'

She rolled her eyes. 'It's for your breath, dummy.'

Malika sat outside the head of year's office. Miss Cullerton. Miss. Another title to work on. She had been summoned there first thing that morning. Ping-Mei told her not to worry.

'Last time I got called up by the Cull,' she said, 'my parents had made a surprise trip from Singapore. Got me out of school for two whole days. It was great. Though last year,' she pulled a face, 'the Cull had to tell Chloe her brother was killed in a car crash. That was awful. She didn't come back to school for a week. And her parents don't even talk to each other, so the funeral was like really awkward. His family on one side and hers on the other. They've been pals ever since.'

'Chloe and Miss Cullerton?'

'Well not her parents, dum-dum.' She sighed. 'I don't know what I'd do if my sister died.'

Miss Cullerton's office was on the floor below the principal's. Malika's heart raced as an office worker and then another marched past, wobbling on their high heels. She lowered her head and studied her hands. Each finger was quivering. It was curious the way fingers were attached to the hand. Five digits. Four might have been equally efficient, six an advantage, although the fingers themselves would need to be finer in that case. Ayesha had said to her once that Malika's fingers were very fine. As they lay together one warm night, she had held them up to the kerosene light inside the hut. 'Fine and long,' she said, 'with almond-shaped nails. The others will be jealous.' As if the good fortune of fine fingers meant a life of finery would follow.

The door opened and a well-dressed woman with very blonde hair and very red lipstick looked at her. So many people at this school had blonde hair. Her pale eyes were not friendly like Ms Catalano's.

'Malika? Come in.'

The office was the same colour as Ms Catalano's; the desk faced the room the same way, and the seats in front of it were just as comfortable. But it was half the size.

Miss Cullerton studied the file in front of her for a minute before looking up with a thin smile. 'Malika, I am afraid there has been a complaint of cheating made. I am sure you understand we can never ignore claims such as these.' She brought her hands together. 'I should add it is unofficial at this stage. I hope it will go no further.' Malika's eyes widened as Miss Cullerton continued. 'You got 100% on a recent pre-test exam. That is very unusual. How did you do that?'

'I wrote the answers on the paper.'

'It has been claimed that you cheated.'

'That is not true. Did you speak to Mrs Batters?'

'I did, and fortunately she denies anything untoward took place.'

'Then why do you not trust your teacher?'

Miss Cullerton leaned forwards, her face earnest. 'This is an important year for all students, Malika. It is my responsibility to be sure that no one feels they are being prejudiced against.' She paused. 'Not just you.'

'Do you have evidence of this claim?' Malika asked.

Miss Cullerton clasped her hands together on the desk and looked at her steadily.

Malika's eyes flashed. 'I will do another test.'

'That won't be necessary. Please understand I must ensure there is honesty and transparency in my classrooms.'

'Perhaps the next test will provide that.'

'Perhaps.' The teacher wrote on the pad in front of her for a few minutes before looking up. 'You may go, Malika. Thank you.'

Malika stood and walked to the door, her insides shaking for reasons she couldn't yet understand. She placed a hand on the door handle, and then turned. 'I do not cheat, Miss Cullerton.'

'Yes, I heard you the first time.' She put down her pen and placed her elbows on the table. Her brown eyes bored into Malika's. 'Just so we are clear, I will be keeping a close eye on things from now. The leeway we show you in permitting your foreign headgear and veil at this school will extend no further.' Her nostrils flared as she inhaled. 'If I had my way, you would be treated the same as anyone else. I am told in your case there are reasons, but we all have to overcome our issues.'

Malika took her hand off the handle. She didn't know what to say.

'This is about standards,' Miss Cullerton continued, 'not feelings. Mine or yours.'

Malika's palms were sweating as she left the room. For a moment, she thought she might vomit. What should she make of this? She did not know how many people would listen to her, or if the rest of the class felt the same as Miss Cullerton. Ping-Mei might help, but she did not know her yet and she might also make more trouble. And it was not her problem. No. It was best she said nothing. That was what she did when Tahir drowned the goat kid. She told no one. She had thought then as she did now: an experience revealed lost its power as it became a story. She was still a stranger in this school; she could not yet afford stories.

That afternoon at lunchtime, dressed in her school uniform and Ping-Mei's black tights, she packed her laptop and notebooks into her weekend bag and walked towards the school gates. She went over the trip Mrs O'Bryan had made with her the previous week in her mind. The teacher had pointed out numbers and shops to remember, and at which stop to get off. It was not difficult. She had marvelled at the tram that swished smoothly along the rails. She had not seen such vehicles at home, not even in Lahore. Buses were plentiful, but this bus was more like a train.

Mrs O'Bryan had told her that morning that Dr Kate would pick her up outside the mathematics building, and that she should wait for her there. She said she hoped the doctor wouldn't cancel again, but she was to ring the boarding school with any problems, as emergencies could arise.

Just before the front gates of the school she left the drive and darted behind a thick clump of bushes. Checking she was alone, she pulled off her uniform and quickly slipped on her tunic and pants, adjusting her hijab before stepping out. In truth, she did not mind if people saw her bare arms. Perhaps even her legs. But she did not belong to this uniform as the principal wished her to. She crossed the road just as the tram appeared at the top of the hill.

2

Sunshine shone yellow-green through the old elms as Kate half-shuffled, half-ran along College Crescent. The closest parking spot had been opposite the cemetery way up College Crescent. Hardly a gift when she was already twenty minutes late. She should have refused that last referral. Stephen would have. She checked the time again as she stopped to catch her breath. She was going to be thirty minutes late. They hadn't given her a mobile number for the girl; the only thing she could do was get there.

She didn't know this side of the uni at all. Her comfort zone was the medical block, about as far from where she was now as was possible. Direct sunlight hit her as she turned onto Monash Road, and she pulled her sunnies out of her bag. Panting slightly, she scanned the street for a girl in school uniform as Verna O'Bryan, the boarding mistress, had told her to. No one even remotely fitted the description. The few serious-faced pedestrians coming towards her looked as tired as she was, and a group of Asians – students, presumably – were heading the other way in tracksuits and gym clothes.

She pulled the details Verna had given her from her bag.

She was in the right place; the maths school was part of the Richard Berry Building, which was the name on the side of the sandstone and red-brick structure in front of her. Its entrance nudged out from the main façade like a miniature chapel, which was shaded by a large melaleuca on the far side. She stepped up the few stone steps and tried the doors. Locked. She checked her watch. Five-thirty. She retraced her steps and placed her hands on her hips. What to do? Had the girl gone back to school? She took out her phone.

'Dr Kate?'

A Muslim girl in full traditional dress emerged from the other side of the entrance, her fine, brown hands gripping an overnight bag. She must have been standing behind the tree. Kate held back a frown. She had been told to look for a girl in school uniform. The girl's eyes crinkled as she walked up and extended her hand. Kate forced a smile as she put out her own.

'You must be Malika. I am sorry to be late.'

The girl shook her head. 'It is no problem, Dr Kate.'

'I'll try and be on time in the future.' The girl did not respond and Kate stalled. What should she say now? Malika's eyes followed her as she put her hands together and looked around for inspiration.

'So,' she said eventually, 'how did the maths class go?'

'It was not a class. Professor Jenkins and I talked about some things. He is a very smart man.'

'Well, of course. He must be. Could he answer all your questions?'

'We talked for a long time. It is much easier than by email.'

'Sure.' Kate breathed deeply and looked around before

returning to Malika's gaze. 'Is it too early for a meal? Perhaps a cup of tea?'

The girl's head lifted. 'A meal would be very good.'

'Anywhere you would like to go?' She should never have taken this on. 'Maybe Vietnamese?'

'Anywhere is good. I am very hungry.'

'Well, let's try something local. We can leave your bag in the car, it's just up the street.' She reached for Malika's bag, but the girl pulled away.

'It is my bag, Dr Kate. No problem.'

Malika pushed the last of her bread around the near-empty plate of pasta with her right hand, first one way and then the other, soaking up whatever juices remained. Finally, her left hand pulling her veil forward, she passed the bread into her mouth. She closed her eyes as she chewed.

'Don't they feed you at school?' Kate asked, nudging her chair forward as a couple moved to the table behind them.

'I missed my lunch today,' Malika replied, swallowing and holding her plate in both hands. She looked around.

'It's all right,' said Kate. 'The waitress will take the plates.'

'I am very able to do this.'

'It's her job,' Kate began, cutting her sentence short as the girl stood and took her plate to the counter. 'The staff expect to clear the tables,' she explained quietly, as Malika sat down again, adding, 'it's what they're paid to do.'

Her eyes widened. 'Have I done a bad thing?'

'Not at all. I am sure the waitress is grateful.' She paused. 'You seemed to enjoy the meal.'

Malika nodded. 'It was very good. I have not tried this food before. When I looked at Australian food on my computer, it was meat pies and chips. I am glad we did not eat that.'

Kate looked around the soft-toned room with its arched windows. 'I sometimes come here when it is late after work. It's quick and good.'

'You are very lucky to have food like this anytime.'

'I was surprised to see you enjoyed the prosciutto.'

'It is much nicer than ham.'

Kate cocked her head. 'I'm confused – your veil and clothes?'

'I am Christian.'

'I see.' Kate sipped on her tea and smiled at the contradiction in front of her. 'You don't get hot covered as much as you are?'

Malika shrugged.

'How hot is it in your village?'

'Do you have mosquitoes here in summer?'

Kate rolled her eyes. 'They attack me in swarms whenever I water the garden.'

'In my village, it gets too hot for mosquitoes.'

The next morning, Kate dragged herself from bed to find the dishwasher emptied and breakfast set on the table. But the house was quiet and Malika didn't answer when she called. She knocked on her bedroom door and eased it open a crack to find the bed made, the covers pulled up, and the pillows sitting proud on top. She pushed the door open. Malika's bag was on the floor next to her bed and her open laptop was on the desk. But there was no sign of her anywhere. She felt between the sheets. Cold. Had she even slept there? How long had she been up – or gone?

She got in the shower. Should she look for her; drive round the streets? Her first Saturday rooms began at eight – and where should she look if she did? Besides, the girl wasn't a baby.

There was still no sign of Malika when Kate was ready to go. She drank the glass of orange juice on the kitchen table and checked her watch. This had been a mistake. The only thing she could think of was to ring the school.

A key in the front door had her hurrying along the hallway.

'Where have you been?' Kate demanded, as the veiled girl walked through the door.

Malika blinked at her a couple of times. 'Am I too late?'

'Well, yes and no. What have you been doing? It's just that I have to go soon,' she added, softening her tone as Malika took a step back. 'I just wondered where you were.'

'I was looking for the church.' Her brow creased. 'It is very safe in this place.'

'Church?'

'It is not far, just up the hill and across the main road. Shall we eat breakfast now?'

'I've had some juice, thanks. I really have to leave.' She frowned. 'Why the church?'

'It is Sunday tomorrow.'

'And?'

'We have Mass.'

'Of course.' She swallowed. 'Mass.' She hadn't been for decades.

She walked towards the kitchen. 'Shall I put on your kettle?'

'You don't understand. I have patients waiting for me.'

Malika's tunic and veil flared as she turned. 'What time will you be back?'

'Not until after lunch. There's heaps in the fridge. I did some shopping. Sorry. I have to get there early. I have no one to –' She stopped. 'You wouldn't like to come, would you? To help? It's only for the morning.' Even if she sorted the payments. 'You don't have to, of course,' she added, 'and I will pay you.'

Malika stared at her a moment. 'Yes, if you would like me to, I can come.' She looked around her and raised her arms. 'You already give me too much.'

'Well, we can talk about it. But that would really help.' She checked her watch. 'How long do you need to get ready?'

Malika wet her finger and dabbed at the plastic wrap to collect the last crumbs of her falafel before scrunching it and placing it beside Kate's wrapper. She leaned back in the car seat and closed her eyes. 'So many problems for you today, Dr Kate.'

Kate glanced across. The girl had somehow picked up the computer system, organised payments for the patients and produced a report at the end, as if she had been doing it for months. It had taken Sam weeks to learn, and even now she would only produce reports weekly. 'Medicare bounced it,' was her stock response whenever Kate quizzed her.

'Do you fix all these people?' Malika asked.

'I operate on many of them,' she said, 'to try and fix what's gone wrong.'

'That is a good thing,' Malika replied. She turned her head and gazed out the window. 'It is different in my village.'

'What happens there?'

'In the village we must live with what happens. Even when it is very wrong.'

Kate raced to take the arrow just as it went amber. 'What shall we do with the afternoon?'

'We should do the chores and then I can prepare dinner.'

Kate laughed. 'There aren't a lot of chores to do – but later we can water the garden.'

'I would like that too.'

'And until then?' She slowed the car and pulled over to the side. The sun was hot through the windscreen and she opened their windows, letting in the noise of the Punt Road traffic. She had given this no thought whatsoever. Weekends usually just sorted themselves out.

'Ayesha, my other mother, said I must see the ocean.'

'You want to see the sea?'

'She said "ocean". If that is the sea, then yes.' She looked at Kate from behind her veil. 'Definitely.'

Kate thought a moment. 'Well, the ocean might have to wait for another weekend. It is a long way. And the bay beaches can be patchy. But I do know a beautiful beach that is not too far.'

Malika nodded vigorously.

Kate restarted the car, checked her side mirror for oncoming traffic, then crossed to the middle of the road. She waited for the lights to change before doing a U-turn and heading up Punt Road.

It wasn't really a surprise that Mornington beach came to mind. It was the way memories worked. They didn't discriminate – there was no filter, no timeline. Good and bad mixed with recent and old, as if they'd all happened together. Although Jake was one of the good ones. They had been an item, of sorts, late in her second year at uni. She wasn't quite sure how they'd got together. Maybe it was when he told her he was going to drop out. He was the most harmless guy she had met, his mind usually in the stratosphere rather than below his waistline. He never wanted to know about her – so they got on fine, he lost in his world and hers safe from probing. He would spend hours pondering how to beat the system, coming up with possibilities in smoke-heavy cafés filled with like-minded souls. Meanwhile she was at her desk in Carlton, occasionally glancing up at a parched strip of garden beneath the low brick fence. One Sunday afternoon she, faint from study and he, itching to escape, discovered Mornington beach. With cliffs that curved swan-like along the shoreline and a bay that sparkled in the afternoon sun, it became their secret summer haunt. Plodding through coarse sand beneath the earth-red cliffs, they pretended the sandstone prominences were their children, calling each of them by name. It didn't last. She heard years later that he completed an immunology degree and joined a biotech company in the States, ending up selling a monoclonal patent for a fortune. He sent her a postcard from Rio soon after retiring. It was the same year she qualified as a surgeon. Thinking about it always made her smile.

An offshore breeze blew her hair across her face as Kate locked the car. She clutched it with one hand as they crossed the road towards tea-trees strong with memory.

'My mother held her hair that way,' said Malika, looking up. 'Against the wind. It was long, like yours.'

'Do you miss her?'

'Yes. It was a long time ago.'

'And your hair?'

'My hair is also long.'

Kate glanced at her and they smiled, before taking the track to the beach.

The breeze met them again as they emerged through the tea-trees at the bottom. Malika gasped at the wide stretch of blue and looked down in surprise as her feet plunged into the sand. Kate pulled off her own shoes and waited as Malika sat on the coarse, warm sand and untied her own laces methodically, her ankles skinny and dark beneath her pants.

They headed to the water.

'I like this sea very much,' said Malika, laughing behind her veil as her feet splashed in the low-tide shallows.

'I should have brought my bathers,' said Kate. 'Can you swim?'

Malika shook her head. 'But I would like to learn this.' She looked at her. 'Will you teach me?'

'Sure,' Kate replied. 'One day soon.'

They wandered along the shore towards the rocks at the far end of the beach and sat at the cliff base watching a group of lanky kids playing cricket on the wet sand in front of them. Along the beach, a few umbrellas fluttered in the breeze. Kate remembered it being more crowded. She glanced at her watch. It was only four, and the sun was still high above the pencil-like masts of the moored yachts at the distant pier. Perhaps people were already at their weekenders, or a few might have been working the yachts crisscrossing randomly on the bay, their white and bright-coloured sails tilting into the wind.

She squinted again along the beach. It was smaller than she remembered. Even shiny Melbourne across the water seemed a lesser place. Was it the job of memory to make the past loom larger than reality? A course lecturer once said we don't remember an event as it happened; we recall its memory. She had asked him after the lecture whether it was the memory or the reality that had the lasting effect. He had said that no one knew.

Beside her, Malika was digging her toes into the warm sand. Then she straightened her legs and let the yellow grains pour freely from the top of each foot, leaving a dusting of damp breadcrumbs on her feet. Kate watched her from the corner of her eye. They had spoken a little in the car, as they had the night before in the restaurant, but she remained a stranger – polite, obliging, but quite inaccessible. Perfect, really.

'We can go into the town,' said Kate, 'if you like.'

Malika shook her head. 'It is better here.' She looked around her, her eyes widening at the stack of rocks leading up to a cliff behind them. 'Can we get to the top?'

'I think so.' Kate squinted at the cliff, thinking back. 'There used to be a path. Would you like to try?'

Malika nodded.

'I seem to remember it taking about fifteen minutes. When I was young and fit,' she added. 'There used to be a bench at the top.'

'Then let us do it in ten.'

Her dark eyes gleamed before she got to her feet and, holding her veil and hijab, scuttled across the sand as Kate chased after her. The bench was still in its original spot: new of course, with expensive timber and perched on a slatted wooden platform, but effectively the same bench. They sat on it as they recovered their breath and gazed across the water. They had done it in twelve minutes.

'That was a hard run,' said Kate.

Malika turned to her. 'Next time, we will do it in ten.'

'All right,' she said, smiling, 'you're on.' She rolled up her sleeves to expose her white arms, then tilted her head back and closed her eyes. Perhaps, for once, a bit of sun wouldn't hurt.

For a time they watched the yachts and the blue expanse before them.

'This is a sacred place,' said Malika.

'It is.' Kate nodded. 'Are you enjoying your time here?' Malika looked at her and Kate felt, not for the first time, that she was being weighed and sorted. 'Just generally, I mean,' she added.

'I am here to learn,' Malika replied. She paused. 'I did not wish to come, but Father Louis, and then Father Michael, insisted.'

'Oh, I see.' Kate thought a moment. 'What was your alternative?'

'There is a very good university in Islamabad.'

'So –?'

'They said I could be in great danger and Islamabad was still too close. Then Father Louis and my friend, Daniel, were gone. And Father Michael feared more would follow.'

'Because of you?'

'I do not know.' Malika studied her feet. 'It is very different there.' She hesitated, and her brow was wrinkled when she looked up. 'It is true that much is the same. Yes. Very much the same advertisements for skin cream and beautiful shoes. And

Pepsi. Many women in the Great City also dress like Western women now, in jeans and t-shirts. And it is much cleaner. But here even the toilets are clean.' She stopped for a moment. 'And you have such organisation here. There is no shouting, or fighting – but also I do not see people laughing. There is much struggle but also great laughter in the streets at home. They are sometimes having a great time.' She looked up at Kate. 'I have not seen that here.' She shrugged and looked across the expanse of water. 'It is hard to explain.'

They arrived back at Kew in the late dusk, each yawning as the car pulled up. Kate hosed the sand off her own feet at the front door and then made Malika laugh when she turned the hose on her, her knees jumping and her feet dancing under the porch light as the warm hose water sprayed off them. She squealed, and then Kate did the same as the spray somehow found its way onto her own clothes.

'Turn it off,' said Kate, laughing and pointing the jet onto the garden for a moment, before splashing it back on Malika who was twisting the tap furiously. She squealed again. When the water died, they straightened and looked at each other.

Kate grinned as she wiped her feet on the doormat. 'I'll make dinner,' she said. 'I'll just change.'

'I will make naan.'

Kate went to her room and dried her legs as she sat on her bed. If it were up to her, she would make toast and go to bed. She glanced at her face in the mirror as she brushed out the knots in her hair. She was sunburnt – she had felt the tell-tale warmth in the car. She would have lectured her patients if they had done the same. But it was worth it this once: the beach was pristine, just as she remembered. Why twenty years between visits, she asked the face in the mirror as she pulled on a t-shirt and black tights. For that matter, how long since she had been anywhere?

'Is something wrong, Dr Kate?'

Kate looked up. Malika was staring at her from the opposite couch, a writing pad on her knees and a pen in her left hand. The empty dinner plates were on the table between them. She realised she had been rubbing her forehead, possibly sighing. But why wouldn't she? The rosters in front of her were impossible: twelve surgeons, each with a specific number of weekends on call according to their sessional allocation, and weekdays on a separate roster – though it was the total on call days that ultimately counted. Add to that their designated conference and annual leave, a sabbatical for one surgeon halfway through the year, and long service leave for another – and at that point her head gave up. Stephen had been wise. He never mentioned it; instead, he would put forward a plan in January and rely on people to sort it out for themselves. No one dared complain about stuff-ups, not to the prof, anyway. She was still smarting from the email that her colleague, Jonathan Hooper, had sent to Andrew Jamieson.

She sighed. 'I got the roster wrong last weekend and got hammered for it. It's a little tricky.'

'Roster?' Malika put her pad and pen down, and sat forward on the couch, her eyes eager behind her veil, her hands clasped.

Kate smiled. 'Do you want to have a go?'

Malika's hands reached out.

She handed the laptop back to Kate twenty minutes later. 'It is done,' she said, running her fingertip across the screen to make sure Kate followed. 'I have made a program so you can add names, time away, and hours to work, and the program will sort it out for you.' Her fingers began tapping. 'Let me show you.'

Kate watched as Malika worked through two examples, then she tested it herself, inputting the details of a couple of the surgeons – Jonathan first. She exhaled. 'I can't believe you've just done that,' she said.

Malika nodded. 'It is not so hard.' She yawned. 'I think it is time for me to be in bed now. What time would you like breakfast?'

'How about we get our own breakfast? It's Sunday, after all.'

'It is no problem. I must wash my kameez.'

Kate realised a moment too late. 'You're actually going to Mass, aren't you?'

They walked together up the hill to Mass the next morning, and again the following Sunday. The hour was as tedious and boring as she had remembered, as if the last time she had been was measured in days rather than years. She stood when she was supposed to, sat through the long sermon in the straight-backed pew, kneeled, and tried not to be too obvious when checking her watch. She looked around her. The place was less than half-full, and the two of them must have dropped the mean age of the congregation by a decade, many of whom stared openly at the two newcomers. Kate stifled a laugh: the presence of Malika in her kameez, hijab and veil must have been a significant challenge.

The young Filipino priest noticed them the first week and gave them a winning smile the second. They couldn't escape him on the stairs on their way out. Unlike the sharp glances and odd scowl from the other parishioners filing around them he was curious, about Malika in particular. They spoke for a minute, before Malika looked at Kate and began to walk away. Kate smiled apologetically to the priest as she departed.

'He was only trying to be nice,' she said, catching up.

'This does not help people.'

'He's just doing his job.'

They reached the main road and Malika pushed the button for the traffic lights. Then she stood back, arms folded, before pushing the button again.

'It doesn't help to push it twice,' said Kate.

She stayed silent.

'What has upset you, Malika?'

She stared straight ahead as she spoke. 'His sermon was about having a drawer in the kitchen that is not neat – three neat, one not neat. What use is this? Father Louis spoke of courage and hope and that we must continue to believe in dangerous times.' She glanced at Kate as they crossed the road. 'And now he is gone.'

'We don't know that. Not yet.'

'In my country, people are gone too often not to be sure.'

They spoke little more on the way back to her mother's place. Kate made coffee and they drank it beneath the umbrella on the back verandah. The late morning glare was bright around them. Malika stared in front of her, her fingers holding the cup near her lips.

'Why don't we miss Mass next week?' Kate asked. 'Especially if it's not really working for you.'

'Mass has no meaning here,' Malika replied.

'We could try a different church, if you like. I could drop you off, or you could just not go at all.'

Malika sipped on her coffee. She shook her head. 'I prefer to go.'

'Do you think God will punish you if you don't?'

'No, it is not that.' She looked up at Kate. 'Have you heard from Father Michael? I have emailed him but there has been no answer.'

Kate shook her head. She had done the same, repeatedly. She had even rung the Jesuit house a week earlier, without success. A polite refusal to discuss him – or anyone, for that matter – was the best way she could frame her conversation. 'He must have limited access to emails,' she said. 'Maybe none at all right now. I don't even know where he is.'

'Father Louis' parish is very large.'

'We can only wait,' said Kate.

She dropped Malika at school later in the afternoon, glancing around the parking lot as Malika climbed out of the car.

'Didn't you say you had to wear your uniform at school?'

Malika turned back to her. 'I decided that it is different on weekends.' She opened the back door and pulled out her bag.

Kate nodded. 'Call me if you need to,' she said.

She watched the diminutive, shrouded figure shuffle towards the boarding school, her body tilted by the weight of the bag. For the hundredth time that weekend, she asked herself if it was all a huge mistake. She was too busy. What would happen when she was on call? Far better that Malika find someone more reliable, a family with a dog maybe, and a swimming pool. She could come over occasionally, stay a night once a month or so. Malika turned and waved before turning the corner, and Kate found herself waving back. Only then did she back the car up and leave.

She headed out the drive, memories leaping at her from each side of the car. Even the smell of the grass reminded her of summer sports. She checked the time. Still enough left to check her pre-ops and make it to drinks with Lucy at six. They had barely made contact since Lorne, which seemed an age ago. What she did know was that the pregnancy was well underway, and that Lucy wanted her to meet the elusive Hamish. Driving into the city, she remembered she had another meeting later that week, her first official one with Andrew Jamieson. Her palms were clammy on the steering wheel as she wondered what he might want to discuss.

3

The phone call from Father Mike woke her from a deep sleep on Thursday night. She couldn't make much sense of it initially; the delay when she spoke and the echo down the line disoriented her – she thought initially it was the hospital calling. And his voice was hesitant, like an on-duty resident phoning her overnight with bad news.

'I can't leave these people right now,' he said, the line momentarily clear enough for him to have been next door.

'But the risk.' She sat on the edge of her bed. 'I mean –'

'You're right, and I need to keep my eyes open, but the danger is in the cities, mainly.' The line went dead for a moment. 'Kate,' he said, when he came back, 'there is other news you must know.'

They spoke for a long time, his voice reverting to its usual consoling tone, reassuring her as the minutes passed. Yet as soon as she hung up, the cold dread that had begun germinating in the pit of her stomach when he told her the news spread through her body, robbing her of any further sleep as it taunted her with calamity. It was like a scalpel cutting the skin, knowing that what lay beneath was bad, just not quite how bad. The chill in her bones was still with her as she prepared for work the next morning.

'Kate?'

She looked up. Andrew blinked at her from behind his glasses, his green mask bright under the theatre lights.

'It's your move.'

She stared down, askance. The wound lay open, raw and red, waiting for the skin graft she had prepared. 'Sorry!' She turned to Peta, her scrub nurse, who passed across the moistened graft Kate had prepared earlier. She picked it off the tray with her forceps, carefully placing it over the raw facial tissue, relieved to see it fitted perfectly in the space created by the excised tumour.

'Well done,' said Andrew. 'Three to go.'

'You were distracted in there today.'

Andrew poured them both a mug of tea, and carried hers across to the table where she was sitting. They had finished their joint list early, and he had asked her if they might meet in his office then, rather than wait until the next day as arranged.

'I'm sorry. It won't happen again.' She sat upright in the green leather chair and nudged her hair behind her head.

'Stephen's absence is a hole. A big hole. I know that.' He pulled up a chair and sat opposite her. 'Jonathan's told me he's willing to help out.'

She tried to read him. She couldn't. It seemed to be the way with really smart people. The only thing she knew for sure was that he was watching her intently. His eyes were as blue as hers.

'He also made an official complaint. About me,' she said.

'That's a little strong. We can all see you're pushed. And we all have a breaking point.'

She swallowed. 'I made a mistake in the roster. It's hardly a crime, and it's been fixed. Today was –' she stopped and collected herself. 'It won't happen again.'

The room was silent as Andrew sipped his tea. For want of something better to do, she did the same. She could hear Ellen, his PA, on the phone outside his office.

'Do you want me to hand over Stephen's job? I'm doing it because he asked me to, no other reason.'

'No.' He placed his mug on the table. 'He asked you because we had discussed it and because he backed you as the best choice. And I can see why, even if you can't. But you have to be on top of your game. It goes with the job.'

She nodded. She thought of the bespectacled man tripping on the steps at Stephen's place a few months ago. Was this the same person? This man was a lion. Quiet, perhaps, but a lion all the same. Already he had changed the department, his presence and his drive permeating even the most ingrained routines. He challenged and supported staff at the same time and, with a deftness that resembled inactivity, was swinging the spirit of the place from negative to positive. People wanted to come to work in the morning.

'You haven't forgotten your talk Tuesday week?'

'Of course not.' She hadn't even started the background reading.

'It's important we start rebuilding our academic standards. To be honest, they are hardly at an international level.'

There was a knock at the door and Ellen poked her grey head into the room. She had stayed when her former boss left, and in the space of a week had also found her smile.

'I'm sorry, Professor, it's your son on the phone.' She glanced at Kate. 'He did say it wasn't anything important.'

He looked at Kate with a half-smile. 'Could you say I'll ring him back in five?'

'I can go,' said Kate, standing. A son?

'Please, no.' He stood awkwardly as the door shut and pushed on his glasses. The man who had stumbled on the steps that night at Stephen's had reappeared. This time, he stayed on his feet until Kate sat again. She tried to ease back into her chair, but the knot in her stomach held her stiff.

'How old is your son?'

'Julian's nine. He and his sister are still in London with my parents. He's having trouble sleeping. They'll fly over in the next couple of months. The plan was to wait until things here were settled.'

'Your family?' She drained her mug.

'My children.'

He turned in his chair and looked out the elongated window to his left. Kate followed his gaze. The suburbs stretched as far as the Dandenongs, a soft indigo in the distance.

'My wife died over two years ago,' he said, speaking to the suburbs or maybe to the sky. 'A long, but ultimately unsuccessful battle with the usual.'

'You don't have to explain anything to me.'

'I know that.' He looked back at her. 'But for some reason I'd like to.'

She picked up Malika late again that Friday. Sam had booked three appointments at the same time, and then had slouched off before Kate finished the last. Liz shrugged when Kate had raised her eyebrows. 'Who knows?' she said. 'Gen Y. Or is it Gen Z? I've lost track. Millennial, perhaps?'

They ate at a local place near her mother's as the sun set. Kate chewed her food slowly. There was no right time to say it; no way she could make this news easier. Perhaps she should have waited until they got back to her mother's, or until Saturday afternoon when they could have walked or hosed the garden. But she didn't. Maybe couldn't. Or perhaps she was responding to Malika, whose senses and instincts had proven finely tuned.

'They found four hands,' said Kate, her hands gripping each other below the table. 'In a plastic bag.' She looked into Malika's eyes as the restaurant door clanged open and a group swept in. 'Father Mike asked me to tell you, before it goes public on Monday.'

'Just hands?' Malika's voice was as soft as butter.

Kate shook her head. 'Don't ask me right now. I'll tell you later.'

'Father Michael is all right?'

'He's fine. He told me to tell you that. And also that he's more sorry than he can say.'

'It is I who should be saying that to him,' said Malika, looking onto the street. Kate's hand reached for Malika's, but she pulled away. 'It is all right,' she said. 'I expected this. In many ways I already knew it. Father Louis would never have stayed silent for so long.' She kept her head turned to the side as, outside, cars hovered in thick traffic and people manoeuvred between the chairs and cleanly set tables on the pavement.

'I'm sorry, too,' said Kate.

Malika turned, her eyes bright with pain. 'We are all sorry,' she said. 'It does not bring them back.' She dropped her head and clasped her hands in her lap.

'Dessert?' Their waitress stood beside the table, menu in hand.

They didn't speak in the car. At the house, Malika went to her room and closed the door. Kate waited in the lounge for a while, pacing up and down and eyeing Malika's door. She hoped she would reappear, but there was no sign of her, no sound. She decided it was better to leave her; she would emerge when she was ready, even if that wasn't until morning.

She was watching TV when she heard the door open again, quietly – like a secret whispered. It closed again and there was silence. Kate found herself listening acutely, feeling rather than hearing the presence behind her.

'You fix things, Dr Kate,' said Malika. 'You fix things very well.' Her inhalation was loud. 'Can you fix this?'

Kate turned. In the doorway, Malika was standing with her head raised, her veil and hijab gone. She met Kate's eyes, her face clear beneath the glare of the downlights. The remote control fell from Kate's hand.

Mel grinned at her as she opened the front door, swinging it wide and then having to haul it back. She held Kate tight before hugging the veiled Malika as well. She led them inside, turning effortlessly on her heels. As they entered the front room, Malika moved to the window and looked across the sun-drenched city.

Kate had called that morning to see if Stephen was well enough for a chat. Mel said it hadn't been a great morning. 'I just wanted his opinion about who I should speak to,' she said, before Stephen's voice came on the phone and she explained.

'For God's sake, bring her across and let me feel remotely useful,' he said, his voice as cross as it was concerned. 'I'm sick of being an invalid.'

Kate sat beside him on the couch. He had aged five years in five weeks. His eyes behind his glasses held deep weariness, and his skin was tinged with grey, either from the treatment or the anaemia that went with it. Probably both. He was thinner. No one could just shrug off chemo cycles.

He asked her about his unit with a steady gaze, and she found herself consoling him. Everything was okay. Fine. They missed him, but it was business as usual. Everyone was asking after him.

'No one's rung,' he said, and she cringed.

'I've not been fair on you,' he said, when she had finished updating him. 'But it's temporary. I'll be back once these cycles are done. Myron's really quite pleased with the figures. Most of them, at least.' He eased back into the couch cushions and winced. 'I must admit, I'll have more respect for my patients in the future. Feels like I've been run over by my tax bill.' He grinned at his own joke. 'Shall we have a look at your charge?'

Kate called across the room. 'Malika, are you still happy to show Stephen, as we discussed last night?'

Malika turned and came over to the couch, her hands working fluidly on the clasps and clips of her headwear. Mel appeared in the doorway behind them, glass in hand. She watched, fascinated, as Malika pulled off her veil and hijab, and then drew her hair out over her back.

'Oh! You poor girl!' said Mel, dropping onto the couch. Her glass clunked on the table.

Stephen pulled out his glasses. He took Malika's hand and gently drew her closer, holding her jaw in his large hand. With her head tilted back, he looked along her nose through his bifocals. Malika's dark eyes stared back at him.

'Be careful, Stephen,' said Mel.

He glanced at her and smiled, then turned to them. 'Let's try the study. The light's better there.'

He struggled to his feet, and Kate and Malika traipsed after him along the hallway.

His 'study' was fitted as a mini operating theatre. Kate stood to the side while Stephen urged Malika to sit on the examination chair. He went through his usual procedure, finishing by shining a light from his pen torch up each of Malika's nostrils.

'Well?' Kate asked.

He exhaled slowly. 'She'll need scans,' he said. 'I'd start with a CT. But any surgery will need an ENT and maybe a facio-maxillary guy too, as well as one of us of course. The nose will be tricky, the zygoma might wait. And it will remould to some extent, regardless.'

Kate nodded. One thing at a time. She had thought the same.

He took off his glasses and rubbed them with the cloth from his holder. He smiled at Kate. 'You're not going to want to touch it. I can't, so Andrew or Martine would be my first choice.' He smiled at Malika who sat upright in front of him, her hands resting along her thighs. 'I'm sure we can do something, young lady, but we will need to do some scans.'

'I have scans,' she said.

'You didn't mention that last night,' said Kate, turning to her.

'I had them done in Lahore. I have a disc at the school.' She looked from one to the other. 'The doctor there said it was not possible to fix.'

'We have very good tools here,' said Kate.

Stephen's eyes narrowed. 'Did he say why?'

'He said it was very dangerous.' She shook her head.

'We need to see those scans,' said Stephen.

'It is no problem,' said Malika.

'Good.' He looked at Kate, and then grimaced as he leaned forward to stand. He laughed. 'Must be time for my afternoon nap.'

They walked to the front door. Mel was nowhere in sight.

'I'll say goodbye for her,' said Stephen.

Kate gave Malika the keys to the car and she headed down the steps. When she was out of sight, Kate turned to Stephen. 'What do you really think?'

'Is she covered for surgery? It won't be cheap.'

'I'm sure she has insurance.'

'I think you might find this will be counted as pre-existing.'

'I'll have to think about it then.'

He lifted an eyebrow. 'You're going to have to watch this philanthropic attitude of yours, Kate.'

'I think I'm stuck with it.'

He smiled. 'That's why I took you on as a partner. Don't forget to show me the films.'

'I thought I should take them to the radiology meeting, too.'

'Good idea. Does Andrew go to those, like Graeme did? I know he went to the first couple, but it doesn't always stick.'

'Usually, yes.'

'That's good. Are you and he getting on okay?'

'Fine. Sure. Why?'

'Always good to get on with the boss.' He looked down the steps. 'What do you make of Malika?'

'This problem with her nose has rocked the boat. The school warned me, but I only actually saw it last night. It's a mess, isn't it?'

'She looks traumatised to me.'

'I'm not good with that stuff.'

He looked at her for a long moment. 'Can I suggest something, Kate?' He waited until she nodded. 'Can I suggest you approach her as you would one of your patients?'

'Really?' She frowned.

There was a thump above them and Kate looked up. 'How's Mel handling things?'

'You know the answer to that. She's lucky to get through to six at the moment. Starts on the juice about ten in the morning.'

'It's understandable.'

He nodded. 'The other problem is she thinks they did her bottom lip wrong with her last treatment. Too much filler on the left side.'

'It looked all right to me.'

'She stares at it all day. Thin edge of the wedge, she says.

It's got her paranoid now about her breasts, though they look perfect to me. I made her an appointment to see Jason later this week. He's the only one she trusts.' They swapped a half-smile and he shrugged. 'Stops her worrying about me at least.' He stepped forward. 'Take care of yourself, Kate. And don't take any shit from Jonathan.'

She looked at him with concern. 'I hope the next cycle isn't so bad.'

'Four to go.' He walked across to the edge of the porch and folded his arms. The city buildings gleamed in the afternoon light, the gum trees were far below them as the Yarra slid past, brown as soil. 'You know,' he said, 'the world's a different place when I look out from here these days.'

Kate stopped beneath a tree in the school car park while Malika fetched the disc. She reappeared after a few minutes and passed it through the car window.

'I have a copy,' she said. She hesitated a moment. 'Perhaps one week I can stay with you on the Sunday night also.'

'If you like, but don't you have friends here to catch up with?'

'Perhaps not everyone here is a friend.'

Kate narrowed her eyes. 'Is everything all right? Anything you want to tell me? It doesn't have to go any further.'

'Yes. Everything is all right.'

Kate got out of the car. She placed a hand on Malika's shoulder; her bones were palpable beneath her kameez. 'This has been a big weekend for you,' she said. 'I know that. No one can bring your friends back, but I hope we can help you with your face.' She paused. 'We will look at the pictures on the disc, but there might be limits to what we can do. What is most important to you?'

Malika looked at her with a resolute gaze. 'I wish to smile at myself in the mirror again.'

Kate nodded slowly. 'We want the same thing then,' she said.

News about a Jesuit priest and his scholastic broke as she was driving home that night after doing her rounds at Cabrini. Now they had found the bodies as well: decomposed and needing to be tested, but there was no doubt in her mind. It could only be Father Louis and Daniel. The newsreader spoke of the atrocity as if it were a weather report. It was his job, Kate told herself. It still seemed wrong. She wondered how the families were coping, now their fears were confirmed. Her mind flitted to Malika and Father Mike, back to the plight of the two Jesuits, and then again to Malika, and her silence. She had simply shaken her head when Kate asked what had happened to her face. It was blunt trauma of some sort, that was obvious. Examining her, she would have suggested a fist. Everyone, it seemed, had secrets that stalked them across the years, secrets casting long shadows across their lives.

She slowed up the ramp as she exited the freeway, flicking on the indicator when the traffic lights loomed bright against the dark sky.

The publicity about the attack on the Jesuits would run for a few days, maybe a week. The foreign minister would have her say, the Church would call for solidarity and there would be Prayers of the Faithful for the two martyrs. For the rest, there might be a vague sense of life's normality disrupted, but nothing that a few shakes of the head and glass of wine – or a sporting event, perhaps – couldn't fix. It was a pity the cricket had ended.

The newsreader had mentioned the Taliban, but what did that mean? If it hadn't been them, it would have been someone else. Did it really matter if the sack dropped on someone's head contained flour or rice? But in the eyes of the media and their public, the baddies had got them and it was now up to the goodies to fight back. That was how it was done, wasn't it? Goodies and baddies: two sides of the same coin. What mattered to her was that Father Mike was still over there and she had no idea whether the Church was planning to leave him there or bring him back.

She gripped the wheel as she navigated the dark, single-lane road from the freeway towards Kew. Perhaps the weekend had taken more from her than she'd realised. She was drained, her mind in free-fall. But regardless of the events and distress that had entered her life, somehow she still had to get through another week, trivial though its problems seemed by comparison: Jonathan, for instance. They'd been in the same year in medicine, even the same tute group at one stage. Now he was trying to turn their careers into a competition. She thought about it for a minute, ending with a wry smile. Goodies and baddies.

She yawned as she turned the car into her street. It knew its own way to her mother's by now.

4

The end of the week rushed up on her and late Friday afternoon found Kate again hunting for parking spaces on a crammed Royal Parade. She lucked into one opposite Naughton's Pub and, with a glance at an ominous sky, grabbed her umbrella before hurrying up Tin Alley. The Centre Quad was a different place from the one she remembered. The old cafeteria had become a blur of cafés with colourful signs and even more colourful outside seating. As she passed, she glanced at the groups lounging as only students could beneath the summer-green trees.

She tracked right, finding paths and cut-throughs to the maths school on instinct. Stray spots of rain smacked her shoulders and hair as she turned onto Monash Street. She checked her watch. Two minutes to spare. She relaxed and found a bench.

She waited outside until five-fifteen, by which time her phone screen shone in the fading light and the air smelled of rain. As the first serious drops fell, she pulled her handbag onto her shoulder and marched up the steps of the entrance alcove. She tugged firmly on the doors inside. To her surprise, one of them opened – a security breach someone should know about. Inside was gloom. She found a light switch and poked around the ground floor. All was silent. Empty. The weekend had begun. Malika had mentioned the professor's office was on the first floor, so she headed up the stairs and walked towards a translucent glass door at the end of the corridor: the sole source of light. She knocked gently.

The door was opened by a man her grandfather might have resembled, had she known one. Squat, with shrewd eyes, his thick grey hair was matched by a large moustache. An earring in his left ear caught the light as his face lit up with a buoyant smile, and his arms extended in welcome.

'Ah!' He turned. 'Well, young Malika, judging by your highly accurate description, your ride is here. It would seem we have delved for too long.' He opened the door fully. 'Please, come in, Dr … ?'

'It's Kate,' she said. She extended her hand.

Taking it, he bowed his head. 'Professor James Jenkins. At your service, Kate.'

His room was deceptively spacious. A large whiteboard on her right was filled with a mix of half-familiar symbols and hieroglyphics, while the long window in front was partitioned into three by sculpted stone. It looked down onto Monash Street. On her left, shelving crammed with books and papers ran to the other end of the room. Malika sat at a square table there, her face behind its usual veil. Their eyes met and Kate smiled.

'I was about to pour myself a drink.' Professor Jenkins marched down the room to a small fridge perched beside the bookshelf. A Woolworths basket on its top was filled with bottles. 'You will have one, of course,' he called over his shoulder.

'Not right now –' she began, and stopped. He had turned midstride, shocked, as if there could only be one answer to his proposal. She smiled. 'Well, why not? Thank you.'

He rubbed his hands. 'Excellent! It's a tradition around here. Anyone still here after five on Friday must share in some convivial enjoyment. At this hour, of course, it has to be sherry.' He poured two glasses and tasted one, smacking his lips. 'One would normally have left by now, but Malika is in the middle of something and Mrs Jenkins thought we could have a walk before our yoga class.' He handed Kate a glass. 'I'm too fat to be walking and too stiff to be doing yoga. And what she doesn't know won't hurt her. Santé!' He tossed his head back, swallowed, and smacked his lips again. 'Perfect. Malika, would you like some more water?'

'No thank you, Professor.'

He cleared a chair at the table for Kate and she sat down as he poured another glass for himself.

'How did the lesson go today?' Kate asked.

'Well, I think,' said Malika. She stood. 'I will be back in a minute.'

'Just use the gents if the lights are still not working,' he called after her. 'Something wrong with the wiring, I fear.' There was a clap of thunder as she closed the door and the overhead lights dimmed for a moment. He looked out the window. 'We may have a damp journey home. Mrs Jenkins will bring the umbrellas, I'm sure. Anyway. Lesson? What lesson do you mean?'

'Yours with Malika.' She frowned. It was plain enough.

He laughed. 'Oh, it's no lesson, my dear. Believe me. She doesn't come here to learn. She is working on something quite novel and well beyond most of us – certainly beyond me. She comes here to use our computers, plot models and consult with my younger colleagues. You can hear a pin drop when she is talking. All the grads and post-docs are transfixed. We simply discuss things afterwards. I might help her link her equations with other theorems, perhaps suggest colleagues who can help, but really it's we who are learning.'

Kate's jaw opened. 'Malika?'

'Oh, yes. There's no guarantee it will eventually come together, but –' he looked at her. 'Do you have any idea what she is trying to do?'

She shook her head. 'She's very quiet.'

'She is, isn't she?' He thought a moment. 'Let me put it this way. You must know the story of chaos theory and fractal equations, and so forth.'

'I've heard of chaos theory but,' she frowned again as she sipped her sherry, 'fractal?'

He looked at the carpet and shook his head. 'Dear oh dear, what do they teach in school these days? The principle is quite simple, my dear. For the uninitiated, it's effectively about resolving non-linear equations. These are things we can't directly measure or that have so many operative factors they are unable to be predicted according to standard Newtonian theory.' He waved a hand at the grey window. 'Like a flight of birds, for instance. Malika says it was a flight of swallows that actually gave her the idea. You see, solving fractal equations is fairly standard these days, with computer modelling and so forth; but we can't get close enough to the things that really matter, what will change at the edges, the extremes. Malika's contention is that it is the things on the edge themselves that hold the key, the outliers that actually make the change. She is starting her equations from the reverse perspective. It has nothing to do with the birds at the front, or the mass behind them for that matter. It's dependent on the fringe.'

He had lost her when he said 'Newtonian'. Medicine was a snap compared to this. She sipped her sherry and frowned. 'Can you give me an example?'

He shifted in his seat, warming to the task. 'Well, think of the weather. She's not interested in the cyclone in Cairns, she's looking at the edges: the anticyclone in Melbourne, the trade winds along the equator, the stable barometer in Alice Springs. We hadn't thought of it. She is *starting* with the extremes, the outliers, the things we can't predict: the birds on the edge of the flight of swallows.' He sniffed and drained his glass again, before placing it on the table. 'It may even apply to human behaviour.'

Kate put down her own glass. The lights overhead had become bright and the rain outside heavy enough to hear. 'And could her theory have practical implications?' She tried to keep her voice calm. In reality she was on the edge of an abyss, perched there, almost toppling. Malika was a girl she was meant to look after on weekends, while she settled in at school.

He gazed at her for a moment. 'Let me put it another way.' His voice was suddenly deeper, his stare intent. 'If we can simplify – harness if you like – the effects of these outliers through a system of equations, precisely and completely, then we can begin to work out how to change things in the direction we wish. How to make it rain, for instance. And where. We could avoid droughts and floods. Who knows what else? But for Malika, that's just the start. To be honest, I haven't seen a talent like hers. What this girl is doing, this mere girl from some godforsaken place on the planet, is formulating novel equations that could turn our world around.' He shook his head again, his eyes alive. 'The consequences …'

Her head spun, and it wasn't the sherry. No one had indicated this about Malika. Not even Father Mike. Did he know? Had Father Louis really understood her potential? Had anyone regarded her as more than 'gifted' before she arrived? If what this professor in front of her said was true …

'And if it doesn't work?' she asked. 'If it's not possible, or perhaps just wrong. Falls short maybe?'

He nodded. 'Very true. There is no guarantee. We shall know soon, I think. She is nearly there. Then, she must publish her equations and her modelling, expose them to the world for it to judge.' He paused, and his eyes found her. 'She's not far from that already but,' he turned his head to ensure they were still alone, 'that in itself will be a battle.'

Kate frowned.

'She fears exposure.' He put up his hands. 'Not just failure. I think she has the capacity to cope with that. She would learn from it and rebuild her constructions. No,' he said, 'there's more to it than that, though what I don't know.'

The door opened as Malika returned. Kate turned and Professor Jenkins leaned around her.

'We were beginning to worry about you, my dear. Are you all right?'

'Yes. Thank you.' She joined them at the table.

'The new food again?' Kate asked.

Malika's eyes creased. 'Yes, Dr Kate.'

'So, this person I was telling you about,' said the professor, 'no one can be sure. But,' he looked at Kate steadily, 'my God. If.' He smiled at Malika. 'Enough for one day, I think, yes?'

'Yes. I think so.' She walked over to the whiteboard and picked up her pad and pens. She put them in her bag. 'Next week, professor?'

'Indeed, my dear.' He stood. 'Two delightful young ladies in one afternoon. I must make sure my wife doesn't hear of this.' He beamed.

Kate shook his hand at the door. 'Thank you for your time – and for the sherry, of course.'

'Please come again,' he said, bowing his head. 'Sherry is far better shared. Malika, I shall see you next week at one. We have much ground to cover. I have ensured the computers will be free for you.'

'Thank you, Professor,' she said.

'What do you think of him?' Kate asked, as they walked to the car.

'He is very nice to me.'

Kate looked at her. 'He thinks his mind is slipping.'

Malika was quiet for a moment. 'At home in the wet season,' she replied eventually, 'the water buffalo only shows his head above the waterline.'

'Meaning?'

'He is the smartest man I have known.'

Kate made sure the umbrella covered Malika's precious head as they hurried through the rain, and that she had as much time as she needed on the weekend for her doodling.

She dropped Malika at school on Sunday afternoon. She had shaken her head when Kate suggested staying until Monday.

'It will be all right,' she said.

'I'm glad,' said Kate, and meant it. She didn't know how she would have managed a Monday morning trip to the school with her early start in the rooms. 'I'll let you know how the meeting on Tuesday goes by Friday,' she said. 'Have a good week.' As Malika turned, she closed the window and headed down the hill towards the school gates. The routine had already become familiar. Waiting at a set of traffic lights before the climb up Richmond Hill, she drew a blue biro line on the inside of her wrist to remind her to take the disc to the meeting on Tuesday. Malika hadn't mentioned her scans since handing over this disc which, Kate knew by now, simply meant she was waiting to hear.

The three groups of surgeons – plastics, ENT and facio-maxillary – filed along the narrow corridor into the radiology meeting room: a procession of the surgical elite. For an hour, they would review scans, decide on what surgery was needed, and reflect on outcomes of recent ops. In the past, Kate had been able to bury herself down the back with the trainees and residents while the big guns, the chiefs, sat up front, their heads a row of bowling balls silhouetted against the front screen. Supposedly, the sole purpose was to reach a consensus – to agree on the best management. But there was another agenda that hovered in the room like tension before a race. Respect. It was rarely offered, but you grabbed it when it was. But fail even slightly to measure up, and though nothing much was stated, in the near dark eyebrows would lift and a quiet but sly comment would follow and invariably stick. Such was the temptation, she had been guilty of indulging sometimes herself. It was just too enticing. She doubted even Andrew could change this dynamic – assuming of course that he wanted to.

It was a cauldron she had never thought she would be immersed in. But here she was, at the front, squeezed between Andrew on one side and Gary Simpson, the hard-eyed head of facio-maxillary on the other. She felt Jonathan's eyes bore into her from the back of the room as they waited for the first images to appear on the screen. She had survived the meeting the previous month, maybe had even impressed a few at the time, but she knew he was lying in wait until the time was right and he could press home his advantage. Patience and timing – the darlings of the ambitious.

One of the registrars began discussing the first case. He presented the relevant issues with style and a touch of arrogance as if his own career depended on it which, to some extent, it did. Canny heads lowered in thought as the prospects of surgery were weighed. Risk versus benefit. That was always the question; only whose risk and which benefit was not so easy to determine. None of them wanted a reputation for complications. They were there to help of course, but at the bottom of that inclination lay decades, even generations, of self-preservation.

It was nearing the end of the hour when they finally came to Malika. Kate had primed Andrew about it, so she could shrink a little into her chair and mostly stay out of it. He had been supportive. 'Keen to see the films,' he said, taking the disc from her. 'Let's see what we can do for her.'

The radiologist took a minute or two to sort out the disc; Kate hadn't been able to open it herself. But eventually, its secrets were revealed and Kate went through the story – the little she knew – as the CT slices appeared on the screen, from frontal bone to mandible.

'Nasty breaks,' said the radiologist, from the back corner.

She nodded. It was awful.

'It's a shocker. Would need ENT as well as one of us. What do you reckon, Prof?' Elliott Thomas was a junior in the plastics unit, trying to establish himself as the go-to cosmetic surgeon for a total makeover. The word was he was booked out months in advance. Subservience was his trademark, his academic credibility relying upon his public hospital appointment.

Kate turned to Andrew, who was studying the screen. The images reflected off his glasses. She could almost hear him thinking, but was it about what to do or how to let her down gently?

'I can see why they didn't want to touch it in Lahore,' he said eventually. 'That bone wedge of the cribriform is pushing right on the meninges. I can't separate them on these views. At least it's stable as it is.'

'We could get another CT,' the radiologist offered. 'Higher resolution might help.'

Andrew nodded in agreement. 'And we could get an MR scan for the meninges.'

'Absolutely.'

'Well, I wouldn't touch her.' Jonathan spoke out from the back. 'Little to gain – her nasal passage is clear on one side at least – and there's a whole lot to lose.'

Silence stretched on for heartbeats while Kate's cheeks burned. How she could tell Malika that they wouldn't even try? 'Do you know what it's like to walk around unable to show your face to the world?' she asked, 'knowing that your punishment will last forever?'

'Sure I do; I was born ugly,' Jonathan quipped. 'Unlike some.' A burst of laughter filled the room. 'But better that than meningitis.' He paused. 'Far too high-risk,' he said. 'That must be obvious even to you, Dr Davenport. Though you could probably do the zygoma easily enough.'

Kate looked at the darkness on the floor in front of her. Andrew tapped her chair.

'What do you think?' he asked.

She stared at the screen. 'I think this girl needs our help.' There was another silence in the darkened room, and she knew she had failed. The risk of complications was just too high. She could feel Jonathan behind her, smirking. 'Isn't there anything positive I can tell her?'

'Tell her it could be a whole lot worse,' said Jonathan. 'Who's next?'

She clenched her fists and then her jaw. And then her fists again. Maybe she could do something herself, she and Andrew. Or Stephen? She crushed the thought as soon as it appeared.

What made it so bad was that at the bottom of it all, she knew they were right. Risk and benefit. Big benefit, sure, but huge risk. Puncture the meningeal lining with one of the bony fragments and meningitis was a certainty. She hardly listened to the remaining few cases.

She followed Andrew to his office after the meeting. 'Is there nothing we can do?' she asked, when he shut the door. 'She thinks I'll make her whole again.'

He walked over and stood at his desk, his head down, his pale fingers leafing through his mail, mostly letters, it seemed. Did people still actually write letters?

He looked up. 'You could do an MRI. We can hope for a surprise. But,' he added, 'she is high risk.'

'I know.' It was something, at least. 'I'll speak to her.'

He put his letters down and faced her. 'Have you got your talk sorted for next week?'

'I – not yet. This weekend.' He must think her stupid. Worse. Uninterested.

'Right.'

'I will get it done.'

'Send Ellen a copy when you're happy with it. Tuesday night, remember.'

And dinner afterwards with everyone, she thought. Why did she agree to it? They stood awkwardly in silence for a moment, until her neck began to prickle.

'I'd better go,' she said, and he nodded. Something about him made her hesitate. 'How's your son?' she asked.

'Julian?' He smiled. 'A bit better, I think. We talk as I drive to work in the mornings. The three of us. Alice chimes in when she's ready.'

'It must be difficult for them at the moment. You over here.'

'Yes.' His face looked bleak. 'I misjudged that, I think.'

'Are their flights booked?'

'We decided end of term. Six weeks or so. I'm ringing schools now. It's very different to back home.'

'I've heard there are agencies who can do that for you.'

'I feel helpless enough as it is,' he said, the strain of living away from his family showing for the first time.

She found herself closer to his desk. 'For what it's worth, I hope I'd be the same. Doing it myself,' she added.

He looked through her. 'It's worth something.'

'Will you go and bring them across?'

'I hadn't thought to.' He paused. 'Do you think I should?'

She put up her hands. 'I'm hardly an expert. But they might think it's cool.'

'Yes.' He nodded, slowly. 'They might, mightn't they?'

They smiled and she turned to leave. 'See you in theatre. It looks like a long and complex list.'

It was many hours later that she tracked back along familiar corridors. Her shoulders and neck ached. Such days had one advantage. The struggles of others always buffered her own, made them bearable, even distant. The trouble was that no buffer worked forever.

She picked up Malika again that Friday. She was in high spirits. The afternoon had gone well. But the light in her eyes spoke of something else too – she was waiting for news of the conference. Hope shone in her furtive, occasional glances, as they wandered the streets and talked of their weeks. As evening settled, they ate outside a restaurant near Lygon Street, while pink-tinged clouds stretched high above them.

Kate found herself speaking about work – hers and Malika's, about Professor Jenkins, about magpies and the Australian bush – anything really, while the news from the conference stuck in her throat. Did she not have the courage to tell her, or did she just not have the heart?

'That is very interesting,' said Malika at one point, as Kate told her about Andrew and his children overseas. But her eyes were dim as she moved her veil aside to draw in a fork wrapped in noodles. She knew, Kate thought then. She already knew. And she stared through the window onto a late summer's evening that had swiftly turned bleak.

She took Malika to her apartment after they finished dinner. Stale warmth enveloped them as they stepped across the doorway. As Kate drew open a curtain, remnants of the sunset glowed fire-red. They moved into the kitchen and Kate wrinkled her nose. Something was off. She checked the cupboards and then opened the fridge door – lifting her wrist to her nose as she did. This was it. Leaving the door ajar, she threw whatever dips and sauces that had been left into the rubbish. Any that weren't past their use-by date soon would be. She had meant to visit weeks earlier. Malika watched her from the other side of the bench as she worked, her head moving from fridge to bin and back again as if attached to a thread.

'You have very much food,' she said at last.

'Too much,' agreed Kate. This was the last thing she wanted to be doing in front of Malika.

'Why do you have two houses?' Malika asked, as the car sped back along the Eastern Freeway.

As Kate explained about her mother, she felt Malika's dark eyes study her, although they passed three of the soaring light columns along the median strip before she spoke. 'The one we are travelling to now is much more your home.'

'Well, it's bigger, yes. Neither feels like a home to me.'

'I know that feeling.' Malika looked out the window. 'You were lucky to have a mother for so long.'

'I suppose.' She steadied the wheel as a maxi taxi and a semitrailer rumbled past, one on either side.

'My mother was beautiful and kind,' continued Malika. 'All the people in my first village would smile at her when we walked to the bazaar. Ayesha, my other mother, is kind but she is not beautiful.'

Kate glanced across. 'I think kindness matters more.'

'I think it is easier to be kind when you are beautiful.'

'I'd like you to remind some of my patients about that.'

She flicked her indicator as they took the ramp to the Chandler Highway. The red light at the top drew them to a stop.

'The conference doctors did not have good news, I think,' said Malika.

Kate wished she had found the courage earlier. 'It's not decided,' she said. 'But,' she swallowed, 'it's not straightforward, Malika. I've made a copy of the films. I'll show you when we get home. Another scan could help.'

'It is all right if you cannot help. The doctors in the Great City were very certain.' Her voice was wound tight as a coil.

'I haven't given up yet.'

Their eyes met.

'Then I will keep hoping, Dr Kate.'

Kate's heart ached as they headed up the hill. When she glanced across again, Malika was staring straight ahead.

5

She still had twenty minutes left to speak and already the yawns had begun. They wanted to be told what to do instead of understand what the latest evidence said or, more importantly, didn't say. To his credit, Jonathan remained silent. Finally she came to the summary slide. It was as simple as she was able to produce in relation to stem cell therapies: one column highlighting the pros; the other, the cons. As soon as it appeared, tablets flicked open and pens clicked. In the corner of her eye, Andrew was watching. Was he cross or half-smiling? The applause when she finished surprised her. She exhaled; it was over.

At the restaurant afterwards, however, it was a different story. She had been held up at the hospital with a call from her registrar, and most of the surgical division – thirty or so she guessed – were already seated around two long tables, drinks poured, the noise level rising. Being a Tuesday, apart from one or two other couples, they had the place to themselves. Andrew had promised to save her a seat, and he chanced a smile at her as she sat down. It didn't go unnoticed. Halfway down their table, Jonathan nudged the ENT guy next to him and angled his head. A quick return glance with the merest flick of an eyebrow followed. She looked away.

Turning her back to Andrew, she tried to strike up a conversation with the woman on her right, Zoe Chiu. An attractive plastic surgeon dressed in red silk, she was rumoured to have been considering leaving before Andrew arrived. She had smiled as Kate sat down, but then rejoined a heated discussion with two colleagues. Kate sat silently until a waitress leaned across with their meals.

'They seemed to enjoy your talk.' Andrew turned to her as the waitress stepped back.

They. Not he. Kate's stomach clenched. Five minutes earlier she had been ravenous – lunchtime somehow missed among urgent emails and the preparation of slides. Now the eye fillet in front of her was a lump of indigestible animal flesh. 'It went okay,' she said cheerfully. 'I was a bit rushed at the end – ran out of time.'

He put down his water glass and picked up his knife and fork, his smile at her a quick back pedal. 'I thought some parts were excellent.' He glanced at her meal. 'I also think you made the better choice.'

She forced a grin as she looked at his small portion of sea bass. 'Perhaps size-wise anyway.' She reached for the mustard in front of her. 'And the other parts?'

He pushed on his glasses. 'Well, the papers you quoted were the same ones I would have used. Mostly.'

'Mostly?'

'I had hoped you would go into some of the new developments on stem cell grafting across open wounds I was reading the other day. I'll send you some papers. It's an area my lab could be interested in pursuing.'

'Sure. Send them along.' She nodded. 'And the rest?'

He put his cutlery back down on the white tablecloth, fork and knife neatly spaced on either side of his plate. 'To be honest, Kate,' he said, 'I think you could do better. Don't get me wrong, it was sound, reasonable, in parts excellent.' He nodded. 'But being you. I think. Yes. At times, it almost seemed …' He paused.

Her hand trembled as she reached for her water glass – she wished it were wine. She forced her head up. 'It seemed?'

He shook his head. 'Nothing.' He smiled. 'It was a fine start. We can talk about it later. Let's enjoy our meal.'

She took a gulp of water and stared for a moment at a small stain on the tablecloth in front of her plate. Jonathan's scorn she could have handled; she was almost used to it. But Andrew only had to say he didn't love it and she was mortified. Stupid.

He cut into his fish. 'You know, in London we used to circulate our talks to a trusted few beforehand. It helped – sometimes a lot.' He paused. 'I'd be happy to collaborate next time if you'd like.'

She smiled and chewed on a morsel of her steak. She was damned if she would send it to him. But he was right; she could at least have sent it to Stephen. She sighed to herself and let her eyes rove the tables for a distraction. That they were all out together on a weeknight hadn't happened before, not in her memory. Everyone seemed to be talking or laughing, a few of them waving their hands or even shouting to be heard above the noise. Jonathan was telling jokes and pouring wines for a small group of trainees on the other side of the table. They hung on his every word – as trainees desperate for a job next year always did. Two female surgeons nearby were head down, deep in conversation. Amanda, a few years Kate's senior, had recently separated and the other surgeon beside her, Jill, was long-divorced. Their meals had hardly been touched. Besidc her, Andrew had turned to the facio-maxillary guy on his right, and Zoe was now arguing the worth – or not – of *Game of Thrones* with another young surgeon, Stewart Li, across the table. Typically, he was the sole turn-up from the cardiothoracic unit. Kate twisted in her seat and checked behind her. No one from orthopaedics, either. Also predictable. She ate as much of the steak as she could and pushed it aside, waiting for an opportunity to leave. That had always been her way: turn up to be seen and leave as early as possible.

'What did you say to your young girl?' Andrew picked a chip out of the bowl in the middle of the table. He glanced at her as he took a bite.

'Malika? It was difficult, though I think she'd already guessed. Did I tell you she's supposed to be a maths genius?'

He raised his eyebrows as he reached for his glass. 'Genius is a big word.'

'That's according to the maths professor at Melbourne Uni, at least.'

'Makes risking an operation on her even less attractive.'

'It does.' She nodded and sighed. He was right, and the dilemma had nagged at her since her meeting with Professor Jenkins: any operation would be a risk; but how was a teenager supposed to fit in at school – or anywhere – with a nose smashed against her face like a cauliflower?

He finished eating and gave his plate to a passing waitress with a cheery 'many thanks'. Then he folded his arms and leaned forward on the table, gazing into space.

Kate watched him from the corner of her eye while she picked at her salad. If asked, she might have said he was struggling to make a decision.

Finally, he pushed on his glasses and eased back, his eyes focussed on her. 'Would you be interested in coming to a small meeting with me? Only a handful of us from around the country are invited, it seems.' He smiled. 'Though I think I could get you a place.'

'A meeting?' She frowned.

'With a visiting researcher from Harvard. We go back a long way.' He crossed his legs under the table. 'This guy's printing a 3D matrix of facial bones and growing up stem cells to cover the matrix.'

She had read about that sort of thing. A bit anyway. It was fascinating, though she wondered about its feasibility.

The two women who'd had their heads down earlier stood up, meals barely touched. They wiggled their fingers at Andrew as they left. Which bar, she wondered. But it gave her the out she needed, once she'd listened to what he had to say.

'I thought combining the tissue and vascular stem cells was a major problem. And I'm sure that's only one of plenty.'

'Absolutely.' He nodded. 'You're right, it's a few years away still. But imagine if we could make it work.' He took off his glasses, his eyes bright. 'Those horrible injuries and congenital facial deformities we spend so much time dealing with could be gone. Effectively, we would just cut and paste.'

She found herself turning towards him. 'Meaning all our reconstructive work would become redundant?'

'Redirected. The work would shift to fitting the matrix perfectly, ensuring the bones are fixed, attaching vessels – getting the connections right, basically.'

She narrowed her eyes. 'I'm not sure what this has to do with me. I'm hardly a researcher.' She waved a hand at the room. 'And there are surgeons here with decades more experience.'

'They're not head of unit.'

'Acting.'

He nodded. 'Acting. And –', he paused as their waitress stopped in front of them again with the dessert tray. He took a plate of cheese and Kate asked for a green tea. It seemed she would be staying a little longer. He continued. 'I was talking to David Casey from St Vincent's the other day. Seems you did some research with him a little while ago.'

'I did.' She tried to ignore the prickles that had sprung up around her neck. 'But it was hardly a little while.'

'He thought you would go on, said you were as gifted as anyone he had seen. Microsurgery and capillary regeneration.'

'Being gifted doesn't pay the bills.' That was true, but it wasn't why she left. In fact, she had loved it; loved the freedom of walking into an empty lab late at night, working solo through the dark hours and watching the sun rise as the city slumbered. Then, as cars jammed Lygon Street in the peak hour rush, it was time for an indulgent coffee and croissant at Tiamo's before tumbling into bed and an untroubled sleep. Until everything changed.

She raised her cup to her lips. 'What else did he say?'

'He said he almost cried when you left.'

'Was that all?' She studied his face, roamed it, every centimetre of it. Did David tell and Andrew was being polite? Or had he actually kept his word? Did men talk? Of course they did.

'Pretty much.' His stare was as intense as hers. She couldn't read it.

Her tea came. She ignored it. 'It was nice of him to remember me.'

'Was it so long ago?'

She shrugged.

'You know,' he said, 'for someone with your talent it's never too late. Research time can be negotiated. There are assistants, techs –'

'I would be a long way behind.'

'You could catch up.' He cut a piece of cheese. 'It was just a thought.'

She swallowed. 'When is the meeting?'

'First Friday next month. After work.'

She pursed her lips. 'It's just a meeting? All work?'

'Well, there's usually a dinner after these things. Maybe drinks beforehand.' He cocked his head. 'Is that a problem?'

'It might have to be just the meeting. I have Malika on Friday nights.' It was a ruse, a reason to escape. Malika didn't need anyone.

She reached beneath her seat for her bag and stood. 'I'd best be going. Early start.'

He pushed back his chair and stood to let her out. 'Will you think about the meeting?'

She nodded. 'Okay.' She should have thanked him for asking her. Any normal person would have done. But it was the sort of thing she only ever thought about afterwards – as she did then while unlocking her car.

He stayed on her mind as she drove home. At times he could be like a boy, yet he controlled the pack of unruly surgeons as if born to it: delving, pushing their boundaries, forcing them to think and change – never raising his voice or being the boss the way Graeme had been. It was always based on logic, science, even strategy on occasion; whatever it took to get them to see what mattered. That was the difference. He wanted them to see. Professors of surgery weren't like that.

She caught another glimpse, of the man beneath, on an early ward round the next week – the only time she now had to see her public patients. Andrew was already on the ward when she arrived, sitting beside a red-eyed registrar in a long, narrow room that had once been a treatment room but now functioned as the junior medical officers' area. The trainee was biting his lower lip and nodding. Andrew smiled at her as she dumped her coat over a chair. She smiled back. She knew the feeling. The registrar had been up all night. Exhausted. Exams in six weeks. She met her own registrar and resident at the door as they rushed up from the ward to meet her, taking them to the computers in the central area to check on blood results. She glanced up the corridor as the resident tapped away on the keyboard. Andrew was leading the registrar to the lifts, a hand on his shoulder. He waited until the lift doors closed and then strode back towards them.

'Seen my residents?' he mouthed to her as he got close, raising his upturned palms. Kate pointed to a room nearby, where his team was filling out blood and X-ray requests while they waited. He called out to them.

'Dr Hassan will be back this afternoon. Let's get these patients sorted, shall we?'

One of the residents fetched the patient files, the other raced to the portable computer, nearly tripping on the cord as she unplugged it from the charger. She wheeled it over and they headed down the corridor. Kate watched his retreating figure. His eyes were just as red as the registrar's, which made sense. They had both been up performing the same operations all night.

Her private lists began to expand, while the increase in her public hospital work pushed her limits. In Stephen's absence, the GPs had begun to see her as their default option. She was able to hand a few cases – cosmetics mainly – to Martine, who had slotted her extra sessions almost exclusively on days when Kate wasn't there. It seemed to suit them both. But to deal with the increased load, she had to arrive at the city rooms by seven. Her meals were eaten at odd hours, if at all, and most of her belts now needed an extra notch. Some nights, on the way home, she would force herself to stop at the local gym and stretch tired muscles in the pool, the echoes of the water lonely comfort as she swam up and down.

She dined late with Lucy one night at a café in South Yarra. She had started to show. Her cheeks were flushed and her hair had grown an inch. Part of the reason to meet was that Andrew had mentioned the research workshop again and despite herself, she had accepted. But to appease her conscience with Andrew for her subterfuge, arranging for Malika to spend an evening at Lucy's had seemed a good idea.

'Sounds great, regardless,' said Lucy, who immediately saw through such subtleties. She giggled. 'I told Hamish about her. He wants to play her at chess.'

'Are you sure it's okay?'

'Is Malika okay with it?'

'Jumped at it.'

Lucy waved a hand. 'So, fine. Don't worry so much.' She paused. 'You know, you look a bit tired.'

Kate stifled a yawn. 'Don't start.'

'I've got some great tonics.'

'It's nothing a bit of sleep and regular meals wouldn't fix. I dropped in at Stephen's on the weekend. He's the one looking tired. And so, for the first time in her life I think, is Mel. I feel for her at the moment.'

Lucy sipped on her tea. 'When's he coming back?'

'He says May.' She had circled the date on the fridge calendar at Kew. The day after had also been circled, and underlined. The start of her holiday.

It had been a long morning. Three bad diagnoses for her first three patients. She was praying for good news and a simple fix with the next. Her heart sank when a kidney transplant patient got up from his chair and followed her into the consulting room. He walked into the room with a quiet shuffle. She knew it well. No reason to rush when illness is your life companion.

They spoke for a few minutes and she helped him onto the couch. She looked him over carefully. The dense spattering of skin tumours across his shoulders, neck and face were treatable, but they would just recur without him stopping his anti-rejection tablets. That probably meant him losing his kidney. She waited for him to get dressed again before talking to him.

He looked at her fish-faced a moment, but wasn't budging. 'I'm not going back to dialysis, doc,' he said, his hands clasped as he leaned forward in his chair.

'They'll come back otherwise.'

He shook his head. 'Six years of being tied to that machine is enough for anyone.'

'Are you sure?'

He leaned back with his hands on his head. 'I'm sixty-four next birthday. Had a good life for most of it. Seen the kids grow. Wife and I've paid off the house. I told her when I got this kidney I wasn't being attached to a machine again.' He thought a minute. 'It's a jail sentence, doc, and there's no end to it.'

'The tumours will get bigger. You know that, don't you? And they will spread. She scanned his medication list. 'Dr Lee has already made the changes to your treatment I would have suggested.'

'The new tablet? Yeah, he said it might help slow things down. You can't chop 'em out?'

'Some I can.' She shook her head. 'Not all. And I couldn't graft that much skin anyway.' She sighed. It was a lost cause. 'You want me to do what I can, don't you?'

He nodded.

'All right. I'll get at the cancers and pre-cancers that look most troublesome. That bunch on your neck there,' she pointed, 'will need a skin flap.' She leaned forward. 'It's not a small operation. It will take two or three hours, and there's the potential for a significant amount of blood loss. Anaesthetics will want to make sure you're up to it,' she paused. 'And I'll have to speak to your nephrologist. That often means tests and delays.'

'How long in hospital?'

'A week to ten days. Depends on what I find.' She scribbled out a theatre list appointment and passed it to him. He looked at it a long moment.

'They said you wouldn't give up on me,' he said, finally.

'Who said?'

'The docs at the hospital. They said to make sure I saw you.'

She looked at him firmly. 'There are no promises on this, Mr Leonard.'

He breathed deeply as he pulled out a handkerchief. 'Give me a break, doc. I'm not after promises.'

'I get it.' She nodded and they smiled, before he blew his nose.

She was reading through the next referral when there was a knock at the door and Sam put her head inside.

'Have you got a minute?'

Kate glanced at the wall clock. Jonathan had tapped his wristwatch at her last week when she showed up in clinic an hour late. 'I have to finish these referrals, Sam. Maybe I can ring you from the car.'

She stepped into the room. 'I've scheduled a break in your list. Your next patient's not due for ten minutes.'

Kate's neck tensed. 'You scheduled a break without telling me?'

'I need to talk to you and there's never any time.' She sat down.

Kate stared at her desk. Sam might have been right about the lack of time, but she would never have tried it with Stephen. 'What is it?'

'I need six weeks off. I'm due eight.'

'When?'

'From next week.' She pulled out her phone. 'Until mid-March. Nearly.'

'Are you all right? Angus? Family?'

She nodded. 'Yeah. Fine.'

Her fist clenched. 'Sam, how am I going to find someone else within that time?' Her mind went to Malika, who had slotted seamlessly into the Saturday mornings. But that was impossible.

'Marilyn's going to cover for me.'

'Marilyn from Tim Mathieson's rooms?' She frowned. 'But isn't she on maternity leave?'

Sam nodded her blonde head and wriggled back in the chair. 'She's due back in two weeks, but she said she'll put her return back a couple of months.'

'Does Tim know? Did you ask him about it?'

'Carolyn is doing fine filling in.' She shrugged. 'He'll just extend her contract for a couple of months. Angus says it happens all the time. Anyway, there's no other way.'

'Sam, I can't do something like this without Tim's approval.' She went to the window and forced herself to count five red cars. 'Do you mind me asking what it's for?'

'I'm getting a makeover.'

She shut her eyes. This was a bad dream.

'Everyone on the floor's done something. Marilyn did hers a couple of years ago. She said if I'm going to do it, to get the lot done. Mr Thomas said he'd throw in my waistline free because I'm in the industry.'

Kate turned. 'Elliott Thomas?'

She nodded seriously. 'The best.' Sam looked at her, frowning. 'I thought you'd be happy for me.'

'Did you?' Kate's lips stretched a moment. 'Maybe it will just take some adjusting. Let me talk to Tim first. I can't agree to anything before then.'

She stood up. 'I'd better get back. Mr Thomas said to say hi, by the way.'

Kate stayed at the window after the door closed, until her pulse settled and the headache behind her eyes eased. She could do nothing about the feeling that she was a ship lost on a wild sea, moved by eddies and currents she had no control over, no say at all in what they would do.

6

Kate arrived at the Park Hyatt and stood, starstruck, in the foyer. It was vast, the opulence disorienting: pillars of white, gleaming chandeliers and floors polished mirror-bright. Large artworks littered the walls. Guests sauntered by. Staff in serious suits or navy skirts and heels higher than hers hurried past.

To one side, mostly hidden by pillars, a piano was being played. The melody floated across the space. She leaned to the side, trying to get a view of the pianist. She glimpsed a black dinner suit and a mane of white hair. She drifted towards him, leaning against a pillar and watching as his hands, white as his hair, shimmered over the keys. He was absorbed, his body swaying in rhythm. She didn't recognise the music; it was something classical though.

Shortly he stopped and she clapped politely. He turned and bowed his head.

'You are too kind.' She couldn't place his accent. European maybe – or Scandinavian?

'It was beautiful.'

'Beautiful music should always be appreciated.' He gazed at her a moment. 'Like all beautiful things. I will play you a song. What will it be?'

She straightened. 'A song?' She glanced around. They were alone. 'Music's not really my thing.'

'That is a pity. Everyone should have a song.' He let his thumb fall on a note in the middle of the keyboard. 'Without music, what is there but noise?'

His other hand joined it and he pressed the keys. Softly. Chords first, a melody slowly building from the middle notes. 'I will play this for you.'

She checked her watch and her heart jumped. 'I'm sorry. I really have to go.'

'No matter,' he said, his eyes closed now and his hands moving more quickly. 'Take it with you as you go. Perhaps it can be your song.'

'It's beautiful. Who's it by?' She took a step back.

'Mendelssohn, but that's not the point,' he said.

The music followed her down the marble staircase to a large tiled area where men in suits stood talking in small groups, while company reps flitted between them. She recognised many from her past life – research powerbrokers. Some nodded to her and smiled. Kate, awkward in heels, moved across to the registration table and picked up an agenda. She bit her lip. The company *had* divided the talk into halves, one before and one after dinner. It was the second talk she was interested in. With discussion and questions afterwards, it would be late by the time they finished.

She noticed Andrew across the room. He had changed his slightly daggy – if truth be told – work jacket for a clean-cut, navy suit. He smiled to see her.

He picked up his name tag and scanned the agenda on the placard, tutting as he turned to her. 'I'm sorry, Kate,' he said, 'I didn't know about this. They must have made a late change.' He frowned. 'If it's a deal-breaker, I can try and change it.'

She shook her head. 'You can't do that. Anyway, I guess I have to eat some time. I'll just ring my friend.'

Her heels clicked on the tiles as she stepped behind the staircase and took out her phone. She had worn Lucy's heels – green, to match the dress – on her advice: 'You can be professional and still have class,' she insisted, holding them in front of her, and Kate acquiesced. Why did she do that? Lucy answered the call quickly.

'Lucy. Hi. Is it all right if it goes a bit late tonight?'

Lucy laughed. 'Enjoy! I can hear the piano from here. We're having fun. Hamish is teaching Malika how to play chess. How's Andrew?'

'Fine. Why?' She moved a couple of metres farther away.

'Does he like the heels?'

'Lucy!' she hissed down the phone. 'I'll be there by eleven at the latest.'

'You call that a night out? Go and have a drink or something together.'

'It's just a talk, Luce. I told you, and Andrew's my boss. Eleven. Promise.'

She hung up and peered between the vertical bars of the descending staircase. She guessed that most of the surgeons were here by now. She had noticed the professor from Harvard, Vihan Singh, when she arrived – tall, a few years older than her, greying at the temples, with impeccable teeth and golden cufflinks. He was chatting with Andrew. She edged farther behind the staircase, checking her earrings and nudging the hairdo that Lucy had talked her into along with the heels. Malika had stared at her the whole time while Lucy fussed, which had done nothing to help matters. She tugged on her dress straps as she rejoined the group.

Andrew held out an arm as she approached. 'Kate, I'd like you to meet Vihan, an old friend –' he turned back to him and smiled, 'sparring partner perhaps is most accurate. We first met in Edinburgh.'

'Both of us presenting papers at our first conference, as I recall,' Vihan agreed. He shook Kate's hand. 'A pleasure. My colleague should bring his talented researchers into the public arena more often. Are you as competitive as he is?'

Her cheeks warmed. 'I think I'm more about collaboration than competition,' she replied.

'Excellent thought, although I fear it's too late for some of us to change our spots,' Vihan replied, winking at Andrew.

They laughed.

'I hope you'll be telling us more about your 3D techniques,' Andrew continued. 'We've headed in a slightly different direction.'

A bell rang and one of the company reps began politely herding them all towards the conference room, where twenty or so writing pads and pens were aligned on top of a long table. A projection screen glowed at one end of the room. Kate took her seat beside Andrew and wondered quite what she was doing seated with this who's who list of the nation's research boffins. She nestled into her chair, took a breath and a sip of water, and prepared herself.

The piano was alone without its player and the lights above it had long since been extinguished when they climbed back up the staircase. Kate and Andrew said their farewells to the others – most of them from interstate and staying overnight – and carried on down the hotel drive, bright beneath the moonlight, towards their cars.

The night's discussions echoed in her mind as they walked. Fleeting, no doubt, but for the first time in years she was enthused: the thought of reigniting her academic career was exciting. Hardly realistic, she told herself, but just then she didn't want to hear that. Her thoughts were alive with research possibilities and the ways to get there.

'Do you think Vihan was serious about collaborating with us?' she asked.

'That was why he came,' said Andrew. 'He's stuck. You saw that. Remember? You raised an eyebrow at me.'

He was right; she had seen it. Vihan had taken them on an impressive tour through his work on combining cartilage matrix and 3D modelling, but he pulled up short at the end, deflecting them instead towards potential outcomes and possibilities. She had wondered whether he had overlooked the final pieces or didn't want to show them, but the thought of interrupting him had been too much. What if she was wrong?

'Why didn't you say something?' she asked.

'He was waiting for me to. After that, it would have been routine.'

'I don't get it.'

'If I had challenged him,' Andrew continued, 'or even asked him a question, he would have asked me what I would do.'

'And?'

'Well, as you might recall, the research world is finely balanced between exposure and protection. If I tell him I don't know and six months later publish a paper showing that I actually do know, we would never be able to collaborate. And I would have an enemy, which would count against me, especially as he would almost certainly be asked to review my papers and grant applications. On the other hand, I'm not going to just hand over my best ideas to him. He would take them back to the US, throw in a million dollars' worth of lab work, and get it all out before me.'

'I see.' She had forgotten about all this, the positioning and the politics. She actually used to love it. A battle of wits. It seemed Andrew was cut from the same cloth.

They took a path through to Spring Street and Andrew stopped beneath a streetlight on the far side. 'Some of your ideas in the discussion afterwards really made him think. I saw it in his eyes. To be honest, Kate, they made us all think.'

'I'm a decade or so behind everyone, remember?' She hoped he couldn't see her face burning

'Ideas are ideas. And not everyone's got them.'

Flinders Lane was crowded with people and cars. It was as if the city was suddenly open for business. She had no idea it would be like this at night. Was it just Friday night? Pedestrians – couples and loud groups mostly – passed them from behind, or crossed the street ahead between the traffic. Headlights from idling cars picked them out as they single-filed like centipedes through the fumes. She checked the time. Already past ten.

They stopped beneath the red sign of the Wilson's car park, and she tried to remember exactly where she had left her car. Downstairs, somewhere at the back seemed right. She had been focussed at the time on not twisting her ankle in Lucy's heels. She rubbed her bare arms in the cool air.

'You'll be all right from here?' he asked.

'Thanks.' She smiled. 'Yours is …?'

He nodded down the hill. 'Somewhere down there. Not far. Would you like a drink before we leave?'

Her heart made a small and unwelcome jump in response.

'I'm not sure where will be open.'

He looked around. 'I don't think all these people are heading home, do you?'

She rummaged in her bag for her keys. 'Well, it's past ten and I told my friend I would be back before eleven.'

'Of course.' He paused. 'Has Stephen spoken to you yet?'

She looked up. 'Has something happened?'

'He rang me this morning.' He pushed on his glasses. 'I thought now might be a good time to discuss it.'

They found a place buried half-underground on their way through to Bourke Street. The dimly lit interior was suited for the news he carried, her disbelief gradually shifting into resignation as he spoke. She had heard similar things before, of course. But this was personal and that made it different. Personal meant people you knew and even loved died. It made your own world unreliable: each life had a final day.

Her fingers trembled as she picked up her spoon and stirred her latte. It churned through the pale froth as if it were something tangible, of substance. When in fact, as everyone knew, the tiny, magic bubbles lasted only moments before popping and vanishing, leaving nothing but residue. She placed the spoon on the saucer. Andrew was looking at her across the blue-chequered tablecloth.

'And you're sure that was all he said?'

He nodded. 'Pretty much. The myeloma's in his kidneys, and it's time for him to retire.' He picked up his coffee. 'He said he'd call you.'

'I see.'

He leaned forward. 'You've gone pale.'

She attempted a smile. She needed to play it cool, to find the right balance between nonchalance and understandable concern. And she had to be okay, for in some small way Stephen might need her right now. He had looked after her professionally, gifted her a career. Being available for him was the least she could do. She ensured the glimmer of hurt that he hadn't yet called her remained hidden in the shadows. Her coffee was lukewarm when she sipped it. She had asked for it hot. A part of her wanted to complain, and if their waiter had not been the genial old man he was, with small, round gold spectacles with matching gold-buttoned white jacket – well, she might have. His bald head shone beneath the downlights as he headed their way again, this time with a dessert in each hand for a nearby couple, beaming as if he had baked the treats himself. He would have been ten years older than Stephen at least. It was ten years that Stephen wouldn't get. The capriciousness of life. Two men. Different paths. No rhyme. Just chance: who would fall first?

A random cheer erupted from a large group in the corner, and she turned to see a young waitress placing extra bottles of wine on their table. Her hair had slipped, and long strands fell forwards across her face as she leaned over the group. She placed her hair behind her ears, before slouching back to the kitchen. Kate felt the ache in her feet.

She turned back to Andrew. 'Well, if his kidneys are involved, obviously he would retire. Is he on dialysis?'

Andrew shrugged. 'He didn't elaborate and I didn't ask.'

Why hadn't she kept in touch more? She forced herself to sip her coffee again. 'I suppose there's no chance of a transplant.'

He took off his glasses and placed them on the table, massaging his eyes slowly. 'He didn't mention it. And he would have.'

'We spoke about five years. More, maybe.' She continued, turning it over in her mind. 'Even Myron thought that.'

He reached his hand forward and placed it on hers. 'I'm sorry, Kate.'

She looked at his hand as it lay there. It was warm. Caring. Instinctively, she went to pull back, but her hand stayed where it was. Maybe her hand did need a little care just then.

'Thank you for telling me. I'll go and see him this weekend.'

Her disquiet finally won out, and she moved her hand to her napkin, dabbing her mouth.

'What can you do?' he asked.

'I don't know, but I wasn't there for either of my parents and –' she frowned suddenly. 'Why didn't he tell me things were so bad?'

'Perhaps he just needs a little time. Perhaps they both do.'

She nodded. The waiter and waitress were standing together now in front of the till. Fifty years between them. The girl looked at her watch and rolled her eyes before flashing the briefest of reluctant smiles at the man. She didn't want to be there. Were they related? He could easily have been her grandfather. One day, would she look at her own grandchild with the same tolerant eyes?

Andrew was right. Mel would be distraught, and champagne might not be enough. 'Did he seem okay?' she asked.

'In himself? I think so. To me, at least.' He paused. 'I can't imagine you not being there for your parents, Kate. You spend your life being there for others.' He frowned. 'Do you mean you weren't there when they died?'

'Dad died in a plane crash when I had just turned eight.' She wasn't ready to say more. She drained her coffee. 'You said that day in your office that you missed your wife's death.'

He was quiet for a moment. 'I left Clara one afternoon to fetch the children from school. She slipped away while we were travelling back to the hospital. It happened quicker than anyone expected.'

'How did your children cope?'

'Not well, for a while.'

'And now?'

He smiled and shook his head. 'Alice likes to remind us all that sometimes girls grow up before they've finished being girls.'

'Let me guess. Mobile welded to her ear; hair never right; her skirts are too long. And her room is always locked.'

'She misses her mum.'

'I'll bet she misses her dad, too.'

She looked down at the chequered tablecloth. Perfect blue and white squares. They fell over the edge of the table like an Escher chessboard or perhaps a Dali painting. She pushed her index finger along a line of blue, stopping when it reached the sugar bowl in the middle of the table. Lines served such a useful purpose: direction and limits at the same time.

'Tell me it's none of my business if you like, but why did you leave London?'

He took a deep breath before looking at her. 'When she was near the end we discussed the future. She asked me to make a new start, said there was time to have a life with someone else.' He cleared his throat. 'She wanted what we had to stay that way. Our own bubble.' He picked up his glasses. 'And for me to form a new one.'

'A man I met before the meeting tonight told me that I should have my own song.'

'Perhaps they're the same thing.'

'I've got one advantage.'

'What's that?'

'Mendelssohn.' She pushed the sugar bowl forward a whole centimetre, before glancing across at him and smiling. It was a careful smile, warm and defensive both. It came from a warm place deep inside her that she had almost forgotten, that had always spelled trouble, a place she had learned to avoid.

She picked up some yellow tulips from an overnight florist's on the way back to Lucy's. She used the key Lucy had lent her to get in. Malika had fallen asleep on the couch, her veil slightly askew. Kate had forewarned Lucy about the veil. 'Poor thing,' she had replied on the phone. 'How horrible for her.'

'Sorry I'm late,' Kate whispered, handing Lucy the flowers.

Lucy smiled and frowned at the yellow bunch. 'Thank you, but what did you do that for? I'll get a vase. And don't be stupid,' she added, crouching in front of the dresser. 'I never go to bed before midnight. Unlike …' She cocked her head and Kate could hear snores tumbling down the staircase. Lucy rolled her eyes. 'His Friday night red wine and KFC combo. I'm working on a remedy. A whole sea of toxins to neutralise.'

Malika opened her eyes and, startled, jumped to her feet. She adjusted her veil and stood there, blinking. 'Will you be ready for your work in the morning, Dr Kate?' she asked. 'Tomorrow is looking very busy.'

'You can sleep in,' Kate replied. 'No problem.'

'No, it will be fine,' she said.

Lucy wanted a rundown of the night. 'You owe me that much,' she demanded, relenting only when Kate explained their early start. 'You'll be working Sundays as well, soon,' she said. 'Okay, so that gives me an idea. You and Malika come over on Sunday. For lunch. We've got nothing on. You can fill me in and Malika can beat Hamish at chess again.'

Kate felt the effects of a long day starting to mount. Sunday sounded ideal. 'Baby behaving himself?' she asked as they walked to the door.

Lucy drew her hair away from her face and held her swollen belly. 'So far, so good.'

Kate called in at Stephen's the following afternoon. She had left Malika at home to work. Mel was out shopping, and Stephen led her to a sitting room overlooking the back garden that was almost cosy in comparison to the vast space at the front. He poured her a mineral water and they chatted on a couch bedecked with cushions in front of an empty fireplace. He was in good spirits – being on the other side of a treatment cycle did wonders, it seemed. It was good to see he had rallied, even for a short while. But he downplayed everything when she asked questions, waving his hands and shaking his head.

'Just time to get away from the main game,' he said. 'I'm still here.' He asked if she was going to apply for his job.

'I don't think so.'

'These things don't come up often.' He stretched his long legs towards the fireplace and looked at her. 'It makes a difference.'

'Meaning?'

'You set the course of the unit, make it count. You leave your mark.' He smiled. 'It's your legacy in a world of transience.'

She glanced away. 'You know how busy I am, covering your patients and mine. I was counting the days until you came back.'

'I guess we both have to make some decisions then.'

She nodded and smiled at him. The ice clinked in her glass as she picked it up. 'They want an academic. I haven't done that sort of work for years.' She took a sip. 'My income would take a nosedive for a start – and for little gain as far as I can tell.'

'I know it's different for me, but is income so important to you? Anyway, you could negotiate.'

'Negotiate? Oh, sure. It's me, remember,' she said. 'I'm hardly the surgeon from the RPA, lauded on national TV and bringing twenty lab staff and three post-docs with me.'

She crossed to a spacious window overlooking the back. Trimmed hedges bordering an elongated lawn stretched away from her towards a gazebo. Beyond it, a swimming pool sparkled in the afternoon sun. It was a place for lazy summer afternoons and barbecues. She folded her arms and placed her feet together, absorbing the scene.

'They'll want at least an associate professor, someone with research gravitas. I can barely persuade our surgeons to listen to me. Jonathan's the one they follow.'

'If that were true, I would have heard complaints when you started.' He paused. 'There were none. Why did you get out of research? You are a natural – and that's rare.'

Her voice was strained as she spoke. 'I'm happy enough where I am, Stephen.' She breathed. 'You know, settled.'

'Sure.' His eyes narrowed. 'But?'

She turned back to the window, her gaze drawn to the pool. What was the problem? She had asked herself the same question for twenty years. 'Maybe I just couldn't stand to fail again,' she said.

He eased himself up from the couch and stood beside her.

'It's a nice pool,' she said. 'Clear.'

'You're hardly a failure, Kate.'

'I know.' She sighed. 'And I've spent my life trying to prove it.'

She felt his hand on her shoulder. 'Do you think we might all be doing that, Kate?'

part four

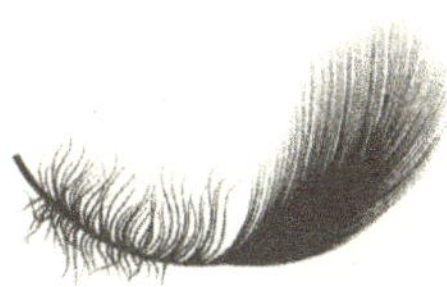

1

Malika rose as the first pink tinge appeared in the sky. She dressed and took the envelope from her desk before making her way down the fluorescent-lit stairway. The air was cool on her forehead as she trod the path between the school buildings. Reaching the main avenue she headed uphill before crossing the playground, the bitumen cold on her bare feet. She stopped before the fig tree.

It was different in the near-dark, no more than a hushed silhouette. Around it, the glass walls of the science building were silent sentries. She made for the far side of the tree and sat on the wooden bench at its base, out of sight. Only the cheeping of a bird somewhere out in the dark canopy disturbed the stillness. She stood and reached for a leaf, plucking it and rubbing her fingers along its smooth belly. How she missed the great tree of her village. Many weeks had passed now since she had been to her home, seen Ayesha and Fatima, made porridge, or even fetched water from the well. Many weeks could feel like a lifetime. She pulled the envelope from her pocket.

Her fingers deftly opened it and unfolded the creamy, blue-lined sheets she had read with a pounding heart the previous night. Fatima's letter had taken a month to arrive. There was not enough light to read the words clearly but they burned in the mind from the night before. Her friend had been married six weeks ago, the ceremony brought forward because Pamard's mother was not well. Malika mouthed the words as she half-read, half-remembered them. *Ayesha sang for our happiness and we prayed that you were well. The party lasted until the men had to leave for work. I cried for you when they told stories of our childhood. I now live with Pamard's family. They are kind, but his mother is very sick. One day we shall have this place. I have found him to be a good man. Dear Malika, she finished, you are always in my heart.*

Her chest ached as she folded the letter and slipped it back into the envelope. She looked straight ahead. Already the morning sky was reflected in the glass panels and she could see the reflection of her own small shape beneath the tree. She would write to Fatima today. And to Ayesha. It might help. Her left hand found the watchband on her wrist and her fingers traced its outline. Father Louis had told her there would be difficult times. 'My mistake,' he said, 'when I arrived was to push them away, to wait and hope that good things would come.' Then he grinned. 'And one day I realised that we need difficult times more than we need good things.' But that night she had been in no mood to listen, fired up at last by the imminence of travel and the thought of being in a new land where she could work on her theories and perhaps one day find relief for a needy world. This was her great wish.

A great wish perhaps, but it was withering like a tree in drought. The past six weeks had laughed at her, at how little she knew – her equations falling down when they most needed to stand, collapsing when she put them to the test. And she had tried with all her might. Professor Jenkins was speaking of publications and putting her work forward as finished, when it was nowhere near ready. There was a central flaw. She could sense it, just as on some days she could almost see the solution. But it stayed just out of reach, like finding the pail at the well did not quite reach the water after a hot day in the fields. She angled back her covered head against the tree and watched a magpie that had landed nearby. It studied her for a moment before searching the grass, head cocked to one side, driving its beak into the short, green shoots. Her challenge had been how to include everything in her equations, for it all counted: the flock of birds, a breath of wind, even the angle of the sun. And, one day, humans. Yes, especially humans, though they were what eluded her most. Their actions could not be predicted. Perhaps only Shiva himself could capture such things. Perhaps she had been a fool to even try.

She began making her way back to the boarding house as sunlight appeared on the grass around her, grimacing as she passed the administration block. She would have little chance to prise the mysteries from Shiva that week. Miss Cullerton had called her to her room twice, for misdemeanours she hadn't known existed, and now her precious Friday with Professor Jenkins was gone. Instead, she faced a 'det'. She did not know what it meant exactly, apart from wasting time inside a hall with other girls who also had better things to do. She looked at the lightening sky as her fingers found the letter in her pocket and wrapped themselves around it.

When she got back to her room, she had time to wash her face and brush her teeth before it was Chloe's time in the bathroom. She nibbled on an apple and sat at her desk, pen in hand, wondering what to write to Fatima. She still had time before lessons began. Perhaps she would start with Ayesha. Fatima could read it to her. A creak came from the bathroom behind her and she twisted round. Nothing. She checked her watch. It was still Chloe's time.

A few minutes later, there was another noise from the bathroom. A louder creak and she turned to see the door fling open and Chloe and two of her friends stumble into the room. They shrieked as they pushed, one against the other, trying to maintain their balance. Their smiles froze when they saw Malika's face. She quickly turned back to the window but it was too late. Her veil lay on the bed where she had thrown it earlier. It could have been a mile away now. They had seen her, her face, her nose. They had seen her as she was, and she drowned for an endless moment in shame.

'Oh my God,' said Chloe. Her hand rose to her mouth.

One of the girls Malika knew was called Megan said nothing. She just stood there, her mouth open. Malika had also met the third girl, but couldn't think of her name. Gabby. That was it.

'Have you been watching me?' Malika demanded.

'Don't be paranoid.' Chloe flicked her hair back as she stood up straight.

'How many times has this happened?'

Chloe eyed the other two girls and shrugged. 'Well, what do you expect, the way your wear that veil the whole time? Like no one's going to wonder what you're hiding.'

'Why do you not ask me, instead of slinking after me like thieves?'

Chloe rolled her eyes as Gabby pretended to hide a smirk. Megan's cheeks had become as red as her hair, which fell like copper coils around her face.

'I'm so sorry,' Megan managed.

Malika's chest was thumping. It was exactly what she had feared from her first day, her twisted face becoming a carnival event, a street show. The entire school would know of it by lunchtime.

'You're basically a freak,' said Gabby.

Malika dropped her eyes.

'She's right, isn't she?' said Chloe. 'What normal person gets 100% in every subject? Or goes for walks by themselves in the middle of the night?'

'And has an alcoholic as their best friend?' Gabby added. She and Chloe glanced at each other.

Malika frowned. Did they mean Ping-Mei?

'Wait. I'm not part of this,' said Megan. She straightened her skirt and turned on Chloe. 'You said you had a surprise. You didn't mention anything about this.' She turned to Malika. 'I'm really sorry, Malika. I mean it. If you hear anything about this from anyone else, I promise you it won't have been through me.' She glared at the other two girls and reached for the door, before marching out.

Megan's words should have helped. But the sight of the tall girl with red hair closing the door only added to her despair. She had never felt more alone.

'What do you want from me?' she asked, quietly.

'Just be like, more fucking normal.' Chloe folded her arms and eased her weight on one leg.

'Not that you can do anything about your face,' said Gabby, matter-of-factly. 'And actually, I think you're right. You're better off hiding that.' Her eyes widened. '*Forever.*'

'Maybe you could get a proper outfit and look like a real Muslim,' said Chloe. 'Then you'd fit in fine.'

Malika's eyes widened. 'You are such disgraceful women,' she said. 'Is there nothing you respect?' She wanted to spit at them. Her fingers searched for her watchband as emptiness invaded her. This was one of the times Father Louis had spoken of. Was she up to it, he had asked the night before she left, his face, for a change, showing the concern he always hid. Was she? Her legs were shaking. She inhaled deeply as she looked at them.

'If being like you is normal,' she said, 'then I do not want any part of it. I do not seek your support or want your acceptance. I want nothing to do with you.'

'Fine with us, pizza-face,' said Chloe. 'But don't say we didn't warn you.'

'You've already got one det,' said Gabby. 'Things can just happen around here, haven't you noticed?'

Malika stared at them. 'Why are you so horrible?' she demanded, her voice rising. 'Do you find meaning only in another's distress? You are like dogs preying on the weak. And like dogs you should be treated.' Her finger shook with rage as she pointed at the door. 'You will leave my room and never come back. You are never welcome in this place. Never!' Her voice shrieked on the last word and it was all she could do not to burst into tears.

'And what if we don't want to?' said Gabby, her hands on her hips.

'You will go now,' said Malika, her chest heaving. 'Right now. Or I will take Megan to the principal with me and we will tell her exactly what has happened here today. I have nothing to lose.'

She watched as they glanced at each other, hesitating. Then they rolled their eyes. She met their glares with steel as they finally left her room.

That Friday at lunchtime, Ping-Mei and Megan kept watch on the teachers patrolling the yard, as Malika slipped out through a rear exit and headed towards the university. She hoped for success, but again her modelling didn't work, her precious equations were still unreliable. Perhaps she was distracted. Or perhaps they never would be successful. Dr Kate was there for her on time and Malika smiled to see her. She placed a hand on Malika's arm. The warmth of her touch was soothing. While they ate dinner Malika asked if she had heard from Father Michael. She'd had an email the previous week, Dr Kate said. And Malika nodded, glad he was all right, but thinking about him made her miss the tender solace of Father Louis. And she longed for the familiar activities and smells of her village. Her home had been very greatly on her mind since the letter. She knew that Ayesha would be missing her. She had asked Fatima to watch over her, but Fatima now had another life. Malika watched the cars speed by outside the restaurant as Dr Kate checked her phone messages.

'You are very quiet tonight, Malika,' said Dr Kate, as she opened the front door for them that night.

'I think like you I am a little tired,' she answered, as she headed to her room.

She closed the door and looked into the mirror on the wall. Her veil covered her face and her kameez the rest of her. This person in the mirror could be anyone. Or no one. She breathed. It was not her. She made the decision there and then that she would no longer wear her veil in this house. If she were to have a home while she was in this country, this would be the place, here with Dr Kate. And she would be herself in it. She unhooked the veil and then released the clasps as she slowly unwound the hijab from her head. Laying it on her bed she fetched her brush from the bathroom. She brushed out her hair and breathed two deep breaths before stepping into the lounge room. Dr Kate was reading, her feet extended along one of the couches. Her long arms were white, and as graceful as a dancer. She was like the princess in the magazine, but more beautiful. Her hair shone beneath the lights, suffused with the colours of the earth as it fell down one shoulder; her lips were full, her eyes tender, and her nose even and straight – balanced like a perfect equation.

Malika sat on the couch opposite her. She smiled when Dr Kate looked up from her book. Dr Kate smiled back.

'It is the first time I have seen you smile, Malika. You have a beautiful smile.'

Malika looked away and rubbed her hands on her thighs. 'Thank you for your words, Dr Kate. But my face is ugly, like a sow's. No one can like it.' She paused. 'Do you mind if I do not wear my veil in this place?'

'I'm glad that you've removed it.'

'When shall I do the extra scans that you mentioned?'

Dr Kate's eyes became uncertain. 'Perhaps I can book them in during the holidays.'

'Or I can do them this week.'

Dr Kate came over and sat beside her. Malika could feel her gaze on her as she looked at her hands. 'Malika, I must tell you that we all feel this might not work out as you hope.' Her voice was gentle, like Father Louis' had been when he arrived to take her to Lahore, all that time ago. 'We can do the scan again, but it is not likely to be different and the other surgeons I have spoken to say it would not make any difference. They say the surgery might kill you. They will not operate in those conditions.'

'It is too dangerous,' said Malika, nodding. The doctors in Lahore had been right.

'The other surgeons think it is very dangerous, yes. Even I can see it would be a great risk.' She placed a hand on Malika's. 'I wish it were different.'

'Wishing will not change this,' said Malika. She took Dr Kate's hand and turned away.

'Is there anything I can do?'

Malika's face softened as she remembered. 'When I was very young, my first mother would sit me in the bath and sing to me as she washed me.'

'Well, I'm not going to wash you, but I could run you a bath.'

Malika looked at her. 'And sing?'

'I don't think that would be a good idea, no.'

They smiled.

'But perhaps,' said Dr Kate, 'I can scrub your back when you are ready.'

'Thank you. That would be nice.'

They crossed through the bedroom that was never used and entered a large bathroom with white tiles and many lights. Dr Kate shut the door and closed the shutters as water poured from the taps into a large white tub. She laid a white towel on the floor and opened one of many bottles on the shelf behind the bath, pouring in sweet-smelling crystals as steam rose and swirled around them.

'I'll leave you now,' said Dr Kate. 'Your towel is here on the stool.' She opened a cupboard below a long mirror covered in mist like a morning fog and pulled out another towel. She placed it on top of the first. 'This one is for your hair.'

'Thank you, Dr Kate.'

'Call me when you are ready.'

The door clicked shut as she left.

Malika gasped as she stepped through a miracle of white bubbles into the hot water. Warmth pressed itself into her body as she lay at full length, easing her head back against a folded cloth. She thought of Ayesha. How she would have loved to find hot water coming from a tap. Even in the Great City, hot water did not always come from the tap in winter. She washed herself slowly: her brown legs, her broad flat feet and her skinny stomach. Then she washed and rinsed her hair. She called Dr Kate.

Dr Kate clicked her tongue, pretending to be cross when she opened the door. 'You have not had long enough to soak.'

'I will rest here when you are finished,' Malika replied,

leaning forward and putting her head on her knees. She heard a sponge squeeze and warm water ran down her back. It made the same sound as when her mother washed her many years earlier. She wondered why she remembered such things.

'I can take you to Mass on Sunday,' said Dr Kate.

Malika shook her head as the sponge moved across her back. 'I will not go to Mass this week,' she said.

'I thought you would want that, especially this week. My mother used to say that God was only useful when things were not right.'

'Perhaps your mother was right,' said Malika, 'but if there is a God, it is not right only to ask Him for help.'

'You have said that before,' said Dr Kate, '– if there is a God.'

'Yes.'

'Yet you go to Mass every week.'

'Yes. It is quite different.'

'I see.' Dr Kate sighed as she pushed the sponge up to her neck again. 'Then on Sunday we can go on a picnic instead. If it's warm, we can take it to the beach.'

'The ocean?'

'The ocean is a long way for one day.'

'I would like to see it one day.'

'One day, of course.' Dr Kate's knees cracked as she stood up. 'We'll see. I don't even know if it will be warm enough to go to the beach.'

'I would like to stay here on Sunday night,' said Malika.

'Why don't you rest tomorrow, and catch up on some sleep? I can cover the rooms easily enough in the morning.'

'I will be ready when you say.'

'Let's see how you feel in the morning.' There was a moment's silence. 'And Malika, I'm really very sorry about your nose.'

'Thank you, Dr Kate.'

Cool air swept across Malika's shoulders as the door opened and she sank back deep into the bubbles. When it closed again, she laid her head back against the flannel and closed her eyes. As fatigue extended deep into her limbs, she surrendered to the quiet of the room and the warmth of the bath, and the knowledge that she would never again be whole.

Stella Catalano opened her office door and welcomed Kate inside, shaking her hand warmly and smiling broadly.

'Thank you for fitting me in,' said Kate.

'My pleasure,' said Stella. 'I'm sure your time is just as limited.' She followed Kate in and they sat at a table at the far end of the room. The sun shone through large windows on a morning that carried the first chill of autumn.

They talked for a few minutes before there was a knock at the door.

'That will be Fiona,' said Stella, getting up. 'As I said on the phone, it is better …'

Kate nodded. 'Yes, of course.'

She stood as a petite, blonde-haired woman entered the room. Tidy was the word that came to Kate's mind as she stepped towards them: neatly bobbed hair, red lips that matched her low-heeled shoes, and a close-fitting cardigan carefully buttoned and pulled down around her hips. She shook Kate's hand formally as Stella introduced her, smoothing her skirt as she sat down.

'Now, let's begin,' said Stella, smiling cheerfully and turning to Kate. 'You're concerned about Malika.'

The two teachers listened as she explained.

'I want to stress that she's not mentioned anything,' said Kate, 'but I know her well enough to know she is struggling.'

Stella nodded seriously and turned to her colleague. 'You're her head-of-year, Fiona. We spoke about this the other day. Have you found out anything since?'

'Well,' Fiona glanced at them both, 'it's difficult to know where to start.' She looked at them. 'I know it must be slightly strange for her in a new school, let alone a new country. And I can understand if she feels she is struggling. But that aside, so far she hasn't won many friends here. In fact, some of our girls feel quite the opposite.' She paused. 'I've had several complaints now.'

'About Malika?' Kate's eyes widened. 'Are you sure?'

'I'm told she holds lessons at lunchtime. Corrects papers, drills the girls. It makes them feel inferior. I know she's very smart,' she added, smiling at Kate. 'Perhaps with you she's different.'

Stella folded her arms and nodded again. 'Who has complained?'

She hesitated. 'The girls did approach me in confidence.'

'I see.' Stella looked at Kate.

Kate had the same feeling as when a patient's relative offered a story that didn't match the patient's. She had to find a way to get below the surface, even if it involved pushing a few buttons.

'She can't have made all enemies,' she said. 'One of them

has asked her to Sydney for the holidays.'

'I didn't say she had no friends,' said Fiona. 'A girl like Malika will always attract girls. She has a very strong character.' She hesitated. 'Unfortunately, she lacks discipline, not that it's all her fault. She behaves as she's been taught.' She smiled thinly. 'For instance, she failed to attend a detention last Friday.'

Kate frowned. 'What did she do wrong?'

'Minor disruptions in the boarding house. But repeated,' she added.

Kate's eyes narrowed. 'Meaning?'

Fiona Cullerton shrugged. 'It began with not attending meals without excusing herself. Mrs O'Bryan has spoken to her about that and I believe it's been fixed. But also playing her jangly music after midnight. It keeps the other girls awake.'

'Perhaps she's lonely,' said Kate.

'It's not fair on the others.'

'Did you talk to her, Fiona?' asked Stella quietly.

'Yes, of course.' Her eyes were steady as she answered. 'We have spoken at length. She hasn't denied anything, and has even admitted to drinking alcohol on the premises, which we are currently investigating.' She shrugged again. 'Things like that are only compounded by two girls approaching me independently with complaints of bullying. Putting it together,' she paused, 'I would only say that a detention is hardly the worst punishment. I thought it would bring home the point.'

'Where did she get the alcohol from?' asked Stella.

'She wouldn't say, but we have a lead.'

Stella wrote something down.

'Do you know what her Friday afternoons entail?' asked Kate.

'Yes, we have all been informed of her gifts. But we also have rules.' She glanced at Stella. 'I'm sure the university won't miss her for a couple more Fridays. It might –'

'A couple?' Kate raised her eyebrows. 'What's happened now?'

The attractive young teacher blinked a couple of times. 'Missing a detention is an immediate punishment of repeating the one missed in addition to a second one. All the girls know that.'

'Malika may not know. Friday afternoons are very important to her.'

'That cannot be helped. She must follow the same rules as the others.'

Kate glanced at Stella, who looked back, her face serious.

'The other thing,' Fiona continued, 'is that when she does leave here on Fridays, she has been seen putting on her traditional clothes at the tram stop.'

'Maybe she feels more comfortable in them,' Kate said.

'I'm a little disappointed to hear that,' said Stella. 'She and I had an agreement.' She sighed and rubbed her forehead with her finger. 'It does seem that Malika has had little opportunity to speak for herself.'

'She can come forward at any time,' said Fiona, 'but she will not get special attention from me. In my opinion, that is a large part of her problem. If she were any other girl –'

'But she's not,' said Kate. 'And she does deserve special consideration.'

'She has refused to speak to our counsellors and religious support people,' said Stella.

'Perhaps it's time to try again.'

'I agree.' Stella checked her watch and placed her hands on the table. 'We all have to get on with our day. Fiona, I will ask you to cancel Malika's detentions. Perhaps we will find another time for her to do them, but I will speak to her first. Kate, thank you for coming to us. Fiona and I will talk about the best way forward. I agree that Malika is a special case, but while she is here she cannot simply do what she likes either.' She stood and looked at them both. 'I think it best that nothing is said to any student at this stage.'

'You should have spoken to me, Dr Kate,' Malika said immediately, when they met outside the university that Friday. She was dressed in school uniform for the first time. 'It is my fight, this one.'

'I'm sorry,' said Kate. 'I thought I needed to do something. I'm new at this.' She peered at her anxiously. 'Did I make things worse?'

She shook her head. 'Ms Catalano was cross that I was not wearing my uniform.'

'She said you had a deal.'

'She asked if I understood what she wanted and I said I did. That is not a deal.'

'I understand, but occasionally we do something we have to so we can then do what we want to.'

'Father Louis used to say a similar thing.' She looked down at her uniform, 'I do not mind Ping-Mei's tights.'

'Did you bring your normal clothes?'

Her eyes crinkled and she held up her bag. 'I will be back,' she said, and headed back towards the maths building.

They walked to Lygon Street when she returned.

'Are you okay with things otherwise at school?' Kate asked, as they entered Faraday Street.

'I think they are not big problems.'

'Watch out for Miss Cullerton.'

'I'm on call this weekend,' said Kate, as they sat next to the window at one of their regular eateries. The apron-clad Italian staff always smiled now when they walked in. A thin young man with orange hair showed them to a table.

'I have much work to do on my equations,' said Malika. 'One night this week I lay awake much of the night. And then I had a thought that is very exciting.'

'Can you explain it? Very simply,' she added.

'It *is* very simple,' said Malika, her eyes bright. 'I was making an assumption. I was thinking that we – people – are part of the whole, and so my equations must include our actions. But I have realised that is not quite right. It is true we are part of the whole, but also we are not. The swallow's path alters as it reacts to the bird beside it. The grass pollen must always be at the mercy of the breeze.' Her hands wove an image for Kate in the space between them. 'But we change the world even as we are part of it; we create our own directions.' She beamed behind her veil. 'That is the secret of Shiva. We think we do not dance, but we do. We are always part of it.'

Kate turned over the concepts in her mind. She latched

onto the idea – just – but the rest was Malika's world. A frown escaped her. 'Why Shiva's secret?' she asked.

'The Nataraja,' Malika replied. 'The Lord of the Dance.'

2

Father Mike rang the following week, as Kate was about to go to bed. He was in Lahore. For a change, the line was clear. They had emailed on occasion, but it was some weeks since they had spoken.

'Are you all right?' she asked, her voice anxious. He sounded tired.

'All's well.'

He was keen to hear her news and she relaxed into the closeness that had developed between them. It was the closeness that could sometimes emerge with the freedom of great distance.

'I wanted you to know I will be out of contact for a little while,' he said at last, his voice quieting.

She waited. What was next?

'We have decided to relocate a village near Peshawa.'

Peshawa. She had heard about it in the news. It was near the Afghanistan border, and had been recently bombed. She shivered. Horrible bombings, in the marketplace.

'How long?'

'A month.' Pause. 'Maybe a little more. It is hard to know.'

'I won't ask if you'll be all right.'

'We are told it is safe at the moment; it's a good time to do it.'

She pushed back a rising panic. 'So can we keep in touch? Phone? Emails? Will I still be able to reach you?'

His sigh echoed down the phone. 'The authorities have insisted on silence. Broadcasts are monitored; there are spies within the police. No one knows what might happen if word got out.'

'I see.' Her mind wandered. 'And Malika?'

'I trust your judgement, Kate. Take care of her.'

She wondered if he had any idea about what that might entail. She changed the subject. 'How do you relocate a village?'

'There are five or six villages farther south that will take the families. It should be temporary.' There was another pause. 'But, yes. Not without difficulty.'

'You know I'll worry.' It came out strained; she had meant to convey the opposite.

'I'm sorry, Kate.'

'Must you do this?'

There was a delay. It might have been the line. 'No, I could come home.' He sighed again, so deeply she could feel it. 'It's difficult to explain, Kate. But the disappearance of the priests has affected the Christian villages greatly. Right now, they are afraid. I can't leave them like this.'

She nodded, uselessly, and rubbed her forehead.

When she hung up, she leaned on one elbow and stared out the window into the darkness. He had promised his next call would be a happy one. She closed her eyes and prayed that one day such a call would come. And she wished she had hugged WestConnex him when she'd had the chance.

In the weeks following Father Mike's call, her private work continued to escalate. She thought it was a coincidence until she caught herself accepting new referrals when there was really nowhere to put them – as if making herself so busy she couldn't think meant she wouldn't have to. To some extent it worked, but then the hospital work also increased and the strain began to show. She almost missed a rare sarcoma, consoling a new patient that the slight bulge on her foot was a ganglion, when she should have booked her into theatre. The bad news at least came through on the MRI scan.

Andrew asked, once, if she was managing. She had felt his eyes on her from time to time. He had ample opportunity as they shared a weekly operating session since she had taken over from Stephen. He hadn't mentioned Stephen's permanent position – or her research for that matter – since the night they were out together. Perhaps he could see she was already at full stretch. And there was no rush. Judging by past appointments, it would be months before the university and the health service could organise themselves.

She tried to keep her Friday evenings free. It didn't always work, but most times she would meet Malika and they would explore areas around Carlton or Brunswick before eating. Or they might shop and then cook at home. Malika, laughing, had persuaded her to eat curried goat once, which she liked, and another week a dish of lentils with strange spices, which gave her stomach cramps the whole night. Somehow she and Malika fitted together; she just couldn't explain how.

One Friday they met Lucy and Hamish in Lygon Street for an early meal before a film. Apart from her swollen belly and hair that now reached her shoulders, Lucy looked the same as when they had first met in November.

'You athletic types,' Kate teased her over dinner.

'It's the naturopathy,' Lucy said matter-of-factly, rotating her fork reflectively in her pasta. 'Western medicine's all about sickness. Eastern medicine's all about health.'

Malika nodded. 'Health and sickness are not the same thing. We treat them this way at home.'

'Well, for a simple surgeon,' said Kate, 'if you're not healthy, you're sick.'

'Yes, but just because you're not sick,' Lucy persisted, 'doesn't mean you're healthy.'

Hamish nodded seriously, and Malika's eyes crinkled when Kate looked at her.

'I can see I'm outvoted here,' said Kate, feeling a weight of fatigue descend on her shoulders. She picked up her fork to avoid getting cross. 'The movie starts soon.'

Hamish glanced at Lucy and refilled Kate's glass from the bottle of red on the table. 'That's the spirit,' he said. 'Never beaten, just change the subject.'

She smiled at him gratefully before noticing Malika turn her head suddenly and stare out the large window onto the darkening street. She seemed to breathe deeply, and then she ensured her hijab was in place before turning back. Her meal stayed mostly untouched. Lucy frowned at Kate and she shrugged before noticing a group of Indian men sitting at a table nearby. They were laughing as they looked at Malika, slapping shoulders and joking in a language Kate didn't understand.

'We could have moved,' she said in a low voice to Malika, as they walked across Elgin Street. 'It wouldn't have been a problem.'

'It is nothing,' she said, shaking her head. 'I am very much looking forward to the film.'

Kate squeezed her arm and Malika's fine-boned hand slipped inside her elbow, staying there until they reached the cinema.

She was glad when the school holidays arrived and Malika left with Ping-Mei for a week in Sydney. Kate insisted on dropping them at the airport before her rooms' session on the Saturday morning. Malika had hugged her and stood on the footpath outside the automatic doors, waving furiously as Kate got back in her car as Ping-Mei tried to pull her into the terminal. Kate smiled, waving back. The sleek-haired, tall Asian teen in three-inch heels and a designer coat beside the diminutive Malika in her veil and shalwar kameez were as odd a pair as any.

It was her first weekend in three months without Malika. She noticed it first at her rooms. Marilyn, Sam's replacement, had kindly agreed to fill in at reception for the Saturday morning – reminding her when she arrived that Sam's return was only two weeks away – it was 'Marilyn speak' for the fact she wouldn't be doing it again. Kate scanned the billing summary Marilyn passed her at the end of the session. She had missed an account on one of the double-booked appointments. One patient had been overcharged, another rebated when they should have been billed privately. Kate smiled as Marilyn picked up her bag.

Her mother's house was eerily quiet when she got back. Not that Malika made much noise. It was more the emptiness, the same feeling she had in her apartment in Carlton. She had a sudden idea that night, as she made a stir-fry and flicked on a film on the telly. Malika was still on holidays next week. She could take a couple of days off work. It would require some organisation, but it might work. Malika would love it. They had hardly been anywhere since she arrived. Her mind raced. Possibly, they could get to the ocean. She would need to check with Andrew, make sure they had nothing urgent on their theatre list – or she could ask one of the other surgeons to fill in. She picked up her laptop. She had their roster. Who was available?

Andrew rang her the following Monday morning, asking if he could see her that afternoon. His face was serious as he looked up from his desk. Scattered sheets of paper surrounded him and his computer, all but covering the brown surface.

'Give me two minutes,' he said. 'A meeting with the CFO in half an hour. Budget issues can make anyone lose sleep.' He sighed as he stood up. 'They expect a clinical service based on profit, as if it's all a business.'

She nodded sympathetically as she unwrapped her scarf, dropping it on his table before sitting down. He joined her when Ellen brought in tea and they sipped it quietly.

'Everything okay?' she asked eventually.

'Oh, sure.' He nodded.

'Okay. Good.' She hesitated. 'I was hoping to take a few – a couple, maybe – days off next week.'

'Good idea. You've got a couple of months you need to take.'

'Three and a half, the pay office tell me.'

He raised his eyebrows. 'All the more reason.'

They fell silent. It had begun to occur of late, as if one was waiting for the other to speak. She busied herself by looking about his office. He had put a photo of his children on the wall. He spoke of them as if they still needed help dressing. Well, Julian possibly. At nine, his brown hair and blue eyes were exactly how Andrew might have looked at his age. Alice was a different equation entirely: her hair had been straightened, a heavy fringe and eyeliner an indication of what might follow. Had he seen it?

She glanced back at him. 'You wanted to talk?'

He cleared his throat. 'I did. There are a couple of things. I thought I'd take your advice and bring Julian and Alice across.'

'How long will you be away?'

'I thought about three weeks.' He smiled. 'Catch up with the family, friends and so on.'

She nodded. 'Good idea.'

'I've lined up Angus Fraser to cover my lists.'

'He's a good surgeon.' She folded her arms. 'They'll be glad to see you.'

'I hope so. They will have grown, of course.' He stood and walked to the far window in his office. She watched him deliberate. 'They'll advertise for Stephen's job while I'm away,' he said eventually.

'So soon?' Surely not.

'The university is keen to expand our base, attract more funds through innovation and links with industry.' He turned. 'But really, it's about stability. It's going to take a while to get all this right.'

He was staring at her. Internally she squirmed, but she held his gaze. 'You know I'm not interested,' she said.

'You keep saying that.'

'When do the applications close?'

'I'm discussing that with the chief medical officer now.' He turned back to the window. 'Would it make a difference?'

'Probably not.'

'I'll ask Colin to make it a month, then. I'll be back by then. I'll see –'

'Can you make it six weeks?' Her cheeks were burning, her hands pushing hard on her chair.

'I can try.'

'I probably won't change my mind. You know that, don't you? But I want to be fair on you. And Stephen.'

'And maybe even you?'

'Maybe even me.' She smiled, despite herself. She fiddled with the end of her scarf. 'When do you leave?'

'End of the week.' He smiled. 'So, back to you. Is cover organised?'

'Jonathan's been asking for more operating time. Or Felicity's always keen if he can't.'

'I'm sure he'll be happy to cover for a few days.'

'You know he'll apply. For the job, I mean.' She knew him too well.

'He's a strong candidate.'

'He is.'

'Colin will advertise internationally. But don't forget you're the acting incumbent.'

'Will you be all right over there?' she asked. 'I mean, with everything?'

'In my home town?'

She nodded and glanced down. Stupid.

'Don't work too hard while I'm away,' he said. He smiled at her and she smiled back.

'Have a good trip. I'll look forward to meeting your children.'

Her lonely rounds were lonelier that evening, and the usual silence in the house at night seemed deeper. Part of her would miss him more than she wanted to admit. But there was nothing to be done. There were ten reasons not to start anything with him, one of which she never wanted him to know. She destroyed lives.

'Now, let me get this straight,' said Lucy, two days later. 'You think you fancy this guy, Andrew – who you've mentioned more than once, by the way – but you don't want to start anything, basically because you think he won't like you if you do.'

'And we have to work together.'

Lucy popped a nut into her mouth. 'Katie, the way you work, when would you ever meet someone else?'

They had met in a wine bar near Lucy's place in Malvern. Kate wasn't quite sure why she'd rung, but Lucy had immediately suggested they catch up. 'Besides,' she had added with a yawn, 'Hamish will be out on Friday night with his mates. And you owe me a drink, even if it's only a mineral water.'

It was past seven, and crowded. As soon as a table had become free, Kate had dived on it, winning out over two guys with similar intent. Chivvying her pregnant friend through while she carried their drinks sealed the deal.

'So, go on,' said Lucy, wriggling to get comfortable in her chair, 'what don't I know?'

Kate shrugged. 'That's about it.'

'Do you relate to your patients better than this?'

'That's different.'

'Well,' Lucy leaned forward, her elbows on the table, 'pretend.'

Kate frowned. What else was there? 'Well, I think he likes me – I know he likes me.'

Lucy rolled her eyes.

'He has two children.'

Lucy popped another nut. 'Do you like him?'

'We work well together, yes.' Lucy waited and Kate sighed. 'I guess I do. Yes. I like him.' She nodded and a tingle ran down her back. So it was true, then.

'So, what's the problem?'

'Like I said, he'll find out what I'm like, or his children will hate me, or both, and then I'd have to find another job.'

'Or maybe he could.'

Kate eased to one side as the two guys from earlier squeezed past, heading to another table. She leaned forward and dropped her voice. 'Luce, there's stuff about me that's not nice.'

'In addition to what happened at school?'

Kate nodded and swallowed. 'That was the first one. Then I had an affair with a research professor when I was in my late twenties. He left his wife and family and then I dumped him. I didn't even leave a message. I was cruel. Heartless,' she added bleakly. 'So, an abortion, a suicide, and two broken families from two failed relationships. That's got to be some sort of record.'

Lucy was quiet for a moment. 'Kate, you're not a bad person. We've all done stuff that's dumb, dumb or stupid. Tell me who hasn't. God, there was a time when I was sleeping with two guys for a while. But it's in the past, and what's there is a locked room. You can't get back in; you can't change it. So you have to pull your knickers and bra on over the person you actually are now, take a chance, and show the world. Or else a part of you stays in that locked room forever.' She pointed her finger and her grey eyes looked into Kate's. 'And those guys didn't have to do what they did.'

'You're right, Luce.' Kate nodded slowly. 'You are. I just don't know that I can break free.' She sighed and drained her glass. 'What's the hardest thing you've ever done?'

'The hardest thing?' She paused and glanced behind her before leaning forwards. Her voice was low as she spoke. 'I had to tell Hamish when we started going out that I'd received an unexpected and painful present from one of those two guys.'

'Oh Luce! Wow! How did he take it?'

'Better than I'd dared hope for. As usual, the rock.' She shook her head. 'And it's fine. It's pretty much gone. And there are tablets now.' She shrugged. 'But like I said, tell me who doesn't have regrets.'

Kate studied her glass, her fingers playing with the stem.

'I know a great counsellor,' said Lucy.

'I spent two years with a psychologist once. She was supposed to be the best.'

'And?'

Kate held up her hands. 'You're seeing the improved version.'

They smiled briefly, and Lucy stood up. 'I'll get another drink.' Her long legs and blonde ponytail headed towards the bar, returning a few minutes later with two glasses of pale yellow wine. Kate's mouth opened as Lucy placed the glasses on the table.

Lucy waved her hand. 'Oh, don't! One glass of wine during the pregnancy won't cripple him, and counselling sessions with you are hard work. Anyway, you won't have one unless I do and believe me, if you don't need a drink after what we've just shared, I sure do.'

Kate sipped her wine gratefully. 'What would you do in my situation?'

'I'd do what you would have done in Year 9. I'd go get him. But,' she sipped from her glass, '– Oh, that's good! – you're not going to do that.' She paused. 'Have you lost him?'

'After yesterday's performance, I probably have.' Kate traced a line through the condensation on her glass. 'Anyway, he's going away for three weeks, so that should take the heat off.'

'Okay.' Lucy took another sip of wine and put her glass on the table. 'Why don't we put this in the too-hard basket for now? Think about it while he's away. Hamish and I were wondering if you and Malika wanted to come to Lorne on the long weekend. Knowing your commitments, I thought I should get in early. Just for a few nights.'

Kate screwed her eyes shut. 'That's in about eight weeks,

isn't it? I don't think I'm on ward service. It might work.' She turned. 'So a provisional yes. Thank you. Sounds great.'

'Do you want to ask Malika?'

Kate waved her hand. 'I'll just tell her. She'll jump at it. It'll be her chance to see the ocean.'

3

Kate stopped the engine just as Malika and Ping-Mei appeared with their luggage. Thank God for delayed flights. Her last patient had needed an unexpected tissue debridement, which, since Liz was not there on Saturdays, had set her back an hour. Malika sat in the front seat and closed her eyes.

Kate smiled. 'Hard week?'

'So awesome,' said Ping-Mei from the back, unwinding her ear buds from her phone. 'Xiu, my sister, knows *every* cool place in Sydney.' She laughed. 'We stayed up one night for a band that didn't start until three o'clock. Malika fell asleep in the taxi on the way there.'

'It was too, too late,' Malika murmured.

'Have you had lunch?' Kate asked. She was starving.

'I'm good, thanks,' came the response from the back. Malika shook her head, her eyes still closed.

'Where shall I drop you, Ping-Mei?' Kate glanced in the rear-view mirror again as they sped along the freeway. 'You can stay with us if you'd like.'

'Nah. Xiu had a look at my exam results. She told me I have to pull my finger out to get the grades I need. I'm gonna get back to school and start on some work.' She pushed back her hair as she lodged the buds in her ears. 'I'm no Malika.' Her head started nodding as she watched the yellow fields flashing by.

They dropped Ping-Mei at the school. Malika got out to hug her but was asleep again by the time they reached the road, and went straight to bed when they arrived at the house. The weekend didn't work out as Kate had planned. Malika was listless when she woke late in the afternoon. She didn't want to go out for dinner, ate quickly, and then settled on the couch with her computer. Kate had spent the afternoon washing – adding Malika's as an extra load – and packing for their days away. She had found a B & B owned by a young couple, nestled between a winery and a small farm in the Yarra Valley. Jo and Pete. Jo was a delight; she needed 'just a couple of hours' to get the place ready on Sunday once the weekenders had gone. Kate smiled to herself as she hung out the washing. They could head off after Malika had been to Mass.

But the next morning Malika slept in, for the first time since Kate had known her, walking into the kitchen in her bathrobe at ten. She sat at the bench yawning while Kate emptied the dishwasher.

'I didn't want to wake you,' said Kate, handing her some glasses to put away. 'I could see how tired you were. Are you going to Mass this morning?'

'I think I will go this afternoon,' said Malika, opening a cupboard. 'I have much work to do.'

Kate straightened. 'But that's not until five.'

Malika looked at her.

'I mean, I have a surprise for you,' said Kate. She outlined the plan.

When she'd finished, Malika turned and put the remaining glasses in the cupboard.

'I thought you would be excited,' said Kate to her back. Perhaps she was not well. Or was she still waking up?

Malika closed the cupboard. 'You are too kind to me, Dr Kate,' she said, turning. She paused and looked at the floor. 'Professor Jenkins sent me an email during the week. He sent me three emails. He wanted to know why I was not with him now that school had finished.'

'You're allowed to have a holiday.'

'He said there is an important meeting of mathematicians next month. I must submit my work to them. But there is a deadline this week.'

'Couldn't you work on it while we are away? I'll understand.'

'My work needs much modelling now.' She looked into Kate's eyes. 'I am sorry, Dr Kate. I will be very busy this week, and I will need to use the computers at the university.'

Kate walked into the lounge room and stood at the window with her hands on her hips. It was too late to reorganise work. She would have to go alone. What would she do by herself for three days in the Yarra Valley? She bit her lip.

A floorboard creaked behind her. 'Dr Kate, can I talk to you? This is making me feel very bad. You have gone to much trouble.'

Kate turned. 'Just give me a moment, will you, Malika? I'm trying to work things out.'

'Yes, of course, Dr Kate.' She walked back through the kitchen. Kate heard her bedroom door shut.

She waited a while, half an hour maybe, but Malika didn't come out and there was no sound from her room. Her stomach tight, she swept the path outside, and then took out the bins, ready for the morning collection. When she couldn't stand it any longer, she came inside and summoned the courage to tap on Malika's door. After a brief pause, it opened enough for their eyes to meet. Kate took a deep breath.

'I'm really sorry, Malika. I was just trying to fix up something that I know you would have enjoyed – that we *both* would have enjoyed.' She put her hands together. 'Can we talk?'

Malika opened the door wide. 'I too am sorry.'

They made tea and drank it in the sun on the front porch. Kate took cushions from the lounge and sat with her back against the bricks. Malika, without her veil, kept her back to the street. Her long hair was out and the sun burnished the outer strands, turning their ends to copper. Kate suggested she stay at the house during the week.

'Will you go to this special place while I am working?' Malika asked her. 'You have made this time to go away.'

Kate shrugged evasively. 'I'll find something.'

'You work too hard, Dr Kate.'

'You know, we could reschedule for next weekend.'

'But I already promised Ping-Mei I would go away with her next weekend. Before school starts back.' She watched Kate's face carefully. 'It is after the deadline for my submission.'

Kate folded her arms. 'Well, perhaps on the Friday evening, then.'

'Yes. Perhaps that is also possible.' She nodded, uncertainly.

They finished their tea and Kate went to stand. 'Dr Kate.'

Malika placed a hand on her forearm. 'I think now is a good time to hear this thing.' Kate sat back on her cushion. She smiled nervously before speaking. 'What is it that you do when you are not at work and I am not here?'

Kate waved a hand. 'Well, lots of things. I read journals, shop on the internet, or just potter. I don't know, whatever needs doing, really.'

'Do you do the things we do, when I am not here? Go to dinner, meet friends?'

Kate's eyes narrowed. 'What are you getting at?'

Malika was silent for a moment. When she spoke, her voice was very soft. 'Sometimes, Dr Kate, it is as if you depend on me very much to do these things, that perhaps you would not do these things if I was not here. Perhaps –'

'It's okay, Malika. I get it.' Kate looked at Malika steely-eyed as anger seethed in her chest. She drew her feet up to her bottom and clasped her ankles. 'You know,' she said curtly, 'you're hardly perfect yourself.' It was something her mother might have said, and her face burned.

Malika lowered her eyes. 'Yes, Dr Kate, that is very true.'

'I thought we were sharing a friendship.' The tendons on her arms stood out as she squeezed her ankles. 'At least, I was.'

'You are my very great friend, Dr Kate. But sometimes friends must do other things also.'

Kate's heart pounded. 'In this country, Malika, a friend wouldn't say that sort of thing.'

Malika's dark eyes dwelled on her. 'Ayesha used to say that things such as these only a friend can say.'

Kate left later that afternoon, sick to her stomach as she turned the corner. Malika hadn't come out of her room to say goodbye, so she left a note. *Stay while I'm away,* she wrote. *We can talk when I get back.*

There were times during her days away when the bleakness of life nearly overpowered her. The grey skies matched her spirits. On Monday, as she traipsed determinedly along a dirt road between rows of crucifixion vines, she asked herself if there were anywhere in the world she could go, anything she could do, what would it be? And no answer came. Her life had become a process, an ongoing diversion while the years passed: emptiness filled only by work. It was a prison with all the comforts of home, but a prison nonetheless.

She ordered a late lunch at a winery on the Tuesday, grateful that some diversions at least were easier than others. She stayed longer than she intended; the wines were too good. Sober again by late afternoon, she took a back route to her B&B and found herself driving towards a low-hanging sun along a road she didn't know. And there was a moment. It was as she got to the crest of a long hill. A golden sun lit the valley before her and she just had to stop. She pulled over to the side of the road beside a hill covered in yellow grass. Stepping out of the car, she hopped up onto the rough beside the road and squeezed through rusting wire runners on a nearby fence. She clambered up the hill. At the top, the breeze was cool on her face and the view as wide as her longing. She sat on a grass tussock and watched the birds revelling in the evening light. And as the sun set behind distant hills, for a fleeting minute she was aware of an easing within her. A settling. An awareness that perhaps ties might yet be loosened, and bindings freed. She knew the name of the settling. It was called hope, and she seized it as a boat on wild seas might seize upon a harbour.

Malika was out when Kate arrived home on the Wednesday. She unpacked, made tea and was reading her journals on the couch when the front door opened.

'Good afternoon, Dr Kate,' said Malika, quietly.

'Hello, Malika.' She glanced up.

Malika went to her bedroom and then returned, sitting silently on the opposite couch, her computer beside her.

Kate put her journal down. 'Did you get some work done?'

'Thank you. Yes.' She smiled.

Kate sat back and folded her arms. 'I suppose we should talk.' The coldness between them was almost painful.

They stared at each other before Malika came and sat beside her. Leaning forward, she wrapped her arms around Kate's neck, laying her head on her chest. For a moment, Kate resisted but Malika persisted, her body a salve. And Kate's arms slowly responded, unfolding little by little, until they also reached around Malika's back, embracing her. Closing her eyes, she buried her face in Malika's hair and let her body say what she could not.

'I have asked myself,' said Malika, 'how can you expect to have a life and work as hard as you do? I do not understand these things enough.'

'Others manage,' said Kate. She kissed Malika's head. 'Let's go out for dinner.'

A bell rang as Kate pushed the restaurant door open. It had been a fifteen-minute walk from the house. Most of the window tables were already filled, and sizzling meat and the smell of hot fries suited the mid-week buzz. A waitress led them to a table near the back. They passed a gentle-faced grandmother, surrounded by her family. But her face turned cold as Malika passed and she clicked her tongue. Kate was about to stop but Malika, seeming to sense it, turned.

'It is not a problem,' she said, as their eyes met.

Kate was still seething when the waitress brought menus to their table. Kate looked back along the corridor, glad the family was out of sight behind a wall.

'Did you get enough work done?' she asked Malika, picking up her napkin.

'Yes, I have made much progress.'

'Will you be ready by Friday?'

She hesitated. 'I think the work will be done, yes.'

'So you're all set.'

'Yes,' said Malika. 'All set.'

Kate picked up a menu. 'You're away with Ping-Mei this weekend, aren't you?' She waited for Malika to nod. 'I changed the roster at work so I'll be on call. Ready for school next week?'

'Yes, there were two books I needed to get. It was easy to do this.'

'How are things going at school?' Malika rarely spoke of it, which Kate knew was a way of not bringing her problems home.

'In Pakistan, a new term was always a good time,' she replied. 'I am hoping it will be the same here.' Her eyes crinkled and

Kate smiled too.

'Well, let's order some food,' she said.

It was dark when they left and they had to watch their footing on the path downhill. As they turned onto the side street, Malika glanced at Kate, the whites of her eyes bright beneath the streetlight.

'Dr Kate, I do not know that I am ready for the mathematicians to see my work. I am very nervous about this. If the work is accepted, Professor Jenkins says I will have to talk about it in more public places.' She lowered her head. 'I do not think I am ready to do this. Even at the university it has been difficult sometimes.'

'Perhaps you can say that you will not travel.'

'Perhaps.' She fell quiet. When she spoke again her voice was soft and Kate had to lean closer to her. 'What I truly fear is that my ideas will not be accepted.'

She didn't speak again until they were inside. Kate made a pot of tea and they took it into the lounge room. Malika sipped hers then leaned forward, hugging her arms as her knees pushed against the table.

'In the Great City,' she began, 'soon after I arrived, I submitted a set of equations to one of the professors.' She turned to Kate. 'You must understand that such men are treated with great respect in my country. Everyone calls them "Sir" and it is not advisable to ask questions in class. Rarely does anyone speak. This professor gave back my equations the next week with a smile. I thought I had done well, but he had marked them all as wrong. Then he made me stand in front of the class. I was very young then and that week I was very sad.

'What was wrong with them?' Kate asked.

'I wondered that also, but then I saw he had made an error each time in his factorisation. So I took them to the head of the department.'

'What did he say?'

'She said I had arrived with a very great reputation and that the professor wished to make an example of me. She said I had two choices. I could let it be, and everyone would forget about it in a week. Or I could take it higher. Then the professor would be exposed, but my year with him would be very painful. He might even find a reason to have me expelled. "You need to know that is a possibility," she said.' She turned to Kate. 'When I asked Father Louis what I should do, he said I should act according to my conscience. But,' she smiled as she held up a finger, '– I remember him holding his finger like this – he said that I should be careful how difficult I made my life. Dying for your faith is one thing, he said, but few people have the strength to live by nothing more.'

Kate nodded slowly. 'So what happened?'

'I saw what he meant. He knew my faith was not his. I had lost my family and my face. If I lost my standing at the university also, what did I have left?'

Kate frowned. 'But here it is different, surely. For a start, you have Professor Jenkins.'

'Not everyone in the department is like Professor Jenkins. I see it sometimes in their eyes. Will mathematicians from other places be different? I do not think so. Trees grow the same in one village as in another. If they say my ideas, my calculations are wrong –'

'But you said they're not. When I was at school, maths was all about proof. If it's proven –'

Malika shook her head, as if explaining to a child. 'My theories depend very much on modelling. It is precise, but there is no absolute proof. There is too much variability, too many factors. It is difficult to explain.' She paused. 'Do you have advice for me, Dr Kate?'

Kate stared at the table in front of her and thought. 'Would you would lose everything if your paper was not accepted by the mathematicians?'

'I think if I lose this chance, I cannot rely on another. Not in this country. And Father Louis was right. What do I have if I do not have my work?'

Kate stood up and paced the room, her hands in front of her, fingers stretched. 'I know so little of your world, Malika. When I operate, it's straightforward. I've done the operation scores, possibly hundreds of times before. It's routine. But then sometimes, now and then, something unexpected happens and I have to act. If I don't act straight away, it's bad news.' She stopped pacing and looked at Malika. 'You're not in that situation. You've got time. If it doesn't feel right just now, maybe it's because it's not. But I know one thing for certain. At some point, you have to back yourself. Whether it's today or next year, that's not going to change.'

Malika nodded slowly. 'That is good advice, Dr Kate.' She stood up. 'I will go to bed now and I will think about this.'

Kate settled back on the couch when she left and stared outside at the clear night sky. She wondered how it had been possible to say what she had with such conviction, and at the same time to feel such a fraud.

4

Kate's plan to visit the art gallery disappeared along with thoughts of sleep when Jamie, her junior registrar, called her on Friday evening. His voice was strained, even through the tinny sound of the car speaker.

'A guy's come off his motorbike, Dr Davenport. No leathers. He's got a massive de-gloving injury along his thigh. All the way to the knee. Must have caught something on the road. His femur's on view. Internal injuries too. ICU is with him now. They reckon they'll need half an hour before we can take him to theatre. The trauma surgeons want to go in with us.'

'That's fine, Jamie. Give them free reign. Our job will take a whole lot longer and isn't so desperate. He may lose his leg, but we'll do what we can.' She turned the car around, hoping the traffic on the freeway had mostly cleared.

The trauma guys had already started when she arrived. They were convinced the spleen had ruptured. She munched on some biscuits and drank hot tea before scrubbing. It would be dinner. And possibly breakfast.

It was four am before she pointed her car towards home. There wasn't anything more they could do. She hoped the seven-hour stretch in theatre might at least save the young man's leg. But as she told his father when she'd finished the surgery, sadly it wasn't likely. She crashed into bed, her body craving sleep. She and Jamie had agreed to meet at nine for the round. Four good hours could do wonders.

Her bedroom alarm woke her at eight. She felt for her phone. And then felt again. She sat up. Where was it? Heart racing, she threw her robe around her shoulders and dashed to the car, flinging open the door. It was beneath the handbrake on the centre console. Where she had left it. She exhaled. Four hours was probably okay, but … She flicked it on and swallowed. Ten missed calls. Eight voicemails.

She looked at the numbers and bit her lip. Cabrini, the private hospital, had rung her four times, Jonathan the same number. There were two missed calls from Malika, and a text saying she was fine and would go to school with Ping-Mei on Monday morning. Was that okay? Kate texted her back and took a deep breath before she dialled Jonathan's number.

'I see you finally got my messages,' he said in his steady, faintly mocking voice.

'I just saw them,' said Kate. 'I'm sorry. Really sorry.'

'Perhaps I'm wrong, but I thought you were on call for private and public this weekend.'

'I am. Long case last night. I'm sorry,' she repeated, as if it would help. Had she checked her mobile after theatre? She always did that.

'I'll cope,' he said, 'but personally I find it helps to know where my sheep are lest they become lost. That transplant guy you did a few weeks back?'

'Yes,' said Kate. She rubbed her hand across her forehead.

'He came in late last night. Septic as hell. Can't remember seeing someone looking as sick. They tried to get hold of you, then rang me – in desperation I think. I had to remove his skin graft. It was a bed of pus.'

'I haven't seen him since the surgery.' She punched her thigh with her fist. Why hadn't she? 'Is he all right?'

'Wish I could say yes. He's in ICU, on a bucket of inotropes when I last saw him at somewhere in the small hours this morning. That's the trouble with these renal patients. One thing goes down and everything else follows. They'll be doing the ICU round soon. If I hadn't heard from you I was going in this afternoon.'

'Have you taken him over?'

'Asked his wife what she wanted. For some reason, she wants to stick with you.'

'I'm so sorry, Jonathan.' She swallowed. 'And I can't thank you enough.'

'Don't mention it.' He paused. 'But you're lucky I was around.'

She joined Jim Wiley, the ICU consultant, at the foot of the bed. In front of them, Stan Leonard's weather-beaten skin was brown against the white of the sheets. He was intubated and on the ventilator, with a collection of drips and monitors fanned around his head. His neck was heavily dressed. The nurse had just finished a set of obs as they walked in.

Kate shook her head. She had shaken his hand and told him to arrange a follow-up appointment three days after surgery.

That was three weeks ago.

'His blood pressure's okay,' said the nurse, looking up at the monitor. 'One-twenty's not bad given how septic he is.'

'It's all the norad,' said Jim. 'Noradrenaline,' he clarified, looking over his glasses with a tight smile. 'Still needing jumbo doses. And now he's flipped into atrial fibrillation. If we can slow his heart rate he should improve.'

'Do we have a bug yet for the sepsis?'

He shook his head. 'But whatever it is, two decades of immunosuppression isn't going to help.' He inhaled. 'His kidney function isn't doing what we want either.' He reached over and held the urinary catheter tube in his hand. 'Nothing since he arrived last night. With luck, it will pick up once we're on top of the sepsis.'

'He doesn't want to go back to dialysis.'

'Yes,' he said, pumping the antiseptic container and rubbing the white foam into his hands. 'Mrs Leonard made that very clear to us and to his transplant physician this morning.' Kate followed suit with the antiseptic and they walked into the main corridor. 'The difficulty,' Jim continued, 'will be if he only needs a few days' or weeks' worth of the wash box until his transplant kicks back in. Which we won't know until it recovers, of course.'

There was no way out. They had to wait.

'I should see Mrs Leonard,' said Kate.

'She's waiting in the interview room.' He nodded towards a nearby exit. 'Down the corridor.' He laid a hand on her arm. 'She's had a rough night, Kate.'

Her hands clutched at her elbows as she walked down

the corridor, her heart rate as fast as Stan Leonard's. At that point, she would have mounted a cross if it would have made a difference.

Angela Leonard's trim figure sat opposite her on the chair in the small, claustrophobic room. Two couches and a square table in the corner comprised the furniture. Fluorescent lights glared overhead.

Every time Kate had seen her during Stan's previous admission, she'd worn the same clean hairstyle swept up and back from her face, the same pale red lipstick that matched her glasses. Today was no different, except small bags were evident beneath her eyes when she took off her glasses, and every so often a tremor appeared in her voice as she related the past forty-eight hours. She sat straight-backed on the lounge as she talked, her shirt buttoned to her neck, her knees held together.

'Where were you, doctor?' Her taut face challenged her.

'I was operating most of last night, Mrs Leonard, and my phone –'

'I don't mean that,' said Mrs Leonard. 'You can't always be available. I've been around doctors long enough to understand that. Most of my life, now I come to think of it.' She inhaled and steadied herself. 'I mean when we tried to book in to see you.'

'I did have time off during the early part of this week,' Kate admitted. 'But I organised cover.'

Mrs Leonard shook her head. 'When we came home from hospital we rang to organise an appointment. Your secretary said you were fully booked until this coming week.' She breathed again, a deep, drawn-out breath. 'We even rang last Friday to see if there was a cancellation.'

'I wasn't given any message,' said Kate. 'I'm sorry.' There had definitely been no message. She counted back. It was the week Sam started back. But she hadn't said anything as Kate passed her on Friday afternoon. She had been rushing, that was true. Should she have stopped, asked if there were any issues?

'Will he be all right?' The older woman's gaze was unflinching.

'I honestly don't know,' said Kate. 'It will be a little clearer by tonight, I think.' She took a mouthful of water. Her head was throbbing so hard it threatened to split apart. 'He is in really good hands here. I promise you we will do all we can.'

'I hope I will be able to say better late than never,' she said. She took off her glasses and dabbed her eyes before clutching her hands. 'He didn't stop trusting you, Dr Davenport. Even in the emergency department after the other surgeon had seen him and they were taking him to theatre, he told me to stick with you.' She blinked three times and looked straight at Kate. 'So I will. To be frank, I'm not sure I would say the same thing if it were our daughter.'

'I understand,' Kate mumbled. They stood up together, as if on cue. 'Is there anything I can do to help right now?'

'Tell me he's improving.' She paused. 'Can I see him now?'

'I'm sure that will be fine. Shall I ask a nurse –'

'I know the way, thank you.'

Kate waited as Mrs Leonard walked out of the room, her back again ruler-straight as she headed along the corridor. A cleaner stopped his mopping to let her pass. When she turned the corner, Kate headed the other way to a ladies toilet in a nearby corridor. It was empty. Locking herself in a cubicle, she sat and wept silently into her hands.

Kate finished her session on Monday and called Sam into her office. She looked a different woman from the one who had sat in the same chair two months earlier. She was ten – maybe fifteen – kilos lighter, with prominent cheekbones, and lips as full as hers. Cleavage probably fuller. Her hair and skin could have been lifted from *Vogue*. But underneath, it was the same old Sam.

'I can't stay long,' said Sam. 'I'm meeting someone for lunch.'

'Then let's get into it,' said Kate. 'A patient of mine rang a few weeks ago, and you apparently told him – maybe his wife – that I was full.'

Sam shrugged. 'Happens all the time. I fit them in where I can.'

'They would have told you they were post-op and that I had asked to see them.'

'I can't remember everyone who rings,' she said. 'You've become too popular since Stephen left. You'd be here until midnight.'

'I think you might remember this one. Mr Leonard? Stan Leonard? He rang again the Friday before last.'

'Oh, yeah. The transplant guy. Yeah, he told me he had a transplant twenty years ago.' She nodded and crossed her legs, her bright green pumps striking against her black tights. 'Friday was tricky. I said he already had an appointment for this coming Friday, so why not just keep it? Or go to emergency if necessary.'

'Why was Friday tricky, Sam? You're here all day Friday. I'm always available if I'm needed, here or elsewhere.' Her skin was prickling all over, but she needed to keep her cool.

'I had another engagement.' Her cheeks flushed. 'I took time in lieu. I do so much overtime as it is.'

'I haven't seen that.'

'You're always gone.'

'Sam, I told him to make an appointment after his operation and he told you that. He rang again on Friday.' She stared across her desk. 'This man ended up in intensive care over the weekend.'

She looked interested. 'How is he?'

'Touch and go.'

Sam returned Kate's gaze. 'Well, twenty years is pretty good for a transplant patient,' she said, evenly. 'I've heard them talk.'

Kate's eyes widened. She blinked. 'Okay, Sam,' she said, placing her palms on the desk. 'Here's what's going to happen. You are going out there and you are packing your things and you are not returning. I want you out of these rooms in ten minutes. Permanently.'

She stood. 'I've done nothing wrong.'

'Don't even start.' She glared at her, but Sam didn't flinch.

'You have to give me two weeks' notice.'

'You can stay here for two weeks if you want. I'd rather just mail you a cheque. You've made decisions you're not qualified to make and have totally disregarded patients who depend on me.'

Sam glared at her. 'This is unfair dismissal and I'll take it further. Don't think I won't. I know my rights.'

'Go ahead,' said Kate. 'I have quite a dossier on you from the past few months. Shall we ask Stephen how far back it goes?' She stood to match her. 'I will take this to the wire, Sam. It's become personal. Don't even try to mess with me.'

Sam strode to the door and turned, her hand on the handle. 'You know what they say about you? You're so fucking uptight you wouldn't know a fuck from a shit.'

'Get out, Sam. I've got real people here to deal with. Consider yourself fortunate I'm not suing you. Although Mrs Leonard may well decide to do so. So I'd watch out if I were you.'

Kate looked at the door for a full minute after it slammed. She had no idea how she would fill Sam's place. But it was worth every moment until she did.

She got a call from ICU as she was finishing the paperwork at her desk. Her fingers clenched when she heard the young intensivist's voice. Stan Leonard. She didn't need to hear bad news. He had been stable both nights when she dropped by early each morning.

'We want to extubate him before it gets too late,' he said over the phone. 'He's already breathing independently. Perhaps we can get him to the ward tomorrow. His inotropes are almost off.'

Her eyes moistened. 'Chris, I couldn't have asked for better news. I'll see him tonight,' she said.

She hung up and leaned forward. What was next? His skin graft would need replacing, but it could wait. Had to wait. He wasn't going back to theatre anytime soon. He needed a cardiologist to look him over again as well. He hadn't flipped into those odd heart rhythms when they ran him through his paces in the weeks before surgery. Thankfully, the tumours she had been most worried about looked not to have spread. The pathologist was reassuring. If she could help him through the next few weeks, he might have a chance. She set her jaw.

May arrived with a blast of icy winds, followed by another hot spell. Events in her life followed much the same path. She struggled for several days at the rooms until she found a temp who seemed half-decent. His readiness to be interviewed at seven in the morning got him halfway there. Absent all week at the university, Malika handed in her first paper to Professor Jenkins on the Friday. They celebrated with champagne that night. She had finished her first glass by the time Kate had filled hers.

'It is so very much better than vodka,' she said, smacking her lips audibly. She held the glass forward. 'I think I will have another.' Her eyes crinkled and Kate raised an eyebrow. She poured a half-glass.

'That might do you for a while, I think,' she said. 'Until I've finished mine, at least. Tell me, what made you decide to hand it in?'

'I thought about what you said, Dr Kate. And I decided this is what I am here for. I would dishonour many people if I did not do this.'

'So you backed yourself.'

Malika nodded. 'I backed other people's belief in me.'

'So now we wait.'

'Now we wait,' she agreed, holding out her glass again.

Two weeks later Melbourne could again talk of nothing but the AFL. Andrew was due back in a week. She had missed him. Angus Fraser was a nice guy, worthy and reliable, but he wasn't Andrew. It wasn't just the operating sessions. She found herself thinking about him as she ran the Tan Track – a new pledge – at least twice a week. Sometimes he just popped into her head, as did the questions. How was he dealing with seeing his children again? What were his friends like? Could he have someone over there, someone he had been seeing before coming across? Was that why he had wanted three weeks?

She sent Stan Leonard home from hospital – Angela giving her a hug as they left – on the same day she ran into Stephen. He was standing inside the main entrance to the public hospital when she passed. Her concerns about being late for the afternoon ward round disappeared when she saw him, although she had to look twice to be sure it was him. It had been weeks since she had seen him and the stooped man standing beside the kiosk who needed a haircut and a shave resembled the elegant, well-dressed surgeon about as much as hide did skin. His jumper hung off his shoulders and his pants fell bag-like from his waist, slippers poking out beneath. But he grinned to see her and they hugged when she rushed over. For the first time he smelled of old man.

'You're lucky to catch me,' he said. 'Mel and I are heading to Sydney for a few weeks. Staying with family. It's taken a bit of organising.'

'What are you doing here?'

'What has become my routine dialysis session,' he said.

'Mel's taking back the wheelchair. Sometimes I prop here for a while.' He nodded at the steady stream of people passing them, many gazing vaguely at the overhead signs as they clutched their papers. 'We forget how emotional these places can be.'

'You look well,' she said.

'I don't. But at least I have an excuse.' He peered over his glasses at her. 'You look tired.'

She was taken aback. 'Work stuff's a bit up and down, I guess.' She paused and her cheeks warmed. 'I had to sack Sam. I meant to tell you.'

'She rang me.'

'Really? What did she say?'

'What you'd expect. I said you had my complete confidence and I wished her well.'

Kate's shoulders eased.

He moved across a few steps to the kiosk and pulled out a chair from an empty table. 'Do you mind if I sit down? I get a bit light-headed after dialysis. They tell me it's the fluid removal.'

She pulled out a chair and joined him. 'Would you like a drink?' She glanced towards the counter, but he put a pale hand on her arm. His fingers were cold.

'I let Sam get away with too much for way too long, Kate. I'm sorry. My fault completely. Have you got anyone yet?'

'Just a temp at the moment. But he seems okay. Even good. I might ask him to stay on.'

'Well, let me know. Mel keeps talking about friends whose educated kids can't find work.' He winked with what she guessed was his good eye. 'I think it's usually more won't than can't.'

Kate smiled. 'It's good to see you, Stephen.'

'Speaking of work, did you put in your application?'

'I'm still thinking.'

'Life is short.' His gaze cut through her.

The lifts opened on the other side of the corridor and Mel appeared. She stood in the middle of the corridor looking up and down, radiant in high-heeled sandals and a white jumpsuit. She nodded when she saw them and swayed effortlessly between the people to join them.

Kate stood and they hugged.

'Kate. It's been ages.' She took a step back. 'You look tired. Are they working you too hard?'

'I'm fine,' she said. 'But yes, it's been busy.'

'Well, work life balance, darling. If there's something Stephen and I have learned from all this, it's that.' She was clear-eyed and poised as she sat holding Stephen's hand, a different woman from the one Kate had become used to in recent months. It crossed her mind to ask, but she held back. Some rocks were best left submerged.

They talked for a few minutes – about Sydney, briefly, and then about everything except what mattered. She longed for an afternoon with them again, just one, when they could talk and laugh as champagne flowed. An afternoon when everything could be the way it was.

'Honey, can you sit with Kate for a few minutes while I fetch the car?' Mel turned to her. 'Would you mind, Kate?'

She checked her watch. 'I do have to keep an eye on the time.' Her team would be waiting for her.

'Five minutes. Out the front. Promise.' She air-kissed and rushed off.

'She's different,' said Kate, as she headed outside.

'We had a talk,' he said. 'It was killing me seeing her half-drunk by midday every day. So I told her the truth – that Myron finally fessed up and agreed it was a massive tumour load and that my life expectancy was less than twelve months.' He paused. 'But as I explained, hers isn't.'

Kate studied him, swapping from eye to eye, trying to read him. 'What did she say?'

'She didn't say a word, just sat there looking at me. She told me afterwards she had never felt pain and relief at the same time the way she felt it then. I told her what I loved most about her was how she was at her best when the chips were down.' He smiled resignedly. 'I said I could be her project for the year, and that I really needed her at her best.'

He looked at his watch and pushed his chair back. 'I'd better get out there.' Kate stood to help him but he waved her away. 'I'll be fine. You get upstairs.' Their eyes met and he placed a hand on her shoulder. 'It came as a surprise to me, but you know, the truth isn't such a bad option.'

She gave him a bright wave as she got in the lift, and he raised a hand. 'Enjoy Sydney,' she mouthed as the doors shut, and he smiled. She was halfway to her floor before the full impact of what he was doing for Mel sank in, and she wished one day she might love someone half as much.

5

The hard yellow ball hit the backboard with a loud smack. Malika stared at it in dismay. It was the third time the ball had done this thing. When it happened, it made the girls on her team sigh, at the same time causing great joy in the other team.

Miss Cullerton, dressed in a maroon tracksuit, blew her whistle again. 'Malika! If you stopped fiddling so much with your headwear, you might find you were able to stop the ball. That is your job as goalkeeper. This is your fourth training session and so far you have done absolutely nothing to help your team. Am I right, girls?' The ones nearby stayed silent, but they looked at Malika with pleading eyes. Even Megan. 'Now, do better or you will be running laps.' Miss Cullerton glared at her.

Malika looked down. Her trainers were covered with mud. They had been white at the start of the session, but heavy rains during the week had made the playing area sodden, like a field in the wet season. Everyone was now covered in mud to their knees, even Miss Cullerton, even the large and solid pads she had strapped on at the start of the session. Her hands were cold inside her gloves and the light was beginning to fade. Malika wished the session would end. She had never played 'sport' before and did not care about this game called 'hockey'. Miss Cullerton told her at the start of the term that playing *a* sport was a school expectation. It would also help her fit in better with the other girls. Malika had read through the rules book twice but it had not helped connect her stick with the fast-moving ball. She picked up the mud-smeared ball and threw it back to Miss Cullerton. It landed with a splosh at the teacher's feet and she glared at her again. Malika stared back as one of the girls sniggered.

Eventually, it was over. Miss Cullerton called Malika over as the other girls trudged off. She waited until Malika removed her face guard.

'I expect a better attitude when you are playing in a team,' she said. 'You don't even try.' Her cheeks were red from running up and down the field and blowing her whistle many times. Her very yellow hair was spattered with flecks of mud. Malika imagined her own veil must look the same.

'In my village, I could catch the chickens as well as the boys could.' Malika replied. 'I think I would do better if I could run in the field.'

'You will play where you have been told to play,' Miss Cullerton said sharply, 'and make the most of it, like everyone else. At this stage I don't expect you to do more than be involved in training, but for once you will show some commitment to a team.' She looked at Malika's pads as they began walking towards the sports complex. 'And make sure those pads are scrubbed clean before you leave.'

'Mr Mick, the curator, told me they had to dry before cleaning them. He said it was better he did it the next day.'

Miss Cullerton pursed her lips but remained silent as they reached the change rooms. Crossing in front of Malika, she strode to the teachers' area. Malika watched her disappear and then headed inside, gathering her things before heading back to her room to shower. It was the one privilege Miss Cullerton allowed. She was like the maths professor in her first year in the Great City, always looking for flaws. By the end of the year she could work with her maths teacher. She did not think that would happen with Miss Cullerton. Megan whispered to her in the first session that everyone hated the Cull. 'Just our luck,' she groaned, as they ran onto the playing field. Malika did not hate her, but like the maths professor, she doubted they would ever be friends.

The following Tuesday Miss Cullerton stayed mercifully silent after the session. Malika was looking forward to her hot shower when Chloe, hot and sweaty from a run, stepped in front of her as she was heading back to her room.

'My father's taking me out tonight,' she warned. 'I need the bathroom in twenty minutes.'

Malika checked her watch. 'I will be finished in forty,' she said evenly, stepping around her and walking up the few stairs to the exit. 'Not a minute more!' Chloe shouted up as she got to the top. Malika could not help a small smile.

She woke early the next morning and lay for a few minutes in the dark, aware of the loneliness that sometimes woke with her. It was strong that morning. She sighed. She would take her letters from home and read them beneath her tree as the sun rose. But when she stepped outside, light rain was falling. She reached for an umbrella from the stand and walked through scattered puddles to the main avenue. Her shoes and feet were quickly wet. She was thinking of returning to her room when the steep silhouette of the chapel roof caught her eye. She had only been in the chapel for the first and last Mass of her school terms. Both times she had gazed at the altar that was bathed in light from the coloured windows around the walls. The teachers at these times wore black gowns, and crossed themselves silently with holy water as they entered the building. She had not seen a teacher or any of the girls enter the chapel at other times, though Ms Catalano said in her start-of-term speech that it was always open. She shivered as the rain began to drum on her umbrella before reaching the cover of the large buildings along the avenue.

She had to raise her umbrella for the run across a small courtyard to the chapel entrance. The heavy door creaked as she pushed it open and then stood in the vestibule for a minute, her umbrella dripping loudly on the floor. Small lights along the walls allowed her to make out the lines of forbidding pews stretching forward to the altar, itself dimly white in the distance. Perhaps this was not a good idea.

'What are you doing here?' Chloe's harsh voice from the end of the back pew to her right made her jump and her hand went to her chest. She squinted. Chloe was staring at her. Even at first light, her wet hair made her look forlorn.

'Nothing to do with you,' said Malika.

'Good.' She sniffed.

Malika picked a pew on the other side of the aisle and sat down. The only sound for a time was Chloe sniffing and then dabbing her nose with a white tissue. Malika shivered as the cold began to seep through her clothes. She pulled her cardigan tight.

As the light improved she could make out the ornately framed paintings along the walls – Stations of the Cross, Father Louis had called them. From the corner of her eye she could also see Chloe glancing furtively across at her before fixing back on the front.

'Do you come here often?' Malika asked her, after this had happened several times.

'None of your goddam business.'

Malika sighed. It would not be possible to spend time quietly here. Perhaps it would be better in her room. She stood to leave.

'Anyway, as if you would care.'

Malika turned and their eyes met. 'Why else would I ask?'

Chloe folded her arms and looked up at the altar, weighing the logic of the answer. 'It's personal,' she said eventually.

Malika stepped into the aisle, genuflected as Father Louis had taught her and picked up her umbrella. She could feel Chloe's eyes on her.

'It's my brother's anniversary,' said Chloe, her voice unsteady.

Malika paused. 'The other girls told me of this. I am sorry. I too have lost family.' She was not sure why she added, 'The pain is always there.'

For an instant, Chloe's eyes showed surprise. 'It's shit,' she said.

'Were you close with your brother?'

'No, I hated him. And he hated me.' She bit her lip. 'But I didn't expect him to die.'

Malika sat on the edge of the pew. 'Is this why you were out with your father last night?'

'The arsehole had a meeting in Singapore tonight so he had to fly out this morning.'

'Perhaps he finds it difficult too.'

'Yeah. Maybe.' She laughed as she wiped her eyes. 'My family is so screwed up. Like, totally screwed.'

They were quiet again. The light was now strong enough to brighten the altar. Candlesticks and white marble glowed.

'I will say a prayer for your brother,' Malika said eventually.

'That won't help him.'

'I was hoping it might help you.'

Chloe sniffed and then stayed silent. She checked her watch and came and stood in front of Malika, looking at her through red eyes. 'This isn't going to change anything between us, you know.'

'I understand,' said Malika.

Chloe shivered as she pulled her coat across her front. 'I'd better get back and shower. Are you coming?' She looked towards the large wooden doors at the end of the chapel. 'You can shower first, if you want.'

The top of Miss Cullerton's hair was perfectly parted, the ends tucked in just as cleanly beneath her jaw, as she read the letter. She looked up at Malika on the other side of the desk when she'd finished. She hadn't told her to sit and Malika knew by now it was a mistake to try until she had.

'What am I supposed to do with this?' Miss Cullerton asked.

'I have an important paper to give in a few weeks' time.

When I saw Professor Jenkins on Friday, he said he wanted me to spend more time at the university to prepare.'

'And let your studies at school lapse.'

'Until the conference is over.'

Miss Cullerton put down the letter and stared at her. 'This is typical of you, Malika. Special treatment. I wish I could say I was surprised. What if I refuse?'

'This conference is very important to me, Miss Cullerton.'

'So, you would try and do it anyway.' Her blue eyes glared. 'Why should I cave in to your demands when the rest of us have to comply with rules and protocols?'

Malika sighed and sat on the chair anyway. It had been a long morning. She had known this would not be easy and had made her plans carefully. She was tired of this teacher.

'Is the reason you wish me to hold to your rules so greatly because I am different?'

The teacher leaned back in her chair and gave a small smile. 'Well, there you have it, Malika. That's the essence of it. You actually think you are better than the rest of us.'

'In some ways I have been most fortunate, yes.' She paused. 'But I have not always worn a veil.'

'It won't help to feel sorry for yourself.'

The words cut and Malika shut her eyes for a moment. What could she say that would not make things worse? She wanted to shout at this woman, but it would be like yelling at a wall. She took a breath. 'This school has been very new to me, Miss Cullerton. I have made many mistakes. But I do not think I am as bad as you say. When Mrs O'Bryan searched every room in the boarding house for alcohol last term, my room was the only one without any. I have not lost points in any of my science and maths tests, my English tests –'

'Are not perfect.'

'Are improving very much. And there are very few girls or teachers who I am not friends with.' She paused. 'But I do not think I will ever be good at hockey.'

Miss Cullerton leaned forwards, her eyes on Malika and her hands clasped. 'You will always be a loner, Malika, as you will always believe your God-given gift entitles you to special treatment.'

She leaned back, and there was silence as she re-read the letter, her face slowly hardening. She put the letter down. 'I am going to say no to this request, Malika. It sets a bad precedent for the other girls in your year level. You will need to engage in your additional studies during your own time. I will speak with Ms Catalano, but I expect to have her support on this.'

Malika gazed at the floor before raising her head. She had feared it would come to this. 'I am sorry you do not approve, Miss Cullerton, but when Professor Jenkins and I saw Ms Catalano this morning she was very pleased indeed to know that I shall include the name of the school on my slides at the conference. The professor also offered to show some of the girls here his maths department at the university.'

'You've already seen the principal?' Her lips tightened.

'The professor and I saw her before school. But she wanted you to sign the form. She was busy this morning but will speak with you later, I think.' She counted her heartbeats in the silence that followed. 'Will you be happy to sign?' she asked quietly.

The teacher's jaw had clenched and for a moment Malika thought she would fling the papers in her face. But eventually, she scowled and picked up her pen.

'Here,' she said, jabbing her biro at the dot on the 'i' and passing it back to Malika. 'Regrettably, I'll see you in three weeks. Not a day longer.'

Kate pushed hard up the long hill. She wanted to make it to the end. She wasn't sure about running the Tan by herself after sundown. The streetlamps produced as much shadow as light. Her breaths were short gasps by the time she reached the top and she let her pace slow, sucking in air as she ran down the slope to the clump of large fig trees on the corner. She finished at the water fountain and paced around for a minute, her hands on her hips, until her pulse and breathing settled. She drank from the fountain and checked her watch. Seventeen minutes. Not bad. Her goal was sixteen by summer.

The air was cool on her damp back and shoulders as she walked back to her car beneath the canopy of the fig trees. Traffic on Domain Road was still heavy, the stream of headlights bright in the gloom.

She heard her name being called as she unlocked her car. She peered across the street. A man was waving at her from the restaurant across the road. It looked like Andrew. She smiled. He was wearing a Melbourne football jumper and jeans. He had arrived back a week earlier, invigorated. In theatre over open dissections he had chatted about his children and how good it was to have them here, what the trip had been like. And, of course, he'd talked about his research ideas. The pang from seeing how little she was involved in his world surprised her, as did the way she clung to their momentary, intimate silences on Monday afternoon in his office. When they'd parted on Friday they had wished each other well for the weekend.

She reached into her car and grabbed her top, taking advantage of a stationary tram to cross the road. 'How do you know about this place?' she asked, stepping onto the pavement.

'You told me,' he replied, 'when I said I'd found a place in East Melbourne. He nodded to his right. 'We're renting just up the hill there.'

She had forgotten. It had been months ago.

'The children and I have just been to a game of the provincial rules. Aussie Rules.' He pronounced it awkwardly, making her smile. 'Do you want to join us?' he asked.

'They're here?' She scanned inside the restaurant briefly before looking down at her lycra and scuffed runners. 'I've just finished a run.'

'I'll buy you a drink. I promise they won't bite.' He smiled again. 'They'd love to meet you.'

She climbed up the few steps, pushing absently on her hair bun and tucking stray strands behind her ears. 'Malika's cooking tonight. I don't want to be late.'

'One drink.'

She followed him in, her heart pounding as she approached the table. His children. What was she supposed to say? Or do? They filled the space around the table more than she would have expected, as they pushed back against the chairs, mobile phones firmly in their grasp.

Andrew introduced them, adding 'phones, please,' as he

glanced at Kate.

Alice looked up momentarily through the fringe she was growing out, her skin as pale as it was in her photo and her eyes as brown as her hair. She nodded and flicked her hair back. 'Hi,' she said, and returned to her phone. Julian grinned, putting two enormous front teeth on display. Kate wondered if Andrew's hair had once been as blond.

'Children.' Andrew's voice carried a hint of warning as they sighed and placed their phones on the table.

Kate took an empty chair and Andrew sat beside her. Her back was sweaty again, the lycra damp between her thighs. She tried to remember how she and Malika had started talking the first time.

'How was the footy?' she asked Julian.

'Okay.' He shrugged. 'They jump really high.'

'I think understanding the rules would help us all,' said Andrew.

Kate turned to Alice, but she was gazing out the window. It was almost dark.

'Alice?' Andrew prompted.

Her attention returned slowly to the table.

'Did you like the footy?' he asked.

'Awesome.' She rolled her eyes and rotated her phone on the table to see the screen.

Andrew shook his head and stood up. 'I was just getting drinks,' he said, looking at Kate.

'Mineral water for me,' she replied.

She waited until he had gone, just catching Alice as she picked up her phone. 'How do you like Melbourne so far?'

'He wants me to say everything's great,' she nodded in the direction of her father, 'but it's not. It's *pus*.' Her accentuation made it seem as if being brought here was a crime.

'What's the worst thing?'

'It's all bad.'

'It's a bit better than that, I hope, but it will take time.'

'Not if he keeps taking me to stupid sports games.'

Kate wasn't winning. She wasn't good at this. 'What do you want to do when you finish school?'

Alice pulled her hair onto one shoulder and began playing with it. 'At home, I was going to be a film director. Mum used to write screenplays.' She looked out at the dark street. 'This place won't even have a course.'

'It probably does,' said Kate, beginning to wonder why she was trying so hard. 'You know, a girl a bit older than you stays with me on weekends. Sometimes, we go to a film on Saturdays with another girlfriend of mine. It's not London, but would you like to come to one? It could be just us girls.' If this didn't work, she was in trouble.

Andrew placed her glass in front of her and sat down with a large beer in his hand. He smiled. 'She would love that, wouldn't you, Alice?'

Alice glanced at her brother, who had picked up his phone again. 'As long as he's not there.'

Andrew looked at Kate. 'We'll work it out,' he said.

There was silence around the table. Alice returned to her phone. Andrew drew deeply on his beer while Julian finished his drink and returned to the game on his phone. It was the first time since they'd met on the steps at Stephen's house that she'd seen Andrew quite this unsure. A struggling dad. He was trying to play families and there was so much that needed sorting, working. Even loving. Her heart went out to him as he smiled brightly at her again.

'Daddy!' Julian's hand had disappeared beneath the table, his eyes round.

Andrew jumped to his feet. 'Okay, little man.' He raised a shepherding arm as the boy scurried past clutching his shorts. 'Back in a minute.'

Alice, absorbed in her phone, commented as they disappeared. 'He does that all the time.'

'Is he all right?'

She shrugged. 'Daddy says he's fine.'

'A touch of enuresis plus a bit more,' Andrew explained, as they stood on the pavement afterwards outside the bar.

'Is he all right?' She repeated her question, acknowledging to herself as she asked that her anxiety might be somewhat displaced: Julian's hair gleamed under the lights as he ran and then leaped up and down on the pavement with his eyes raised and his arms high in the air. Alice, her jeans tight and arms folded, wandered up to the restaurant next door.

'As you can see, he's mostly fine,' said Andrew. 'I'm sure things will settle down.' He laid a hand on her shoulder and she let it stay there. It was warm and just then, felt right. 'Thank you for helping with Alice in there.'

'I did nothing.'

'You did more than you know.'

She shivered and rubbed her shoulders. 'I'd better get going.

Malika will be waiting.' She would ring her from the car. 'Can I give you a lift up the hill?'

She dropped them outside their place just before Punt Road and drove down the hill towards the freeway, humming to herself.

The email that arrived late the following night came from an evening she had all but forgotten, subconsciously let go of as if it had never happened.

Dear Kate, it began, *I hope I have not left it too long and that you still remember me. It was a pleasure* … Kate's hand rose to her mouth as she read on. It finished with an electronic signature, *Vihan Singh*.

She read it again. And then again. He had researched her publications – was highly impressed by the quality of her work, and her ideas when they had spoken at the conference – and was delighted to be able to offer her a research secondment – to take up anytime in the next twelve months.

She went into the kitchen, her hands trembling as she poured a glass of water and leaned against the sink, drinking it slowly. Her mind was a whirl. A research secondment at Harvard? She shook her head. Twelve months to begin, but after that who knew? She was due for sabbatical leave from the hospital. That, in addition to her annual leave, would almost get her there. She would have to find someone to do the rooms. That would hardly be a problem; they'd be falling over themselves.

That Thursday after theatre, she followed Andrew to his office.

'You said you had some research ideas,' she said.

He looked up from his desk. 'Can it wait until tomorrow? I did say to the kids –'

'I just need fifteen minutes.'

He checked his watch and nodded. 'I guess they'll still be serving pizza at seven-thirty.'

He made a pot of tea and they sat at his small table. As always, he quickly warmed to the task. 'I think we can make the breakthrough,' he said, 'at least a significant development through that major block.' He cocked his head and his eyes narrowed a little. 'Is there a particular reason you're asking?'

'Well, for a start the applications for head of unit close tomorrow.'

'That's true.' He raised an eyebrow. 'And?'

Her palms were clammy as she rubbed them together. 'And Vihan Singh has offered me a research fellowship with him.' The words came out in a tumble.

When she had the courage to look he was staring at her impassively. 'He was very taken with you.'

There was a strained silence. She hadn't expected that.

'What will you do?' he asked eventually.

'I thought I'd discuss it with you.' Her heart was beating hard. 'Isn't that what I should do, discuss my career options with the people I report to?'

'It's challenging when I've introduced that person to my direct competitor and he makes a play for her.' His face was pale.

'I haven't replied yet.'

'What is he offering?'

'Salary?' She shook her head. 'He didn't mention payment.'

He snorted. 'That'll come. It's Harvard.'

'It's only for twelve months.'

'Places like Harvard can be a one-way trip for good researchers.' He stood up and went to the window – as he would do when he was upset. 'Apart from it being Harvard, I don't believe his science is any better than what we're doing here.' He paused. 'In fact, he's the one who's hit the wall, remember?'

'You want me to be head of unit. How would I find time to do any decent research here if I did that? Stephen couldn't.'

'I said we could negotiate.'

'Andrew, the job's full time without research. Unless I stopped my private work.'

He looked at her. 'I don't want you to go.'

'Why? You have a host of people you can call on aside from me.'

He inhaled deeply as he turned to her. 'For a start, we make a good team. Clinically, and potentially academically.' He paused. 'And …'

She swallowed, but there would never be a better time to say it. She found herself on her feet. 'Andrew, if I was head of unit, *if* it happened, we'd see each other almost every day. We'd operate together. I would report directly to you. Anything else would have to be out of the question. You know that.' Something in her gut shifted as she was saying it. She wasn't running this time. It was the right thing to do. Yet she could hardly stand it.

He nodded and was silent for a long time. Minutes.

'Will you put in an application?' he asked eventually.

The space in the room disappeared as their gaze met. She saw it then. The professor was asking a valued colleague to stay. But the man was asking for her trust. And somewhere between the two lay a zone her heart yearned for but couldn't enter. And it made her sick to her stomach.

'It looks like I have some thinking to do,' she said at last. She looked at her watch. 'And you'd better go and order pizza.'

She did her rounds, stopping for a swim on the way home. She had hoped the clarity of the blue water and the repetitious monotony of the unchanging black line beneath her would provide solace. But it only made her feel more alone. She submitted an application in the end: late at night, while the world slept. She hadn't made a decision. She couldn't say she had done that. But she hadn't ruled it out, either.

6

June arrived with no word from Father Mike, which Kate convinced herself was a positive sign. Any news of the dead priests had also long passed; now not even mentioned in the Prayers of the Faithful on the odd Sunday that Kate accompanied Malika to Mass. Both Melbourne's newspapers were instead focussing on the defection of a rising AFL star to Melbourne City FC and whether the Brownlow Medal favourite would recover from his leg injury in time for the finals. Melbourne in winter.

Lucy called on Tuesday night, before they were due to go to Lorne for the long weekend. Kate took the call in her car on the way back from a late operation at Cabrini Hospital.

'Everything sorted? You hadn't forgotten?' Lucy's voice was anxious.

'Absolutely not.' She hadn't given it a thought.

'You haven't pathetically rostered yourself on call or anything, have you?'

'I've cleared the weekend, Luce. I'm looking forward to it.' It was the one thing she had done, some weeks earlier, after the near-disaster with Stan Leonard.

'And Malika is still up for it?'

'Bells and whistles, I think.' She recalled a packed bag near the door in Malika's room the previous night.

'We'll pick you up on Friday night then. I can't believe it, Kate. You're actually taking a long weekend.'

Malika's bag was placed neatly beside the front door when Kate walked in on Friday evening. She was sitting upright on the sofa in the lounge, and smiled at Kate before glancing out the window as a car passed.

'You seem keen to get going,' said Kate, pausing at the doorway with some quickly ironed tops.

'I am very excited to be seeing the ocean, yes,' said Malika. She sniffed, and dabbed her handkerchief to her nose.

'You're not getting a cold?'

'Perhaps,' she said.

Kate stepped over to her and felt her forehead. 'You don't have a fever. It's probably just a cold. You've been working very hard.'

'You are right,' she said. 'This weekend I shall rest.'

Kate dropped her bag beside Malika's just as Lucy texted, saying they would be ten minutes late. *Hamish!!!*, she wrote, and Kate smiled. She put her hands on her hips and went through her mental checklist. Lucy had said to bring nothing fancy – it was Lorne. She had made sure they'd both packed runners and waterproofs for beach walks, though how far Lucy would last at this stage of her pregnancy was another matter. They seemed to have everything. She checked her watch. Expect them now around seven, Lucy had said. They still had half an hour. She poured herself a glass of wine and sat opposite Malika.

'I think I will not wear my veil at this place,' said Malika.

Kate nodded slowly. 'Will you be okay with that?'

'Yes.' She thought for a minute. 'But I shall bring it in case Lucy or Hamish is not at ease with this. And if we walk along the street,' she added, and sniffed again.

'At least it will be easier with your cold,' said Kate.

It was a clear drive down, most of the traffic well over by the time they reached Werribee. They arrived in the dark again, the house a cold silhouette against the night sky as they trundled in with their bags. As Lucy turned on the lights and Hamish the electric heaters, Kate took Malika to the bunk room she had used before. A single globe in the middle of the ceiling lit up the red doonas on the two top bunks.

'I slept like the dead the first night I was here,' said Kate, dropping her bag on a lower bunk. 'It's so quiet.'

Hamish drove into town for pizza while Lucy lit the fire and turned on the hot water. Kate tried but was too tired to eat, let alone make conversation. Malika seemed much the same. They both bundled into bed after packing the dishwasher.

'The sea air will be good for your cold, Malika,' said Lucy, standing at the door. 'The salt will boost your immune system.' She waited for them both to clamber into their bunks before switching off the light. Kate barely remembered falling asleep.

When she woke the next morning, Malika's bunk opposite was empty, while Hamish and Lucy's door farther along the corridor was still closed. She threw on her bathrobe and padded around the house for a minute before finding Malika in the bright sunshine outside on the deck, already showered and dressed. She was leaning over the railing looking through the eucalypts to the ocean. Kate stepped outside to join her, shivering as the sharp breeze cut against her face and bare legs. She pulled her bathrobe tight.

'Meet expectations?' she asked, coming up beside Malika.

Malika turned and grinned at her. She said nothing.

They stayed there for a few minutes, each in their own thoughts, as sulphur-crested cockatoos squawked and swooped overhead. Surf pounded faintly far below.

'I'll get some breakfast going,' said Kate eventually. 'Do you want anything?'

Malika shook her head. 'Thank you, Dr Kate. I am fine here. When can we walk along the sand?'

'Lucy says that's the only rule at Lorne: no plans.' She cocked her head. 'Any special reason?'

'Ayesha has never seen the ocean. She very much wants me to bring back some sand and some water.'

'Then you should.' She frowned as Malika dabbed her nose again. 'Perhaps you shouldn't spend too much time out here in the cold.'

'Just another five minutes,' said Malika. She moved back to the row of deck chairs that Hamish had aligned along the window the night before. Sitting down, she closed her eyes and turned her face to the sun.

'I'll bring you a cup of tea,' said Kate. 'And I'll sit with you once I put on something warmer.'

Malika turned, opening one squinted eye, and smiled. 'This is very beautiful, Dr Kate.'

The morning slid away from them. By the time Lucy and Hamish had stirred, Kate had picked up the paper and some bread at the shop, and they had cleaned up after a late breakfast, it was mid-afternoon. Eventually, Lucy said she was ready to head to the beach and Malika ran and fetched two small jars from her room. She slid them into her bag, which she slung around her shoulder.

'I'll explain on the way,' said Kate, responding to Lucy's quizzical look.

Deep grey clouds had moved in during the morning, filling the sky as they headed downhill. They crossed the road and continued to the foreshore, passing beneath a thick canopy of cypress branches. Malika clutched her bag as she stumbled on the roots that protruded snakelike through the sandy soil. They turned down a narrow track flanked by shoulder-high tea-trees and emerged onto a wide, empty beach. Beside them, a collection of boulders and large rocks stretched finger-like into the sea. Lucy called it the groyne. The tide was out and the only visible people were a few distant surfers working the swell on the far point. With Malika following, Kate climbed onto the rocks, stepping across them before jumping on to the cold, soft sand. Hamish and Lucy walked around the front of the groyne, splashing in the ankle-deep water. The sweeping stretch of wet sand shone eerily in the gloom and the onshore breeze hadn't warmed since morning. Kate hugged her coat close as she joined Lucy and they ambled towards the water, leaving divots in the sand.

Malika ran ahead a little way, pulling a jar from her bag. She fell on her knees, filled the jar with dry sand and screwed the lid on firmly before placing it back in her bag. She beamed at Kate and then ran to the water, walking steadily through the shallows up to her knees. She waited for a wave and then scooped the empty jar through the gentle foam. Screwing on the top firmly, she walked back to the others, triumphant.

'Ayesha will be very happy,' she said. She handed the bag to Kate. 'Can you mind this while I run?'

Kate hung the bag from her shoulder, smiling as Malika spread her arms wide and twirled in front of them before releasing her veil and hijab. She ran ahead to Hamish who, in cotton shorts, had marched ahead briskly. Coming up from behind, she tagged him and, with a high-pitched squeal, ran for the water, looking back to check he was following. Her long, black hair flowed behind her in the wind.

Kate glanced across at Lucy. She couldn't hide the waddle of her hips in the wet sand. Her swollen belly pushed balloon-like against her blue duffel coat.

'You're very quiet,' said Kate.

'Am I?' Lucy's cool eyes appraised her, and they smiled.

'That was the smile you used to give me at school when you got your test results,' said Kate. 'Then I knew something was wrong. Baby's okay?'

'Oh, baby's fine.' She tucked her hair behind her ears and took Kate's arm. 'The obstetrician says everything's perfect – and it is.'

'Hamish?'

'He's so excited.'

'Well, that's good isn't it?' Kate swept her own hair off her face with her free hand. Its thick strands had taken on a life of their own in the breeze. She held it at the base of her neck.

'Oh, sure. We were trying for three years, you know.'

'You didn't tell me that.'

'It doesn't matter, does it? It's not exactly true, anyway. We just let it happen. No contraception, I mean. We only really tried for about a year. But I was starting to wonder.'

They stopped walking and turned to the sea, the wind blowing in their faces. A large wave fifty or more metres away dragged up streams of sand as it reared and hung for a moment, crashing with a loud clap onto the water below. Already behind it the next wave was forming. On the horizon, a super tanker lumbered its way across the leaden seas.

'The ocean scares me on days like this,' said Kate.

'No place for kayaks today,' said Lucy. She nodded across to the point. 'Those surfers are quite mad.'

'Or perhaps we're just getting older,' said Kate. 'Kayaks notwithstanding,' she added.

Lucy laughed and squeezed her arm and they began walking again. Hamish and Malika were now a long way farther up the beach, their shapes indistinct through the spray. Every so often, Kate would hear a faint squeal.

'You know,' said Lucy, 'I'll be fifty-eight by the time this baby's twenty. Over sixty if I have another. I think I'm going to grow my hair long and keep it that way.' She glanced at Kate. 'Your length at least. I'm terrified of the day I cut it all off. After that, it won't be long before I need a Horlicks before bed and I start sleeping in pyjamas.'

Kate turned her head. 'You're not really okay, are you?'

Lucy sighed. 'It's just – I've suddenly realised my life won't be mine anymore. It takes a little getting used to.' She stepped awkwardly over a large piece of driftwood and turned to Kate. 'Can you do two things for me?'

Kate turned, wondering if she was serious.

'Don't let me drink any wine tonight, will you? I had another glass this week.'

'And the other?'

'Remind Hamish on the way back that we need this driftwood for the fire at home.'

They rugged up after dinner and set themselves up on the deck: three chairs around a gas heater that hissed orange and blue into the blackness. Malika had stayed inside, eating only a mouthful of dinner before lying on one of the wide, ochre-coloured couches in the living room. Kate watched her for a few minutes through the sliding door. Her eyes were closed and her face had become pale. Every so often, she raised her handkerchief to dab her nose.

Hamish poured the last of the wine into Kate's glass and leaned back in his deck chair, the glow from the heater turning his face red. He smiled at Lucy. 'It doesn't get better than this, does it, honey?'

The door opened behind them and Malika poked her face out.

'I shall go to bed,' said Malika. 'I am very tired.'

'It's probably your cold,' said Lucy. 'Or you haven't had enough water to drink. I'm sure you'll feel better in the morning. If not, I've got some Rescue Remedy somewhere. That always works.'

'Too much running on the beach this afternoon,' joked Hamish.

She smiled at him. 'You are a very slow runner.' She turned to Kate. 'Do you have a tablet for a headache?'

'Come with me,' said Kate, standing. She led her to the bathroom and punched out some paracetamol from a blister pack. Malika swallowed the tablets with a glass of water. 'You hardly ate any dinner,' said Kate.

'I think Hamish is right. I ran very hard this afternoon.'

'Lucy might be right, too. Have another glass of water.' Kate felt her forehead. It was warm. 'Now you do have a fever,' she said. 'Let's see how the paracetamol goes.' Malika gave her a tired smile and Kate smiled back. 'I'll help you into bed.'

'I had a most perfect day today,' said Malika, as she eased into her bunk. She shivered as her head touched the pillow.

'Let's see if you're feeling any better tomorrow,' said Kate.

She turned off the light and wandered back onto the deck.

'She looked exhausted,' said Lucy.

'Yes,' said Kate. 'She did.'

She slouched back in her deck chair beside the heater and folded her arms, frowning as she stared hard into the dense blackness of the trees. Fevers and colds often went together, as did frontal headaches and sinus inflammation. No surprises there. And anyone at a new school – let alone a new country – had to get the occasional cold. That was inevitable. She shook her head. It all fitted fine. Just why there was a gnawing pit of anxiety in the centre of her stomach, she couldn't say.

'You okay, sunshine?' Hamish was staring at her and she smiled.

'Must be tired like Malika. I should get to bed.'

'It's the damned sea air,' he replied. 'Gets you every time.'

'Dr Kate.' Malika's voice was a whisper in an endless darkness. She might have been saying it for some time, Kate thought, as she forced her eyelids apart.

'What is it, Malika?' The darkness was stultifying.

'Dr Kate, my head feels very bad. I have great pain. Something is not right.'

Kate eased out of bed and crawled across to the other bunk. She groped about with her hand before finding Malika's forehead. She was on fire. Kate got to her feet, shivering in the cold. She stumbled over some clothes as she found the door and fumbled for the light switch. Malika groaned and rolled her head to the side as light filled the room.

Kate pulled on her robe and came back to Malika's bed, kneeling beside her. She looked at her carefully. Her nostril was crusted, her hands – she squeezed them – cold. She leaned over to her bed and picked up her phone, squinting at it. Six hours since she had given her the tablets.

'I'll get you some more paracetamol,' she said.

'Please,' whispered Malika.

She was halfway back from the bathroom, water glass and tablets in hand, when she put it together. She knew exactly what was happening and it stopped her mid-stride.

7

Kate's legs were jelly as she hauled on her tracksuit pants and a jumper. She knelt by Malika's bed.

'Can you hear me, Malika?'

'Yes, Dr Kate,' she whispered.

'I think you are not very well. I am going to take you to the hospital. Is that okay?'

'Thank you, Dr Kate. Please hurry.'

Kate tapped on Lucy's door, pushing it open as she did. Narrowing her eyes, she could make out two vague forms beneath the pale bedding. She went to Lucy's side.

'Lucy,' she whispered, leaning forward. She shook her shoulder gently. 'It's Kate.'

'Kate!' She fumbled for her light and switched it on, squinting at her. 'What time is it?'

'About three.' Her heart was thumping. 'It's Malika.'

Lucy sat up rubbing her eyes as Hamish groaned and rolled over. 'What's wrong with her? Has she vomited or something? There's a bucket in the laundry.' She yawned.

Kate hesitated. 'I think she has meningitis. It explains everything. I have to take her to the hospital. We don't have much time.'

'Meningitis?' Lucy started. 'Will she be okay?'

'I hope so,' said Kate. Now wasn't the time to go into it. 'But I need your car keys.'

Lucy blinked at her for a moment before nudging Hamish. 'Honey, wake up. Now. We have to get going.'

Kate threw all their things into their bags and bundled them into the back of the car, the metallic clank of the door invading the dense stillness that lay around them like a cloak. While Lucy locked up, Kate helped Hamish carry Malika to the car, taking her from him in the back seat. Malika groaned as Kate placed her head on her lap. Hamish started the car as Lucy eased herself in, and reversed cautiously out of the drive. Kate stroked Malika's forehead as they sped downhill.

'It's going to be okay,' she whispered in her ear, over and over. 'It's going to be okay.'

Malika's eyes rolled open as they passed beneath a street-light. She shut them immediately.

'Turn right. The hospital's at the far end of town,' Lucy said to Hamish, as they reached the main street 'It's not far.' She glanced back at Malika and flashed Kate a hopeful smile.

Hamish stopped the car outside the emergency department, its name glaring fluorescent red above automatic sliding doors. Hamish took Malika from Kate, and she and Lucy hurried inside, the automatic doors sliding open with a hiss. The overnight nurse was sitting behind a desk enclosed by glass. On the wrong side of middle-aged, with bushy grey hair and black-framed glasses, she watched them approach. The name on her badge said 'Agnes'.

'I believe the girl behind us,' Kate turned as she spoke, 'has meningitis. She needs urgent treatment. I'm a doctor,' she added.

Agnes stared at her steely eyed for a moment, then stared at Hamish, standing with Malika in his arms. She turned off her radio and reached for a form from several piles in front of her. Her heavy arm quivered as she filled it out, signing the bottom. She posted it through the glass slot in front of her.

'That will be four hundred dollars,' she said.

Lucy gasped, as Kate reached for her wallet. 'Card okay?' she asked.

Agnes nodded.

'We need a cubicle now,' said Kate, looking around. She counted five, all empty.

'Put her in resus,' said Agnes. She nodded at the large, bright room behind them.

'Can you call the doctor now?' Kate said over her shoulder, as they took Malika into the room. She groaned again as Hamish carried her to the trolley, before turning her head and vomiting what little dinner she had eaten onto his shirt. He ignored it.

He looked at Kate. 'Will she be all right?'

'I hope so,' she said.

He nodded, only then looking down at the large stain on his shirt.

'I'd better clean this up,' he said.

'I'll help,' said Lucy, her face pale.

They disappeared, as Agnes banged her glass cabin shut. Pushing aside the curtain, she shuffled into the room. Moving slowly and deliberately, she began a set of observations, the stitches on her white uniform stretching wide as she leaned across Malika to check her breathing. She pulled out a thermometer from a nearby stand and placed it in Malika's ear, checking it when the machine pinged.

'Child's burning up,' she said. 'No place for her here.' She unfurled the cuff on the sphygmomanometer and wrapped it around Malika's arm.

Kate looked around the room. Sterile packs, trolleys, a defibrillator, an overhead mini-theatre light – it was enough for what they needed. She hadn't managed meningitis since she was a resident, but one thing had stuck. You didn't get more than one shot at it.

A doctor with a tanned face, about the same age as Stephen, pulled across the curtain and walked into the room. If Agnes had mentioned to him that Kate was a doctor he didn't show that he'd heard. He blinked at Malika several times, then tugged on his pullover and extended his hand to Kate.

'Dr Whiteside,' he said, smiling congenially. 'What seems to be the trouble?'

He nodded several times, stifling a long yawn, as Kate explained as quickly as she could.

'It sounds like we need an ambulance,' he said when she finished, his face a mask of relief.

'How long will that be?' She folded her arms.

He checked his watch. 'What is it now? Nearly four.' He twisted his face as he weighed the options. 'An hour, maybe two if they're busy. They're often caught up in Geelong after midnight.'

'We don't have that sort of time,' said Kate.

'It would be quicker if you drove,' he said. 'In reality, it's a minimum of ninety minutes for the ambulance.' He paused. 'And a forty minute drive at this hour.'

Kate looked at Malika on the trolley. She hadn't moved. Her head was turned to the side, her feet splayed wide on the white cotton. Her breathing rate had increased.

'What's her blood pressure and pulse?' she asked Agnes.

'BP ninety over fifty, pulse one-twenty,' she said crisply, writing the numbers on a large sheet.

'There's another option,' Kate said firmly.

Dr Whiteside frowned. 'What's that?'

'We do our job.'

'Now, hold on,' he said, raising a hand and glancing at Agnes for support. 'There are limits to what we can do here.'

'I realise that, but you have to understand that what we do right now might be the only chance this girl gets.' She took a breath. 'Tell me truly. Can we do it?'

He hesitated. 'Technically, yes,' he said eventually. 'Technically.'

Kate nodded towards the well-stocked wall opposite, as Hamish and Lucy reappeared. 'We'll need an IV line, three lumbar puncture tubes and two sets of blood culture bottles.' She turned to Agnes. 'What sort of antibiotics do you have?'

'Only ampicillin and cef-t at this time of year.'

'No chloramphenicol or penicillin? Really?'

Agnes shook her head.

Kate turned to Dr Whiteside. 'How long since you've done a lumbar puncture?'

'Quite a while.'

Kate recognised the look in his eyes. 'I'll do it,' she said.

She turned to Malika, who was moving an arm feebly as if reaching for her head. 'We don't have much time.' Lucy and Hamish were standing in front of the cubicle curtain, their faces strained. Hamish's hands were clenched. A large, wet stain covered the front of his shirt.

'You two will have to leave,' said Agnes. She looked at them, her face reflecting new purpose. 'We're busy.' She pulled out a pile of sterile packs and towels and laid them on the bench.

'I think we might need them,' said Kate. She looked at Agnes. 'Is that okay?'

'If you say so,' she said, shrugging.

'Is that okay with you two?' Kate asked.

'Of course,' said Lucy.

'Great.' She thought through what she had to do. 'Luce, come and stand by her head. Just keep talking to her. It will help. Hamish, I'll have to roll her onto her side and bend her knees up. She won't like it. You need to hold her there. Yes?'

He nodded and moved to the other side of the trolley.

'Are we ready?' Kate asked Dr Whiteside. 'Agnes?'

They nodded.

She breathed deeply. 'Okay, let's go. Where do I scrub?'

The lumbar puncture was as easy as she could have hoped: the long, fine needle passing easily through the skin and ligaments of Malika's back. With her gloved hand protruding from her long-sleeved gown, she withdrew the trocar from the hub and held the first of the sterile tubes beneath it, as she waited for the cerebrospinal fluid to emerge. It took only a moment for fluid to fill the small chamber and start dripping into the waiting tube beneath. She replaced the first tube with the second, and held the first up to the light, hoping against hope for the fluid to be as it should: clear as a cut diamond. But it wasn't. It was turbid. Faint, but definite, like sand inside a wave.

After the third tube, Kate withdrew the needle and they rolled Malika onto her back again.

'Lights,' she moaned, as she lay back.

'Can we turn them down?' Kate asked.

Agnes strode over to the doorway and the room suddenly became mellow. Kate recalled the same glow surrounding Peter, the young lad with melanoma, and clenched her jaw.

'Can you do blood cultures?' she asked Dr Whiteside.

'Of course.'

'Great.' She turned to Agnes. 'Can we get an IV going in her other arm? Just an 18-gauge should be fine.'

'Me?' She started wiping her hands on her uniform.

'It's okay,' said Kate. 'I'll insert the IV. But I'll need you to set up a bag of saline. And tell me when the antibiotics are ready to go.'

Ten minutes later, antibiotics dripped steadily through the IV flask into the vein on Malika's forearm. Kate watched her for a moment. She had stopped moaning and lay quietly. Kate wasn't sure if that was a good or a bad sign. Her breathing was just as rapid.

'How's her blood pressure and pulse now?' she asked Agnes.

'Same,' she replied. 'Temp's up to forty, though.'

'We have to move her,' said Kate. 'And get these samples processed. Ambulance time?' she turned to Dr Whiteside.

He checked his watch. 'It's almost five. A bad time. Just about handover, I think. I can try.'

Kate sighed. They should have called for the ambulance when they arrived. She looked at Lucy, sitting on a chair that Hamish had found somewhere. He stood beside her. They both looked as if they had run a marathon. Kate felt the same. She wiped her forehead with the back of her hand.

'We have to do this,' she said. 'Or at least I do.'

'You're not leaving us behind,' said Hamish. He took a step forward. 'I'll drive; Lucy can navigate. Geelong Hospital, right?'

Kate nodded. She glanced at the IV flask. 'This'll be through in five minutes. We'll go then.'

They sped along a darkened Ocean Road at speeds that sometimes dropped close to the proposed limit. Towns and communities rushed by. At one point, Lucy laid a hand on Hamish's forearm.

'It won't help if we crash, honey,' she said.

He nodded, visibly slowing. 'Sorry.'

Kate was in the back with Malika's head on her knees. She had remained quiet since they started, responding feebly whenever Kate stroked her forehead but little more. Outside, the ocean was a shadow in the false dawn; strips of white appearing and then vanishing like ghosts. Kate's stomach churned as her mind raced. She knew what was needed from here, knew it as clearly as if it were printed on a sheet in front of her. Malika's runny nose had been no cold. It was cerebrospinal fluid. The meningeal lining, always at full stretch from the fractured bone plate, had finally given way and now the leaking fluid was mixing with bacteria in her nose. The course was straightforward from here in one sense, utterly unknown in another.

They needed to treat the infection, and they needed to fix the leak the fractured bone plate had created. Both depended on how much damage the infection did before they could stem it. Assuming that was possible. She forced down images from her residency; she had seen what meningitis could do. She needed to hope. Had to. She licked her lips. They were dry and cracked, her tongue as coarse as the sand they had walked on the previous afternoon.

'It says fourteen minutes to Geelong Hospital,' said Lucy, holding her phone and turning round. 'How's she doing?'

'About the same, I think.'

'They'll sort her out at the hospital, I'm sure. We're nearly there.'

Kate looked down at Malika's face and foresaw the scenario. Her gut was telling her something, and it didn't include Geelong Hospital. More than ever, they both needed friends right now.

'How long is it to Melbourne from here, Hamish?' she asked. His large, hunched shoulders hadn't altered since they set off.

He glanced in the rear vision mirror. 'Not Geelong?'

'I can't help her in Geelong. It'll be out of my hands. I'll be the pushy outsider. They'll want their own assessment.' She glanced at the small Esky on the floor with the samples inside. 'They'll probably repeat the lumbar puncture and the blood cultures. Then it'll be a matter of finding someone who knows what to do on a Sunday morning. They could well end up moving her to Melbourne anyway.'

'It's your call,' said Lucy, turning around.

She pursed her lips, weighing the odds. It was the right call. She felt it. 'I'll show you the short cut to my hospital,' she said.

They reached the ring road and Hamish planted his foot. 'Always wanted to see what this baby can do,' he said.

They were five minutes from the hospital when Malika had her first seizure. Her feet thumped against the car door and her arms shook senselessly as her mouth frothed through clenched teeth. All Kate could do was hold her firmly on her side and pray for it to subside. It took a minute. A whole minute.

Kate had called in advance and the emergency team was waiting at the door with a trolley. Two male nurses wheeled it across to the car and, taking her slender, limp body from Kate, carefully moved Malika onto it. Her skin was dark against the white cotton sheet and pillow slip.

The air was sharp, the morning light clear as Kate stepped out of the car.

'She's just had a full-blown seizure,' she said. 'Is ICU coming?'

'I'm the ICU registrar, Dr Davenport,' said a tall young man in t-shirt and jeans. He moved to the top of the trolley and pulled out a torch, lifting up Malika's eyelids. She responded feebly.

Kate looked him up and down. He really was young. 'Do you have a bed?'

'I thought we should stabilise her down here in emergency first. Then we can move her up. The scans can wait until we know where we are.'

She nodded. He already had that air of quiet efficiency that intensivists radiated. 'I can live with that,' she said. She quickly outlined Malika's background and then the events of the night as they wheeled the trolley away.

She was about to follow it when a nurse in blue theatre fatigues holding a clipboard stopped beside her. She pulled a pen from her ponytail.

'Whose bed card?' she asked, her pen poised.

'Mine,' said Kate. She would sort that out later.

'Thanks.' She smiled and scribbled.

Kate turned to see what had happened to Lucy and Hamish. They hadn't moved; the car was precisely where Hamish had pulled up. She crossed the bitumen and leaned in through the open back door.

'I can't thank you guys enough,' she said. 'I'll take it from here. Go home and get some sleep.'

Lucy's face was chalk white as she turned round. 'I hope it goes well,' she said. 'Let us know?'

'Of course. Hold on.' She leaned across and plucked the esky from the floor of the car. 'I'd better get these to the lab.'

'Are you okay?' Hamish asked.

'I'll be fine,' she said. She almost believed it.

It was a tight morning, one action dictating the next and everything dependent on what would happen in the next few hours. Malika's future was on a knife edge. The ICU registrar decided initially that she could get by without being intubated, but changed his mind after speaking to his consultant.

'She wants to blow down her carbon dioxide,' he told Kate. 'To keep the brain swelling to a minimum.' He paused. 'We'll have to increase her inotropes. Her blood pressure's going to struggle if she's intubated and ventilated.'

Kate nodded. She was in their hands. She spoke to the neurology and infectious diseases consultants herself, took the samples to the lab – where the on call tech guaranteed her a gram stain result within two hours – and finally, after she had done every other thing she could think of doing, made the call she had known since Lorne she would have to make.

'Kate?' Andrew's voice was surprised.

She closed her eyes as emotion welled within her. 'Andrew, I really need your help.'

8

An hour later, she and Andrew stood on opposite sides of the bed in the bleak ICU cubicle. Behind the bedhead, the fine slats of a venetian blind allowed measured streaks of sky. Malika was surrounded by machines; all attached to her by tube, line or wire. A nurse leaned over the recording charts, and then squatted to check the catheter bag. Young and slim, her bob haircut swung forward as she dropped her head. She worked around them with an air of purpose as if they weren't there.

Kate's chest ached as she gazed at Malika's face. It was even more distorted with the endotracheal tube down her throat. The tube fogged slightly with each breath as the ventilator wheezed and sighed beside her.

Andrew stood there silent: dishevelled hair, faint stubble and jeans; he had clearly rushed.

'Yesterday, she was running on the beach,' said Kate.

'Was her blood pressure any better than this before they intubated her?'

'I think so.' She glanced at the nurse, who nodded.

He peered at her through his glasses. 'And the lab is sure it's staph?'

'Gram stain only, but they're pretty confident.' They had rung ten minutes before he arrived.

'Has Prue O'Connell seen her yet?'

'Her registrar rang. He said she would be in by eleven. She and Chris from infectious diseases both said it sounded like we are on track.' It was what they didn't say, the caution in their voices that made her chest ache. She looked at him. 'Will you take her over, Andrew? She needs surgery, but plastics is hardly her primary problem.'

He took a moment, weighing up the implications. 'Of course, Kate.' He smiled briefly.

The nurse was fiddling with dials on the ventilator. 'The MRI's booked for this afternoon,' she said.

'But she won't be stable enough for surgery until tomorrow at least,' he said. 'At least.' He emphasised it. It was her only chance. Control the infection and then fix the leak. 'You still have the old films, haven't you?' he asked. 'We'll need to compare them. And consent?'

'I have to contact the school. It's not as if I'm her legal guardian or anything,' she replied. 'We're flying free on the emergency at the moment, but that can't last. And then there's insurance. The school must have protocols for this sort of thing.' She'd ring Verna O'Bryan.

They fell silent, both watching the nurse as she tapped hard on an IV line before circumventing Andrew and filling in dots on the chart at the end of the bed. She smiled vaguely at them as she frowned and tucked her hair behind her ears. Kate saw it then. She was nervous. And why wouldn't she be? With two senior surgeons standing by as she tried to work, she would have felt her every move was being watched and judged.

Kate took Andrew outside and they walked back along the corridor.

'I have some other calls to make, too,' she said.

'The university professor?'

He was right onto it. 'That's one.' She nodded. She would try Father Mike as well, for what it was worth.

They stopped at the end of the unit and her throat tightened as she turned to him. 'She could die, couldn't she, Andrew? Or be left brain damaged? I'm not imagining things.'

He took off his glasses and gave her a gentle smile. 'You know we'll do all we can.'

She swallowed. 'She'll need plastics work as well.'

'Jonathan's on call, I think.'

'He is, yes.' They waited as two junior doctors walked past with all the jaunty swagger of young registrars – Teflon-coated with their new skills. 'Don't even think of asking him,' she said.

His eyes narrowed. 'Are you sure, Kate? You and Malika are very close.'

'I've never been surer.' No one else was going near her. She matched his gaze, but had to force herself to stand straight, her body was nearing its limits: the stress, lack of sleep, nothing even to drink since last night. Her tongue was cottonwool in her mouth, the headache behind her eyes slowly working itself into a migraine.

'I'll speak to him,' said Andrew, 'but you need rest.'

'I know. But first I'll speak to Jonathan.'

She showered, changed, ate some breakfast and fell into bed.

She woke with a start and stared at her bedroom clock. Midday. The house was deathly silent as she picked up her mobile. She got through to Verna O'Bryan who gasped at the news. When she could talk, Kate suggested they meet at the hospital that afternoon. Professor Jenkins was equally upset, but more forthright.

'Good God,' he said, 'not Malika. How much does one poor girl have to go through?' There was a pause. 'Will she be all right?'

'I wish I knew,' she said. 'But she certainly won't be at any conference.'

'Conference be damned!' he said. 'There will be others. She's beyond us, anyway. Oh my God,' he said, as reality dawned. 'That is, of course –'

'We're doing our best,' she said.

She hung up, her hands shaking. She made herself a cup of tea and sat at the kitchen table as she drank it. When she tried Father Mike there wasn't even a ring tone.

Her phone rang when she was halfway back to the hospital. It was Margaret Donohue, the ICU consultant.

'We think she's had another seizure,' she said in her usual, crisp tones. 'Hard to be sure, but one foot was twitching for several minutes before we could stop it. Her nurse picked it up. We've increased the antibiotics and Prue's switched her anti-epileptic medications around. She's settled now. Andrew's happy with everything, but he wanted you to know.'

'I should be there in ten,' she said. She glanced across at her overnight bag on the seat beside her. She had packed it on instinct. Now, she just had to find somewhere to sleep.

She met Verna outside the unit. She was a different person from the one Kate knew. It was to be expected. Kate guided her by the elbow into the cubicle. They stopped short of Malika's bed and Verna burst into tears.

'I'm so sorry,' she sniffed, wiping her eyes. 'I told myself I wouldn't do this. Oh, the poor girl.'

'We really need to sort out some legalities – authorised signatures and so forth,' said Kate. 'Who has legal power of consent, insurance cover, that sort of thing. Not my area, but the intensivists here are used to it.'

Verna cleared her throat and nodded. 'Yes, that's all easily covered. I can sign for her. Do whatever you need to do.' She hesitated. 'The only thing I'll need to check with Stella is the medical fees. I think we're only covered –'

'No one here's going to charge her,' said Kate, firmly.

'Thank you.' She nodded. 'There is one other thing. I rather think the girls should know something at least. I would say just her friends, but that's – impractical.'

Kate glanced at the nurse, who had stopped what she was doing and was looking at her. Kate knew what she was thinking. 'I understand. But perhaps no visits for a while,' she said.

That night, she found a bed in the residents' quarters. There was nothing she could do but being close by felt better. She got a few hours somewhere after midnight and in the morning trudged bleary-eyed down the corridor to the bathroom. She stepped into one of the empty shower cubicles. In her time they would have all been full, their inhabitants' tired bodies forced into waking as the overnight shift ended and an early ward round beckoned. Fatigue was a fact of life. Thankfully times had changed.

They had agreed to meet at nine: she, Andrew, Prue and Margaret. A team meeting to decide on proposed surgery. She was deliberately early, so she could see Malika. The same nurse was in the cubicle. Kate read the name on her badge. Raechel. She hadn't seen it spelled that way before. She glanced at Kate as she entered.

'How's she been?' Kate asked.

'They said she was stable overnight.' She glanced at the monitor. 'Inotropes are down, obs stable, afebrile. They began to ease back on the propofol on the evening round.' She nodded. 'She's doing fine, though the docs haven't seen her yet.'

Kate remembered Margaret's phone call from the day before. 'You were the nurse who picked up her seizure, weren't you? That was a good pick.'

She smiled.

'Not many would have seen it,' Kate continued. 'Especially as she was almost paralysed on the ventilator.'

Raechel spoke to the IV line, a flush rising on the back of her neck. 'I used to want to be a neurologist, but my grades were nowhere near good enough.'

'It's tough,' Kate agreed. 'Too tough, I think. Would you still want to be?'

'A neurologist?' She turned. 'Nah. I'm good at what I do. We want to have a baby next year. We can't all be astronauts.' She nodded at Malika. 'I hear she's really smart.'

'She'd knock Spock off the bridge of the *Enterprise*,' said Kate.

'Let's hope,' said Raechel.

The meeting was brief. Margaret thought she was stable enough for surgery. Her face was taut but definite.

'Her inotropes are almost off. Blood pressure and respirations are fine.'

Prue agreed. 'No problems my side.' She was dressed in a long woollen frock, her trademark handbag over her arm. Her motherly appearance was at odds with her clear, penetrating voice. 'I'll get an EEG scan tomorrow, but as far as we can tell, she's had no further seizures.'

Kate's shoulders eased a little. First hurdle down.

Andrew brought up the MRI scans on the large computer screen at the end of the room. They crowded around.

'That right side looks tight,' he said, pointing to the ethmoid area, just below the brain's frontal lobes. 'We'll inject some fluorescein pre-op and find the leak as we go in.'

Kate looked at the old films. It was really tight. Had the broken fragments been pushed to the right? 'Why is it so tight, do you think?' she asked.

Andrew shrugged. 'It might just be the angle difference between the scans. We'll find out when we're there. Main thing is to stop that leak. It's usually straightforward.'

Kate studied the film again. 'And if we can't get to it?'

'I discussed that with the neurosurgeon yesterday. They could help if needed, but they would have to lift off her scalp, cut through her skull, and then pull up on her frontal lobes to gain access.'

'That doesn't sound good.'

'They would also have to cut her olfactory nerves to create space to reach the cribriform plate.'

'She would never smell again.'

'I said we'd call them if we were in trouble.'

'So we're agreed?' Margaret challenged them. 'Surgery for six tonight?'

Andrew caught her as she headed down the corridor. 'Did you have any trouble with Jonathan?'

'I'm going there now. He's on the ward.'

'The kids are away this weekend – Julian's got a school camp and Alice has found herself a friend for a sleepover,' he said. 'I'll be in my office if you need me.'

'I'm sure we'll be fine.'

She rehearsed her approach to Jonathan in the lift. It was her call at the end of the day, but it shouldn't come to that. It was less work for him, after all.

Jonathan was sitting at the computer in the vacant registrars' office. He turned when she arrived, smiling briefly. She shut the door and sat in the chair beside him. They talked – she explained – for a few minutes.

'So let me get this straight,' he said, once she'd finished. 'You want to do this girl – a high profile case for the hospital by the sound of things – and override my on call duties.'

'That's a harsh way to look at it.'

'Really?' His broad lips curled into a smile. 'The way I see it is you'd inveigle yourself with the Prof yet again, at a time when it's all starting to matter.'

'That's out of line, Jonathan.'

He stared at her. 'There's not a chance I'll let you do it,' he said eventually. 'I'm on call and that means I catch what comes in. This would signal a massive vote of disrespect for my abilities. Besides,' he narrowed his eyes, 'aren't there other irregularities here you haven't mentioned?'

Her eyes narrowed.

'You're emotionally compromised, for a start.'

'That's absurd.'

He smiled again. 'You said as much yourself. Why don't we talk to the Prof?'

'Why don't we?'

Ten minutes and a phone call later, they were facing each other at the round table in Andrew's office. Ten minutes had been time enough for Jonathan to clarify his thoughts. Angling his body away from her, he faced Andrew directly. He was forthright and unforgiving.

'If she operates on this patient – who we all know is someone very close to her – I shall formally complain to both the medical and the hospital boards. It is inappropriate and her emotions could certainly compromise the care of the patient.'

'Why would you do that?' Andrew asked. 'Kate is an excellent surgeon.'

'So am I.'

Andrew nodded slowly. 'This wouldn't have anything to do with the head of unit applications, I presume?'

'I'm merely thinking of the patient.'

Kate had had enough. Gripping the arms of the chair, she fired back at him. 'This is bullshit, Jonathan; it's not worthy of a formal complaint to anyone. This girl is sick, I'm the head of unit and I choose to operate on her.'

Jonathan ignored her, and kept looking at Andrew. 'What selection committee would appoint someone knowing they were being investigated for compromising patient care – particularly in light of past complaints?' His narrow-set brown eyes swerved from Andrew and fixed on her. 'And not only mine.'

'You are doing your own chances of appointment few favours,' said Andrew coldly.

Jonathan smiled again and crossed his legs. 'Well, Prof, as you know, it is a panel of ten and you get to know a lot of people when you've been in one place as long as I have. Generate tons of support.' He sat back, at ease. 'I'll take my chances.'

Andrew turned to her, his face serious. 'Kate, I can't stop Jonathan from doing this. You have the authority to override him, but you can see the potential cost. I can't disagree with him that your chances of appointment are substantially lower if there is even a hint of concern.'

She looked from Andrew to Jonathan and back again. 'This is what you've been waiting for, isn't it? A way in, a chance to throw me.' She paused and stared directly at Andrew. 'So my chances as head of unit are shot if I operate on Malika?'

Andrew nodded slowly, weighing the situation. 'I agree it's not something you would want unresolved at the time the appointment's being made. At the very least, you'll have a battle to be supported.'

She forced her breath through her nostrils as she stood up. Her career was on the line in a way she had never considered. After all the work, the dreams, the commitment, it came to nothing. Her career blown away. For a girl from nowhere. She turned to them. 'For me it's straightforward,' she said, 'I'm operating.' Her lip quivered as she turned to Jonathan. 'And I'll take my chances, too.'

Kate stood facing Andrew across Malika's anaesthetised body. She turned to Jack, their anaesthetist.

'All good here,' he said. 'Let's get on with it.'

Andrew positioned Malika's head and they worked as a pair, prepping the area with antiseptic and then carefully laying the sea-green cotton drapes above and below her face, and pinning them around her head. As the ventilator heaved and sighed in the background, Kate took the scalpel from the tray, breathed deeply to quell the butterflies in her stomach, and made the decisive cut.

As she lifted the nasal flap and exposed the septum, she exhaled heavily. 'You see it on the scans, but it's not real until you're there,' she said, half to herself. The septum lay sideways, obliterating the nasal passages. The break extended farther than she had seen before.

'Can you right it?' asked Andrew.

'I think so.' She nodded. 'Yes, the septum itself is intact. But I'm going to have to go deep. It will take a while.'

'Take all the time you need,' he said.

'Let's keep going, guys,' said Jack. 'I've got a party to go to tonight.'

Kate shook her head, glad for the pressure release. She flicked him an appreciative glance. Eventually, she had it right; the septum was fixed firmly in place. It stood upright like a shark's fin, for the first time in years opening up the right side of Malika's nose. She stood back.

'You've got access,' she said. And Malika had her nose back. She exhaled deeply.

Andrew moved in and peered through his magnifiers into the recess at the base of the nose. 'I can see the fluorescein,' he said. He had asked Jack to inject the brightly coloured stain into her spinal fluid before they wheeled her into theatre.

Andrew gently suctioned the area before taking a probe from the tray. Kate watched as he pushed it towards her brain. He retracted it, frowning. 'It's badly stretched. I think that's why the meninges tore. I can patch it, but I'm not sure we'll be able to keep it closed.' He looked up at Kate. 'I thought that fixing the septum would do it.'

'I did, too,' she said. She looked at the monitors. 'Do you think we should call the neurosurgeons?'

'I'm not sure they'll be any more successful.'

'Can I have a look?'

He stepped back, letting her pass around to his side. She peered into the exposed area, her headlight exposing the temporary packs she had placed. Above them, beyond reach, a sharp, bony plate was angled directly into the meningeal lining, stretching it like a layer of lycra. The bright orange dye leaked slowly through the rent in the tissue.

'I can try and fix it,' Andrew repeated, 'but we'll only get one shot. If it doesn't work –'

'We have to try,' she agreed. 'As long as we don't cause any harm.' She bit her lip. This wasn't right. Something at the back of her mind kept nagging her. What was wrong? She looked across Malika's face. The soft tissue of the nose wasn't in place at the moment, but the depressed contour of her other cheek was clear as it ran up into the enveloping drape, dragging that side down. It was acting as a splint. The problem was that her nose attracted all the attention. A memory of an operation with Stephen flashed across her mind. A young man's face. 'The bones want to sit in their correct positions,' he had told her that afternoon in theatre. 'It eases the pressure.'

Kate looked back at Andrew. She blinked. 'I know what's wrong,' she said. She pointed to Malika's cheekbone. 'It's the pressure from her zygoma. It's splinting her upper face.'

'Can you fix it?'

'If I were Stephen, I'd say of course.' She looked at Malika's face. 'Yes. I think so.'

'We can call for help.'

Her eyes flashed at him. 'Yes, I know that.' She paused. 'I'm going to have to break her zygoma and reset it.' She turned to her scrub nurse. 'Andrea, do we have a small bone lever and saw?'

'I'm sure there's one in the ortho theatre,' the stout woman replied. She turned to the assistant behind them, who was already on his way.

She turned back to Kate. 'Two minutes.'

Twenty minutes later Kate nudged, eased and pushed the freshly broken pieces of bone into place. She took a step back and leaned towards Andrea, who mopped her brow. Kate's hands beneath the gloves were also covered in sweat, and her heart was racing faster than Malika's pulse on the screen, but it was done.

'Now it's just a matter of stabilising it,' she said, half to herself, half to Andrew. 'Give me fifteen minutes.' She looked at Andrea. 'Are the screws and plate ready? And I need a change of gloves.'

As she leaned in again, an emotion took hold of her. Was it a sense of good fortune, perhaps? It wasn't, but that was as close as she could fathom just then. Fortune. Luck. It had been fortune she was in theatre with Stephen that night, years ago, luck certainly that she remembered any of what he said, and an unforeseeable stroke of grace that she was here now for Malika. None of it was actually related, not even remotely, and yet it all was. And luck, good fortune or grace, she was part of it. An overwhelming sense of gratitude pierced her as she fixed the last screw in place. She looked up at Andrew as she stepped back.

'I think it's okay now.'

They met afterwards in the surgeons' lounge. Another case had started in the theatre next door, which meant the room was empty.

'That was an amazing thing you did in there,' said Andrew, lounging back in his chair behind a mug of hot tea. 'Really.' He stared at her. 'You might have saved her life.'

Kate drew one foot up onto the chair and hugged her ankle. 'Stephen showed me once. I was lucky to remember it.' She rested her head on her knee. The last few hours had drained her. Her back ached and her chest was still sticky with sweat.

'I'm sorry about Jonathan,' Andrew continued. 'I had a feeling he might try something.'

She looked up. 'I'm glad I did what I did.'

'So am I.'

They smiled.

They checked on Malika later in ICU. She was stable, although her heavily bandaged face hid what would become massive bruising in a couple of days. The ICU registrar was in the cubicle fixing various lines and scribbling orders. She looked at them both.

'Go home,' she said. 'We've got it covered. I'll call. We should have her off the ventilator within twenty-four hours.'

There was a casserole from Lucy on the front doorstep when she arrived home, together with a brief note and a kiss at the end. Kate's heart warmed. She took it inside and put it straight in the oven. She had hardly eaten for days. While it warmed, she collected the mail from her desk, where she had thrown it on Friday. It seemed like weeks ago. She leafed through it. Mainly bills, but there was a plain envelope she didn't recognise. She ripped it open. It was from the hospital. Her interview for Head of Unit was at three pm on Thursday.

9

Kate woke early on Tuesday morning. She blinked a couple of times before rolling over and checking her phone. No messages or missed calls – probably as good as it was bad. She headed to the shower and decided to make her morning as normal as possible: there was time for an early run around the Tan and she could still get to her rooms by seven. Keep busy. Keeping to her schedule would help her most to get through the day.

Alex, her temp, had the histories in her tray and her patient list ready when she arrived at the rooms. With Liz on time and no awkward complications to surprise her, for once she was able to get away by midday.

She had intended to head to her office and give the ICU team a break, but it was hardly a surprise when her feet took her directly there. She nudged aside the curtain to Malika's cubicle and a look at the nurse – an overweight, older man she hadn't seen before – told all as he shook his head. No change. He glanced at Kate with concerned eyes and continued cleaning Malika's eyes and mouth with large cottonwool swabs. She put her bag down and sat at the bedside opposite him.

'The bruising around her face is really starting to show now,

Dr Davenport,' he said, looking at her badge. 'I'm Malcolm, by the way.'

'That's expected,' she replied. 'Where's your badge?'

He grinned, showing teeth yellowed by age – or more likely smoking. 'We all have our little rebellions.'

Kate looked at Malika carefully. She was breathing by herself through the tube. Most of the pumps and lines had been removed and her blood pressure was stable. Kate hung on each positive, willing each to be part of the sign she was desperate to find.

'Dr O'Connell was looking for you,' Malcolm said, an antibiotic syringe in one hand. He grasped the IV line in his other hand.

'She didn't call.'

'She rushed through.'

Kate dived for her phone. No messages. She stepped out of the cubicle and dialled Prue's number. She answered quickly.

'Are you around?' She had her neurologist's voice on. 'It's a good time to talk. But better face-to-face.'

Kate's blood ran cold. 'Is she all right? There's no change that I can see.'

'Why don't you come up? I'm in my office.'

Prue's office on the eighth floor was narrow. Kate hadn't been there before. Bookshelves on each side gave it a library feel, with texts and journals cramming the shelves. A computer and printer jostled for space on the desk. They had both worked in the hospital for more than five years but had met perhaps only five or six times in passing until now. It was the way of work in a large hospital. Prue nudged some papers off a chair beside a grey filing cabinet, so Kate could sit down. She had a view of the back of the door as she did, where a photo of two gap-toothed children grinned at her.

Prue turned her chair around and clasped her hands, pushing herself back in her seat. 'Thanks for coming, and sorry if I seemed mysterious on the phone. Andrew was keen that I speak to you in person.'

'No problem.' She faked a smile.

Prue cleared her throat and smiled reassuringly. 'We all hoped Malika might have woken by now, but it's always a guess. That's the problem. We'll scan her brain again tomorrow, but it's really up to her.'

Kate forced herself to think. 'So a week, do you think?'

'Maybe. Maybe more.' She pulled her phone out of her pocket and glanced at it before killing the number on the screen with her thumb.

'More?'

'The last one we had took two months to wake. She was older though, almost sixty, I think.'

'Two months couldn't be good.'

'It's a long time, yes.' She nodded.

'Could she,' Kate leaned forward, 'could she not wake up? I mean, at all?'

'It's possible.' She paused. 'The thing is that it's probably better if we take over her care now. There's still a lot to do regardless of what happens.'

Kate studied Prue's face. Was she as intense as this when she spoke to other families? Family. She hadn't thought of that before. Was Malika family, in any sense of the word? It seemed like she was.

'What is there to do?' she asked, quietly.

'Turning, toileting, those sorts of things. Active physio. I'm pretty big on starting feeds too. We'd normally run a nasogastric tube, but Andrew was keen we avoid the whole nasal area.' Her face relaxed a moment. 'I'm sure you feel the same. So we can easily pass the tube down her mouth for now.'

'Was he happy to transfer her?'

'We both agreed that now would be a good time.'

Kate nodded. She didn't trust herself to speak. Her control over Malika's future was slipping already. She dreaded what would come. The weeks, possibly months of coma that Prue intimated, would take their toll. She would become the 'poor thing' in the single room at the end of the ward as she developed bed sores and catheter infections, her wasted arms and legs slowly contracting. Things like that just happened. Conscious patients always demanded priority. Inexorably but inevitably, hope would die.

She became aware that Prue was still watching her and she smiled bleakly. 'Sorry, is there something else?'

'Is that okay with you?'

'The feed?' She nodded. 'Yes. Of course. She'll be highly catabolic right now.'

Prue frowned a moment and Kate realised she had been asking about the transfer. Perhaps one meant the other.

'Good. Okay.' Prue scratched the back of her head. 'There is one other thing. I'm also big on early trachies. I don't want her languishing with a tube down her throat in ICU for too long.'

'A tracheostomy? Malika?' The thought of a long-term tube

feeding into her lower windpipe – with all the suctioning, stubborn sputum plugs and scarring that went with it – threw her even as she saw the sense. It made it official, a partial recovery the best they were hoping for.

'Can't that wait?' she asked. 'I mean, she might wake up, mightn't she? As you said, it's early days.'

'Probably,' Prue nodded. 'And you're right. Though, if she's still not awake by this time next week –'

'Let's pray,' said Kate.

'Now's the time to pray,' Prue agreed.

Kate left Prue's office and headed to her own. Three hours of emails and paperwork awaited her, yet she couldn't even make a start. Instead, she stared out the window from her desk, watching dusk turn to night, before making her way to the ICU. Andrew's door was open as she passed. She hesitated, almost stopped, but kept going.

She sat by Malika's bed, chatting to Malcolm a little, and sometimes, during the long silences, stroked Malika's hair. Why it felt better to be at her side, she didn't know. Perhaps it helped her to fool herself.

She left for the car park when the nursing shift ended, pulling her keys out of her bag and forcing her mind to think about the next day. She saw her phone on the centre console when she opened the car door. It must have lain there the whole afternoon. Her heart sank. Hadn't the last time been warning enough? Anxiously, she checked the screen. Two missed calls, both from Andrew.

He answered immediately. 'I was getting worried.'

She explained quickly and switched the subject to Prue.

'Are you sure about transferring her care?'

'I'm sorry, Kate. I really am.' His voice was firm. 'They can do what we can't.'

'It's just hard.' She closed her eyes, emptiness engulfing her.

He was silent for a minute. 'Kate,' he began finally, 'I want you to take a couple of weeks off. From the public side at least.'

'Weeks?'

'You're trying to do the impossible, and something will snap. Or someone will suffer. Elliott Thomas has agreed to cover for a couple of weeks.'

She should have objected, insisted. Instead, relief washed over her like a cleansing wave. 'Starting when?' she asked.

'Tonight. Now.'

'Was he okay about it?'

'He said he would do whatever he had to do.'

'I see.' She thought a moment. 'I'm still looking after Malika. If there are any problems, I mean.'

'I'm sure no one will argue with that.'

She sighed. 'The transfer's a good idea, Andrew.'

'Are you ready for the interview on Thursday?'

She paused. 'More or less.'

'Good. I'll see you then.'

She had to wait when she arrived at ICU the next morning. Malika's nurse – Kate was relieved to hear Raechel's voice through the intercom – had just begun to bathe her. She sat on one of the hard beige seats in the waiting room, holding the two vials – one of sand, one of sea water – that Malika had collected so earnestly from Lorne. It didn't take long.

'How's she doing?' Kate asked, as they walked along a corridor so clean it gleamed.

'Breathing on her own, doing well, but no change.' Her young face was serious but untroubled.

Without most of the drips and syringes around her, Malika's shape beneath the sheet seemed even smaller. Kate checked the observations on the charts.

'They talked of getting a trachie done some time later this week,' said Raechel.

'No!' said Kate. 'I mean, Prue, her neurologist, and I have discussed it.' Her mouth had gone dry. 'Maybe next week, we thought.'

Raechel nodded understandingly. 'It's just that we're not doing much for her here, and she can't go to the ward with her airway unprotected.'

'Did they talk about timing?' She tried to sound casual.

She shook her head. 'Not that I heard.'

Kate stood and took her phone outside, ringing Prue when she was out of Raechel's earshot. She was apologetic, but unyielding.

'If she's not waking, it's the best thing,' she said. 'I'm sorry Kate. ICU is keen to get her out. To be honest,' her voice carried a tinge of surprise, 'is it that big a deal?'

'No. I guess not.' She shut her eyes as she hung up. She left soon after, making sure to leave the vials she had brought clearly visible on the set of drawers beside the bed, in case Malika woke.

Andrew was in theatre when she dropped by his office. Ellen said he had a meeting in the city later. Kate walked back down the corridor and had a sudden urge to get out, to go somewhere – anywhere away from thc hospital. She rang Lucy as she drove out of the car park. She had clients until midday but could see Kate then. They agreed to meet at the Tan. 'Do my waddle a power of good to have a walk,' said Lucy.

She was already waiting when Kate arrived. They set off along the flat section towards the city in bright sunshine as serious runners pounded past and proud mothers in bright lycra tights pushed their strollers. At the top of the hill, just after the Shrine of Remembrance, Lucy put a hand on Kate's shoulder. She was panting.

'Time for lunch?' Kate asked, nodding towards the shops and cafés on the far side of the conservatory.

'No sweeter words uttered.' She smiled through her breaths. 'This pregnancy caper's way overdone.'

They found a table outside, near a group of older women who were chatting easily in the sunshine. Kate ate slowly. When she glanced up, Lucy's grey eyes were watching her.

'I was just wondering,' said Lucy, 'is this trachie operation such a bad thing, if everyone else thinks it's okay?'

'Probably not.' Kate feigned a smile. 'It must be the plastic surgeon in me. I'm allergic to scars.' Lucy raised an eyebrow and Kate sighed. 'And what they're expecting after.'

'The coma?'

Kate nodded. 'And the rest.'

'You said it was early days.'

'It is.' She sighed and squinted across the table. 'I just want her back, Luce.'

Lucy nodded slowly. She finished her sandwich before answering. 'Maybe we won't have that option.' She held up a hand. 'Don't get me wrong. I would be devastated, Hamish worse. We all would be. But it's possible that when she comes back she won't be the same. You must know that.'

Kate looked at her hands. 'I thought when I had finished the operation on her face, she would be perfect. All she had to do was wake up.'

'Perfect's a big ask.' She stared absently at the group of women as they groaned their way out of their chairs. She looked back at Kate. 'I didn't tell you I had to have a screening for Down's Syndrome early in the pregnancy, did I? It's standard, with my age and all. I freaked out. I was convinced after trying for three years that the test would be positive, and Hamish and I would have to make a horrible decision.' She smiled. 'The naturopath in me wouldn't let me do IVF.'

'What did Hamish say?'

'He said he would back me. As always. But I knew that really he wanted a healthy child he could grow up with, someone to go to the rugby with, play tennis.' She paused. 'Anyway, of course the test was negative.' Lucy pushed at a crumb on her plate. Her hair shone in the sun, as it always did. 'But there was a whole week when I had to face the fact that my perfect life might be gone forever.'

'Would you have kept it?'

'I told myself I would. A baby just needs love, right?' She squinted at Kate. 'But I really don't know.'

'At least you would have had a choice.'

'Perfect wouldn't have been one of them.' She did her Lucy smile. 'I'm starting to wonder if it ever is. Sooner or later, we have to make the best of things.'

Kate looked at her. 'I haven't given up on perfect for Malika.'

'Just don't expect it.'

Kate finished her soda water and they headed downhill to the cars. She hugged Lucy and watched as she drove off. She stood there for a minute. It was time to think through some imperfections of her own, perhaps even make decisions. She continued along the broad sandy track, completing the circuit twice before finally driving back to her mother's house in the glow of the late afternoon sun.

They met the next morning in the ICU consultant's office: Andrew, Prue and Kate. Nic Derrigan was the intensivist. He was tall and skinny with a long nose and piercing eyes. He must have been new, as she hadn't seen him before. He sat at his desk while the other three looked on from straight-backed chairs. Raechel appeared with the obs charts and laid them across the desk. Then she leaned against the door, her arms folded.

Nic clasped his hands on top of the desk and looked at Kate expectantly.

'I know Malika will wake,' she said. 'I know her. The nurses have mentioned separate incidents in the last few days. Something is starting.'

'As far as I've heard, there's been nothing definite,' said Nic. 'And a tracheostomy is a very low risk operation.'

She knew the tone. It was the 'deal with the troublesome

relative' voice. Put her off nicely, but put her off. 'It's still a risk,' she replied, 'and we're rushing into something that doesn't need to happen. Not right now, at least.'

He spread his hands. 'I'm sorry, Kate. We need the bed.'

Kate's cheeks warmed. 'Doing the wrong thing for a good reason doesn't make it right. We're treating a patient, not managing expendable resources.'

She had leaned forward, her elbows on the desk. They stared at each other for a moment, and then she twisted round to Andrew and Prue. 'You both know I have a reputation for accepting a decision when it's right. But this isn't.' Nic was checking his watch when she turned back. She had to find another way. 'Do we have consent from the school?' she asked. 'You'll need that, at the very least.' She could ring Verna if she had to; she knew she would back her stance.

Nic glanced at Raechel, who shook her head. He looked at Andrew and Prue.

'I'm happy to give her the weekend,' said Andrew. 'The post-op bed we thought we would need this afternoon has had to be rescheduled. The chap's got flu.' He glanced at Kate. 'And I've found Kate's judgement is usually right.'

'I'm happy either way,' said Prue. 'We would have to magic up a bed on the neurology ward for her now, anyway.'

Nic looked up at Raechel. 'Have you noticed anything?'

'Not myself,' she said. 'But a couple of the other nurses have wondered if there's been something occasionally – a flicker of her eyelids, or maybe a quick cough on her tube.'

Nic rubbed his jaw with his hand and sighed. 'How many spare beds do we have?

'One at the moment,' Raechel answered. 'Maybe another later this afternoon.'

'Better hope we don't need more,' he said. 'Alright. We'll keep her until Monday. We'll work it somehow.' He looked at Kate. 'Are surgeons always this much trouble?'

'Always,' she said, her heart pounding. She had done it, even if it was no more than a stay of the inevitable.

Prue disappeared down a corridor as Kate followed Andrew to his office. Ellen let her through and she poked her head through the door.

'Do you have a moment?'

He studied her face from his desk before joining her at the table. 'You did well just then,' he said. 'Malika is lucky to have you.'

'Thanks. You and Prue helped.' She placed a hand on the table as if to physically steady herself and inhaled. 'Andrew, you need to know that I'm withdrawing my application.'

He didn't move for a long minute. 'This is very late,' he said eventually. His voice was distant. She had expected worse – cold perhaps, or angry. Either would have been easier to deal with.

'It's the only thing that makes sense,' she continued. 'I knew it when I chose to operate on Malika the other day. The head of unit position may as well not have existed. Having it out of reach should make me fret. It doesn't.'

'I see.' His eyes were steady but his jaw clenched. 'I presume you're thinking of joining Vihan?'

'I was thinking about it. With your support. I've been out of research for a decade. Despite what you say, we both know I can't just pick it up again as if I were peeling oranges. And with my patients, let alone with the extra load as head of unit – not that there's much chance of that after the other night – there would never be time to retrain.' She raised her palms. 'Working with Vihan for twelve months would have its advantages. I would come back independent, able to set up my own lab again – we could be colleagues.'

'Or you could stay there and build your career.'

'I could.' She nodded. It was true, and a bridge that Vihan might well put in front of her. 'But I can't go unless you approve.'

'You could.'

'I'm not prepared to resign at this stage.' She had considered it. For a moment.

'So if I refuse?'

'You've got me, just as you asked. I'll stay and do what I was doing before. It's hardly a bad life.'

He nodded and eased himself to his feet. Head down in thought, he wandered over to his desk and picked up her CV. He thumbed through it. 'And you're not just caving in to Jonathan's threat?'

'I'm hardly looking for trouble, but no. That's not it. Anyway,' she shrugged, 'there are worse things than Jonathan telling me what weekends to work and signing off on my conference leave.'

'He hasn't been handed the job yet.' He looked at her for a long minute. 'I'll think about it,' he said eventually.

10

If someone were to ask her, she would have said she spent the next few days at Malika's bedside. It wasn't true, because her work life also continued. Friday for instance, she saw her private patients, operated on several others in the afternoon, and saw them again post-op before her rooms on the Saturday morning. But the intent at least was true – every spare moment found her sitting by the bed in ICU.

She left Malika at nine o'clock on Saturday night, before the beginning of the night shift. She was there again by seven the next morning, as two bouquets of flowers arrived and were ferried to the utility room with the others. At the back of the cubicle, scores of cards lay in a large basket below the window, mostly unopened. Kate had leafed through several of them, all from the school.

Malcolm, Malika's night nurse, smiled at Kate when she walked in, raising her eyebrows. 'All good, but nothing new,' he said. His face wore the fatigue of an all-night shift. He handed over to another nurse called Cindy, who beamed winningly at Kate and then spent the next half hour on her phone, texting.

The hours dragged on. Malika breathed through the

ventilator, was turned, and then turned again. Cindy emptied the catheter bag and repeated the obs. She did both again around eleven, before the ward round lumbered through with the consultant and ten or more in tow. When they finally left, Kate went downstairs for lunch. She managed a salad and called Lucy, before returning to the steady lines of the mind-numbing screens above Malika's bed. By mid-afternoon, she was reading a book at the bedside, her arm across Malika's legs.

At eight o'clock, they were in a huddle at the desk: Margaret, the registrar and the resident. Kate knew what it meant. Malika's time was up. That was the deal.

Malcolm arrived again for the night shift, around nine. Brushing aside the curtain, he stopped in his tracks when he saw her.

'I'm staying the night,' said Kate.

'I see.' He looked around uncomfortably. They both knew she was pushing the rules.

'I have to,' she said.

He nodded, slowly. 'Then I'd better tell the boss.'

'I'll come with you,' she said. 'It might help.'

'Do you mind if I stay?' she asked, as they headed down the corridor.

He grinned. 'Long live the revolution.'

It was a stupid idea. She didn't sleep at all. Her back ached, her forehead kept hitting the bed, Malcolm came in numerous times – to do the obs, give the antibiotics, turn Malika one side or the other, drain the catheter. She stepped outside once as he bathed her, and became cold around two o'clock as the air conditioner switched on. She pulled her coat around her shoulders. Her mouth was dry and her teeth chalky, as she ran her tongue over them.

'What time is the tracheostomy booked?' she asked Malcolm about four o'clock.

'You know about that?' he raised his eyebrows.

She wanted to reply with something clever, but her brain was too fogged to think. She nodded.

'Around eleven's usual.'

She looked at Malika. Her facial swelling was subsiding and her bruising was already shifting colour from blue-purple to brownish. Another two weeks and her contours would be clean again. Another month and she would be as nature had intended. Would she ever know?

It was Raechel who woke her with a mug of tea. A butterfly clip held back her bangs on one side and her hair was tucked behind her ear on the other. She smiled.

'Here,' she said. 'It's a bit against the rules, but you've earned it.'

Kate held out her hands for the hot mug, wrapping her fingers around it. Her throat ached with thirst. 'I must have dozed off about five.' She yawned. 'What time is it now?' She peered through the venetians at the end of the cubicle. The morning outside was pale and clear.

'About seven,' said Raechel. 'Malcolm said to say goodbye.'

Kate nodded, her brain not quite functional. She drank half the tea, placed the mug on the computer station, and went to the bathroom. When she returned, Raechel was flicking the IV tubing vaguely with her pen while looking intently at Malika.

'Everything okay?' Kate asked.

Raechel held up a hand, one finger extended. She squeezed between Kate and the end of the bed, making a small cross on the large white chart to mark the respiratory rate.

Her finger pointed Kate to the spot. 'See? Her respiration rate has gone up. At four, she was spot on fifteen per minute. Fourteen at three, fifteen again at two. But then at five she's sixteen, and seventeen at six.'

'And now?'

'Still seventeen.'

'What does it mean?' Kate asked.

'She could be getting a chest infection or,' she sighed and squinted up at the monitor, 'she might be lightening.'

'Is a chest infection likely?'

Raechel frowned at Malika's face at the top of the bed. 'Most of what happens in this place isn't likely. It still happens. Even so, her pulse is steady, venous gases are unchanged, temperature normal. I wouldn't guess at an infection. The chest x-ray should help.'

Kate vaguely remembered stepping outside the room at six for the radiographer with his portable machine.

As if on cue, Malika turned her head to the side and gave a single, sharp cough. Kate grabbed Raechel's arm.

'I'll get the doctor,' said Raechel.

Prue, Nic the intensivist, Kate and Andrew were gathered around the bed by eleven. They had pulled the tube an hour or so earlier, as Malika coughed and gagged. She lay quietly in the bed now, her respiratory rate back to fifteen.

'What now?' asked Kate.

'We'll watch her,' said Nic, studying the screens. 'For a few hours, anyway.'

'Then we can get her up to my ward on Level 9,' said Prue matter-of-factly. She glanced at Kate. 'The question now is how far she'll come.'

'It's still something,' said Kate.

'It is,' Prue agreed.

'So, are we all good?' Nic asked. He looked at them.

It seemed so, for the group began to disperse without a direct answer. Prue headed back to the ward and Andrew crossed his fingers at Kate before he marched in theatre scrubs in the opposite direction. Kate stared after him. As he disappeared through the doors at the far end, a part of her followed him.

'Everything okay?' Raechel asked, when Kate stepped inside the cubicle again. She was removing wires and tubing from Malika's chest and arms.

'As good as it's going to get,' she said. She watched the tall, slim nurse for a minute, until her eyes began forcing themselves shut. 'I should go home and get a few hours' sleep,' she said, yawning.

'Sounds like a plan. Before you go,' she reached behind her and handed Kate the two vials she had left there the previous day. 'These sorts of things tend to get lost in the move.'

She left as Malika was wheeled into her room on the ward. It took a crew of ten – she had become a celebrity. They would want to get her settled.

Kate paced the floor that night back at her mother's place. She moved a vase from the table in the hall to the kitchen – and then to the lounge – something inside her was churning, not letting her rest. She walked outside, looked at the sky and came back in. Finally, she headed to her mother's bedroom. She hovered a moment at the doorway before entering. She couldn't remember when she had last been there. It had been months. She sniffed. It smelled of dust and disuse.

Her fingers traced across the top of a set of drawers and an old photo frame as she walked across the thick carpet. Sitting on the edge of the double bed she looked into the darkened dressing room. A word kept playing in her mind. Home. She had told the ward staff they could find her at home. It surprised her how easily the word came to her; home was a place she had longed for but never found. She had envied how Malika chose this place as her home, in Australia at least. Her figure had appeared dwarfed by the bed as they wheeled her into her room. Had she looked after her charge well enough? Andrew would say she had done all she could. A generation back, perhaps her mother would have said the same about herself. She laid her hand on the pillow beside her. How hard had it been for her mother? She had never asked, never thought to do so. Did she live with regrets, clinging to her fading looks to compensate for the life that had been denied her – a cherished family, a loving daughter? Would she have wound back the clock, too? Would everyone? She smiled softly as she gazed deep into the dark space in front of her, the outline of the mirror just in view. As Lucy said once, the past was a closed room.

Yet perhaps she and her mother had more in common than she had ever considered. Regret and guilt were her mother's steadfast companions. Must she carry the same lifelong burden? Would freedom always be so distant? The dance that Malika spoke of, like the pianist's song, was always there. If her mother had the chance, would she have listened? Might they have shared a different journey? She would never know. Kate bowed her head and as the transience of life swelled before her, she finally opened her heart to the woman who had always been beyond her.

Prue rang her at midday the next day while Kate was still in her private rooms.

'She's woken,' said Prue, in her straightforward way.

Her heart caught in her throat. 'Is she all right?'

'She's okay.' She paused. 'Coming and going a bit. She's asking for you. When can you come in?'

'I'm on my way.' She glanced at the rotund, middle-aged man in front of her. His fingers could do with another week's splinting, but it was nothing Liz couldn't sort out.

'Can you call me before you see her?' said Prue.

'Of course.' She pushed the phone against her ear. 'Anything I should know?'

'Call me before you see her.'

Prue joined her outside the room. She smiled as she approached, and Kate tried to smile in return.

'Tell me,' she said up front. 'What do I need to know?'

Prue nodded. 'There is something. The infection has

destroyed the nerve fibres to her inner ear. It's not uncommon after meningitis.'

'I see.' Kate bit on her lower lip as the words penetrated. 'How bad?'

She pushed on her glasses. 'She's lost her balance and her hearing. I'm afraid she's completely deaf – and very nauseated with the vertigo. Unfortunately,' she added.

'I see,' Kate repeated for want of something better to say. She put her hand against the wall and forced herself to think, for her mind to penetrate the gas-like haze that had sprung up around her. 'Will she improve?'

Prue's thin lips widened a little. 'The balance probably, yes, although it could take months. We'll know more after some rehab.'

'And the deafness?'

She shook her head. 'Usually permanent, I'm afraid. In all the cases I've seen, anyway.'

'My God.' Kate raised her hand to her mouth. 'Totally deaf?'

'I'm afraid so.' She frowned. 'I said it was her right side, didn't I?'

'No, you did not.' She gulped at the air. 'You said nothing of the sort.'

'I'm sorry, Kate. Yes, it's her right side.' She allowed herself an apologetic smile. 'That's why I am hopeful about her balance. The young often learn to adjust.'

Kate let out a long, quiet sigh. 'At least that's something.'

'Yes.'

'And everything else is all right?'

'We haven't tested her yet, not formally. It's early days. But she spoke softly to us and she seems okay. Whether –'

'Whether she is who she was.' She nodded. 'Yes, I understand.' She looked at her feet. She would know that. She would be able to tell. But Malika was back, and everything else they could work through. What had Lucy said? Something about perfection. Was this close enough?

Prue stepped aside. 'Don't stay too long, and it's just you for today.'

Kate tiptoed into the room. The semi-prone figure from the night before was lying half-propped on large white pillows. Her eyes were closed, her black hair brushed around her head. The flowers and cards from ICU had been placed on shelves, beside her bed, and on any additional spare spaces available. Malika's eyes opened as the floor creaked.

'Dr Kate,' she whispered. 'It is good to see you.'

'Hello, Malika.' She came up to the bed. 'Welcome back.' She struggled to keep her voice steady as she placed her hand on the thin, brown arm.

They smiled and Malika gave a small, hoarse cough.

'Take it really quietly, sweetheart. It's going to take a while to get better.'

'My ear.' She pointed to it and wiggled her fingers. 'Nothing. And the room, it spins so fast.'

Kate began to explain, but Malika raised a hand. 'Dr Prue told me. I am glad you know.' She yawned. 'Why does my face feel tight?'

'We had to fix –' Kate began, but stopped as Malika's eyes closed again.

Kate watched her breathing for a few minutes, her chest rising and slowly falling. Her clean, facial lines had started to show through the bruising. She pinched her leg hard but tears came to her eyes regardless. She looked up as one of the residents appeared at the door.

'I have to sort through some medications on her charts, Dr Davenport,' he said. 'Is that okay?'

She smiled. 'I'll come back later.'

Needing a distraction, she went back to her office and screened her emails. Many she could delete without reading. There was one from Andrew – actually sent to Colin. She was copied in. She checked the time. It must have been written straight after they met in his office.

Colin, I'm sorry for the late notice but Kate has decided to withdraw her application. I will speak to you more about this, but she is likely to take up a 12-month secondment at Harvard with a colleague of mine. It might be longer. This has implications, but as always I trust her judgement and her wishes implicitly. She has my full support. I'll see you at the committee meeting this afternoon. Andrew.

He was letting her go. She read through the message twice and shut her eyes, whether to block the images of him from the last six months or to let them in, she wasn't sure. Her hands were clammy and something in her, somewhere, knew gratitude and her heart longed to respond.

Andrew wasn't in when she walked around to his office.

'He's flown to Sydney for the afternoon,' Ellen said. 'His taxi arrived an hour ago. Could you see him in the morning?'

'Do you know when his plane gets in?'

'It's Qantas,' said Ellen absently as she tapped her keyboard. She looked up. 'Seven-thirty pm. You can always ring him if it's urgent.'

'It's okay,' said Kate.

She drove along the rain-soaked freeway to the airport, her wipers flicking steadily. Red tail-lights surrounded her in the dark. Why was there always a jam around Mickleham Road? She clucked her tongue as the car ahead stopped again without warning. A text pinged on her phone and she glanced at it while waiting for the car ahead to move.

Gave Malika's talk this morning. A triumph for her. Trust and pray no news means it's all good. Ring when free. JJ. She smiled. A triumph. She would ring tomorrow from Malika's room.

Rain stung her face making her raise her umbrella as she hurried from the car park to the arrival hall. Was she too late? He wouldn't have luggage so he could just stroll through arrivals without seeing her. She waited, her eyes riveted on the stairway leading up to the flight arrivals. Her coat was damp and her hair sticky wet. This was stupid, pointless. She should have arranged to see him in the morning, as Ellen suggested. She counted ten faces, all of them looking forlornly at the taxi queue outside.

His face was pale as he walked down the stairs, briefcase in hand. He was tired. She could see that from afar. She waited until he reached the ground and walked towards him. He stopped when he saw her, his face impossible to read.

'Kate!' he said. 'Are you off somewhere?'

'I thought you might like a lift home.'

He looked outside. 'There are plenty of taxis.'

'There are. Lots.'

He frowned. 'It's been a long day, Kate.'

'Yes.' She swallowed. 'Did you hear Malika's news?'

'Mostly good, I believe.'

'Mostly.'

They stood facing each other. Always facing each other, it seemed.

'I got your email,' she said. 'Thank you. I didn't expect it.'

He was silent for a moment. 'I would never try and hold you,' he said.

Her hand trembled as she ran it over her hair. 'A lot's changed recently.' She paused, inhaling deeply. She hoped it would come out right. 'Andrew, I need to know if it's too late.'

'Too late?' He frowned again.

'For anything between us.' She blinked. 'You and me. Maybe.'

He took off his glasses. 'I thought you were getting ready to travel.'

'That'll take months to organise. And it won't last forever.'

His blue eyes fixed on her with an intensity she hadn't let herself hope for. 'To be honest, Kate, this time yesterday I would have said it was. Too late, I mean.'

'This time a week ago I would have said the same.'

He smiled briefly. 'Then it's as well we didn't speak at either of those times.' He reached for her umbrella, touching her hand as he did. His fingers were also trembling. 'Where's your car parked?' he asked.

'Not far at all,' she said, turning to the exit. 'I'll show you.'

She took his arm as they walked through the sliding doors.

Malika was lying back on pillows and cushions when Kate walked in. The flowers around her were already beginning to wilt. She held the two vials in her hands.

She looked up. 'Dr Kate.'

Kate smiled as she sat by the bed. 'How are you feeling?'

She frowned. 'I cannot sit up. I am like a newborn goat.'

'They say that will improve.'

'Yes. They tell me that.' She looked at Kate. 'I have been doing calculations in my head.'

'And?'

'The answers come slowly.'

'But they come.'

'Yes, they come.'

'You are still recovering.'

'That is true.' She closed her eyes and breathed deeply. 'Always it seems I must live with loss.'

'There is no other way,' said Kate.

'That is also true.' She nodded seriously and turned her dark eyes to Kate. 'I will forever thank you for my face, Dr Kate. I have been looking at it in the mirror. It is the face I was born with; in it I see my parents again.' Her eyes became bright and she paused. 'The nurses tell me it was you who did it.'

Kate squeezed her hand. 'We did it together. All of us. No one more important than the other.'

'Like swallows.'

'Just like swallows,' Kate replied, and they smiled.

'Dr Kate,' said Malika, 'I have a request.' She picked up the vials again from the bed, her fingers wandering over the glass.

'I have spent much time in your home for six months. I would like to take you to see my village. My home. My life is not here.'

'I would like that,' said Kate. 'When you are well enough.'

'Yes. That is a good plan. I think we do not really know people until we see them in their home.'

Kate looked into Malika's eyes and leaned forward, kissing the top of her forehead as if it were a benediction, a blessing, a celebration of life. Her heart was filled with possibility, more than she had known in all the years she could remember. Perhaps since her father died. Perhaps ever.

'I couldn't agree with you more,' she said.

epilogue

Six months later

They drove past eucalyptus groves and fallow fields for nearly three hours, the train line always on their left. The road was busier than Malika remembered; cars and bright-coloured buses passed them at speed – their faint, jangly music disappearing as quickly as it had arrived. The air outside was still cold, as Kate discovered when she wound down the window. Malika smiled at her as she wound it up again.

'I told you,' said Malika.

Finally, the low skyline of her village came into view, its whitewashed walls and layers of dust distinct against the winter countryside. It was a small village, Malika thought, smaller than she had remembered. They waited until the road was clear, and then Dr Kate turned the car into a space near one of the huts. She pulled on the handbrake and looked at Malika.

'Perhaps we should leave your stick in the car. You managed well in Islamabad last week.'

'I had to give a good performance for the university.'

'They seemed very happy. "Delighted", I think the chancellor said.'

Malika looked at Dr Kate. 'Are you sure that Ayesha and

Fatima do not know we are coming?'

She smiled widely. 'Father Mike said it had been organised. I haven't heard him so excited.'

Malika pushed her stick onto the back seat and they got out of the car. They ambled carefully towards the village, their feet tracing the same lane that she, Tahir and Razzaq had walked so many years ago. She could feel the dust settling beneath the straps on her ankles. Steadying herself with one hand against a wall, she pulled her scarf around her shoulders and raised her face to the wind, breathing in its scent. Soon there would be rain.

'How long will you stay in my village, Dr Kate?'

Dr Kate held her thick plait to one side as she turned around. 'I have two nights. Father Mike wants me to travel with him to Peshawar, and I must be in Melbourne for Christmas.'

'We have great merriment at Christmas here also.'

'I think Andrew and the children would be disappointed. They voted for Christmas at my place. And then I fly to the United States in January.'

'You have a great opportunity, Dr Kate.' She raised her arm and pointed ahead. 'See there,' she said. 'The branches. It is the great tree of our village.'

They entered the square, where all was silent. It was puzzling. Perhaps they were waiting at Ayesha's hut or in the new hall that Father Mike had mentioned. Malika stopped and gazed up at the tree she had missed so much. Like the village, it was smaller than she remembered. But its roots touched the ground and its leaves lay in clusters around its base.

'I am home,' said Malika.

Dr Kate looked at her and smiled. 'I am glad,' she said.

Acknowledgements

Novels are written through the experiences of few, but the input and influence of many.

My sincere thanks and gratitude to Dr Antoni Jach for his dedication, illuminating and inspiring workshops, and sage advice on so many occasions; and to Matthew Hooper for pointing the way and teaching me how to rewrite a novel. Particular and lasting thanks to Toni Jordan for her steadfast belief and encouragement – her wit and fearless critiques always seamlessly intertwined. Thanks also to my agent, Jane Novak, who remained stoically optimistic when her client did not. In regards to both, *sine qua non*.

I am indebted to my writing groups for their boundless support and encouragement, especially my current partners in fiction: Rocco Russo, Michelle Almiron, Stella Glorie, Linda Kemp, Patsy Poppenbeek, Diana Lawrenson, Sara Bannister, and Mira Robertson.

I am deeply appreciative of their generosity of spirit and the willing sharing of expertise by many, especially the participants of the various masterclass workshops at the idyllic Wheeler Centre over (too many) years. In no specific order, these include Moreno Giovannoni, Jacinta Halloran, Leigh Redhead, Jennifer Green, Sarah Schmidt, Yvette Harvey, Rosalie Ham, Mick McCoy, Janine Mikoszka, Tiffany Plummer, Jacqueline Muller, Kylie Doye-Vella, Carolyn Marshall, Lyndel Caffrey, Lyn Yeowart, Clive Wansbrough, Jane Leonard, Nick Gadd, Toby McCorkell, Antonia Pont, Margaret Geddes, Meredith Jelbart, Joss Kasperczyk, Maria Abbatangelo, Bridget Haylock, Maggie Baron, Scott Robinson, Miriam Zolin, Adriane Howell, Anthony Ham, Katrina Watson, Peter Kenneally, Kerry Munnery, Deborah Wardle, Ariella Gild, Kim Kerr, Luke Batten, Pauline Schokman, and Michelle Wright. I know there will be some I have missed. To them, my apologies.

Special thanks to my children, especially my daughter, Claire; my brother, Paul, and brother-in-law, Danny; and to select friends and extended family (Cathie, Mary, and Mariette) for their reading, support and suggestions. Finally, my gratitude and deep thanks to my wife, Penny, who bore the endless months of writing, the late nights and lost weekends with cheer and remarkably few sighs.

About the Author

L. P. McMahon was born in Melbourne. His writing career began as a medical student, and he has since won or been shortlisted for multiple national and regional short story competitions. He has travelled, lectured and published widely in his medical career, living and working in Oxford, Berlin, Pakistan, Newfoundland and New Zealand. He currently directs a busy medical department as Professor of Nephrology at Monash University. *As Swallows Fly* is his debut novel.

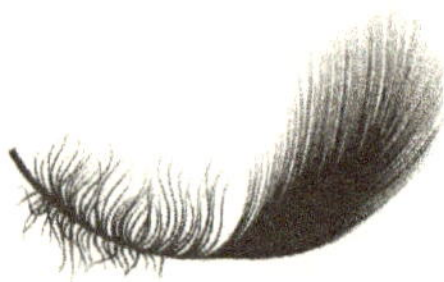